TEMPTED

by the

VISCOUNT

SOFIE DARLING

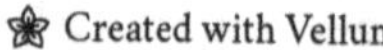 Created with Vellum

2

Jake couldn't remember a time in his life when he'd been so thoroughly ogled by a room full of strangers. He may as well have entered the ballroom wearing nothing but his smalls and a tiara for all the rapt attention centered on him.

And on Mina.

Pride swelled within him for the way she stood, facing down a visibly inquisitive *ton*. "Ready to board the first ship back to Singapore?"

Her lips twitched, and her gaze cut toward his before returning to the crowd. They were here to stay. Any suggestion otherwise was pure fantasy. Reflected in one hundred pairs of eyes below them was reality.

Misgiving snaked through him as he stared across that uniform sea of faces. These people would make a spectacle of Mina. They would never accept her, not fully.

Even though she was the daughter of a viscount, her father's birthright would be the condition of her position. Not her beauty...or her intellect...or even her father's wealth. Forever she would be reduced to a novelty.

This was his fear and sometimes, like now, it threatened to erupt into a full-blown panic. Yet he had no choice. This was the life they'd been handed, and the one they'd accepted.

The gossipy tongues of London wouldn't know more than the truth presented them. He and Mina were safe here, half a world away from Japan, from the truth of her birth. If the people populating this room ever uncovered that particular truth, they would do more than observe her in idle curiosity, they would shun her, completely, forever.

Well, that wouldn't happen. The past was locked away, and he alone held the key.

Below him, a thoroughly bejeweled matron began ploughing up the staircase with an alarming tenacity for a woman of middle-to-late years. This must be the Dowager Duchess of Dalrymple.

"St. Alban, my dear," she puffed, placing her hand on his arm for support, "it has been entirely too long."

Too long? He wasn't aware of ever having set eyes on this woman in his life. Still, he inclined his head in agreement. "Your Grace."

"You were such a tiny lad when last I saw you." She snapped her fingers. "And now you're a man full grown. One can't tell from letters how very tall a person might be. And you were a sailor all these years on the Eastern seas?"

He nodded. "All my life in one form or another."

Until now, he stopped himself from adding. Until he'd become a landlubbing viscount stuck in a soggy country that proceeded along much in the same manner as its weather: invariably and predictably.

The duchess pivoted toward Mina. "And you must be Miss Radclyffe? Nearly match your father's height, I daresay. Must be the Dutch blood."

Jake took this as his cue. "Your Grace, may I present my daughter, Miss Radclyffe, to you?"

"Now, now, St. Alban, no need to stand on ceremony with family. After all, your paternal great-grandfather, the First Viscount St. Alban, was my paternal grandfather. My father was the second viscount. My brother, the third. And my nephew, the fourth. Such a tragedy about your distant cousin Georgie, but the man had no business stepping foot onto a boat. He couldn't keep his footing on dry land." She paused out of respect for the dead before continuing, "As far as the St. Alban title goes, nothing was ever expected to come of your particular branch. I suppose that is why you know so little of your English family. But, now, here you are. We shall make the best of it. You do, at least, look the part."

Her eyes narrowed, and she began doing what appeared to be a complex computation, which required the use of her fingers. Jake smiled and winked down at Mina, who gave him a serious smile in return.

"Ah, here we have it, St. Alban," said the duchess. "You and I are first cousins once-removed. That's twice-removed for you, Miss Radclyffe, but I would like you both to call me Aunt Lucretia. Now, about Miss Radclyffe." She paused for a gulp of air. "St. Alban, I understand that you've not yet learned the rules of society, but you've made a grave *faux pas* in bringing her here tonight. She is not yet out. I shall escort her to my private suite of rooms, where she will remain until you are ready to leave."

She held up a forestalling hand as Jake opened his mouth to insert his opinion on the matter. "I've been around men all my life, and I know that look. You can save it. Miss Radclyffe's reputation is at stake." She turned to Mina. "Do you happen to have a sampler in your reticule?"

"I have a copy of Newton's *Opticks* in my reticule," Mina replied.

The duchess's eyebrows shot up. "Indeed?"

"Miss Radclyffe," Jake inserted, "has a keen interest in astronomy and is intent on constructing her own telescope."

"Oh?" chirped the duchess. She pursed, then un-pursed, her lips and, at last, rallied. "How original of you, my dear. Now, if you will come with me."

Jake made eye contact with Mina to ensure she was agreeable to the plan. Mina nodded once, and that settled the matter.

The duchess was leading Mina away when she threw one last parting command over her shoulder. "St. Alban, you must make yourself at home."

A snort escaped Jake as the duchess and Mina disappeared into the crowd. Home? Several fingers of a Scottish single malt might convince him that this room felt like home.

He slipped through the crowd, making his way to its periphery and ignoring the three-foot radius of silence that surrounded him. He would stumble across a cart stocked with whiskey, sooner or later.

One year ago, the first royal summons had reached him in Singapore, informing him that a distant English cousin, who happened to be a viscount, had died without having produced an heir. He'd ignored the letter. The English aristocracy had naught to do with his life.

His father had been the younger son of a minor branch of a noble family. Few career options open to him, he'd purchased a commission in the Royal Navy and rose to the rank of admiral before his untimely death at sea when Jake was still in leading strings. As a result, Jake had been raised by his widowed mother and the Dutch family she'd left when she'd fallen in love with the older English admiral, only to return after his death. The Van Rijn's were successful traders in the Far East, and Jake had spent the first thirty-five years of his life assured of his place in that unpredictable, always fascinating, world.

The English, however, had a different opinion on his place in the world. A month after the first summons arrived a second summons. He'd ignored that letter, too.

When the letters from the duchess began trickling in, relentlessly one after another, he began paying attention. Her message was clear and increasingly frantic: if he didn't accept the title, it would revert to the Crown. There were no other male heirs.

No longer could he ignore his English relations. He'd never shirked his familial obligations a day in his life. He'd accepted his fate. A fate that had led him to London, the possessor of an English viscountcy and a mountain of debt left by the previous viscounts, George and Georgie.

While this crowd didn't reflect the sort of company he was accustomed to keeping, it did offer a distraction, albeit a temporary one, from the dreary balancing of Georgie's books. The man's idea of "business ventures" had involved blindly handing over large sums of money to "gentlemen" capitalists. It was clear to Jake that those "gentlemen" had speculated the money away on their own doomed and uninformed interests.

At last, his feet found the oasis he sought: a shiny brass cart stocked with crystal decanters of various shapes and sizes. He deferred to a silver-haired gentleman seeking the same before pouring himself two fingers of a deep amber whiskey and taking a long draught. That was the stuff. This cavernous ballroom wasn't like home, but the light felt warmer nonetheless.

The old gentleman gave him a knowing smile and a silent toast as they turned in unison to take in the crowd. Jake was about to practice his rusty social skills by introducing himself—life aboard an East Indiaman didn't prepare one for a London "small" salon—when a pair of lords sidled up to the whiskey cart behind him.

"A widow for a decade?" asked a sloppy voice. "And now a divorcée? That would make her a follower of Mrs. Wollstonecraft or a slut and—"

"And," an equally sloppy voice chimed in, "she's too handsome to be a bluestocking."

A round of laughter, grating and repulsive, rang out. The old gentleman stiffened and stabbed the obnoxious duo with his piercing blue gaze. Jake turned in time to watch the blood drain from their faces, eyes as round as sovereigns.

"Might there be," the old gentleman began, "a wide spectrum of possibilities for the fairer sex between bluestocking and slut? Perhaps I'm acquainted with this paragon?"

"Oh, no, Your Grace," one of the louts stammered out, "you're not familiar with this particular, *erm*, paragon."

The pair mumbled a few indecipherable inanities and halved in size as they slunk away, entirely sobered, Jake suspected.

Your Grace. A duke. The company one kept in London.

His Grace tossed back the remainder of his whiskey, set the glass down, and pivoted toward Jake. "Don't believe everything you hear about Lady Olivia. They," he said, gesturing toward the room at large, "have the upside-down of it."

The man sauntered away, and Jake couldn't help wondering who this Lady Olivia might be. Then a too-near voice called out, "St. Alban!" and his curiosity died an instant death.

He tried not to cringe. It was a name he had difficulty accepting as his own. The Viscounts St. Alban were distant relations on distant shores. And now he was one of them. Beyond belief.

"Have you considered taking a wife?" asked the duchess without prelude.

Jake's brow wrinkled, equal parts shock and bemusement. "Actually," he began, "I've reconciled myself to the idea."

"Oh, my dear, it isn't so grim as all that."

Perhaps it wasn't. But he hadn't expected ever to marry for reasons other than true affinity, even love. This move to London had changed that expectation, and his obligation to Mina demanded precedence. He would find her a stepmother of impeccable reputation and lineage, one who could guide her and cement her place in society.

He wouldn't fail Mina, not the way he'd failed her mother.

"St. Alban," continued the duchess, a matchmaking gleam in her eye, "your bride is in this room, I can feel it."

Jake scanned the cavernous space, surely full to the brim with every member of the *ton*, and feared she might be right.

Her eyes narrowed in on an indeterminate figure in the distance. "In fact, I may have the perfect candidate."

Dread, pure and unfettered, shot through his veins, turning them to ice. His life just might be slipping out from under him.

"Now, the Duke of Arundel has agreed to my request," she stated, again without preamble. Her hands and fingers flitted about in perpetual motion, sliding rings, shuffling bracelets, toying with necklaces, or whatever happened to be movable on her person.

Jake hesitated. "And what request might that be?"

"To mentor you in the duties of a viscount, of course. You appear a capable enough young man, but my dear papa was a Viscount St. Alban, and I won't stand idly by and see the title run into the ground due to ignorance."

Jake blinked once but held his peace and the smile that wanted release. He appreciated honesty in all its forms. Besides, he wasn't obliged to accept or decline the duke's mentorship at this moment, although decline he would. If the Duke of Arundel's financial acumen mirrored that of the late Viscounts St. Alban, he would be better served seeking the advice of strangers on the street.

"I see, *Aunt* Lucretia," he replied at last. "If I'm to call you Aunt, then you must call me Radclyffe, or even Jake will do."

Her active fingers froze mid-air, one finger looped through a long strand of pink pearls as if showcasing them to the room. Her sharp gaze held his for one... two...three seconds before she relented. "You are St. Alban. Better you accept that fact now and get on with it." Her fingers resumed winding their way around the pearls as if they hadn't missed a beat. "Now, you must meet the Duke of Arundel. Connections, my dear. One needs them in environs such as these."

Jake resisted the urge to search the room for armed assassins, even as he suspected assassination came in subtler forms in *environs such as these.* "After you, *Aunt.*"

She threw him a *that's a good boy* smile and set off, trusting him to follow in her wake. The density of the crowd pressed in on Jake as the duchess—he couldn't think of her as *Aunt*—guided him, stopping every few feet to introduce him to whomever was unlucky enough to stray into her path, usually yet another lord and his coquettish lady.

He was well-acquainted with a certain flutter of lashes that intimated a specific sort of interest, which had naught to do with ballrooms and husbands. A young man navigating coastal colonies learned quickly about other men's wives, and the trouble they could cause.

"St. Alban!" the duchess called over her shoulder. "There he is."

In the distance, the silver-haired duke from the whiskey cart stood engaged in a discussion with a lady half his age. She was the sort of lady typical of English gatherings: petite, blonde, and invariably dull.

Then his brain caught up with his eyes. The fact of the matter was this: even though she wasn't his type in the slightest, the lady was remarkably good-looking.

There were the obvious details, of course: delicate, round face; narrow, pert nose; Cupid's bow mouth with a plump lower lip. But it was another detail that intrigued him more than her physical perfection.

When she smiled up at the duke, one top tooth peeked out and slightly overlapped its neighbor, the sole imperfection on her otherwise ideal English face. And, yet, somehow this flaw rendered her face all the more perfect.

The duchess slowed her clip and squeezed his forearm, jolting him out of musings both uncharacteristic and discomfiting. The duke lit up at their approach and stepped forward. While Jake could take the gesture as welcome, he sensed it was less a friendly step and more a defensive one. It was possible the man was protecting the lady with the intriguing, crooked tooth.

"Your Grace, the Duke of Arundel," the duchess intoned formally, "may I introduce Lord St. Alban to you?"

"Ah," began the duke, pinning Jake with his piercing blue eyes, amusement crinkling their corners, "so you're the latest Viscount St. Alban."

"At your service, Your Grace." He made his bow to the duke, even as the lady at his side remained captivated by the string quartet some thirty feet away. Viscounts must come two a penny in her world.

"From what I understand, Lucretia has plans for us."

"Oh, Nathaniel," the duchess rapped the duke with her fan, "that is quite enough."

Then Jake felt it: *her* attention locked onto him. His gaze slid toward her. His first impression of her typicality held true, but certain details subverted it.

Platinum streaked through her hair as if she spent her days beneath open sky, instead of inside close drawing rooms that a duller shade of blonde would suggest. And her face was unfashionably tanned a few shades darker than her décolletage, doubtless caused by the same source. Speaking of her décolletage...

His mouth went dry. It was the way her dress, a suggestive shade of newly flushed skin, clung to her body.

His eyes lifted to meet hers, and he detected knowledge there. She knew what he'd been thinking, and she wasn't at all impressed. Further, he couldn't help noting a cautious light within those eyes the blue of a Polynesian sky, determined not to give anything of herself away. How ironic, then, that they revealed the opposite.

Behind her guarded manner he sensed a raw, vulnerable nerve. An unusual quality at a gathering where most people's sole purpose in attending was to appear as grandiose and invulnerable as possible.

An urge, immediate and strange, compelled him to protect this woman to whom he'd never spoken a word. He made an automatic movement forward, and she responded with a skittish step backward. A jarring image of predator and prey came to mind, at odds with the protectiveness he felt. A part of him relished the idea of playing shark to her minnow, even as another part understood that it made him a scoundrel.

The duke must have noticed the subject of his attention for he neatly side-stepped and gestured toward the lady, whose circumspect gaze never once strayed from Jake. "Lord St. Alban," said the duke, "may I present my daughter, Lady Olivia, to you?"

This was Lady Olivia? The woman the pair of louts had been disparaging at the whiskey cart? And she was the daughter of a duke? *This* duke?

From what he could gather, the woman was a walking scandal. Impossible that she was the duchess's candidate for his bride.

He gave himself a mental shake. *His bride?* Where had that last bit come from? Even so, disappointment, distinct and unmistakable, reared its head and as quickly lay down. He didn't need a walking scandal for a wife.

On a step forward, Lady Olivia extended her hand toward him. The instant he touched his fingers to hers, a happening occurred, unexpected and confounding: a tiny shock of electricity sparked between them.

A startled chirrup escaped her pink lips, and she snatched her hand back, a surprised smile flashing across her mouth. The smile dropped in an instant, as if she remembered that she didn't smile for strangers.

Another tug of disappointment pulled at him. Lady Olivia had the sort of smile that reached all the way up to her eyes. A rare sighting in *environs such as these*, he suspected.

"Daughter by law, Your Grace," the duchess was saying, either unaware of or indifferent to any sparks that might be flying between him and Lady Olivia. "And former at that."

Jake's brows drew together. An entire conversation seemed to be taking place below the surface of the current conversation. And he wasn't invited.

Lady Olivia angled her body toward the duke and placed her silk-gloved hand on his forearm. There was no mistaking the affection the two held for one another. "I shall call you Father as long as you wish."

"Forever, my dear," he returned, a doting twinkle in his eye. He gestured toward Jake. "St. Alban happens to be my new protégé."

"Your protégé?" Lady Olivia asked. She pinned Jake with a glare equal parts confusion and horror. He rather enjoyed the hitch he heard in her voice. "You don't appear to be the sort of man incapable of managing his own affairs."

The duchess gasped, and the duke's bushy silver eyebrows lifted, but Jake took her outburst in stride. "Too often appearances can be deceiving," he said. "One never knows what sort a man might be. That is, until you've known him long enough to take his measure. Wouldn't you agree, my lady?"

Lady Olivia's mouth snapped shut, and a blush crept up her décolletage. She hadn't missed the double entendre located within his words. He tamped down a swell of satisfaction. For the first time since setting foot on English soil, Jake felt interested, engaged, and alive.

Even though he wouldn't be marrying this walking scandal, her restraint made him want to poke and prod her until he'd stripped her of her exquisite control. Lady Olivia was petite and blonde, but boring and dull she wasn't.

Oh, why had she spoken those preposterous words to Lord St. Alban?

Anyone with eyes could see that, aside from the duke, he was the most capable man in the room. In all of London, mayhap.

But her reason for speaking so rudely was clear, if only to her. She needed to put distance between herself and this viscount, who had faced this entire gathering and silently dared them to speak a word crosswise against his daughter. She couldn't help admiring anyone who stood up to these people. It was a most attractive quality, which was the absolute opposite direction her thoughts should be taking.

It wouldn't do for her to admire any man or find him attractive. That part of her life was over. Her future self would enjoy a different sort of life. One that didn't involve attractive, admirable viscounts.

She cleared her throat and found the duke observing her, a speculative cant to his head. "I must bid you all a good night, I'm afraid," she said. "I have an early morning meeting at the school."

"Lady Olivia, about that *progressive* school," began the duchess. Olivia sensed the other woman building up to a scold. "Why must you invite even more scan—"

"Of course, my dear," the duke cut in, effectively shushing the duchess.

A determined tilt to her chin, Olivia wouldn't risk another glance at Lord St. Alban or squirm beneath his steady, serious gaze. It was possible he saw through to her very soul. "Your Grace, this salon will be declared *the* crush of the Season."

They were the exact, correct words to speak to her hostess, which was yet another reason she should stay far away from Lord St. Alban. The correct words seemed to perform a disappearing act in his presence.

She turned to make her escape when a pair of green bucks, with no more than forty years between them, rushed forward as if the house was on fire. "Duchess Dallie!" they cried in unison.

"Yes? Yes?" The duchess's face tensed in alarm. "What is it?"

Flight arrested by this sudden burst of activity, Olivia paused mid-step. *His* attention was still fixed upon her. She felt its blue ice down to her bones. How she longed to rid her body of its betraying blush.

"Your Grace," began one of the bucks in a studiously measured tone, "we must have dancing tonight." The youth had imbibed a touch too much champagne punch.

"Dancing?" The tension in the duchess's face released in relief. "My dears, this isn't a ball."

"But it is a ballroom, Duchess," pointed out the other young buck. "A glorious one."

"Its magnificence is unrivaled by any other in London," added his cohort.

Olivia suspected the two had been knocking back something a little harder than champagne punch. She risked a quick glance at Lord St. Alban, his serious gaze taking in the frivolous scene. She had a feeling they were all frivolous beings in his eyes.

Yet his close proximity had her body coiled tighter

than a piano string, and she suspected all he would need to do was stroke a single key to make her vibrate and sing out...

She pressed cooling fingers to burning cheeks and inhaled a fortifying breath. She'd rather he not notice, but if he did, he did.

She needed air.

"What sort of bet?" the duchess inquired, calling Olivia's attention back to the conversation around her.

The one young buck nudged the other. "To see if a certain lady will dance with Bletham."

A smile, equal parts delight and mischief, teetered about the corners of the duchess's lips. "For a dance, you say?" She glanced at the duke. "I don't see why not?"

"A waltz?" one of the bucks pressed, boldness winning the day.

"Well, we've come this far, haven't we?" the duchess stated more than asked.

Before Olivia could blink, the young bucks and the duchess rushed away to inform the string quartet of their new duties. The duke hesitated, his gaze finding Olivia's and holding it. She nodded once, subtly, decisively, and the duke strolled idly in the duchess's wake.

Now, in the midst of an ocean of lords and ladies, she stood alone with Lord St. Alban. She should acknowledge him. After all, he was standing directly in front of her. She possessed enough social acumen to deal with this viscount. He was a mere man, and if she chose, after this night, social protocol allowed that she never had to acknowledge his existence again. Besides, she'd already spoken her good-byes.

Then it happened: the string quartet struck up the opening notes of a waltz, the crowd raised its voice in a unified cheer, and Lord St. Alban held out his hand to her. "May I have the honor of this dance?"

She should say no. She *needed* to say no.

She couldn't. Not without inviting more scandal from the odd curious eye that might be observing them. She'd endured enough scandal these last six months to last her a lifetime.

She stepped a hesitant foot forward and held out her hand, willing herself to look up at him. Most extraordinary were Lord St. Alban's eyes: arctic blue rimmed in navy. They should be frosty, but they weren't. They burned with the whitest heat of a blue flame.

She'd never entertained the idea that one could be incinerated by a waltz. But when he took her hand and her pulse jumped, she suspected that she would be lucky to escape this dance entirely unsinged.

She steeled herself and asked, "Shall we begin?"

On a nod, he pulled her toward him and set their bodies into motion. Her gaze remained resolutely fixed over his shoulder in the hope of foiling any attempt at small talk on his part. Her hope was immediately dashed.

"It is a strange sensation," he began, "to have your body so completely in hand and, yet, the essence of you so far away."

A shocked laugh escaped her. Words like *body* and *essence* could make a lady go speechless. They weren't words used in polite circles, particularly in the way they'd crossed his lips, as if a promise was located somewhere inside.

Desperate to summon an upright ancestor or two, she said, "You know nothing of my body or my essence."

"Would you rather I ask how you find the weather?"

Yes! she ached to shout at the dratted man. She wanted simple, and he wasn't having it.

Further complicating the matter was an unruly desire to have the firm hand piously fixed to the middle of her ribcage slide down and settle on the curve of her hip. A simple contraction of muscle would close the remaining gap between them, and he could…*what?*

That wouldn't do. It was possible his words—*body, essence*—had awakened a dormant desire within her. A desire so long unused she'd thought it entirely disappeared. Her mutinous body yearned to hear such words again.

"What is your scent, Lady Olivia? I detect lavender and…is that sandalwood?" She nodded, and he continued, "In my experience English ladies don't smell of exotic spice. Rather they smell of—"

"Stale rosewater?" she finished for him.

A too-charming look of abashment crossed his features. "My apologies, it was intended as a compliment. You are a most unexpected Englishwoman."

A surprising wave of pleasure unbalanced her, and she stumbled over her own feet. His fingers tightened protectively around her waist, holding her steady while she recovered herself. Lord St. Alban wasn't the sort of man who let a woman fall.

She gave herself a mental shake and searched for the words that would right this dance before it went completely topsy-turvy on her. "Have you never heard of idle chit-chat, my lord?"

"I've never had much use for it," he replied, the tilt to his mouth more wry than remorseful.

"Surely you can locate a middle ground somewhere. Here, let me help. I shall ask you a perfectly innocuous question that pertains to nothing personal in your life, and you will answer in kind." Oh, why was she doing this? All this talk of the impersonal felt oddly personal. "Is this your first foray into the *ton*?"

He nodded. "My newfound duties as viscount have prevented me from enjoying the frivolities of society until now."

"We are nothing if not frivolous, my lord." That was better, *bodies, essences,* and *scents* banished from the conversation. A pang of regret for their loss hadn't flashed through her. Not at all. She almost believed it.

Lord St. Alban cocked his head. "Do I detect irony in your tone?"

"Irony? Careful, you're skirting the edge of the personal again." She pointed her gaze over his shoulder. The sooner this dance was done, the better.

"Could you tell me about the school the duchess spoke of? It happens that my daughter is in need of a good one."

"My sister and I founded a school for girls a few years ago. The Progressive School for Young Ladies and the Education of Their Minds."

"A mouthful."

"Yes, well, our headmistress, Mrs. Bloomquist, was adamant that the school's mission be evident in its name."

"So you aren't involved in the daily running of the school?"

"No, but I am on the board of directors."

"Ah, that makes more sense."

"And what is that?" Olivia asked in her best imitation of Mrs. Bloomquist. Something in his tone told her she wasn't going to appreciate the direction of this conversation.

"You don't exactly strike me as the schoolmarm sort."

"And why is that?" she shot back.

Slowly, with the heat of a thousand suns, his gaze raked over the curve of her arm, across her clavicle, down toward the gently rounded mounds of her décolletage. A blush spread across her skin like wildfire. She tried to tell herself that it burned so hot due to justifiable outrage, but she suspected a different cause at its root, one it would do no good to dig up and examine.

From the last stronghold of her composure, she summoned a limp measure of righteous indignation.

"And here I thought," she croaked. She cleared her throat and began again. "I thought you were less of a nitwit than the others occupying this room. Appearances can, indeed, be deceiving."

He pulled her close, and his lips feathered against her ear. "My apologies, if I implied your physical beauty and mental acumen are mutually exclusive entities. You might be the rare lady who possesses both."

Her breath suspended in her chest. She might never breathe again.

She pulled back from him, hoping to encourage a measure of cool reason. But it was no use. Her focus was entirely concentrated on the points of contact between his hands and her body.

At last, a sliver of good sense came to her rescue, and she was able to say, "Let us finish this waltz and go our separate ways."

He gave a curt nod of assent, and the arctic chill returned to his eyes. A sigh might have escaped him, even as they waltzed on, narrowly avoiding another couple.

What was happening to her? Not an hour ago, she'd been an ice queen, untouchable. Now rational thought was abandoning her, and all she could do was *feel*. The pressure of his fingers against her flesh, even through several layers of cloth...the rumble of his words from deep within his chest, even as his soft Dutch accent lent them a clipped quality...and, oh, the content of those words...

This wouldn't do. She knew next to nothing about this man. Which didn't matter, not in the least. She knew herself. She didn't need, or desire, an entanglement with a man, particularly not with a man she met on a ballroom floor. She'd done that once, and it hadn't ended well.

She hadn't divorced one husband only to find another.

Her eyebrows crinkled together. Why had that conclusion come to her? She'd barely had ten minutes of conversation with this man.

But she knew why. The Right Honourable Jakob Radclyffe, Fifth Viscount St. Alban, was the sort of man a woman could marry.

But she wasn't the sort of woman a gentleman married, not anymore. Not that she would; it was simple fact. Besides, she would never be wife to any man again. The bloom was off that particular rose.

With a sudden contraction of hardened muscle, he pulled her body into him to avoid yet another couple. The touch of his breath along the exposed line of her clavicle sent tiny bolts of lightning through her. Her gaze flew up to meet his, to see if he felt them, too. But his countenance remained aloof and stoic, giving nothing away.

Lord St. Alban aroused in her a reaction unlike any she'd ever experienced, not even with Percy. This feeling was dark and complex and mysterious like an underground cavern that wound round and round far below the surface. It insisted that he alone could illuminate its dark depths and satisfy this nascent ache...

She planted her feet, halting their swirling momentum and eliciting a few murmurs of displeasure from the couples who had to swerve to avoid them. Scandal be damned, she needed to leave this room. "My day begins quite early, my lord," she said, her eyes refusing to meet his.

His hands dropped from her body as if singed, yet he made no other movement. No move to hold her in place or insist that she finish this waltz with him.

She inhaled the sigh of disappointment that wanted release and whirled around. Her feet kept pace with the rapid tattoo of her heart, leading her away from him... away from this room...away from this night. Lately, it felt as if she was ever fleeing one thing or another.

Well, in this case, there was no help for it. It was an

absolute imperative that she flee Lord St. Alban. The man made her feel...

Well, he made her *feel*.

And she had no use for feelings elicited by any man.

Determination steeled her as a pair of words swirled through her head: *freedom, independence*. No man would ever make her forget them again.

She must find a Mayfair townhouse posthaste. She couldn't abide the possibility of Lord St. Alban arriving at the duke's manse for his *viscount lessons*. It was all too much, too fast.

Her footsteps trilled down the duchess's front door stoop and crisp night air hit her lungs. She snugged her shawl secure about her shoulders and allowed a footman to hand her up into her waiting carriage.

Tonight, she would lay her head on her pillow and dream this night away.

Tomorrow, she would awake clear-headed and her real life would proceed. That marriageable man and the unsettling confusions of emotion he provoked would be part of a future left behind and better unbegun.

4

NEXT DAY

Some days were born perfect.

On the bridge of an East Indiaman, with the open sea beneath his feet, the clear sky above his head, and a crew to command, the outside world didn't stand a chance of touching Jake.

His head snapped around and another command issued forth. "You there, haul that crate to the foc'sle." A cooling breeze lifted off the water and caressed the back of his neck. "And you, see to it the mainsail is trimmed and secured."

On a trading vessel as well-run as the *Fortuyn*, every man understood his task and set about it with utmost efficiency. There were times when the deck of a ship resembled nothing so much as a hive of bees in springtime. It was a joy to behold.

Deep within him settled a feeling of peace. This was where he belonged. This was home.

A pair of watchful eyes drew his attention. In them, he saw the truth of the current situation reflected back at him. They reminded him that today wasn't a perfect day.

The open sea didn't roil beneath his feet, only a thin layer of muddy Thames kept the moored ship afloat.

The sky above wasn't clear. In fact, above his head hung a sky oppressive with London fog.

And this wasn't his crew to command. Not anymore.

Nylander, the man observing him and his closest childhood mate, was now captain of the *Fortuyn*. This was *his* crew to command.

Jake stood on the verge of crossing a line, if he hadn't already. His function today was purely administrative on behalf of his family's shipping interests. "Are you on schedule to unload her at the Pool before night-fall?" The Pool of London was a bureaucratic mess, but a necessary destination for all trade vessels making their way up the Thames.

Nylander nodded sharply before replying, "The men are anxious for home."

Although the ship sailed under the protection of England's colors thanks to Jake's patrilineal line, home for many of the crew was the Kingdom of the Netherlands. It was obvious in the efficiency of their movements that both captain and crew were anxious to be on their way. They would have been separated from their families for more than a year.

Disappointment shot through Jake. "Ah, well, next trip I'll buy you a pint, and you can regale me with a seaworthy tale or two."

"Next trip." Nylander paused, avoiding Jake's gaze, before adding, "*my lord.*" The Dutch weren't known for mincing words.

Jake's past life had slipped through his fingers. No longer a sailor. No longer one of them, Nylander's tactfully averted eyes told him. A viscount didn't risk his precious, noble hide to captain ships or partake of any occupation that hinted at trade. He dutifully split his time between London and his country estates.

The bitterness of it clogged his throat. Christ, how he missed the open sea. He suddenly wanted nothing more than to be done with this meeting and off this ship. "All looks in order." He passed the paperwork to his steward, Payne. "Captain, Godspeed."

He held out his hand to shake Nylander's. Rough callouses lined the captain's palm, and Jake realized with a start that his own were fading. Soft hands, one of the many privileges of the soft life of a gentleman. He'd spent too much time in a seated position, attempting to balance a dead man's books that refused to balance. A cord of wood must need chopping somewhere in Belgravia.

Another curt nod and Nylander's sun-bleached head whipped around as he issued commands to the active crew, his attention concentrated on the monumental task of accounting for cargo accumulated over several months from myriad ports lining the Pacific and Indian Oceans.

Jake stepped off the gangway and onto dry land, Payne, mosquito-like, racing to catch him. Payne had also been the previous viscount's steward. "Shall I summon your coach, my lord?" The tip of the servant's thin, needle-like nose moved in unison with each word he spoke. A nose, Jake couldn't help reflecting, which was a perfect counterpoint to the rest of the man's rotund, yet compact, body.

"That won't be necessary." Jake quickened his step. "You take the carriage, and I shall walk."

"Walk, my lord?" Payne called out, winded trying to keep up.

Jake came to a sudden stop and pointed his face toward a gray sky that precisely mirrored his mood. "I shall place one foot in front of the other until I've reached my destination."

"Through Limehouse?" Payne struggled to keep up. "And the East End, my lord?"

"We shall review the ship's accounting in the hour before tea," Jake called over his shoulder, each step separating him from Payne, propelling him toward freedom as he set out onto damp, narrow streets.

"My Lord St. Alban," Payne acceded, defeat evident in his fading voice.

St. Alban.

The duchess had been right: he was St. Alban. It was time to get on with it.

However, she'd been wrong in one regard. He wouldn't play protégé to the Duke of Arundel. He didn't trust the advice of any man from a social class whose sole purpose was to lead as unproductive lives as possible. He couldn't understand a man who didn't want to dirty his hands from time to time or enjoy a frothy pint at the end of an honest day's work.

To be fair, the duke did appear to have a shrewd brain in his head. But Jake was determined to stay away from the man for an additional and entirely different reason: Lady Olivia.

He wasn't sure what had been in the air last night, but in the light of day, he saw matters more clearly. And the fact of the matter was this: Lady Olivia may be connected to every lord and lady in London, but the woman was a walking scandal.

He would stop thinking about her and focus on any number of the ladies the duchess had introduced to him last night after Lady Olivia left. Like Miss Fox, the only daughter of a baron and an ideal match, according to the duchess. The lady had a spotless reputation with not a hint of scandal hanging about her. And if she was a little plain, well, he couldn't hold that against her. Every woman was a little plain compared to...

Lady Olivia.

There she was, popping into his head—*again.*

The woman intrigued him too much by half. Perhaps that was why he'd relentlessly provoked her.

It was possible he owed her an apology, except he didn't feel apologetic. Not when she held her tongue in such controlled reserve, yet her eyes flashed hot and pretty blushes crept up from the creamy depths of her décolletage.

He would be willing to wager that he hadn't been the only one interested, engaged, and enlivened by their banter.

No matter. He must banish her from his mind. She wasn't right for him. More importantly, she wasn't right for Mina. Mina needed a guide through society who was wholesome and unblemished, who never spoke a wrong word and never took a wrong step. And Lady Olivia, well, she exemplified none of those qualities.

"Sir! Sir!" he heard behind him. A quick backward glance revealed a street urchin on his tail, a plaintive cry on his lips. "Milord! Milord! A penny, sir? A farthing, milord?"

Jake stopped and pulled a crown from his vest pocket. He watched the boy's eyes go canny and wide as the coin glinted silver in a fleeting ray of sunlight. Before he could reconsider his offer, the urchin snatched it from his outstretched fingers and ran down a rancid alley as fast as his scrawny legs could carry him.

The fact that he carried coin had probably shocked the boy speechless. English gentlemen were above matters as trivial as money, pockets righteously empty of filthy lucre. And judging by his cousin's papers, so, too, were their bank accounts. A thorough gentleman to the end, the late Fourth Viscount St. Alban.

Jake glanced about his surroundings before resuming his westward trek. He hadn't the faintest clue as to his whereabouts, except that he should keep heading toward St. Paul's Cathedral. He was definitely still in the East End, judging by the putrid smells pouring in from every direction: over from the filthy river, up from the filthy sidewalk, down from filthy chamber pots. Filth was the common thread that linked one slum to every other slum around the world.

He breathed it in, let it coat his nostrils. The air smelled real and like home. He'd never lived in a slum, but it wasn't a stretch to say close quarters on a ship at full capacity could resemble one.

Here in the East End, surrounded by cutthroats, thieves, venders, beggars, and whores, he was able to experience that wildness of life missing from the tame drawing rooms of Mayfair and St. James. He was a duck out of water in those rooms.

And Mina?

His body tensed, ready for battle, as the buzz of the *ton*'s scrutiny, their speculation, their unkind titters returned to him. In her fourteen years on this earth, what a large amount of tumult Mina had endured.

From the very beginning.

A face appeared in Jake's mind's eye: a clammy, labor exhausted face, the light fading fast from it, content in death at the promise she'd exacted from him. *"Protect her, Jakob...she'll have only you..."* Her weak grip on his arm had taken on an unexpected tenacity. *"Only you can do it...for Minako, my little Mina."*

Familiar pain spiked through him, and Jake banished the anguished face to the past where it belonged. His focus sharpened on the present.

The narrow London view was still gray, still filthy, and ever crowded as the morning progressed. He glanced at his pocket watch and picked up the clip of his stride. He didn't want to be late for his appointment with yet another girls' school.

He'd already interviewed three candidates with no luck. Mina needed more than piano lessons, drawing lessons, French lessons, and tea pouring lessons. Her brain tended toward natural philosophy and mathematics. The writings of Sir Isaac Newton excited her in a way that the newest dance step might for other girls.

The problem was that he had yet to find a school willing to teach to Mina's intellect, and he resisted the idea of private instructors. She must form relationships with her peers if she was to have a chance of entering society with a measure of success.

What was the name of the school Lady Olivia was connected to? The Progressive School for Young Ladies and something or another?

It mattered not, for he wouldn't be pursuing that particular school. He needed to stay as far away as possible from the scandal-prone and, therefore, unmarriageable Lady Olivia Montfort.

Marriage. That was another way he would ensure Mina's success. A stepmother of impeccable reputation and lineage would provide invaluable connections and assistance in the endeavor. He needed a partner in a wife. Whether or not she made him feel interested, engaged, and alive was of little consequence.

He shook his head, as if he could as easily shake Lady Olivia loose, and made to cross a street when a carriage whizzed past, splashing water fetid with street grime onto his boots. He snapped to. He would be run over and killed, if he wasn't careful. A quick left-to-right glance confirmed the intersection was clear, and he jogged across uneven cobblestones until his feet hit sidewalk once again.

A voice called out, "Hey, guv, ye ain't passin' by without tastin' one 'a tha misses' buns, are ye?"

Jake half-turned to find a rotund man coated in a fine dusting of flour belligerently eyeing him up and down. The man was a caricature of a baker come to life. "What have you there?" he asked, approaching the open window with the man's substantial belly hanging out of it.

"We got yer stickies," the baker said in a sheepish tone, clearly not anticipating Jake's interest in his wares. He craned his head back and shouted, "Fanny! You got yer hot crosses out?"

"Out in two if a minute," came Fanny's shouted reply.

"Oh, come on, woman. Got a real gent'ulman customer 'ere." The baker pulled a beleaguered face as if to say, *Ain't it like a woman.*

"A what?" The woman rounded the corner from the back of the shop and stopped dead in her tracks, straightening her apron as she puffed out her low-slung chest. "Oh, a real gent'ulman is right, I say." She smiled what Jake would have called a toothy grin, if she hadn't been missing her two front teeth. "Ne'er seen tha likes o' ye 'round here. New to tha area?"

"Something like that," he said, his lips ticking up to the side.

Fanny sucked in a deep breath, further enhancing her breasts. In a whispery voice, she asked, "Wha' canna git'cha?"

"A single sticky?"

"I can git'cha more 'n that, guv."

"Awright, Fanny, to tha back wi' ye." The baker shooed Fanny away, but not before she flashed Jake one last toothless smile. The baker shook his head in mournful fashion. "Sorry 'bout that, guv. She gits like that 'round yer lot. Mem'ries o' days spent 'round the street corner, if ya catch me drift."

Jake set a coin on the window ledge. "Will this do?"

"And then some if ye can wait for a few hot crosses," the baker said, pocketing the coin and shoving a sticky bun into Jake's hand. "Tha missus won't mind seein' the front o' ye agin, tha's one thin' for sure!"

The baker's parting words were lost to Jake's retreating back, the entirety of his attention now fixed on the not insubstantial task of managing the sticky bun. True to its name, it right and truly stuck to his fingers, a bit on the lapel of his dove gray overcoat, a drop on the top of his right boot. As soon as he was out of sight of the baker's storefront, he tossed the thing into an alley and appraised fingers shiny with caramelized sugar.

Well, there was nothing else for it: he began licking. He had no intention of sticking to everything he touched all day. By the time he reached his third finger, he was distracted by the sensation of sugar-coated fingers in a way he hadn't been since he was a tot in leading strings.

His footsteps slowed, and he felt...

Pleasure.

The sort of simple pleasure he hadn't experienced in years. Here, on a street where no one knew him, he could luxuriate in the freedom of a simple pleasure.

A smile, wide and unruly, played about his lips, and his eyes blinked open. When had they drifted shut?

The question was destined to remain forever unanswered as his brain registered a sight he'd had no way of anticipating. A nondescript woman, her head down, with no concern for any but her own forward trajectory, about to charge directly into him. Between the tick and the tock of his pocket watch, time did a funny thing and elongated, even as it compressed and intensified. He had only a blink to brace himself for impact.

The instant their bodies bounced off each other, the woman's round, blue eyes met his and clung to him in speechless shock. A heartbeat later, the heat of recognition thrummed through Jake.

This small-scale typhoon was none other than Lady Olivia Montfort.

His right hand shot out when it became apparent that Lady Olivia wasn't only bouncing backward, but backward into a street full of late-morning traffic in the form of fast-moving carriages and delivery carts. His hand clamped around her forearm and jerked her upright to safety.

A loud, "Oof!" whooshed from the parted "O" of her lips as a sheaf of papers flew out of her hands and scattered across the fetid East End sidewalk. A confused moment followed as their bodies pressed full-length against each other—chests heaving, breaths mingling—for a heartbeat too long. Her head tipped back, and her eyes met his.

Gone was last night's measured reserve. Now the primitive emotion that came from having cheated death blazed across their blue depths. A spark of lust shot straight through him, and his hand dropped from her arm as if scorched.

Her eyebrows knit together, and her head canted to the side. "Why on earth are *you*—" she began before stopping short. Her face animated in wide-eyed panic. "My sketches!" She sprang away and began weaving through annoyed passersby in a desperate attempt to retrieve the sheets of paper strewn haphazardly across the sidewalk. She cut him a sharp glance. "Are you going to stand there all day, or help me?"

Jake found himself following her lead as he blindly crouched his way through a forest of tetchy legs and impatient feet. A few filthy minutes later, every sheet was accounted for.

Eyes slinging arrows his way, Lady Olivia closed the gap between them and snatched the sheets from his hands. "A bit of advice?" she began. "You should watch where you're walking."

An air of expectancy hung about her, as if she were trying to tell him something without saying it.

It hit him.

The woman expected an apology.

"*I* should watch where *I'm* walking?" he asked, astounded by her cheek.

"You mustn't go around knocking ladies into the street. Or is that yet another social nicety neglected in your education?" She drew herself up in a show of righteous indignation. "I could have been killed."

"You very nearly were," he replied. "But 'tis you who must be careful. A narrow London street in the East End might not be the most inviting location for a lady's daily stroll."

"You know nothing about me."

Her demeanor returned to its familiar state of studied calm. A pang of loss flashed through him for the other Lady Olivia he'd glimpsed, the one who blazed with emotion, raw and open.

"Or where I should be *strolling*."

She glared at him from below, her fullest height no more than a few inches over five feet, her hair styled in a severe chignon. If they hadn't collided, he would have walked right past her without a second glance. Impossible that the curves he'd glimpsed last night hid beneath the drab, serviceable overcoat that camouflaged her like some sort of slum chameleon. He couldn't decide if the overcoat deserved a funeral pyre or a medal of honor.

As he watched her shuffle through the sketches, examining them one by one, a wisp of memory tickled at the back of his brain. He'd seen these sketches before or, at least, this subject. The material itself was typically representative of Japanese motifs—a serene depiction of nature both botanical and animal—but a specificity lay within these sketches that extended beyond their familiar subject matter.

It was in the brush strokes. A delicate, feathery quality characterized much Japanese art. But not these pieces. Here were brush strokes dense and bold, too singular to be ordinary or forgotten. Indeed, he'd seen these pieces before, but the context eluded him.

He caught Lady Olivia watching him. How had she, of all people, come by such a subject long enough to sketch it?

The baffling woman narrowed her eyes. "I would thank you, Lord St. Alban, but for what, I'm not precisely certain."

"For saving your life?"

"When you are also the same who introduced the danger into it?" she shot back in that soft, yet steely, voice of hers.

He nodded once and allowed her the last word. Lips pressed in a firm line, she rolled up the soiled sketches and hailed a hackney with a short, sharp whistle. Lady Olivia surprised at every turn.

As soon as a hackney stopped, he tipped his hat and made haste to keep his appointment, resisting his body's urging for a single backward glance. He'd gone only a few steps when out of the corner of his eye he glimpsed a shock of white amidst the sidewalk's sea of grime. In three quick strides, he stood over the sheet of paper and snatched it off the ground. She'd miscounted and forgotten a sketch.

He started toward the carriage to return it when a detail at the bottom left corner caught his eye. A tall girl standing apart from a small group of other girls.

He stopped dead in his tracks. Context crashed down on him with the violent force of a hurricane, memories of when and where he'd seen the original paintings slamming through him.

Fifteen years ago. The Kimura compound in Nagasaki. *Her*, captured reading a book, a sliver of light catching the lines and angles of her face, immortalized in a priceless set of Japanese Kanō paintings.

At the time, he'd barely questioned how she'd come to be part of that painting, in that particular room. Six months later, he'd known exactly why. But, by then, it had been too late.

Another memory asserted itself: this set of paintings had been stolen in the dead of night, shortly after his departure from Dejima with Mina. The Kimura family had tried to hush up the details, to ensure they didn't leave the Bay of Nagasaki, but word had leaked out anyway.

How had the paintings surfaced here in London? How was it possible that this piece of a long-buried past had followed him and Mina all the way to England? That someone else held the key that would unlock Mina's secrets?

With the certainty and efficiency of a ship captain, Jake's mind worked out a course of action. He must locate the original paintings and determine how much their "owner" knew about Mina. He didn't know for certain that the person now in possession of the paintings stole them, but he did know that person, by virtue of owning them, was connected to the theft. It was safest to consider that person dangerous and a threat to Mina. It was possible this person—the thief, for expediency's sake—intended to trade on her connection to the paintings and her true heritage. Her Japanese descent was obvious, but that only scratched the surface of the story.

Further, she wasn't merely the daughter of Jakob Radclyffe, but of the Viscount St. Alban, exalted peer of the realm. With a few well-chosen words in the wrong ears, the thief of those paintings could destroy the new life Jake was constructing for his daughter.

He wouldn't fail Mina the way he'd failed her mother. The truth must never find its way to the surface—or to the wagging tongues of society. He must silence the thief.

His head whipped around. *Lady Olivia…* She was connected to the thief somehow.

And he'd just let her go.

He pivoted and sprinted down the sidewalk against the flow of foot traffic, ignoring cries of half-hearted protests. On the run, he scanned the carriages lining the street, all black and ominously the same. He must reach her before she slipped away.

He caught a glimpse of wispy blonde hair showing through a back carriage window, making its way up Ludgate Hill and onto Fleet Street. His feet slowed before coming to a defeated stop, his heart an unrelenting hammer in his chest.

What did Lady Olivia know about the stolen Kanō paintings? His mind raced as the full import of the discovery crashed in on him.

Even if she was a walking scandal, Lady Olivia remained a glimmering jewel of society. A lady with no business navigating London streets like a shop girl. She had the power of a dukedom behind her, quite the opposite of a shop girl who could be plied with a trinket or a night on the town. A literal fortress surrounded the blasted woman, likely a moat, too.

How could he get close enough to a woman like her to unlock her secrets? As soon as the question formed, two answers revealed themselves: the Duke of Arundel and The Progressive School for Young Ladies and the Education of Their Minds.

Immediately, he dismissed the idea of the school. Along that path lay too many unknowns.

But the duke was an altogether different matter. The dukedom wasn't the obstacle, but rather the key. It would place him directly inside her home as the Duke of Arundel's protégé, allowing him access to her. Access to the paintings and the thief was only a step removed.

The uncertain and scandalous future he feared for Mina began to recede into a more manageable state.

Lady Olivia would provide him the information he needed.

It wasn't a matter of *if*, but *when*.

5

NEXT DAY

Olivia settled into her seat at the breakfast table and considered the letter resting beside her coffee and croissant. It looked official.

Another morning, she might allow this letter to sit unopened until she'd considered all of its possible consequences. This morning, she hadn't the time to be patient. Lucy and the duke would be joining her in a few minutes. Without further ado, she took up her butter knife and sliced open the missive.

6 April 1825

To the Estimable Lady Olivia Montfort:

We would like to thank you for considering our services for your estate acquisition needs. However, we deeply regret to inform you that our staff will be unable to assist you in this undertaking. As long-standing retainers of the Montfort Family, it would be a conflict of interest to act in any way contrary to and/or without the Earl of Surrey's explicit instruction.

Furthermore, we would caution you to reconsider pursuing any line of action which does not involve your gracious father's express consent. As you are presumably aware, he and the Countess are not expected home from Italy until autumn. Until such a time, we strongly advise that you remain under the protection of the Duke of Arundel.

Your faithful servants in all, but this,
Wortham, Netheram, & Howell

Olivia slapped the letter down. The cheek! What right had these…*men!*…to put her in her place? She was the possessor of a significant fortune in her own right, the duke having returned her dowry after Percy's "death." How dare they insinuate that she needed a man's name to obtain her townhouse?

She needed no man's "protection," or anyone else's for that matter. Mariana would assist her, as surely would her parents, but that wasn't how she desired to achieve this end. She wanted to accomplish it alone, only then would the life she attained be entirely her own.

She bit down on flaky croissant with more force than necessary. This wouldn't do. She hadn't the faintest idea when Percy would return from the Continent, but he would, someday. And she would be firmly established in her own home before that eventuality occurred. She'd clung to the duke's safe harbor for too many years. It was time for her to venture out on her own. Why wouldn't these…*nodcocks!*…let her?

She reached for the *London Diary* to her left and began skimming its vacuous pages in the hope that they would calm her. She hadn't gotten far when Lucy bounded into the room, followed by the more sedate pace of the duke.

"Good morning, Mum." Lucy landed a fat kiss onto Olivia's cheek and plopped into her usual seat to Olivia's right.

From the corner of her eye, Olivia watched Lucy pick up the unopened letter that lay beside her place setting. Her mouth pinched tight and released before she half slid it under her plate, seal intact.

It was another letter from Percy. And like every other letter he'd sent his daughter these last six months, it had suffered the same fate of utter disregard. At least, outwardly. Inside, Lucy must feel pained and confused. But Olivia must wait for Lucy to broach the subject when she was ready.

Across the table, the duke took his customary place. "I trust all is well with you this morning?"

"Thank you, Your Grace, all is well," she replied, relieved by the welcome distraction of routine.

Lucy, familiar mischievous glint returned to her eye, reached out and lifted the *London Diary* from Olivia's hands. "Let's have a little gossip for breakfast, shall we?"

Olivia couldn't resist an indulgent smile toward her daughter. And judging by the smile tipping up the duke's lips as he perused his serious *Morning Chronicle*, neither could he.

Doubt, subtle and sly, wormed its way into her goals for her future independence. The duke doted on his granddaughter. Wouldn't it be easier to stay?

No. She couldn't allow uncertainty to undermine her resolve.

"What have we here?" Lucy began, thumbing through the pages. "A few changes to Almack's...Lady Jersey said...boring, boring, and more boring... Ah, this is a new feature," she said, her tone growing bright. "It's a haiku." She cleared her throat before reading aloud:

> *Returned to Albion*
> *How to Orient himself?*
> *Breath held, ladies plot.*

"WHO COULD IT BE?" Lucy stared off into the distance, eyes narrowed.

The Right Honourable Jakob Radclyffe, Viscount St. Alban.

Olivia knew it instantly and with a certainty she would rather not consider. It hadn't taken long for thinly veiled riddles about him to start popping up in the gossip rags now that he'd officially entered society.

Two days, it turned out.

"Oh, I know," Lucy cried out. "This must be the dashing new viscount everyone is talking about."

"Everyone?" Olivia asked, unable to resist.

"Oh yes, everyone," Lucy confirmed, but a faraway note sounded in her voice, indicating she'd lost interest in the subject.

Their dance with its talk of *bodies, essences,* and *scents* wedged itself into Olivia's mind, softly insinuating that, indeed, *everyone* found Viscount St. Alban irresistible.

She gave herself a mental shake. The haiku was simply a few lines written in a rag. He was nothing to her.

A little more than nothing.

The memory she'd been suppressing since yesterday refused to be subdued any longer: her collision with him on Ludgate Hill as she'd been returning from Jiro's studio. While she tried to dismiss it as mere curiosity—what had the dratted man been doing in the East End anyway?—her body overrode all the intellectual considerations she threw at it.

Perhaps the high drama of the moment explained her reaction. After all, the instant her footing had slipped out from beneath her, and her body had begun to fall backward into the street, the thought had flashed across her mind that it might be the end for her.

Instead of the inevitable impact of a horse's hoof against her skull, she'd been snapped upright into full—there was no other word for it—*carnal* contact against Lord St. Alban, the insistent pressure of his body against hers. She'd only wanted to soften against the long, rigid length of him.

Oh. That wasn't quite the correct way of putting it.

It was simply that over the last decade she'd forgotten the specific pressure of a man's body clasped tight against hers. And Lord St. Alban's body...

Best she didn't consider the particulars of his body.

She swallowed, hard. What was a lady's proper reaction after having been snatched from the jaws of death supposed to be? Etiquette books offered no guidelines for that particular scenario.

A servant's voice cut in. "Lord St. Alban has arrived, Your Grace."

"Please show him into the room," the duke said without looking up from his newspaper.

Lucy's face lit up, and she squealed. Olivia's butter knife clattered onto her plate. Had her thoughts the power to conjure the dratted man out of thin air? She steadied her voice before asking, "Why is Lord St. Alban—" She considered her next words. "Your protégé?"

Movement caught the corner of her eye, and her gaze swung over to find Lord St. Alban striding through the doorway, looking every inch the noble lord from his hunter green cutaway coat to Wellington boots buffed to a mirror shine. He was the viscount of a young lady's fantasies.

Of course, given the clamor surrounding his arrival at the duchess's salon, it wasn't only young ladies who fantasized about this particular lord. *Everyone* did.

Why did the thought unsettle her so?

"Speak of the devil," the duke said over his paper, an ironic twist to his mouth. "If it isn't the most dashing viscount in London."

Lord St. Alban's brow lifted. It was possible he had the most handsome face she'd ever laid eyes on. From an artistic perspective, of course.

"Perhaps I'm interrupting," he began.

"Nonsense," the duke dismissed, "I instructed the servants to bring you through." He pushed away from the table and stood. "St. Alban, this is my very silly granddaughter, Miss Bretagne." Lucy giggled. "And you've met Lady Olivia."

St. Alban turned and found Olivia's eyes. "My lady."

Across the table strewn with various and sundry breakfast items, their gaze held, and Olivia's heart accelerated as she returned a simple, "My lord." It was all she could manage. For such a short acquaintance, they had certainly accumulated a fair amount of history between them.

"Now," the duke said, "if you will follow me to my study, we can converse about the only five matters a gentleman of means need attend to." He held up his hand and ticked the items off, finger by finger. "Lords to befriend. Lords to avoid. The right tailor. The right club. And the right horse."

The duke strode out of the room, and St. Alban turned to follow his host, but not before casting one more glance in Olivia's direction. The look was one part bemusement, one part curiosity, and wholly familiar. It struck her that she was beginning to be able to read the dashing viscount. How very disconcerting.

Then he was gone. Next, Lucy was pressing a good-bye kiss against Olivia's cheek. "Drummond has brought the carriage around."

Drummond was the duke's ancient, mostly retired valet who saw it as his sacred duty to escort Lucy to school every morning.

"I'll see you later, my love," Olivia said to Lucy's retreating back. Like that, she was alone in the room. Life tended to happen fast around Lord St. Alban.

She'd vowed to leave that man in the past, which was, of course, an impossibility when he collided with her on fetid East End byways and arrived during breakfast for viscount lessons the next day. He wasn't part of a past left behind and unbegun. In fact, with each passing day, their lives grew ever more entwined. How very curious.

She pushed away from the table and stood, intent on proceeding with her day. Her plan was to spend the morning salvaging her sketches, *if* they were salvage-able. If not, she would return to Jiro's studio tomorrow to begin a new set from the original paintings. Another example of the strange way this new viscount kept influencing and entangling himself in her life.

When she reached the doorway, her resolve faltered. To her left, lay a short series of hallways that led to her studio and the rest of her day. To her right, she picked up a low murmur of voices drifting from the duke's study. She supposed they were discussing one of five topics.

Of their own volition, her feet hooked a right. It would be only a minor detour.

As she drew level with the study, his voice rang out, "Lady Olivia, my dear, can you answer us a question?"

She hesitated. They weren't supposed to have noticed her. That wasn't part of the plan. She should make an excuse and continue on her way. Yet her body continued moving forward, and she was inside the room in three steps.

The duke turned to St. Alban. "You're on Cleveland Row, you say?"

"Aye," Lord St. Alban responded in the curt manner of a sailor, calling to Olivia's mind the rumor that he'd been a ship captain.

"Then you're all set with horses. The Russell Court Mews is just up the street from you. Mention my name, and you'll find yourself the owner of a fine piece of horseflesh. Now, Olivia," the duke said as he pivoted toward her, "how many servants would suffice as the skeleton staff of a closed estate?"

"It depends on the estate, Your Grace." She stepped deeper into the study, which smelled of old leather, rich mahogany, and earthy tobacco. "Is it a working agricultural estate with tenants and cattle? Or an ornamental estate with a grand house and nothing much else?" Keen awareness of Lord St. Alban's steady gaze on her profile suffused her body, cell by cell. Why hadn't she turned left and gotten on with her day? "Mrs. Landry might be a better source for the information you seek."

"Excellent point, my dear," said the duke, already moving toward the door. "I haven't yet had the bell in this room repaired. Keep the *dashing* viscount company while I seek out Mrs. Landry, will you?"

She responded with a gracious, "Of course."

One didn't refuse the request of a duke lightly.

Except now only she and Lord St. Alban occupied this room.

The study, immense and airy with its floor-to-ceiling windows and vast swaths of uncluttered space, had ever been a place of refuge and safety where the mind could wander unfettered by concerns outside its four walls. But now it contracted into a tight cocoon, dense and close, as its rich woods and scent of earth turned stifling and dangerously intimate.

In desperate need of distraction, she skirted a leather chaise longue and made her way to the bookcase running the length of an adjacent wall. She pulled the first book at hand and set about feigning interest in a collection of Alexander Pope's poetry. She abhorred Alexander Pope.

"Can you answer me one question?" Lord St. Alban asked from his place at the periphery of her vision.

"Possibly." She kept her gaze fixed on the Pope as if riveted. Nothing could be further from the truth.

"Why does the duke keep calling me *the dashing viscount?*"

Her eyes flew up to meet his bemused gaze, and a surprised chirrup of laughter escaped her. "I take it you don't read the *London Diary.*"

"Never heard of it."

"You may want to acquaint yourself with its pages. According to the *London Diary,* you are the most dashing viscount in all of London this Season. I suspect its readership agrees."

"And are you counted amongst its readership?" he asked, his sharp focus pinning her into place.

"To my everlasting shame, I am," Olivia said and stopped dead. She'd stumbled neck-deep into that one. Her cheeks flamed with sudden heat.

He cocked his head, and amusement warmed his pale, glacier-blue eyes. "I must admit you fascinate me more with each passing day. Yet I know so little about you or your past."

"My past has naught to do with you."

He took a step closer, and she instinctively pressed back against the bookcase. She inhaled the huff of pique that wanted release. Such a reaction was so very silly of her. The man was all the way across the room.

"Perhaps," he began, drawing out the word, "but I can't

help wondering what is true and what is false. Or should I look to the pages of the *London Diary* for my answer?"

"You will find no truth in those pages."

"Then tell me the truth from your own lips."

He was pushing her. *Why?*

She cleared her throat. "My past is just that. The *past.*" It was a weak response, but it would have to do. A stronger defense might further provoke his curiosity.

He nodded his acceptance, even though she sensed he wasn't satisfied by her answer. He stepped forward, and her heart pitter-pattered in her chest. He was coming to join her at the bookcase. He moved with a fluidity unusual for a man of such great height, his body a vertical line of power and grace, mayhap a product of his years spent at sea.

"From what I've gathered," he said, stopping one row of bookcases removed from her, "you've had two marriages?"

He'd drawn near, too near, and was distracting her from her purpose, which was to busily feign indifference to him "I can see how you might reach that conclusion, but, no, I've had only the one marriage."

His brows creased together as he surely added one and one together and calculated two. "How is it possible? You are a widow and a divorcée."

"I divorced the man who first made me a widow," she replied in a matter-of-fact tone, thoroughly unmoved by the observation that his voice had become very like the consistency of crushed velvet.

"That seems improbable."

"Indeed."

The silence that followed pulled taut, and he began scanning the book titles at his eye level before reaching up and running his fingertips across embossed leather spines. She followed their unhurried progress, and her mouth went dry as Saharan sand.

His hands were gorgeous…and large. But it wasn't just the size of them, it was the sheer capability of them. They'd saved her life. What more were they capable of?

Her body heated up by a degree.

His fingers hesitated on a title, tilted it, and slid it out. She watched, transfixed, as his forefinger rose to his lips and he touched tongue to its calloused tip. It dropped to the book and began ruffling through its pages. When had she last blinked?

By sheer strength of will, she tore her gaze away from him and swiveled around on a deep inhalation. How long had it been since she'd last drawn breath?

She'd allowed him to get too close to her. Close enough that she noticed his scent of cloves blending with the study's aroma of cigar and earth. They combined to add a sweetness to the air. It was nice, if she was being honest.

Honesty was an overrated virtue.

She pretended indifference and meandered away from him, her heartbeat present and insistent. She'd never really noticed her heartbeat. A simple function that she took for granted every day, every moment of her life. Yet she was so very aware of its ceaseless pounding.

Because of him.

And his hands.

And his sweetish scent.

And the tip of his pink tongue.

What was keeping the duke?

"At the duchess's salon," she heard behind her, "a few words were bandied about you. *Unconventional. Bohemian.*"

She placed a steadying hand on the elegant maple curve of the pianoforte and set the dreadful Pope onto its polished surface. Lord St. Alban's serious, unrelenting gaze sent pinpricks of heat racing down her spine.

It unnerved her. It quickened her pulse.

"They would use those words about me."

"Why is that?"

"For developing a different point of view."

"That answer only purports to be an answer."

She deserved that. She could remain silent and give him nothing more. He would deserve as much. But she felt a strange urge to reveal more.

She steeled herself and faced him, her back against the pianoforte. "In the years between my widowhood and my divorce, I developed a *most scandalous* interest in the arts."

"As a patroness?" he asked. "Or an artist?"

"Both."

He moved forward, again cutting the distance between them in half, a concentrated alertness about him. He was truly, intensely interested in this conversation. How very odd.

"About the sketches you dropped yesterday—"

"Oh? I don't recall *dropping* any sketches, my lord," she interrupted, drawing herself up to her fullest, primmest height. Her feet, at last, found firmer ground as she took refuge in self-righteousness, possibly her only escape from being swallowed whole by quicksand. "As I recall, they were knocked from my hands."

"Are they ruined?"

"I'll know later."

"If they are, will you still have access to the originals?"

"Yes."

He cleared his throat. "It must be unusual for such subject matter to be seen in London, much less strewn across a rank sidewalk."

"I daresay, my lord."

"Might I view the originals sometime?"

She detected a strange tentativeness not only in his voice, but in his entire demeanor, as a puzzling ribbon of tension twisted through the air between them. "That isn't a request I can grant."

"But you know who can?" he pressed. Was that a note of frustration in his voice?

Even across the colorful expanse of an intricately Aubusson carpet, she detected in his bearing a burning desire to have her reply. She opened her mouth and shut it. She would've never taken Lord St. Alban for an art lover. The sketches were part of a world that was hers alone, and she wasn't about to share it with this man who was no longer a stranger, but not a friend either. A change of subject was in order. "I take it you're unfamiliar with the running of English estates."

A subtle, but distinct, flicker of dissatisfaction crossed his features. She might be developing too sharp a sensibility of the viscount, if she was able to gauge his moods by his facial expressions.

At last, he replied, "That's correct. Life aboard a merchant vessel is simple. Buy, sell, trade, transport. Land in England, it seems, has none of those qualities."

"Then the rumors are true?" she asked, unable to resist being drawn into this line of conversation, to know him better. "You captained a ship?"

He nodded. "My mother descended from a long line of Dutch traders, and my uncles were only too happy to show me the ropes. I took to it like a duck to water."

An undeniable note of bitterness underlay his admission. A bitterness that spoke of a life lost, not one gained. She understood something essential to this man: he had no desire to be a viscount. He would be sailing a ship this very moment, experiencing the adventure such a life offered, if he had his way.

In its stead, he had London, a gray sort of life. While she experienced the vibrancy of London, she could understand that a man accustomed to sailing the Seven

Seas would feel hemmed in by the city's walls. Sympathy for him stabbed through her. She knew what it was to have one life suddenly end and another begin without asking for permission.

"I can see how the lure of freedom and adventure would be impossible to resist," she said.

"Not impossible."

A wry smile curled about his lips, and she intuited his meaning. He was here, a viscount, in England. Not impossible.

She followed his lead and tried to lighten the mood. "And now you're learning how to be quite the conventional viscount?"

"Oh, yes, *quite*. Complete with club memberships, fine horseflesh, and a proper wife."

Wife. The word, like the prick of a needle, shocked Olivia upright. "A wife?"

"Really, a stepmother for my daughter."

"A stepmother for your daughter *is* a wife to you." The seed of an unwanted emotion sprouted open within Olivia, and she tamped it down. She wouldn't give it water or light to grow. How entirely inappropriate, silly even, to feel jealousy over a man who wasn't and never would be hers.

"I haven't given that part much thought, to be honest. It could be a matter of semantics."

"Hardly."

"Well, the duchess has a great number of proper candidates."

There was another word. *Proper.* "I'm sure she does."

Olivia fixed her attention on smudging out a fingerprint, likely her own, on the shiny finish of the pianoforte. Why did her tone have to sound so pettish? What was Lord St. Alban's proper wife hunt to her anyway?

The duke strode into the room with the housekeeper, who looked flustered, flattered, and delighted all at once, and spared Olivia from having to consider an answer. "The most capable Mrs. Landry has the answers to all our questions," the duke announced. As if he'd only just registered the positioning of Olivia and Lord St. Alban, his gaze darted back and forth between them. "Have I interrupted something?"

"Your timing couldn't be better," Olivia said, perhaps too fast on a wave of relief. "I need to get on with my day before it gets away from me."

She pushed herself off the pianoforte and neatly sidestepped the towering Lord St. Alban—and his gorgeous, capable hands. She crossed the room to land a quick kiss on the duke's cheek. Without another glance toward Lord St. Alban, she fled the room in a graceless exit, if ever there was one.

Her heels clicking across gleaming white marble, she gave her head a tiny shake. The sanctuary of her studio lay ahead. She tethered the dashing and problematic Lord St. Alban to the far reaches of her mind.

Where he belonged.

6

———

NEXT DAY

Jake shifted in the unforgiving wooden seat constructed for the proportions of a school-aged child and attempted to find a measure of relief.

In the usual course of events, he suspected viscounts didn't submit to such treatment. However, the formidable headmistress, Mrs. Bloomquist, had left him here, and he dared not risk incurring her wrath—or, at least, any more than he already had.

Their meeting had begun on a promising enough note. At his request, the duchess had arranged a tour with Mrs. Bloomquist of The Progressive School for Young Ladies and the Education of Their Minds. After yesterday's encounter in the Duke of Arundel's study, he'd realized his preferred plan of gaining access to Lady Olivia through that mentorship was doomed to fail. The blasted woman was as slippery as water streaming across smooth stone. So, today, he'd proceeded with his other possibility: to seek her out through the school. And, miraculously, the school had proven an ideal fit for Mina.

Half an hour into the tour, however, Mrs. Bloomquist had asked the fateful question, "And Miss Radclyffe's age?"

Jake hadn't hesitated. "Fifteen years next month."

"Lord St. Alban." A sour frown twisted the woman's mouth. "Miss Radclyffe is well advanced beyond the admissions age for prospective students. I'm afraid you will have to look elsewhere for your daughter's educational needs. A reputable finishing school would be a better match."

A few dumbfounded seconds passed before Jake choked out, "You're refusing my daughter?"

Mrs. Bloomquist looked to the ceiling as if gathering her patience to proceed forward with a room of inattentive students. "We like to mold our girls from the youngest age possible. That is, from the time they are capable of acting like proper human beings. That is, from the age of ten." Her gaze lowered to meet his. "You see, by age fifteen, the clay is quite set. Unmoldable, if you will."

"Ten? Is that number derived from a scientific analysis?"

"Please, take a seat, my lord. You appear agitated."

He searched the room for a suitable chair, but saw only five or so empty school desks arranged in a semicircle. "In one of these?"

"If you please."

His mistake became apparent the moment he squeezed himself into a desk. First, he was going to have one hell of a time extracting his six-foot-four frame from its grasp. Second, he'd ceded the power position to Mrs. Bloomquist. Was that the hint of a smile curving her lips?

She glanced at her pocket watch and made her way to the door. "My lord, if you will please wait here, I must attend to a matter of some importance."

"Must attend to one of your proper human beings?" he'd asked. He regretted the acid in his tone when the woman flashed him a suppressive scowl before exiting the room.

Ten minutes later, he still sat. If he ever succeeded

in disengaging himself from this desk, he might consider kicking himself for having goaded the woman. This school was an impeccable match for Mina. Its emphasis on mathematics—"*Not just sorting household ledgers,*" according to Mrs. Bloomquist—and natural philosophy, including physics and astronomy, led him to the conclusion that here was a place where Mina would not only fit in, but one where she would thrive.

Additionally, the students learned French, piano, tea etiquette, dancing, and needlework. "After all, that is the world in which they live," Mrs. Bloomquist had added on a resigned note.

In short, within these four walls lay the exact school for which he'd been searching since he and Mina had arrived in England. And he'd irritated its headmistress.

He began formulating a strategy for how best to deal with the woman. He would try charming her. If that didn't work, he would cajole. If that didn't work, he would bribe.

Mrs. Bloomquist had her price. His days in the sea trade had taught him that everyone did. What made a Mrs. Bloomquist tick?

A body sailed past the doorway, and he braced himself for the woman's return. His anticipation turned to shock when a wispy blonde head peeked around the doorframe and wide, blue eyes blinked once. A beat later, the rest of her followed. There, framed by the doorway, stood a perturbed Lady Olivia Montfort, staring a hole through him as if she could obliterate his presence with the heat of her gaze.

Her mouth opened, then closed. It opened again, then closed again, her discomfiture evident by her flawless imitation of a fish gasping air. At last, she got out, "Lord St. Alban? How is it that you keep popping up everywhere I am?"

* * *

OLIVIA HAD FINISHED meeting with the board of directors and was about to get on with her day when she caught a glimpse of a large form seated inside what was supposed to be an empty classroom.

Was her mind playing tricks on her? Or was that form a man?

A quick first glance confirmed the room's sole occupant was, indeed, a man. A second glance revealed the man to be none other than Lord St. Alban crammed into the smallest desk imaginable for a man his size, legs splayed out into the aisle like a recalcitrant schoolboy in need of a good paddling.

Oh. Where had that come from? She didn't even believe in corporal punishment for children.

Her eyes traced long muscular thighs outlined by tight-fitting buff buckskins that conveyed the illusion of naked skin. This man was no lad.

She gave herself a mental slap. What was it she'd last said?

Oh, yes… "My question stands, Lord St. Alban." Her insides gave a tumble at the use of his name. She must collect herself. The man's powerful thighs were of no consequence. "What is your business here? I thought you a burglar. We don't get many men in the school."

The horizontal line of his mouth firmed. "I'm here to discuss with Mrs. Bloomquist the possibility of a place for my daughter."

Olivia nodded. "I imagine our school would benefit from adding Miss Radclyffe to its ranks. She strikes me as most impressive." She absently picked up a piece of chalk from the board beside her and pivoted toward it. The burn of Lord St. Alban's gaze threatened to set her back aflame.

"Has Miss Bretagne been here long?"

"She was the school's first student two years ago." A face began to emerge from Olivia's hand.

"That would make her twelve years of age?"

Olivia's hand stilled, and she half turned toward him. "I'm not certain that is any of your business, but yes."

"Your daughter must be a proper human being then."

"Well," Olivia began, setting the chalk down and dusting off her fingers as she turned around, "she has her moments, but I wouldn't go that far. The word *barbaric* has escaped Lucy's teacher Miss Scace's lips on more than one occasion in reference to Lucy."

His gaze shifted left. "Your likeness of Mina is remarkably lifelike for so few strokes."

Olivia's cheeks blazed into twin flames, and her heart banged out a hard thud. She had, indeed, drawn Miss Radclyffe's likeness. How bothersome that his praise elicited the unruly wave of gratification now coursing through her.

He sat forward in his ridiculous chair, his gaze, intense and penetrating, pinning her into place. "Such mastery must take years of practice."

"I'd hardly call myself a master." She shifted on her feet. The movement was an obvious indicator of her discomfort, but there was no help for it. "That appellation belongs to Jiro."

He cocked his head. "An unusual name for London. In fact, I haven't heard the name *Jiro* since I was last in Japan."

She should make her excuses. She didn't want to discuss the details of her life with this man. He knew too much about it already. In fact, it was possible that he knew more about her than ninety-nine percent of her acquaintances. "This drawing has to do with naught other than the fact that I sketch when I'm—"

"Nervous?"

Poised on the edge of flight, she froze. Now he was finishing her sentences?

It wasn't his presumption that unsettled her, but

rather his accuracy and familiarity. He'd not only finished her sentence correctly, but had done so without hesitation.

"Why would you be nervous, Lady Olivia?" he pressed. "Not when we've become such old friends over the last few days."

Like an old married couple.

Oh. Why had *that* phrase come to her?

Well, it wouldn't do. She must leave this room and find a way to avoid this man. When she saw her future stretched out before her, it didn't include any man, particularly not this one. "I bid you good day, Lord St. Al—"

"Have you any insights?"

A few feet shy of the doorway and freedom, she stopped, curious. "Into what?"

"Into how to gain Mina's admittance into this school."

Olivia's eyebrows drew together. "Is there a problem? I'm fairly certain that if this school had an exemplar, Miss Radclyffe would be she."

"She's too old."

"Ah," Olivia breathed out. "You've been speaking with Mrs. Bloomquist. She has firm ideas about young ladies and their malleability, or lack thereof, at certain developmental ages."

Olivia found herself standing one desk removed from Lord St. Alban and saw only now that their conversation had drawn her forward. Separated by no more than five feet, a memory came to her, unbidden: the night of the duchess's salon, when they'd danced the waltz, his breath had tickled the fine hairs of her neck. Its impact on the rate of her breathing was not insignificant.

"This school is the best I've found for her."

"Is that so? Most of London considers our little

school unnecessary and inappropriate." She couldn't resist challenging him. Women likely never did.

He shifted in his seat and crossed his powerful legs. His gaze never wavered from hers, radiating a seriousness and confidence that she couldn't help envying. She wanted some of it for herself.

"Have you heard of Sir Isaac Newton's *Principia*?" he asked.

"The school has a copy in its library."

"Mina has all three volumes memorized from cover to cover."

"Impressive."

And it was impressive, truly, but her proximity to Lord St. Alban made it difficult to appreciate Miss Radclyffe's intellect. Somehow she was standing so close to him that, had he liked, he could have lifted his foot and her dress in a single, swift motion.

"It's beyond impressive, Lady Olivia. Mina has the sort of brilliant mind that could make her one of the great thinkers of her generation. That's what is at stake."

Olivia set a balancing hand on the window ledge to her right and looked through its clear pane of glass in an attempt to slow the conversation, to reassert rationality over herself. Below, a group of girls were pruning rosebushes in the back garden, preparing them for their first spring bloom, but she watched them almost sightlessly.

At issue was the not insignificant problem that her brain, and her body, were refusing to think of Lord St. Alban as a viscount in this intimate space. Stripped away were society's constraints and dictums about who he was, who she was, and who they were in relation to one another. In the small patch of air they shared with no one but each other, it was simple, even elemental: he was a man, and she a woman.

Yet society's rules would reassert themselves, and she remembered precisely who she was: a *mere* woman.

"What I wouldn't give," she began, a burgeoning righteousness increasing with each word she spoke, "to navigate life with your utter privilege. Have you never been denied anything a day in your life?" A silent huff of a laugh escaped her. "No wonder Mrs. Bloomquist's refusal has you stymied. But fret not, you will prevail. Your kind simply does."

"My kind?" he asked, his voice low and deep, wary.

She was being unfair, but she cared not. Life was unfair.

"You take me for nothing more than an entitled viscount who must have his way?"

"My characterization of you tends more toward the general. An entitled *man?* Absolutely." She rested her hip on a neighboring desk. A sleeping beast had awakened inside her, and it wanted, demanded, release. "It isn't only that you can do whatever you please; you can do whatever *pleases you.* What a heady feeling it must be to have the world at your fingertips."

He didn't answer her immediately, allowing the moment to stretch out and the import of her words to sink into the air. All the while, he continued to regard her with eyes cool and penetrating. At last, he spoke, his voice a velvety rumble in his chest. "And what in this world doesn't a woman under the protection of a duke have at her fingertips?"

Her own Mayfair townhouse, she didn't reply. Instead, she pressed her lips together and held his piercing gaze.

A possibility stole in. He wasn't only a man. He was an opportunity.

She and he each had something the other wanted. And they each had the power to give it to the other. It was simple.

Misgiving seized her. This was Lord St. Alban. Nothing would remain simple with him for long. She felt it in her bones. But how badly did she want her independence?

It felt like a test question. And Lord St. Alban was the correct answer.

She cleared her throat and spoke the words before she thought better of them. "As one of the school's founders, I could request a reevaluation of its admittance policy."

He sat taller in his seat. "Is that so?"

She hesitated. Every *no no no* clanging through her head was countered by a *yes yes yes* that this was her opportunity, and she dare not miss it. "I could even put in a good word for Miss Radclyffe. That she be the first student admitted under this new policy."

"Only good?"

"Persuasive," she replied, unsure how she'd come this far. She would be further entwining her life with this man whom she hardly knew. How badly did she *need* her independence? "On one condition," she added.

"Which is?"

"For a favor in return."

"Yes?" He was prodding her along, rightly sensing her ambivalence.

She screwed up her courage and finally said what she needed to say. "Buy me a Mayfair townhouse."

* * *

A LIGHTNING FLASH of anticipation shot through Jake and quickened his pulse. Lady Olivia stood tensed before him, every ounce of her body awaiting his counter. He saw it in the tightness about her lips, the clench of her hands, the rawness of her gaze. Every cell in her body wanted him to say *yes*.

And he would. But he sensed that he could get more out of her if he held off.

After all, in the span of ten minutes she'd confirmed

her connection to a Japanese artist, had even revealed the man's name. *Jiro*. What would another ten minutes yield?

Still, he couldn't allow the opportunity to provoke her further to pass him by. "A gentleman doesn't gift a lady with property." He was being a scoundrel, no doubt. "Unless, she agreed to be his—"

She held up a forestalling hand. "Do *not* finish that sentence."

His rational brain, at last, asserted itself. What was he thinking? Among other things, this woman was an aristocrat. One didn't offer to make such a lady one's mistress in exchange for a townhouse, even one located in Mayfair. "Would you care to elaborate on your proposition then?"

"It's simple," she said. "I'm in need of a new residence, and I've exhausted all acceptable options for obtaining one."

Her eyes told him what her lips wouldn't: there was more to this story.

And she wouldn't be revealing it to him today.

Was she aware how near her body was to his? How easily he could reach up, cup the back of her head in the palm of his hand, and draw her face toward his…

He cleared his throat, as if his mind could be cleared with as little effort. *Focus.* "No doubt the duke—"

"I would like to accomplish this transaction without the duke's knowledge."

"Behind his back?"

"The duke isn't to know until the purchase is finalized."

"The man clearly dotes on you." Jake didn't relish the idea of going against the Duke of Arundel. "He would give you anything you wish."

"I need to accomplish this on my own." She hesitated. "With your assistance, of course."

He didn't like the hard edge racing alongside her

words, but that was the world they inhabited. Like that, he understood something central to this woman: she wanted to forge a life on her own terms.

"And in exchange—" she began.

"You will help Mina gain entry into this school," he finished for her.

She nodded. "All must be done in your name and through your solicitors. I require absolute discretion from you. And, of course, this won't be a gift. I shall re-imburse you with my own funds. In fact, I can't imagine there will be any need to involve you beyond the use of your solicitors and, of course, your noble name."

"On the contrary, my lady," he persisted, "I couldn't, in good conscience, allow you to navigate the vagaries of the townhouse hunt unescorted. It would be un-gentlemanly."

"Lord St. Alban, I must decline your most gen-erous offer," she countered. "I need only your solici-tors and your name, not your...*person*." Her mouth snapped shut on that last word, and she shifted on her feet, a habit of hers. "Secrecy would best serve both of us. Your hunt for a proper stepmother for your daughter needn't be compromised if no one knows of your dealings with the scandalous Lady Olivia Montfort."

What was that strange, sharp note he detected in her tone? If he knew her better, he might suspect re-sentment. But he didn't really know her. Not yet, anyway.

He held his tongue, and waited. It wouldn't do his cause any good to keep arguing his point. But that didn't mean he'd ceded it.

This bargain was exactly what he needed. Here she stood before him, offering him this opportunity like it was her idea: *time*. Her time, even though she had yet to accept that fact. She would lead him to this Jiro, and

Mina's future would be secure. All he had to do was spend time with her.

Now to extricate himself from this desk and properly shake on their arrangement before she reconsidered her proposal. Another chance like this wouldn't land in his lap again. If he wiggled left—

"You're ridiculous in that desk." The side of her mouth tilted up into a mean, little smile. It was more charming than it had a right to be.

He stopped cold. "I think that was the idea."

"You wouldn't be the first man to regret underestimating Mrs. Bloomquist."

Again, he began muscling his way to freedom, and her mouth crept wider into a smile that revealed the tip of her crooked tooth. He saw with no small amount of gratification that when he stood, the mean, little smile slipped.

How very small and vulnerable she could appear in the blink of an eye. That curious instinct to protect her pulsed through him, and he squelched it. Instead, he held out his hand. "Lady Olivia, you have a bargain."

Pointedly, her gaze lowered and met his. "Gentlemen do not shake hands."

"Sailors do."

Her fingers inched forward until they touched his as gently as a butterfly alighting upon a petal. He squeezed her silk-gloved hand within his grasp and gave it a quick shake. A surprised laugh escaped her, and their eyes met, holding for a beat too long. Her smile faded.

She dropped his hand like a hot coal and stepped backward until her skirts touched the wall at the front of the room. Afraid to move and break the spell, he held still. In a matter of seconds, he could close the gap and have her pressed against the chalkboard, legs wrapped around his waist.

But what good would that accomplish? No good.

None at all. Untold depths resided within this woman. If her depths could be reached, how far would he have to fall?

She blinked once, twice, swallowed, and the moment was gone. "I expect to hear from your solicitors in the next few days," she murmured, her gaze refusing to meet his one last time. She neatly rounded the corner and stepped out of sight.

Alone in the room with his thoughts for company, a possibility came to him. A possibility unworthy of a gentleman. But he was a man who shook hands, so what sort of gentleman was he, anyway?

He strode to the doorway and poked his head around the corner just as the front door closed behind her.

She wasn't getting away that easily.

7

J ake rushed down the corridor and slipped through the front door. The conclusion of his conversation with Mrs. Bloomquist would have to wait for another day.

A quick scan of the sidewalks just caught the familiar swish of Lady Olivia's skirts rounding a corner. One blink, and she was out of sight. What was the woman up to?

Before he knew what he was about, he was making the bend around the same corner. The ugly truth wouldn't be denied: he was following her. That thought in mind, he was careful to stay a generous distance behind her. Should she look backward on a whim, he wouldn't stand out in the crowd.

It wasn't long before the air began to ripen into a distinct *odor*. A smell that could be rightly characterized as a stench. She'd led them far afield of Mayfair and directly into the heart of a slum. He wasn't sure which one, but that detail hardly mattered. Why did Lady Olivia insist on spending her time hanging about slums?

As if she'd intuited his question, she set about answering it. Stride shortened, pace slowed, she approached a woman scrubbing a length of coarse linen across a washboard. Jake crossed the street and kept his head down so as not to attract undue attention.

However, he needn't have concerned himself on that score. The entirety of Lady Olivia's regard was fixed on the washerwoman. He couldn't help noticing the other woman's scarlet, cracked hands and stony expression.

The two women exchanged a few words before Lady Olivia reached inside her dishwater dull overcoat and pulled out a coin for the woman. The washerwoman slipped it between her considerable cleavage and settled back against the wall, her arms crossed in front of her in a pugnacious stance.

Pad of paper and pencil emerged from Lady Olivia's flat black case, and she began scratching charcoal across the blank surface. The washerwoman's face never once altered its expression. This woman had seen it all, and there were no surprises left in this world, not even a posh lady offering a bit of coin to take her likeness.

Jake slipped inside a dark alcove and watched, feeling like the voyeur he undoubtedly was. While he was ostensibly following Lady Olivia to find the art thief, he couldn't deny that he was enjoying himself too much and experiencing the same set of emotions he'd felt the first night he'd met her: interested, engaged, and alive.

Her face had taken on a beatific aspect rivaling that of an Italian Renaissance Mary, so deep was her content in this interaction with a washerwoman. He would have never thought to combine a society lady —daughter-in-law to a duke, no less—in the same body with an artist who delighted in sketching lowly washerwomen. As far as he knew, such occurrences were as rare as unicorns gamboling across misty meadows.

Yet here was one such unicorn.

She possessed untold depths, indeed. How did these depths relate to the stolen paintings?

It was becoming apparent to him that she, a woman whom he hardly knew, was capable of anything. Only a fool would think her incapable of connections to the underworld. After all, here she was at ease in a slum, a place where he was certain no other *ton* matron had ever set foot.

She would lead him to the thief. He was more certain of it than ever.

Beneath his unblinking eye, she slipped the sketchpad back into its case, handed the washerwoman another coin, and proceeded down the street. Several minutes and winding streets later, she nearly tripped on a beggar slumped against a dingy wall, legs extended across half the sidewalk.

Nothing new in this scene. Jake gave away too many coins to count to this sort of man, woman, and child every day. He watched her drop a few coins into the beggar's extended cup and retread the same routine with the beggar as with the washerwoman.

She had a way with people that put them at their ease, that rendered their difference in station insignificant. She was no ordinary lady. He would do well to remember it.

A sudden commotion ripped through the air, snapping Jake's attention to the street. Not a block away, a large draught horse, harnessed to its top heavy cart, was rearing up on its hind legs, obscuring his view of Lady Olivia. With each movement, the horse alternately threatened to overturn the cart or race down the street with it.

The driver jumped to the ground, shouting at passersby to clear the area, before he began repeating the horse's name over and over in an attempt to soothe the frightened animal. The horse was having none of it, neighing and whinnying and creating a general fracas.

Jake was about to bypass the entire scene when a small child, with no more than two years on him, toddled forward, hand extended, smile dimpling cheeks chubby with baby fat. Before he could give rational thought to the situation, he leapt out and swept the child behind him. The boy toddled off to his mother.

It was only Jake and the horse now. The massive beast shook its head from side to side as if to let him know this wasn't going to be easy.

What the hell was he thinking? Only this morning he'd met the master of the Russell Court Mews, who'd imparted no small amount of advice on the soothing of a spooked horse. Jake wracked his brain for the man's exact instructions and called a few to mind.

He stepped in smooth, deliberate increments toward the distraught horse, clicking and cooing all the time. A transfixed silence stole over the crowd when he came within three feet of the distressed beast. After a few minutes of this, the horse reluctantly relaxed and came down, ears flickering in response to the clicks and coos. It was as if they spoke the same secret language, and Jake was the only living being attuned to his distress.

Lay a hand on 'im, confident like, no fear in your eyes.

His hand found the horse's muzzle and stroked down the curve of the beast's glistening neck. The horse snorted a wet breath that caught Jake full in the chest, but he discerned a budding trust in the gesture.

Make certain it innit a rock in the hoof. More like than not, it'll be the culprit.

Jake's hand trailed down the horse's proud chest, further down his left leg to his fetlock until his fingers dared reach the underside of a lifted hoof and pluck out a piece of debris visible only to him. The horse gave one last whinny and a toss of his shiny black mane before settling his hoof firmly on the ground, drama over.

The crowd released its collective breath, and, like

that, Cannon Street returned to its usual bustling self. The crowd dispersed and carried on with a hundred individual days.

Jake gave the horse one last pat as he glanced toward the place where he'd last seen Lady Olivia. The beggar remained in his place, but she was gone. Jake raced forward, craning his neck to get a better view. Nothing. The frustrating woman had slipped away from him yet again. Unexpectedly closer to his goal, it galled him to find it snatched out of his grasp.

Yet he also experienced a vague feeling of uncertainty regarding this underhand means of locating the art thief. It had to do with the depths he sensed within her. At the duchess's salon, he'd assumed her the type of Englishwoman who would bore him within two sentences of conversation. But the last few days had shown him that Lady Olivia Montfort wasn't the person her exterior suggested.

She wasn't a type. She was, in fact, very much her own person.

And very like the ever-changing sea. One had to gain experience with the sea in order to read it correctly. Otherwise, its currents would carry a ship far off course before a sailor realized his error.

He did, at least, have some experience with the sea.

Would it be enough?

* * *

OLIVIA ROLLED her tongue against the roof of her mouth and attempted to rid it of its copper taste, the taste of bitterness.

Why had that acrid note sounded in her voice when she'd spoken of Lord St. Alban's future, *proper* wife?

Even in her head, it sounded bitter. He'd caught it, too. She could tell by the tight narrowing of his eyes on her.

Why should she be bitter anyway? It was her choice not to be a proper wife. She'd once been a proper wife, and once was enough.

She increased her pace, her heels a purposeful click-clack against the sidewalk. It wouldn't do to dwell on such musings. They could be sorted out later by the Olivia who dwelled in the West End. The Olivia who had just struck a bargain—and shaken hands on it!—with Lord St. Alban.

A gentleman doesn't gift a lady with property, unless she agreed to be his—

She'd stopped him right there, she'd had to. He'd been offering to make her his—

She exhaled a forceful breath, hoping to rid her mind of the dratted man at the same time. She was striding toward the East End, a striking world that increased in vibrancy and vividness with each step. These environs never failed to offer respite, however temporary, from her small West End life.

Over the years, she'd come to expect any number of situations from a morning spent roaming the East End on her eventual way to Jiro's studio: filth, poverty, rancidity, the odd moment of fright, the odd moment of kindness, but, most of all, she'd come to expect the unexpected.

Her purpose was to dash off quick sketches of street subjects. Jiro had insisted that this exercise was essential to her development as an artist. She needed to understand all walks of life in order to paint life in its full depth and complexity. How was it possible that a decade had passed between now and then?

It had begun with a simple scribble on Lucy's watercolor set. She'd found herself invigorated in a way she hadn't since Percy's supposed death. Painting, creating something from nothing, connected to something deep inside her: it was hers alone. She'd never experienced a pursuit so reliant on her own skill and drive.

Within the week, she placed a discreet ad in the paper and found an art master, the recently immigrated Jiro of Nagasaki, and began painting: Lucy, the duke, the household staff, the aged family dog Poochie, bowls of fruit...anyone or anything that would sit still for half an hour.

With Jiro's encouragement she explored other parts of London, too. It was during this period that she began to evolve into the woman she was today. At least, that was how she viewed it in retrospect.

Instead of having Jiro come to her in St. James's Square, she began going to him in Limehouse for her lessons. She'd hired a nanny to spend mornings with Lucy and began painting like a madwoman, paying her street subjects—like the washerwoman she'd just finished sketching—to sit for five, ten, fifteen minutes... whatever time they could spare.

For the first time in her life, she experienced the real world, and it fascinated her. It was a solitary venture, but she never felt lonely. She saw the dirty, impoverished, fetid side of London hinted at on the streets of St. James. But she also saw the various ways people lived with dignity in reduced circumstances. The poor were no longer an abstract concept for her.

This experience not only deepened and expanded her palette as an artist; it deepened and expanded her as a person. She evolved into a woman, a whole woman, not just some confection of a girl, the girl she once was.

Face tilted toward the cloudless sky, the first in weeks, she nearly tripped over a pair of legs, one of which was missing its foot at the end. "'Ave ole Boney to thank for that," the legs' owner piped up.

Olivia averted her gaze. She'd been staring. "Beg pardon, sir." She dropped a few coins into the beggar's cup. "Which campaign, sir?"

"The Peninsula, milady."

The air arrested in her lungs. For a decade she'd believed Percy's body buried in a soldier's grave on the Peninsula. She drew enough breath to ask, "Which division?"

"Second, milady." A cough rattled through the old soldier's chest. "Signed on in 1809 and didna stop 'til '14. Nearly had me whole leg blowed off. Lucky ole Boney just got me one foot."

She cleared her throat, which had gone tight. "Do you mind if I draw your likeness?"

"Fine wi' me. I ain' goin' nowhere fast," he quipped and settled into the wall at his back.

She opened her case, removed charcoals and paper, and briskly set about sketching the old soldier. First came the shape of his face, hollowed out and coated with street grime. Then it was on to red-rimmed eyes sunk deep within their sockets, parched lips shriveled to the thickness of wrapping paper, pock-marked skin the texture of old leather. In all, a face as ravaged by war and poverty as one was ever likely to see.

Once her pencil found its rhythm on the paper, she began, "My—" she interrupted herself. She'd almost said *my husband*. She began again, "I once knew a man who served in the Second Division. Captain Lord Percival Bretagne. Perhaps you knew him?"

"Knew of 'im, milady, to be sure. Seen 'im sit 'is 'orse real pretty like." The old soldier shifted his weight on the unforgiving sidewalk. "But we didna travel in tha same circles like. Unless 'is 'orse needed a shoe or tha like. In such case, Jem's yer man." The man jabbed his thumb into his chest. "I was told more 'n once that I was the best 'ostler on the Peninsula."

She felt the heat of incipient shame brighten her cheeks. Of course, this old soldier and Percy hadn't traveled in the same circles. Percy wouldn't have had the faintest notion of this man's existence.

Yet another lesson the London streets had taught

her: places like St. James and Mayfair existed within their own social stratum, insular and impenetrable. The rest of London was the hinterlands as far as much of the *ton* was concerned. The masses were to be used for war and service and forgotten. She quashed the rise of anger that threatened, channeling it into her drawing, which was proceeding at an erratic pace.

"Seem to remember," the old soldier went on, undeterred, "that 'e came to a bad end, if ya didna mind me bringin' it up. Kill't by one o' our own at the Battle of Maya, wadn't 'e?"

Olivia's pencil scratched a dark, incongruous mark across the paper. "As it turns out, he wasn't." This old soldier must be the last person in London who didn't know that Captain Lord Percival Bretagne was alive. "In fact, he surfaced in Paris last year, very much alive. The gossip rags had a field day when his wife petitioned the House of Lords for a divorce." She blended out the errant stroke.

"You don' say?" the old soldier said on a whistle. "If ya don' mind me sayin', the wife must be a right selfish and unnat'ral wench to do such a thin'."

Her hand came to an abrupt stop. "Something like that," she murmured. She began stuffing her materials back into her portfolio.

She glanced at the old soldier, his chatter filling in the blank spaces of absent conversation. "Treatin' a war 'ero that way. Whate'er 'appened to a warm welcome 'ome?"

A sudden ruckus involving a horse cart on the opposite side of the street half a block away incited a confusion of activity around them, but Olivia took little notice. Her body had gone numb. She dug inside her breast pocket for another coin. "Thank you for your time, sir."

She dropped the crown into the old soldier's cup. He fished it out and tested it with the few good teeth remaining in his head. She was gone before the coin was out of his mouth.

Heedless of direction, she fled as fast as her legs would carry her and her dress would allow. It was imperative that she move as fast and as far away from that man and that past as possible.

She was aware of how the world must view her, but this was the first time she'd heard the words spoken aloud.

Selfish. Unnatural.

She must be a selfish and unnatural wench to divorce her resurrected war hero of a husband. She must be a selfish and unnatural mother to deny their daughter her father.

Perhaps it was all true, and she was, indeed, selfish and unnatural. Except no one making those assertions had been in her marriage. Only she and Percy had been in their marriage, and only she and Percy knew the truth about it.

Actually, that wasn't quite true. She was fairly certain Percy didn't know the truth about their marriage either, as it hadn't impacted him in the least.

She glanced around, recognized the cross street, and cut a left. Her pace slowed, and her breath caught up with her. This business with Percy wouldn't leave her be. And they weren't in the same city. Not even the same country.

She found herself a single street removed from Jiro's studio and ducked into a deserted alley, only slightly fetid, and stopped. She couldn't arrive looking harried and devastated. Eyes closed, she called to mind an image that had comforted and calmed her these last six, tumultuous months since she'd heard Percy was alive: a single freestanding column of brilliant white marble rose into the sky, steady and unassailable, dependent on nothing and no one for support.

From the instant she'd decided to petition the

House of Lords to set her marriage aside, she'd known this must be her. She would do anything to preserve the integrity of this column. It relied only on itself.

Decently composed, she stepped out of the dank alleyway, dashed up the street, and down another before landing on Jiro's doorstep. After a quick double-rap on the front door, an aged servant opened it and silently motioned her inside. She paused to remove her sturdy boots before following the servant through to the back of the house. Once seated at the large white studio's square central table, she slid the day's drawings out of her case and patiently awaited Jiro's arrival.

Her gaze rested on the paintings hanging on adjacent walls, their luminous gold-leaf background an exquisite contrast with the stark white of the room. A skylight and a north-facing wall provided the studio with perfect light and illuminated the paintings, even on the grayest of London days.

As the eye proceeded from right to left, it first happened upon a pair of young cranes being tended by their mother. Next came a clump of summer lilies and a bamboo forest in the background inhabited by a pair of aged cranes majestically settled upon a snow-covered pine.

Although the final painting showcased a group of young women engaged in one activity or another, cooking, sewing, gossiping, even reading, Olivia gravitated toward the serene nature scenes and the meticulous technique involved in the piece's overall portrayal.

The way the colors of the stylized scenes positively vibrated against the gold-leaf paper was unlike anything she'd ever seen. Someday Jiro would teach her this technique perfected by his art masters in Japan, the Kanō school, if she stayed the path. For now, she would humbly accept the privilege of reproducing them on simple white paper with charcoal.

A feeling of guilt and doubt crept in. Her access to

this masterpiece was a privilege. Yet when she'd set to work on it in her studio yesterday, her mind had wandered and her focus sharpened on an entirely different image: Lord St. Alban.

The man had invaded her thoughts, her home, and now her school within a matter of days. If she was a paranoid, she would think it part of a nefarious plot. But, of course, it wasn't. Nefarious plots were best left to the gothic romances that Lucy devoured at an alarming rate.

An agile movement at the door announced Jiro's arrival. Tall and slender, he cut a handsome figure in the loose-fitting white tunic and trousers he wore in his studio. When he ventured out onto London streets, he exchanged this clothing for the Western-style attire of an English gentleman. Olivia suspected it was a choice designed to help him fade into the background, to observe and not be observed.

His stride energetic and direct, he took his place at the low table across from her. Olivia saw a man entering his prime years. His long fingers reached for her drawings and slid them across the table. He sifted through the pages, preferring complete silence while he sorted her day's work.

First, he examined the washerwoman, her defiance and vulnerability at odds with one another. Next, he found the old soldier and went motionless, studying and absorbing the old soldier's battle-hardened, poverty-stricken features. Then he was on to the next sketch.

Except she hadn't done any other sketches today.

She leaned over to catch a glimpse of what now held Jiro's rapt attention and nearly tumbled off her seat when she saw the subject.

Lord St. Alban.

She resisted the urge to snatch the paper from Jiro's hand. It was simply a drawing done in the middle of a sleepless night. That was all. From an entirely artistic point of view, the man had the kind of face that must have inspired the very first silhouette. It was all angles and planes. A study in geometry, really.

She should have read the *London Diary* to settle last night's restlessness. Instead, she'd been productive. And what had that gotten her? The portrait of Lord St. Alban now resting in Jiro's hand.

Jiro met her gaze, a question in his eyes. "This is not the usual sort of man that you sketch."

Before she could respond, he again bent his head to study Lord St. Alban's profile. His eyes in constant motion across the sheet, it was as if he was committing it to memory.

Unable to restrain herself any longer, she asked, "Is there something more you wish to know about the man?"

Oh, let his answer be *no*. Sometimes Jiro wanted more information about a subject, usually related to coloration or the time of day the likeness was taken. If he inquired about the subject's scent, for example, she could tell him. Cloves. And something else, too. A warm, earthy quality uniquely male, uniquely Lord St. Alban.

She would keep that last part to herself, even in the unlikely event she was asked.

Jiro's gaze startled up to meet hers, as if he'd forgotten she sat across from him. "How do you English say this?" His eyes drifted shut. "A ghost crossed my path?"

"A ghost walked across your grave?"

He inhaled a long, deep breath and exhaled. "A grave from long ago."

8

NEXT DAY

A gentleman doesn't gift a lady with property, unless she agreed to be his—

Well, she'd disabused him of that particular notion.

But what notion in particular? a tiny voice wouldn't stop nagging. How had he been about to finish that sentence?

Unless she agreed to be his…

Wife?

Or something else?

Oh, how her heart had raced, how it raced today, faster than her feet as she strode along Curzon toward her destination, Queen Street. With so many parts of their conversation she could dwell on, it was those pesky words that refused to leave her alone. Like bad company, they popped in unexpectedly, vying for her attention with their boorish manners.

She gave her head an imperceptible shake, as if that could rattle them loose and free her of them. Free her of *him*. Except she hadn't freed herself of him at all. She'd done the opposite.

For the hundredth time, she ran through the events of yesterday. She'd happened upon Lord St. Alban crammed into the tiniest desk imaginable for a man his size. They'd begun conversing. Miss Radclyffe needed a school. Olivia needed a powerful man's name. An idea bloomed—and a bargain was struck.

Panic streaked through her. It wasn't too late, no papers were signed. She could call off the deal and allow her family to take care of her for the rest of her life. It was what any woman of her class would do.

No. It wouldn't do for her. She'd shaken his hand on the matter.

It was a bargain sealed.

Her pace quickened, her heels a determined click-clack across gray cobblestones, her surroundings familiar—after all, she'd spent nearly her entire life in the West End—but also novel. Now that she might become an owner in this neighborhood, she took in with fresh eyes the busy street ahead, uniform rows of town-houses to either side, Shepherd's Market one street over to her left. Even though their deal had been struck only yesterday, Lord St. Alban's solicitors had moved swiftly, informing her first thing this morning of an available property and an arranged viewing.

Anticipation replaced panic. This could be it. This house could be the perfect launching point for her and Lucy to begin a new era of their lives.

But it might not be, fussed a thought the size of a sticky burr. Falling in love with and buying the first house she saw was a bit like falling in love with and marrying the first man she ever met. She'd all but done that with Percy. And that venture hadn't worked out quite as planned.

A sliver of guilt forced its way in. She didn't regret Percy. Never. It would be tantamount to regretting Lucy and not under any circumstances could that ever be. What she did regret was something in herself when it had come to Percy. Her eagerness. An eagerness that he be perfect...that she be perfect...that they be perfect together. A perfect fairy tale come to life was what she'd expected from her future with Percy.

And it hadn't come to be.

Not even close.

It would be best if she lowered her expectations for the first house she viewed. She needed to sample a few others as well. The second, or even third, house might be the better fit.

A gentleman doesn't gift a lady with property, unless—

Why? Why wouldn't the silly words go away? Why wouldn't she let them?

She released a gusty breath. She knew why.

Lord St. Alban had shot an arrow straight to the heart of her insecurities regarding the method she was using to carve out this new life for herself. By involving him in her quest for a townhouse and her independence, she wasn't really leaving men in the past. In fact, she was certain she'd undermined her vow.

In the moment, she'd seen an opportunity that she must seize. Today, she viewed it in a light more in line with reality: she'd again entangled her life with a man. A man who intrigued her. A man on the hunt for a wife, a *proper* wife.

She had no interest in opening herself up to all that could follow with an intriguing man on the hunt for a proper wife. Flowers. Family gatherings. Engagements. Marriage banns. Complications.

Yet there was an exception that allowed her to bypass all the usual rules surrounding courtship. She was a scandalous divorcée, after all. So rare was her particular sisterhood that no rules existed.

There could be another arrangement between herself and an intriguing man, one less formal. One that didn't involve flowers or family gatherings or engagements or marriage banns. One that would remain uncomplicated.

A gentleman doesn't gift a lady with property, unless she agreed to be his…

Mistress.

Like a siren's song, those words, the very idea of them, called to her. It would most certainly end with her dashed across the rocks. No dealings with Lord St. Alban would long remain uncomplicated.

Ahead, Queen Street slipped into view, and in a score of steps she was rounding its corner, scanning the row of townhouses until she found the one at the end. *Her* townhouse, she couldn't help thinking. It quite banished all thoughts of uncomplicated *affaires* to the periphery of her mind.

Like its neighbors, the townhouse was built in the plain, but classical, style of the last century. She approached the tidy, unobtrusive front stoop and, instead of taking the steps up to the crimson front door, she ducked her head and made her way down the side steps to the servants' entrance. The key should be to the right of the glossy black door beneath a flower pot.

She'd agreed upon this arrangement with Lord St. Alban's solicitors to avoid gossip. If the rags caught wind of his activities on her behalf, *complications* would follow. All she wanted was a house and a fresh beginning. Not a scandal and a potential forced marriage.

Ha. She wouldn't be forced into another marriage.

She tilted the flower pot onto its side and palmed the key. As she slipped it inside the lock, she took note of how very still an empty house could be. She'd never experienced a house that didn't also contain, at least, five other souls. Such was the life of a woman born to an earl and married to the son of a duke. Not a bad life at all, but perhaps an inhibiting one.

As she made her way through the empty kitchen, up the servants' stairs, and down the long dark corridor toward the foyer, the freedom of a truly and utterly empty house enlivened her more with each successive step. She could do whatever she pleased without a whiff of self-consciousness. On a whim, her feet spun her around, skirts swishing around her ankles as she came to a stop after a single rotation. An approximation of a giggle escaped her.

As an adult, she'd never spun through the halls of her home, rarely even as a child. It was exhilarating. She closed her eyes and did it again and again until she was dizzy with the sensation.

The image of a Flemish painting from the last century came to mind. *Whirling Dervishes in Mevlevihane in Pera*. The smile on her face grew wider and wider with each turn. An ever strengthening light filtered pink through her closed eyelids, and she sensed she must have entered the foyer.

Her eyes popped open, and her stomach gave a lurch. A small cry burst from her throat, and her heart clanged about her chest. Her smile froze in place, a gray shadow of its former self.

A man stood in the shadow of the front door, facing her. In less than the blink of an eye, she knew him.

Lord St. Alban. *Here*. Watching *her*.

His arctic-blue gaze holding her prisoner, he lifted his hands and began a slow clap, the firm line of his lips at odds with the levity of the gesture.

Flame shot into her cheeks. Feet suddenly turned to clay, she opened her mouth to speak before snapping it shut. She began again, "Lord St. Alban, what a…" *Pleasant?* No. *Unpleasant?* That wouldn't do either. "*Surprise*."

Not every sentence needed adjectives or adverbs or even verbs.

The lift of a single eyebrow was the dratted man's only response.

* * *

Cheeks soft with pink and chest heaving, Lady Olivia's face looked impossibly open and fresh.

Well, her formerly open face. It was now entirely closed off to him. The hand clapping might have been beyond what was sensible, but he hadn't been able to contain himself. She'd made a truly spectacular entrance with her arms spread wide and her face tilted to the ceiling. *Unbound* was the word that came to mind. He'd never seen an English woman so unbound.

His travels had taken him to locales that allowed women certain freedoms of dress and movement, but staid, old England wasn't one of them, not by any stretch. Yet Lady Olivia defied his notions about who she should be at every turn. Yesterday's ramble through London only reinforced that idea.

Her graceful throat undulated in a swallowing motion, and her eyes blazed. "Your solicitors informed me that I would have the house to myself," she said, each word emerging on a note of rising virtuous pique.

"My day's plans changed, and I was curious," he said from his place across the room. He'd learned over the past few days that her physical proximity to his person had an inverse relationship with the rational functioning of his brain. Better he stayed over here and shout across the distance, if necessary.

She bit her plump bottom lip between her teeth and released it. "Is it your intention to inspect this house with me?"

"I don't have anything better lined up for the afternoon."

Incredulity spread across her face. "Can that be true, *Lord St. Alban?*"

A swell of pleasure expanded inside him. He couldn't help it, he liked when she challenged him. "Might you be aware of the previous viscount's penchant for indiscriminate spending?"

He caught a transient spark of humor in her eyes. "I might have noticed his affinity for bejeweled pinky rings on more than one occasion."

"Ah, yes, the pinky rings." He cleared his throat. "In the process of amassing his vast pinky ring collection, the late viscount also acquired a mountain of debt that could be rightly compared to the height and breadth of the Matterhorn. However, this morning I received my first bit of good news regarding the late viscount's affairs. It seems that the Dowager Viscountess St. Alban, Georgie's widow, has been running a Devonshire estate at a profit and is content to keep doing so for the remainder of her days. Her words, not mine. You should see her five-year agricultural plan for the property."

Lady Olivia's eyes widened, and he knew he'd overstepped the mark and struck an overly familiar tone. "I cannot imagine a scenario where that would be necessary."

Again, he cleared his throat, if only to mask the groan that wanted out. "All of which is a long way of saying that I have nothing but time for you, Lady Olivia. Into the evening, if need be."

Her right foot tap-tap-tapped white marble, effectively conveying simmering vexation. Perhaps he'd gone too far. Except what he'd said didn't feel untrue. Truth be told, he enjoyed spending time with the woman. But that particular truth had no place in this room. It was a different truth he should be pursuing.

Pointedly, he glanced around the room and set about using his time with Lady Olivia toward that end. "You must see immense potential in these blank walls. Like blank canvases to an artist's eye."

"Are you an artist, Lord St. Alban?" Her head canted to the side in assessment. "The subject often comes up in our conversations."

"You mistake my meaning. 'Tis you who is the artist." Now that he had her attention, here was his opportunity. "For example, the sketches of the Japanese scene that you—" He just stopped himself from saying *dropped*. Their recent conversation in the duke's study assured him no good would come of using that word. "*Rendered* were quite well done."

"A few drawings *rendered* do not an artist make," she said, irritation unmistakable in her tone. "I do not care to be patronized."

Jake swallowed another groan of frustration. There had to be some combination to her locks. He pressed on with yet a different configuration. "I was always interested in art," he said, sounding no better than a floundering suitor. "But I never took the time to learn much about it."

"Hmm," was all the response she gave.

She didn't want him here. That was clear. Whatever joy she'd been experiencing as she spun into the room had been effectively quashed by the sight of him. But she wouldn't be rid of him just yet. Not until he'd maneuvered some usable information from her.

"Much of the Eastern art for sale in the London market comes and goes on long-haul ships like the ones my mother's family operates."

"Undoubtedly," Lady Olivia replied, her tone transitioning from annoyance to disinterest. He wasn't sure which was worse.

"Some paintings are gotten by honest merchants. Others have provenances less transparent, shadowy at best."

He waited for a glimmer of recognition, even the scantest hint that she knew of one such painting. A set of paintings, in fact. But no such admission emerged. "To be sure," was all she replied, her face now tilted up toward the skylight.

"In fact," he continued, "I've only seen that sort of art in Japan, in a Japanese residence to be exact."

Her gaze swung to meet his, curiosity kindling a light in her eyes. "Were you invited into Japanese homes often?"

"Once. Europeans aren't allowed on the mainland of Japan, only on the trading island of Dejima in the Bay of Nagasaki."

"Yet you were allowed?"

"By special dispensation. My uncles had been a year negotiating a trade deal with a powerful Nagasaki family, and they brought me along to observe the final signing." He shifted on his feet, readying himself for the meat of the conversation. "In the room, there was a set of paintings—"

"What was it like?"

At last, he was getting somewhere. "The paintings? There was more than one of—"

"The residence."

A disgruntled snort wanted release. He suppressed it. *Patience.* "Spare, sumptuous. Rich woods of cream, red, and brown. Somehow it was more than the sum of its parts."

She nodded, slowly, as if confirming something to herself. "You mentioned a set of paintings?"

"Yes, the subject was very like your sketches."

"Is it such an unusual subject?"

"Not at all. But what's unusual about these paintings is that they were stolen a year later."

Her shoulder gave a little shrug. "Art isn't like English land. It can be bought, sold, traded, and transported," she said, tossing the words he'd spoken in the duke's study back at him. "It can be stolen, too."

"But you're a lover of art. Doesn't it bother you that someone would take it from its rightful owner?"

"Who truly owns art? Or has the right to?" she asked, her passion for the subject evident in her voice, her eyes, her entire demeanor. "What matters is that it's appreciated and loved. Besides, it's rare for art to stay in one set of hands for any length of time. Consider how many paintings from the Continent landed in England after the wars with Napoleon. It wasn't that long ago."

"Who knows where the Japanese paintings ended up. Is that what you're saying?"

"Indeed," she replied, unbothered, indifferent.

The point was this: *she* was exactly who knew. But did she *know?*

His gut told him *no*, but he couldn't pursue the matter further right now or she might sense that he was fishing for information. He slouched back against the front door and waited for her to make the next move, but she seemed incredibly interested in the gray veins twisting through the white marble floor at her feet.

The tip of her tongue began absently worrying her crooked tooth, and he caught himself gazing at her mouth, captivated. He had to get her talking if only so her distracting tongue would be otherwise engaged and he could stop leering at her like a perverse wretch. "In your opinion, what would be the best type of art for a room like this one?"

"In a perfect world?"

He nodded. She was giving him something, even if it was a crumb. He could live on crumbs from her table.

For now.

Eventually, he would have the whole cake.

"A work by a Flemish artist called Vanmour. His paintings of the Ottoman court caused a bit of a commotion a century ago." Her lips curled into a secret smile. "Particularly his painting of the Dervishes. And in a perfect world that painting would be right..." She looked up at the skylight and advanced to a specific point along the wall before tapping it with her forefinger. "*Here* in the crook of the staircase."

Encouraged by her sudden openness, he continued along this improvised path. "Your eye would see possibility in every wall of this house."

"Not every wall needs to be filled. There is beauty in negative space, too, my lord," she called out as she left the room, the click-clack of her boot heels echoing through the empty house. He liked the way *my lord* sounded on her lips. It almost felt like an intimacy.

He followed her into what would be the front drawing room as she made her way toward its bow window. A sudden craving unfurled within him to see her spread her arms wide and take a spin, again offering a flash of slender ankles and a flash of her true self. There was apparently no end to his reactions, desires, and cravings around this woman.

A part of him—a part he would rather deny—longed to know more of her beneath the façade, more of her beyond the information she could provide him.

But it couldn't be. He had a use for her. Just as she did for him, he reminded himself. In his experience, women didn't take well to being used, and he couldn't risk telling her the secret of Mina's birth. He didn't know enough about her relationship to the thief and the paintings. Mina deserved better than exposure to unknown risk.

"And this room, my lady?" he asked. "What pieces would you use to fill its walls?"

She glanced at him over her shoulder, a subtle smile playing about her lips. "I'd paint the walls crimson and hang *Las Meninas* by Velázquez. I've never seen it in person, but I've heard it's quite magnificent."

Graceful as a swallow in the sky, she turned in an efficient, swift swivel to face him, cheeks flushed and eyes brimming with excitement. Lady Olivia had thoroughly warmed to her subject, embodying the air of youth, bright and fresh. He couldn't look away.

"It does seem strange, doesn't it?"

"What's that?" he asked, his voice a frayed rasp in his chest.

"That a proper Mayfair townhouse could contain something so magnificent as the work of a Spanish master. Have you ever attended a dinner at Wellington's address, Apsley House?"

He shook his head.

"Suffice it to say that we English are insatiable when it comes to having the best at the world's expense."

"The Dutch might rival the English when it comes to insatiability."

Surprised blue eyes widened, and her ivory throat emitted a small, self-conscious laugh. A nervous tic of a laugh. An intoxicating laugh. He felt like sharing in it. Like forming a conspiracy with her.

"Shall we see what more this house has to offer?" she asked.

A buoyancy to her step, she flitted past him into the next room, leaving behind only her scent of lavender and sandalwood. The scent was much like her: simple and expected on the surface, but complicated with the earthy and unexpected just below. He inhaled, helpless to the urge, no choice but to follow.

"In here," she said, her voice echoing out as she performed a slow three hundred and sixty degree turn, "I would rein in the drama. A soothing robin's egg blue for these walls." Her eyes drifted shut as if her entire being was concentrated on absorbing the essence of the room. "I would bring Sir Joshua Reynolds back to life to paint a four-year-old Lucy in the style of his *The Age of Innocence* and place the piece adjacent to the fireplace."

Eyes shimmering with passion and vibrancy found Jake's. And the light within no longer faded at the unwelcome sight of him.

"Perhaps even a portrait of Lucy's first dog, Poochie the First. We now have Poochie the Second." A smile, diffident and helpless, pulled at her lips, and she lifted one shoulder in a Gallic shrug.

Jake followed, like a pup at her heels, as she led them back to the foyer, occasionally poking her head into an empty room. Lady Olivia had never been the same woman twice around him. She'd always been an adversary in one form or another, but somehow in this empty house she'd become more companion than combatant. In this state, she was an intriguing wonder to behold.

"This foyer... Have you ever seen anything like it?" She didn't pause for an answer. "Observe the way the staircase winds around the room like a loose coil all the way up to the skylight." The same beatific smile he'd witnessed yesterday in her interaction with the washerwoman illuminated her face now.

The full glory of her beaming gaze landed on him, and he basked in its warm glow.

"Shall we investigate the bedrooms upstairs?"

9

Shall we investigate the bedrooms upstairs?

The air whooshed out of the room the instant the words crossed her lips, transforming the unexpected camaraderie of a minute ago into an uncomfortable sort of intimacy. She might burst into flame. It was possible.

Everything was wrong with that sentence.

We. There was no *we*. *We* implied togetherness. And he and she most definitely were not *together*.

He was Lord St. Alban. She was Lady Olivia Montfort. That was all.

Then there was the separate, but entirely too related, issue of the bedroom investigation upstairs. How unaffected by it he appeared as his hand ran along the fine wood grain of the banister. Women must invite him to investigate their bedrooms on an hourly basis.

His gaze held hers, steady and stoic. Or was that an amused glint in his eye? "After you, my lady."

Her voice caught in her throat, and she nodded her assent. Shoulders squared, she turned away from him and toward the coiled staircase. It was a lovely staircase, calling to mind a nautilus fossil she once held as a girl. This might be *her* staircase...

Her house.

So why had she said those words in it? They were words spoken from the lips of a wife to her husband. From a mistress to her lover.

She set a boot on the bottom step and began to climb, the heat of his gaze setting her back ablaze. She tried to imagine all the places his eyes could rest, but her mind kept returning to one: her derriere. Displayed at eye level. The cool, open space of the foyer turned close and hot, stifling.

To make matters worse, it seemed she couldn't keep the sway out of her hips, try as she might. She was a woman. She had hips. And, apparently, they would sway. What further indignity must she suffer before this day was done?

At last, she reached the second level, and her oblivious feet led her to the first door on the right. Her mistake instantly foregrounded itself. This was the master's bedroom suite with its high corniced ceilings, rich mahogany paneling, and floor-to-ceiling bow window overlooking a peaceful back garden. The echo of his footsteps increased in volume as he followed her into the room.

Her body tensed, anticipating the inevitable question. The same question that had delighted her no more than a few minutes ago. He'd asked it in every other room. It only followed that he would ask it here. Such was the current state of her luck.

"Lady Olivia, what masterpiece would you hang in this room?"

The last word sounded as if it had been bitten off. As if the realization of which room they occupied dawned on him in the process of speaking. Her gaze flew to meet his, and she saw confirmation in his eyes. It was possible her assumption that this sort of scenario was nothing new to him was premature.

She rather relished the idea of a discomfited Lord St. Alban. She might be able to preserve, or, more accurately, regain her state of balance if she further upset his. She hadn't spent the last six months scandalizing the *ton* for naught. Perhaps it was time she profited from her *outré* reputation.

"What would I hang in my bedroom?" She racked her brain for a shocking sequence of words. "A rather...*salacious*...option would be..." Ah, she had just the thing. "One of Goya's Majas."

She braced herself for his reaction. Would he blush? Shuffle his feet?

His features remained unmoving. Not even the palest spark of recognition.

"Are you not familiar with the Majas?"

Lord St. Alban's hands—his gorgeous, capable hands—splayed wide in a gesture of surrender, and he held his tongue.

"There are two," she began, trying to keep the exasperation out of her voice. "First came *The Nude Maja* at the turn of the century. It depicts a woman reclining unclothed on a chaise longue. Some have called it obscene as Maja's *mons pubis* is entirely exposed to her audience."

Again, she paused for a reaction. Again, in vain. He simply stared through the bow window toward the back garden.

Olivia crossed her arms in front of her chest. "The scandal over *The Nude Maja* was, in fact, so great that Goya was compelled to produce *The Clothed Maja* three years later."

"And which would you have in here?" he asked so softly that his words just reached her.

Her heart had no choice but to accelerate. "*The Nude Maja* would be the obvious pick, but..." She hesitated, uncertain. How was it that she was revealing herself? Wasn't he the one whose equilibrium should feel *off*? Yet she couldn't *not* answer him. "I would have *The Clothed Maja.*"

In the window's reflection, his eyebrows lifted in silent query. An inexplicable urge to explain herself propelled her on. "It's the subtly differing expressions on the Majas' faces. Even as Goya yielded to public pressure, he did so with a bit of rebellion. The clothed Maja is the saucier of the two Majas, the one more knowledgeable about her seductive prowess than her nude self."

He met her gaze in the reflection and held it. "As is often the case with a woman confident in her own sensuality," he spoke on a low vibration.

The air quaked between them. Her heart thundering in her chest, she remained as still as a startled deer, unable to blink, unable to draw breath. Under no circumstances should she take this house. She'd allowed him to put his stamp on every room.

Ha. She'd not only allowed it, but had assisted it.

"No nudes?" His eyes refused to release her.

She opened her mouth to tell a lie, but it refused to form beneath the acuity of his focus. As if pulled by a strong magnet, her feet carried her forward, inch by inch, until she was close enough to touch her fingers to his back, broad and strong, and trace tense muscles corded beneath his impeccably tailored overcoat.

"Here," she said, pointing an instructive finger over his shoulder, "two or three small nude sketches. Titians. Or Botticellis. Stacked one on top of the other."

"There?" He touched a forefinger to the right of the window pane. "On that intimate sliver of wall?"

An involuntary shiver pulsed from the juncture of her legs. Throat dry, she rasped a husky, "Yes," her eyes fixed on his flawless profile.

She could stare at him all day, except she suspected looking wouldn't be enough. Part of her begged to touch him, to stroke her fingers across his bare skin and know his every texture. Looking would never be enough.

He pivoted to face her, and she became acutely aware of how close she'd ventured. Only a scant bit of air separated her chest from his. Her head tilted back, and his gaze reclaimed hers. She detected latent ferocity within those depths. The sort that wouldn't let her go if he ever got her between his teeth.

She wasn't sure she would want him to.

Free will abandoned her, and she became a being motivated by pure instinct. Words like *fierce* and *desire* swirled around her head. No part of their bodies touched, yet every fiber of her being vibrated with the possibility of where those words could lead them.

To be sure, there was no bed in this room, or in this empty house, but that hardly seemed relevant. Trivialities, like beds, didn't matter with this man, whose gaze alone incited such a wave of lust within her that all she could do was squeeze her thighs together. What further havoc could he wreak upon her?

Her eyelids lowered, and her heels lifted, the distance between their mouths closing with each additional pound of pressure she applied to the tips of her toes. Separated by the slimmest millimeter, his lips parted, his breath a silky feather across her lips.

"A Titian? Or a Botticelli?"

Her eyes startled open. "Yes?"

"Pardon me for saying," he spoke, the words gravel against his throat, "but it seems that you would bring the past back to life wholesale."

She blinked, and the spell evaporated. Reality, sharp and precise, stabbed through her. She took one, then another step backward, obeying her instinct to escape the sting of his words.

From a safe distance, her answer emerged hot and most definitely bothered. "And you'll have to pardon me for saying, Lord St. Alban, that you haven't the faintest clue of what you speak." She shuffled another step back and spread her arms wide. "This house is a move in a forward direction."

"Yet," he began with frustrating deliberation. The Dutch reputation for stoicism was an absolute fact. Good thing the window wasn't open. She might be tempted to push him through it. "You would decorate this house in paintings from past centuries, even going so far as to resurrect an old master or two. A future decked out in colors from the past isn't exactly a move in a forward direction."

She opened her mouth to issue a scathing retort before closing it. None was coming to save her. She hadn't avoided his sting. Her weak reply was to retreat another step toward the door, toward escape.

"How about the works of painters living today?" he pressed. The dratted man was like a terrier with a bone. "How about your own pieces?"

A startled laugh burst from her. "My pieces? They aren't open to public inspection."

"But in the privacy of your bedroom?"

A sketch of him flashed across her mind. The near obsessive detail with which she'd drawn the firm curve of his lips certainly made it fit for a bedroom. Or a bordello. Or a stack of discards never to see the light of day.

And here she was now, staring at his real, live lips. Her eyes lifted to meet his, and she found there a keen interest. As if every bit of him was attuned to her response.

Well, too bad. She didn't have to explain this part of herself. Not to him. He hadn't earned it, and she wasn't about to give it away. "You think me obsessed with the past?"

"Possibly." His gaze continued to penetrate, refusing to let her go.

"You know nothing of my obsessions."

A single eyebrow lifted. "I wouldn't presume."

Radiant heat spread through her. The cheek! They both knew his words were the opposite of his thoughts. She must change the subject before she became nothing more than a walking human blush. Perhaps it was time they return to the subject that had brought them together in the first place. "Do you think this a suitable house for entertaining?"

"Pardon?" That too-knowing eyebrow dropped. Good. She'd surprised him.

"I host a monthly art soirée where I showcase a *current* working artist. Among other things, I need a house that can accommodate up to one hundred guests."

He shuffled uncomfortably on his feet. "I, uh, might not be the most informed person to ask."

"But you're here to help, aren't you?" she asked, her eyes wide and disingenuous. At last, her footing found purchase on solid ground. "In fact, my next soirée is tomorrow evening."

* * *

Jake went stone still. Had he heard those words correctly? Or did he want to hear them so badly that his mind was playing tricks on him?

An invitation to Lady Olivia's soirée was the opportunity he needed. Except he was expected to dine at the duchess's manse tomorrow evening. Miss Fox would be there, too. She'd been invited expressly for the purpose of furthering their acquaintance.

Well, he would have to beg off. There would be other dinners. Finding the thief and securing Mina's future must take precedence over the stepmother hunt. And one thing was certain: his dealings with Lady Olivia Montfort were an entity altogether separate from *that*. The duchess's matchmaking schemes could wait.

"I would be interested in attending your soirée."

Lady Olivia's head cocked to the side, and the mean, little smile he'd caught yesterday as he'd clumsily extricated himself from the tiny desk now curled about her lips. "But I haven't invited you."

He blinked. It was true. She hadn't. He needed to say something, anything, but she'd caught him out. So he did the only sensible thing and remained silent.

One tense second ticked by, then another, and another. At last, she took pity on him. "Of course, with your keen interest in art, and my sketches in particular, you might enjoy it. Guests will begin arriving at eight o'clock."

She strolled toward the door and stopped. He would have sworn an oath that he'd glimpsed a confident swagger in her step. "And bring Miss Radclyffe. She and Lucy might enjoy an introduction, particularly if they will be attending school together."

"Lucy attends your parties? It's my understanding that young ladies aren't allowed such liberties before they are out."

Amusement crinkled the corners of Lady Olivia's eyes. The words had come out wrong. He sounded like a ninny. Like a society harebrain.

"Of course she does, my lord. I hadn't thought you such a stickler for the *ton*'s rules. It's somewhat, hmm..." she trailed and pivoted before striding down the corridor.

Disappointing, he finished for her silently as his ears picked up the echo of her light step trilling down the stairs. An assessment he likely deserved.

It mattered not. He'd secured what he needed: an invitation into her inner circle. An invitation to sniff out the thief. His plan was beginning to bear fruit.

To be sure, he'd somewhat unmanned himself and come across as a society blockhead—her mean, little smile had assured him of that fact—but he didn't need her to see him as a man. And he certainly didn't need to see her as a woman composed of flesh and blood, wants and desires. He didn't need to see her *unbound*.

He needed her to lead him to the thief, and, increment by increment, she was doing so. Today was a small victory. In no way should he feel dissatisfied by the idea that he'd disappointed her and that she might now see him as a popinjay.

His blood wasn't simmering over the thought. He had nothing to prove to her.

He would sharpen his focus on the silver lining. At the last moment she'd returned to being the woman he needed her to be. Not the one who twirled her way through a house on a wave of pure abandon. Not the one whose flick of a tongue tempted him in ways no other ever had. Not the one who revealed the vulnerabilities of her past through a transparent shell of sophistication.

He respected that woman, he might even be in awe of her, the brave choices she'd made, the path she was forging, alone. But he didn't *need* that Lady Olivia. He needed her to be hard and difficult, not soft and unguarded.

He needed her to be easy to walk away from.

* * *

SHE WAITED until the echo of his footsteps faded across the foyer and the front door snapped shut. Only then was Olivia able to release the bravado suspended within her lungs.

Not five minutes ago, his scent of cloves had enveloped her, and all she could think was that she wouldn't mind if his arms enveloped her, too.

No. Nothing so tepid as that. In the privacy of this empty house, she could face her true response to him. Body aflame with desire aching for release, her mind had them horizontal on the bare floorboards, pressing, pulling, tugging, begging for more and more and more until—

Until what? Certain salacious poems and novels detailed quite intimately where such gambols led, but she'd never discovered that place for herself, not with Percy.

But with Lord St. Alban? Her intuition told her she'd find out rather quickly. And, oh, how very much she wanted to know.

On a shaky breath, she forced her body into motion, as if in doing so, she could as easily move away from opaque curiosities that nipped at her like tenacious little fleas that wouldn't leave her be. Her feet crept to the rear of the kitchen, toward the staircase that led up to the communal, secret garden shared with several other townhouses. A cooling outdoor stroll was what she needed.

She ascended the steps and pushed open the door. Her feet came to a dead stop, and the breath caught in her chest. Images conjured up by a too-attractive viscount fled.

Marvelous. No other word captured this garden, ripe with fresh greenery peeking out after an overlong winter and blessedly devoid of another human soul. A narrow footpath wound through the first buds of spring roses not yet in bloom: yellows, pinks, reds, oranges, lavenders. Soon this garden would be a thing of beauty. It was enough to inspire one to take up painting the botanical sort of beauty instead of the human variety.

Now there was a thought. Still life would be so much easier than people. So much more predictable.

She paused beside a vibrant fuchsia rose and brushed her fingertips across petals wound in a tight, velvety bud. Take the life cycle of this rose. From the moment a bee pollinated an ovule to form a seed, its fate was determined. With the proper amount of water, dirt, and sunlight, its path toward dazzling effulgence was secured.

Humans were an altogether different matter, their life cycle fraught with uncertainty and unpredictability. And it seemed to her that they preferred it this way, not knowing what surprise lurked around the corner.

Be it pleasant or unpleasant, it was in a human's nature to root it out. It could be glory on the battlefield, colors flying high, or a death faked in a war-scarred mountain pass on a sunny afternoon. The cost to self or others rarely figured into these risks that came down to an all-or-nothing scenario, that never considered the black void left to others when it ended on the nothing side.

She approached a small bench and perched on its edge, the green carpet of grass before her extending toward a lively fountain, its bubbling stream a distant, soothing hush. How readily she could return to this dark place.

How dare Lord St. Alban proclaim that she would bring the past wholesale into the present. He wasn't there, in her mind, when Mariana had delivered the news that Percy was alive. How all she could think was that she wanted—*needed*—to be set free from a marriage she'd long believed herself liberated from.

Never again would she place her fate in the hands of another. Or again be fooled by the first rush of love, heady, beguiling, and unreliable.

She would choose the life cycle of an English rose. The view might be limited, but her future would be predictable and her own. For here was the other point about a rose: it had thorns. She would employ every last one to keep her independence.

Yet by inviting Lord St. Alban to her monthly soirée, hadn't she undercut that intention? Hadn't she stepped into the realm of unpredictability and invited him to further complicate his life with hers?

Tomorrow, she would see him again. Did she *want* to see him again tomorrow? Did her blood sing through her veins at the thought? It was entirely conceivable that both possibilities were true.

She strove for another controlled breath, but it refused to obey, instead entering her lungs ragged and shallow. Whatever emotions Lord St. Alban stirred within her, she must resolve and silence.

For her present.

For her future.

10

Jake crossed Lady Olivia's threshold and succumbed to the spell she'd cast.

With each step forward, the known world transmogrified into one strange and mysterious, opaque and enchanting. Spellbound partygoers mingled around him and Mina in hushed, almost reverent tones as their vision adjusted to dim, indigo light.

Beside him, Mina went still, observing the room quietly, but without her usual outward restraint. A rapt smile lit across her face, and the corners of her eyes crinkled in what could only be described as delight. She, too, was charmed. "Father, look up."

He followed the direction of her gaze toward the twenty-foot ceiling. Above their heads, hundreds of tiny candles individually set within faceted glass globes glittered like a twinkling night sky against a ceiling dark as the deep blue night. "Do you recognize the constellations, Father?"

He hadn't seen her this enthralled by anything since they'd left Singapore. She resembled the child she still was, if only in years. His heart threatened to lift out of his chest. He narrowed his eyes to inspect the starry ceiling more closely. Scattered throughout the tiny glass globes shone larger ones laid out in the pattern of the constellations. "Which ones am I seeing?"

"There is Orion," she whispered, pointing. "You can tell by the three larger stars of his belt." Eyes shining brighter than the stars above, she angled her arm to the left. "And there are Orion's dogs, Canis Major and Canis Minor. Do the animals he hunted continue into the next room?"

As Jake watched Mina surrender to the charm of the soirée, relief washed over him at having brought her, his few misgivings somewhat mollified, if not entirely erased. After all, the thief remained at large. The man could be in this very room, or the next, and it was vital that he cut off the possibility that the man have any interaction with Mina. He hadn't formed a solid idea about the man's intentions, except thieves tended not to be upstanding citizens, and he wouldn't give the man the opportunity to begin a whisper campaign about her past, if that was his intent.

And, then, there was his wobbly relationship with Lady Olivia. A specific quality charged between them that wouldn't bear up beneath his daughter's discerning eye.

He resisted the pull of his mind toward yesterday, the empty bedroom, and the almost kiss. In that mad instant, he'd summoned his will and resisted his body's carnal response. That was the important part. He also understood he wouldn't be as successful a second time.

"Oh, Father, look over there."

He followed the tug of Mina's arm as she guided him to a scene staged in a far corner of the room. It resembled a nativity one might see around Christmas. A pair of white lambs lay nestled comfortably within a bed of hay, curled into each other and fast asleep. As they drew closer, it became apparent that the painting hanging above the lambs was the focal point.

A wolf, not the sort who hunted in a pack and grew

fat from its bounty, but rather one who had left his pack long ago, stared malevolently into Jake's eyes. So lifelike was the painting, he half expected the predator to jump off the canvas and come straight for his throat. He glanced at Mina. "What do you think?"

"Unnerving," she said, subdued and thoughtful. "I prefer the stars."

"Shall we pursue them into the next room?"

They'd taken no more than three steps when their progress was cut short by a blonde bundle of curls and energy. Lady Olivia's daughter certainly knew how to make an entrance.

"You must be Miss Radclyffe," the girl said, her words tripping over themselves in a breathless rush.

Mina nodded. "And you are Miss Bretagne?"

The girl's lips pulled to the side in a crooked smile. "Egad, finally, we meet. I've heard all about you."

Jake detected a blush brightening Mina's cheeks and started to get a word in, but he decided that it would be nigh on impossible with the ebullient Miss Bretagne. A personality trait she didn't in the least share with her cool and collected mother.

"But no one mentioned that you might be the most beautiful girl in all of London." Miss Bretagne turned toward Jake. "If you do not mind, my lord," she intoned in a studied, polite voice, unlike the one from moments ago, "I would like to rescue Miss Radclyffe from this boring old party."

He caught Mina's eye. "With Miss Radclyffe's consent, of course."

"I would be delighted by the pleasure of your company, Miss Bretagne," Mina said. "Will you lead me through the rest of the rooms? I should like to see your night sky in its entirety."

"Oh, goody!" Miss Bretagne exclaimed as she slid her arm through Mina's to better lead her through the crowd. "Oh, and Lord St. Alban?" she called over her shoulder. "My mother says to mingle as you please. It's an informal affair."

They turned away, and Jake caught one last snippet of their conversation. "And, Miss Radclyffe, you can drop the *Miss Bretagne* bit. It's too ladylike, and I'm not sure I'll ever be one of those. In fact, technically I'm a bastard. You can call me Lucy."

"And I'm Mina."

Lucy grabbed Mina's hand, and the two girls melted into the crowd, leaving Jake alone in the receiving room. Miss Bretagne, a *bastard*? He supposed, in the strictest sense, it was true. Still, none in this room, in all of society, would dare utter that particular truth, not beneath the Duke of Arundel's own roof.

A servant's tray caught Jake on the elbow. This was quite the crush. Not on the scale of the duchess's, but the room was full enough that one must take care where one stepped. This gathering had a strangely selective feel to it, which made little sense considering the guests appeared to be a mixture of the high and the low.

A few faces struck Jake as familiar in the vague way of social acquaintanceships formed in thirty second introductions at a salon or soirée. Others bore aspects of the bohemian sort not received in polite society. Their hues shone just a little brighter; their laughter rang out just a little bolder; and their accents ranged just a little broader. In total, many of the assembled were persons entirely vulgar to the refined eyes of the *ton*.

Yet in her wing of the duke's mansion, Lady Olivia's apartments offered these two disparate strata of society the freedom to enjoy one another's company. On the street tomorrow, it would be a different story. But, tonight, these rooms provided a sanctuary where the two could socialize without constraint.

And it was Lady Olivia who had created this space where art could bridge the gap. She was more fascinating than she had a right to be. It was no wonder she excited gossip.

As he strode through the doorway connecting to the main set of rooms, Jake passed a small sign:

Scenes Beneath a Night Sky

This room was much larger, but no less crowded than the last. He skirted the edge of the crush, scanning the space for his quarry. His height of four inches above six feet made it easy to determine that the thief wasn't in here.

Even though he'd never met the man, he knew one fact about him: he was Japanese. *Jiro.* In a closed society like London's, a foreigner—particularly one whose features were unmistakably *not English*—didn't pass unnoticed. While it was possible another artist of Japanese origin could be here, it wasn't probable. Were the man in the room, he would create a stir without once opening his mouth.

"Champagne, my lord?" a servant's voice intoned.

Jake lifted a crystal flute off the servant's proffered tray and downed the drink in a single swallow before venturing into the crowd and wending his way toward the room's focal point, another staged scene like the one in the receiving room.

This scene was wholly different from the previous one. Where the other possessed a soft palette in color and theme, this one ratcheted up the drama ten times over. Hundreds of full-blown poppies filled every square inch of the tableau not occupied by the painting at its center. They even appeared to grow out of the floorboards to resemble a field lush with effulgent crimson blooms.

However, the cheeriness generated by the spectacular poppies was replaced by unease when the subject of the painting sharpened into focus: an opium den, and not the sort of the Romantics. No indulged lords lolled about on overstuffed sofas, content and oblivious to the world around them. In their stead, emaciated addicts, a puff away from starvation and death, lay about at odd angles, their gazes inward and grim.

To say that the cheery poppies threw the dire realism of the painting into sharp relief would be gross understatement. The irony was undeniable: beneath the surface of a thing of beauty could lay the seeds of one's undoing.

An image of tonight's hostess came to mind.

Of her surface…

Her eyes fluttering shut, lashes dark against her pale skin, parted lips reaching up, up, up…

And her depths…

The quality that made him want to forget his place, his purpose, himself, and dip his head and claim those lips until they were satisfied, sated.

As if a mere kiss could accomplish satisfaction and satiety between them.

A soft swish of skirts whispered behind him, and a voice sounded in his ear. "Does it disappoint? Disappointment can leave one feeling decidedly *unfulfilled*."

Jake looked right, and the room fell away. There she stood, throwing that word at him again. *Disappointment.* The idea that he'd disappointed her had gnawed at him since yesterday. And now she was throwing another word into the mix. *Unfulfilled.*

While he had no desire to leave this woman disappointed, he certainly didn't want to leave her unfulfilled. In fact, under a different set of circumstances for their acquaintance, he wouldn't walk away from this woman until she was thoroughly—*exhaustively*—fulfilled, satisfied, sated…

He reined himself in and cleared his throat. "I've never encountered art like this."

A subtle smile curled the corners of her lips. "Let me

guess. To you, art is pretty and facile and forgettable." She gestured toward the painting. "And this is none of those things. It's brutal, dark, and unforgettable." The blue of her eyes deepened to match the sapphire of her gown. "It's real."

"I may have misjudged you," he said, the words out of his mouth before he could contain them.

"You wouldn't be the first, my lord."

Their eyes held for a beat longer before he broke the contact. Her directness had a way of muddling his intentions. It was time to snap back into focus. He was here to find an art thief.

"I must admit," he began, "your knowledge of the art world fascinates me."

He sounded like a disingenuous prig even to his own ears, but he needed to right this conversation before it fell off the edge and into uncharted territory.

"Does it?"

"Did your family or the duke introduce you? Or, perhaps, his son?" He couldn't bring himself to say her *husband*, or whoever the blasted man was to her now. He despised the man sight unseen. If ever he came within arm's reach of the man, he would clock him directly in the mouth.

"Percy?" An incredulous laugh escaped her. "My interest in the arts has naught to do with my marriage. I was a girl so in love with love that I didn't have room for other interests."

"In love with love?" An unexpected pang of jealousy flared through him, even as her words caught him a bit sideways. "You must have fallen in love with your husband during your courtship to have married him."

"Our courtship was the most romantic courtship anyone had ever seen, I daresay."

"And the marriage?" Why was he pushing the conversation in this direction? He had no desire to hear the details of that marriage.

"Not in the least," she stated matter-of-factly. "And is love a requirement for the wife you're seeking?"

"Of course not," he said. A beat later, the weight of his confession hit him. He shouldn't be speaking of love with this woman.

"Then what is the hurry, my lord? If you believe in love, you should wait for it."

"My daughter needs a stepmother before the year is out. She's of an age where the guidance of a lady who knows the ins and outs of the *ton* is necessary."

Lady Olivia's head canted to the side. "Did you never know young love?"

"I did."

"And you weren't caught in its sticky web?"

"I was."

"Yet here you are, disavowing it."

"And you?"

"What about me?"

"Need I ask?"

Her brows knitted together, and her gaze darted away from his. "Perhaps not. Perhaps we are both done with love." A brittle crack sounded in her voice. "It can never live up to the perfection of its promise."

"Yet—" He hesitated, attempting to slow the conversation. It seemed to possess a momentum that he was powerless to control. "I find that perfection bores me within minutes. Perhaps a little mess is—"

What you need. The words stuck in his throat. A blush spread across Lady Olivia's décolletage and pinked her cheeks. He rather liked that blush. It spoke of knowledge, of connection.

He was unable to pursue that tempting line of thought when a statuesque lady stopped before them and dipped into a shallow curtsy. "Olivia," the woman said in a low, contralto voice, "will you introduce me?"

Lady Olivia's body tensed beneath the request, firing up a spark of intrigue. It was clear she harbored no desire to do any such thing. However, society's rules required a hostess to accede to the desires of a guest. Even he understood that much.

"Lord St. Alban, may I introduce Lady Nicholas Asquith?" she said, her tone rote, mechanical. "My sister."

His eyebrows shot skyward. "Your sister?"

"My twin, in fact."

Lady Nicholas's eyes sparkled playfully. "You don't see the family resemblance?"

It was immediately apparent that the sisters were, in fact, complete opposites, but in such a way that one complemented the other. They must have excited a bit of a stir when they debuted.

"It's true that we don't much favor," Lady Nicholas continued. "A not uncommon occurrence for twins, I hear."

"No one would take you two for common," he replied, the words flattering, but genuine.

Lady Nicholas met her sister's gaze, and her brow lifted, a world of silent conversation happening between the sisters. Then her amber eyes shifted to continue her evaluation of him. She looked privy to a joke that he hadn't yet caught onto.

"Olivia, this is quite possibly the most morbid soirée you've held yet."

A long-suffering sigh escaped Lady Olivia. He couldn't help feeling charmed by the push and pull of the sisters. "I was explaining to Lord St. Alban that art isn't simply sunshine and rainbows. Must I explain the concept to you as well?"

"Well, I prefer the sunshine and rainbows."

Lady Olivia held her tongue, but a grudging smile for her unconstrained sister tipped at the corners of her mouth. These two were opposites, but they were close, too.

Lady Nicholas's determined hand snaked its way

into the crook of his arm. "Shall we take a turn about the room?"

Jake held out his free arm for Lady Olivia, and her body, her entire being, went motionless, her eyes glued to his extended hand. She didn't want to touch him.

A possibility slid in: perhaps she *couldn't* touch him.

Not without a little...*mess.*

She began backing away, for all the world a skittish deer in the crosshairs of a bow. "I've only recollected that I must see to a guest with a special dietary request."

"Lady Bede's goat milk?" Lady Nicholas asked.

Lady Olivia stepped forward and landed a quick kiss on her sister's cheek before vanishing into the crowd, which appeared to have doubled in volume since his arrival.

"Shall we?" Lady Nicholas asked.

Jake nodded, and they strolled together in silence, the crush creating a raucous cacophony that both surrounded them and strangely insulated them from its din.

"What do you think is the true purpose of this soirée, my lord?"

"I haven't the faintest idea, my lady." In truth, he hadn't considered it beyond its usefulness to him. Again, he scanned the crowd for the thief. Again, he turned up nothing. "Would you care to enlighten me?"

"About a year ago," Lady Nicholas began, "an artist, who was a vital part of the arts community, perished of a long and painful lung ailment brought on by malnutrition and lack of medicine. He was only four and twenty years old. Olivia's response was to begin hosting a soirée featuring a different artist every month. Each piece you see is for sale, and every last farthing goes to the artist with Olivia shouldering the cost of the soirée." Lady Nicholas gave a short laugh. "She claims to be no crusader, but I have my suspicions."

"It looks to be quite a monumental and meticulous undertaking for no—"

"Return?" Lady Nicholas interrupted. "Careful, my lord, one might catch a whiff of trade about you." She cut him a speculative glance and slid her arm out from his as easily as she'd slipped it in. "Now, if you will excuse me, I see a dear, old friend to whom I simply must give a piece of my mind."

Jake pitied that dear, old friend. He suspected Lady Nicholas's curious and playful exterior masked an intellect and will of tempered steel.

Alone, he glanced about this new room. Corner to corner, a sumptuous spread of delicacies lined its four walls, tables heavy with roasts of all varieties: lamb, ham, pheasant, quail, even an entire roast pig. It was a feast fit for royalty. Yet there were no dining tables, no chairs, no silverware, no servants offering to fill plates, no invitation to feast on this banquet.

It struck him: the room itself was the stage. He pivoted by degrees until he located it: above a table laden with the most desserts he'd ever seen outside a sweet shop was the painting at the heart of this tableau.

The subject was a small boy curled into himself in sleep. Except this child bore no resemblance to the cozy lambs fast asleep in the receiving room. This child slept on a squalid sidewalk. His only shelter, a stone staircase; his only protection, himself. Where the lambs were white as snow, this child's skin was stained with filth.

But these details were only background for the focal point of the painting: the boy's face, pointed up to a vast, indifferent sky, a hollowed-out shell resembling a man of eighty years, rather than a boy of eight.

Again, Jake surveyed the room. The roar of the crowd hadn't followed him in here. Instead, the atmosphere was silent and chastened. Just as it wasn't for the nameless boy, this feast wasn't for them. He and his fellow guests were part of the performance of the piece.

We English are insatiable when it comes to having the best at the world's expense.

Yesterday, he hadn't given her words much thought, but tonight, in the context of this room, he understood what they said about Lady Olivia Montfort. How had a beloved daughter of the *ton* come to embrace such a radical perspective of the world?

All at once, a tingle raced down his spine, and he turned unerringly toward its source. There *she* stood, engaged in a conversation with a group of her guests. Presented in profile, he was confounded by how small she appeared. She'd begun to loom so large in his imaginings that the reality of her took him by surprise. From this distance, he could take in the entirety of her at his leisure.

She wore a simple, elegant gown of sapphire silk, deeper than the translucent blue of her eyes, expertly fitted to her petite body and cinched at her waist. He could only guess that she was dressed in the first stare of French fashion. Yet any woman who could create this atmosphere out of thin air and sheer will wouldn't be a slave to fashion. After all, she tramped about London clad in an overcoat the hue of sidewalk sludge.

Still, she possessed a sense of her station. In here, she would dress the part. Lady Olivia understood roles, and when to play them to suit the moment.

The corner of her mouth quirked up into a smile for a male guest, and Jake's insides gave a lurch. Then he noticed a detail that allowed him to relax: her smile for that man was polite, controlled, the sort of smile one offered a guest as a token. Quite unlike the one that had spread across her lips and shone for him yesterday. That smile had been glorious, lacking any hint of politeness or control. *She* had lacked the slightest hint of politeness or control.

Again, that word came to him. *Unbound*. And, again, he wanted her that way.

Her face angled to the side, and her eyes cut toward his. The room shrank down to him and her. Time had a funny habit of standing still around her. The indulgent smile dropped from her lips, and her expression transformed, as if she was considering him in some way.

A guest leaned forward and spoke a few words, pulling at her attention. It would be rude for her to ignore the guest, yet he refused to release her. But, alas, she didn't need his permission, and she returned her attention to her guests and her duty. Time resumed its steady tick-tock.

He resisted the impulse to stride over and reclaim her for himself. Instead, he forced his feet to move in another direction, away from her. A strange restlessness simmered at her easy dismissal of him. It made it simpler to do what he needed to do. If the thief wasn't here, then perhaps he could churn up some evidence of the man.

A quick glance to his right revealed a stocked sidebar. He wasn't sure which variety of amber-colored liquid he was pouring into a tumbler, but it hardly mattered. Two, nay, three fingers of whiskey would make the task ahead more palatable.

He strode through to the next room and located an unobtrusive door tucked away in a shadowed corner. He turned the handle and was through it before anyone could notice. The door clicked shut behind him, and he stopped, allowing his eyes to adjust to the darkness.

A strip of light peeking out from beneath a door some twenty feet ahead of him revealed that he stood in a narrow corridor. He began moving forward, his stride purposeful and direct.

Lady Olivia's apartments were bound to house secrets.

11

L ord St. Alban wasn't exactly *forbidding*.

That was the first thought that popped into Olivia's mind as she cut a discreet glance his way, his eyes already upon her, watching her, absorbed in her as if she was the only person who mattered in this room, even in all of London. No one had ever looked at her like that.

Her pulse wanted leave to gallop through her veins. She inhaled to tamp the feeling down. It wouldn't do to let gratification sway her into a course at odds with her goals.

She shifted her perspective and attempted to view him the way the rest of London must see him, as distant and unapproachable. It was his impeccable, physical perfection and those inscrutable eyes that refused to surrender a hint of his private thoughts.

Yet her perception of him continued to differ from society's. Their encounter on Ludgate Hill, for instance, away from the prying gaze of the *ton*, the informality of it, the intimacy of it. The way he'd snatched her from certain death and held her against his long, adept body for one, two, three heartbeats too long. Indeed, he wasn't the sort of man who let a woman fall.

He wasn't distant and unapproachable to her.

She tore her eyes away, determined to rejoin the conversation around her. "Lady Olivia," said Lady Bede, a lively, if slightly eccentric, society matron, "you must tell me about this artist. He is quite good, I'd say."

"Lady Bede," Olivia began, "*he* is a *she* who works from Le Marais in Paris."

A few scandalized titters rippled through the small group. A shock borne of delight rather than of narrow-mindedness.

"A woman, Lady Olivia? A woman painted these?"

She couldn't contain a smile at Lady Bede's enthusiasm. She'd provided the woman a delightful *on dit* that would have her enthusing for days.

"But the paintings in the final room," Lady Bede said, appearing both flabbergasted and captivated at once. "Such sensuality created by a woman's hand?"

"Indeed," replied Olivia, relieved to feel engaged by someone other than *him*, even if only for a moment. "A new style is emerging from the Parisian schools. A realism in painting unlike anything that has come before it, except perhaps by the hand of Caravaggio. Exciting, isn't it?"

"Hear! Hear!" cheered a lord on the periphery of the group, eliciting a host of snickers.

Olivia used the commotion to step away. They wouldn't miss her. Her gaze cut toward Lord St. Alban. *Gone.* Impossible this heaviness in her chest was disappointment.

An arm slid through hers from behind, and, before she knew it, she was secured fast to Mariana's side. "You will be delighted that I have brought a bank check, but no husband." Mariana wasn't one for small talk. "So I am free to spend said check exactly as I please."

A laugh complicated by nothing other than pure, familial love bubbled up from deep inside Olivia. "Is Nick traveling?"

"He and Lavinia have hied off to the north country

in search of the perfect bay stallion. That girl loves horses more than just about anything, and that man loves our girl more than just about anything. So there you have it. A father who will do anything for his daughter, and a daughter who knows it."

Domestic bliss radiated off Mariana in waves. Olivia still hadn't adjusted to her sister's wifely happiness. It was difficult to imagine now, but Nick and Mariana had been estranged for most of their marriage.

Then, six months ago, Paris happened. Like a magic trick, one moment, their marriage was smashed into pieces, irreconcilable, and the next—the wave of a hand, the flourish of a cape, *et voilà!*—they were whole again, reconciled with nary a chip on the surface. It was as if their preceding ten years of estrangement never happened.

Except it wasn't only Nick and Mariana who were affected when they'd emerged from those Parisian shadows, bringing with them into the light a resurrected Percy. Olivia hadn't been able to breathe when she heard the news, the life she'd built for herself threatening to collapse on her. To be a wife again...to lose her hard-won freedom...

Unthinkable.

The old soldier's words came back to her. *A right selfish and unnat'ral wench.* She could accept that descriptor if it meant keeping her freedom.

"But, Olivia, I'd like to change the subject," Mariana said, a spark of mischief in her tone. "Have you been holding out on me?"

"Pardon?" she asked, buying what little time she had left.

"Come now. As your elder sister, I can see straight through you."

"You are older by three minutes. I hardly think that qualifies as *elder.*"

Like a bloodhound on a scent, Mariana pressed on.

"When I spoke with the *very* handsome viscount tonight, I formed the distinct impression that the two of you are, let's say, *acquainted* with one another."

Olivia turned away from Mariana on the pretext of fixing a flower arrangement. Her *elder* sister would see the truth in her eyes in a second flat.

"Lady Olivia Montfort, you have been holding out on me!" Mariana said, her voice an excitable whisper. She snuggled closer. "Tell me everything."

"Mariana," Olivia began in the most patronizing tone she could muster, "you make it sound so...so..." What was a good word for it? "*Tawdry.*" Maybe that was too good a word for it. "He's simply interested in our little progressive school for his daughter. The Duchess of Dalrymple sent him my way, and I answered a few questions for him. That is all."

As lies went, it wasn't bad.

"Oh, we must make that happen."

As Mariana rhapsodized about the possibility of having Lord St. Alban's brilliant daughter at the school, Olivia's mind drifted. She didn't enjoy lying to her sister, but her dealings with Lord St. Alban existed in a peculiar limbo that she didn't yet understand. She felt strangely protective of it.

And then yesterday, she'd almost—

Her eyes squeezed shut in mortification. Oh, what had she done? Or almost done?

It was no surprise that last night thoughts of him had pushed sleep out of reach. Frustrated with tossing about and twisting the bed sheets into knots, she'd padded down to her studio to purge her system of him in the only way she knew how: by drawing her obsession into submission.

Her pencil had gone at him from every angle, even introducing different lightings to accentuate the strengths of his firm lips, his chiseled jawline, his angular cheekbones, his piercing eyes that surely saw through her contrariness, her protests, to her true wants, desires, *needs*.

By the time the first rays of the sun had streamed through an open window, she was spent. Dozens of drawings littering the walls of her studio, she felt that she could be done with him. Surely, her system was thoroughly purged.

Tonight, however, that purging had felt less than thorough when she'd spied him from two rooms away. She'd vowed to stay away.

Instead, she'd spoken of love with him. And she'd spoken of Percy. And they'd spoken of perfection and messes.

What a perfect, little mess she could make with him.

Oh. Where had that come from?

"Olivia."

She could hear the gasp in Mariana's voice. No mean feat.

"You must explain this series of paintings to me."

They stood in the final room, the climax of the show. Three portraits lined one wall while facing them on the opposite wall was an oversized map of Europe. Unlike the scenes in the other rooms, these paintings weren't presented with an extravagant contextual vignette.

"Do you think they're too much?"

"I can't imagine what you're talking about," replied Mariana, a tease in her voice. "Whores and grande dames share wall space all the time."

Olivia closed her eyes, took a deep breath, and opened them, hoping to see the portraits in a fresh light, as a new viewer might take them in.

To the left was the first portrait of a self-satisfied lady seated in front of her equally self-satisfied husband, who stood behind her, a proprietary hand on her shoulder.

In the middle was a portrait of a sensuous opera

singer lounging on a sofa, head tilted back to better hear the coercive whispers of the young buck stretched out behind her, clearly on the precipice of an amorous diversion. The woman's saucy gaze remained fixed on those of the viewer as if they shared a naughty secret.

The last portrait portrayed a prostitute, her stare direct and bleak, as a shadowy man cupped her chin in a possessive and sinister manner from behind. The sad resignation within her eyes made Olivia want to look away even as she was drawn into the woman's plight.

"Was the map directly across excessive? Earlier, it seemed like an excellent idea."

"A way of underscoring the show's message about the casualties of empire?" Mariana asked. Leave it to Mariana to cut straight to the heart of a matter.

"Has it strayed into melodrama?"

"Perhaps," Mariana replied absently, transfixed by the impudent opera singer, "but some people you just have to bash over the head before they understand the subtleties of a situation."

Of the three subjects, it was the opera singer who had made Olivia the most uncomfortable from the first moment she'd laid eyes on her yesterday. The woman's frank, sultry gaze suggested not only her own pleasure to come, but also an invitation to watch. Or to participate.

Her heart fluttered a few beats, sending a warm throbbing sensation to the apex of her thighs. She shifted to study the young buck's face. His eyes appeared to have only just drifted shut, lost to the anticipation of pleasure.

Percy had never taken her from behind in that way. Their amorous interactions had been, well, they'd been a respectful husband and wife in the bedroom. Lights out, covers drawn, domestic, proper, typical of their class, she suspected, but could never know with certainty as one never discussed such things. Not even with one's sister, especially when one suspected one's sister had an altogether different bedroom relationship with her husband.

But when she gazed upon the painting with Lord St. Alban in mind, well, she had no trouble envisioning him lost to such a moment and ensuring his lover was, too.

"He left some minutes ago."

Olivia startled into the present. A thin sheen of perspiration rushed to the surface of her skin, crawling along the nape of her neck, coating her palms. "I beg your pardon?"

"And he walked through *that* door."

"Oh?" Olivia replied, blithe nonchalance breezing through the syllable, even as her gut churned in panic. The hallway beyond *that* door led to... The fine hairs on the back of her neck prickled to a stand. "Mariana, I never saw to Lady Bede's goat milk." She landed a distracted peck on her sister's cheek. "Lovely of you to come tonight."

As the door closed behind her, she heard, "But, Olivia, the kitchens are the other way." She didn't need to see her sister's face to envision the familiar sarcastic quirk of her lips.

It mattered not. Not now. Now that Lord St. Alban had entered this corridor.

Perhaps he'd left the soirée. Or had become lost. Perhaps.

Except both were impossibilities in this particular corridor, which had only two doors.

One led to a storage closet.

The other to her studio.

12

How long had she been standing here, peering at Lord St. Alban through the narrow crack between the door and the wall? Thirty seconds? Thirty minutes?

The amount of time hardly made a difference. A single second was too long for him to have been in her studio. Surrounded by drawings of himself.

Drat it all, what had she been thinking during last night's bout of insomnia? She hadn't. What had once been a deliberate means of healing had become instinct. Something interested her, she must draw.

But it didn't feel therapeutic, standing here, breath held, fingers curled into tight fists, sweat trickling down her spine, watching him through a gap in the door like she was the interloper. The impulse to push the door open and confront him grew weaker the longer he stood inside her studio, judging her work, violating her privacy.

How many sketches littered the walls? She had no idea of the precise number, but dozens. Some drawn from a mid-distance perspective, others more intimate, focused on individual features in a manner bordering on the...*deviant.*

Yes, that was the correct word.

Obsessive was another correct word.

She clenched her eyes shut in mortification as he strolled over to yet another image of himself and swallowed another dram of whiskey. A few swigs of whiskey sounded like a brilliant idea right now.

What was the expression on his face? All she was able to see was his unreadable profile. Was he bewildered? Amused? Or would his face reflect what she felt for herself?

Utter embarrassment.

He took another gulp of whiskey and set the tumbler down. Before she could draw breath, he shrugged his shoulders, shed his overcoat, and draped it over the back of a chair. In the next blink, his vest was off his body. She moved not a muscle as she drank in the muscled length of his torso visible through the fine lawn of his shirt. She'd never seen him without overcoat and vest. What she'd only suspected was now confirmed.

In short, he was well-built. In expanded form, there was no denying the width of his shoulders or the trimness of his waist or the tautness of his backside through the superfine of his pants.

She nearly jumped through her skin when he began examining one of the smaller sketches, facing her. But his expression, neutral and emotionless, gave no sign of awareness that he was being watched. In fact, his fingers loosened the folds of his cravat before flicking open the top two buttons of his shirt. The whiskey found its way to his hand again as if it was a natural extension of him.

Lord St. Alban had made himself thoroughly comfortable. In her studio. Another layer of sweat broke out across her body. And she'd thought she'd drawn him into submission, purged her system of him.

Seeing him now at ease in her private space, she understood that the feeling she'd experienced at dawn hadn't been completion, only complete exhaustion.

There was no completion where Lord St. Alban was concerned. Not even close.

He ambled out of sight, and she pressed forward into the door, straining to keep her eye on him. Dressed down to his unbuttoned starched shirt and black breeches with that tumbler of whiskey carelessly in hand, he looked every inch the female fantasy of manly dishabille. So long had she spent drawing him in black and white, she'd almost forgotten that he was a flesh-and-blood man. Almost.

She inhaled deeply and caught a trace of cloves. His scent.

This limbo couldn't go on any longer. She must face him tonight, now, if she was to have a measure of peace. If she was to face him again. If she was to face herself again.

On a bracing exhale, she pushed the door open on silent hinges and slipped into the studio, her heartbeat a ragged roar in her ears. His back to her, he remained unaware of her presence. She found the nearest wall and slumped bonelessly against it, her body a quivering bundle of anxiety and anticipation.

She wanted this man.

It was no accident that the hazy idea of taking a lover had begun to coalesce around the time she'd first set eyes on him. Her only hope lay in the unreliable notion that it would be uncomplicated.

It could be true. He didn't have to be as complicated as she made him out to be. She could be the one complicating the air between them.

His back muscles tensed, suggesting he felt her presence in the room. He swiveled around, his gaze meeting hers, unwavering. An energy pulsed between them, sinuous and dark. An energy that would no longer be repressed. Victorious, it flared to the surface and dared them to ignore it.

His feet began a slow prowl forward, steadily

erasing the distance between them, inch by deliberate inch. She should feel panicked, or, at least, unsettled, by his purposeful approach. But those feelings refused to take hold. The anxiety and anticipation of seconds ago flared into a single overwhelming sensation: desire, white hot, ravenous.

He drew within a foot of her and stopped. The only sound in the room the jagged in and out of her breath.

So this was what it was to be a wanton? Aching from the nearness of his withheld touch, excruciatingly delicious and exquisitely tortured all at once.

"Why are you here?" she muttered.

"How should I answer that question?" he returned, his voice a low, masculine register that quaked her to the core of her sex. His head lowered, lips hovering just above hers for one, two, three rapid heartbeats, his breath a whisper across her lips. "Like this?"

He thrust forward, closing the remaining gap between their bodies, the full length of him pushing her up and against the solid wall, and their bodies went still, their gazes locked. If there was a time for turning back, this would be it.

She wasn't certain she could survive another night after an almost kiss. And she had no intention of finding out.

Her heels lifted, her body grazing his full length. A groan escaped him, and his mouth lowered, his lips brushing hers, once, twice, her nipples hardening in want, in expectation, before another groan sounded and the kiss deepened in a tidal wave of pent-up desire too long held at bay.

The tip of his tongue swirled around hers, toying with her, teasing her. An animal moan sounded, and she realized it had come from her. His hands slid down and around to the small of her back, coursing lower until he had her bottom in hand. His knees bent, and, of a sudden, their bodies fit together like a perfectly joined puzzle.

Well, almost. She gave a quick thrust of her hips, and her foot snaked around his ankle.

Oh, they could be joined so much more perfectly…

As if intuiting her thoughts, his long, capable fingers wrapped around her knee, and he pressed himself against her until she felt the rigid length of his shaft through gossamer layers of silk. Again her hips pushed forward, this time a more deliberate, slow grind against him. She went mindless with pleasure, pure, raw, clamoring for, nay, demanding release.

This was no uncertain first kiss. This was madness.

He tore his lips from hers, only to trace his slippery tongue down the exposed column of her neck. Her throat emitted a ragged moan as his mouth trailed lower until he reached her breasts and his hands reached up to cup them from below. One expert tug of silk, and suddenly her nipples were free. She didn't wear bindings.

A hard glint of hunger shone in his eyes, coaxing her arousal higher. His mouth covered one nipple, his tongue flicking the taut bud, and his fingers toyed with the other until she bucked beneath his touch. A cry erupted from her throat, a primal plea for more, for everything.

She clutched the lapels of his shirt, intent on rending the cloth, if need be, her sole concern to feel his undressed skin upon hers. She hardly knew herself, a feral wild thing concerned only with pleasure.

Then, she noticed it. He'd gone still. A moan of frustration unwound inside her.

"Shh. Do you hear?"

She exhaled a rough, frustrated breath and quieted her unruly self, listening, waiting. Every muscle in her body tensed, and her eyes flew open. She heard them.

Footsteps echoing down the hallway with only one realistic destination: this room.

No mistake, she and Lord St. Alban had ten seconds before discovery.

"Olivia?" he asked. "What do you need me to do?"

"You can begin by unhanding me," she said in the precise notes of a prim miss.

His hands dropped to his sides, and she could hate herself.

"The servants know to look for me here when they can't find me."

Free of him, too free of him, she slid along the wall and far away from him, too far away from him. Her fingers rushed to right her bodice, smooth her hair, straighten her crushed silk skirts. All the while, his serious gaze never wavered from her, but gone was the sensuous heat from moments ago. He watched her dispassionately as if from a great distance.

A full cry of unrequited lust sought release. She didn't want his dispassion. Quite the opposite.

"You look the perfect lady," he said once she'd finished. "Almost."

She cut him a staying glare before stepping to the doorway, blocking any possible view into the studio. Even the most loyal servant couldn't be trusted with a tidbit of gossip as choice as this one. "May I help you, Mrs. Landry?" Olivia called out. The click of the servant's heels came to an abrupt stop.

After a quick, hushed exchange, Olivia turned back toward Lord St. Alban, Mrs. Landry's footsteps receding down the hallway. She cleared her throat. "Your daughter will be awaiting you in the duke's main foyer."

He looked as if he would say something, but, then, he didn't. What did she expect? That they would pick up where they'd left off?

Again, she longed to cry out. She wasn't finished with him yet.

She was being unreasonable, but her body didn't care. It wanted what it wanted, and it wanted him.

He picked up one, then another, article of clothing and calmly dressed as if this night was a usual occurrence. A storm gathered inside her. The dratted man was entirely too self-possessed for her liking. A need to throw him off balance and keep him that way until he was gone from this room rose.

"Who would have thought you could kiss like that?" came out of her kiss-crushed lips. Surprise sparked in his eyes, and a little thrill fired through her. Good. It was a lie. But it was one she must tell herself, one she must tell him, and one they both must believe.

He cocked his head. "Who wouldn't?" he asked, daring her to continue with the lie.

"You're so very reserved. I would've thought your lips starched as stiff as your shirt." Her fingers skated up and down the doorjamb, as if she was bored.

"Lady Olivia, I think we both know what's as stiff as my starched shirt."

She made herself go very still and keep her eyes locked onto his. She wouldn't look. She wouldn't use her peripheral vision, either.

He began walking toward the door. Toward her, her traitorous heart suggested. Her attempt at controlling the situation was reversing on itself. She held up a defensive hand. "I think that's enough—" She stopped mid-sentence. She'd almost completed it with *for now*.

"They're lovely, you know."

Her arms crossed protectively over her chest.

"The sketches, my lady," he clarified, the beginnings of a smile playing about his mouth.

"A narcissist, are you?" she threw out, a cover for the satisfaction that streaked through her at the sound of his praise.

He shook his head at her, like she was an obdurate

schoolgirl. "The beauty isn't in the subject, but in the artist's rendering of it."

He came within a few feet of her. She would have to step aside or risk letting his body collide with hers. For a split second, she considered the latter. Its risks. Its rewards. But, at the last second, her feet acted sensibly and allowed him room to pass.

When he drew level with her at the doorway, his stride shortened and his pace slowed. For one wild second she thought he hesitated, that he would stop. But he didn't. He rounded the corner without a backward glance.

Her gaze fixed absently on the room before her, she slumped against the wall. This time she permitted herself to collapse to the floor in a puff of ballooned silk skirts.

The taste of scotch lingered on her lips…

The imprint of his gorgeous, capable hands lingered on her skin…

The unrequited demand of lust lingered in her sex.

And she thought she'd drawn this obsession into submission?

Perfect little mess, indeed.

* * *

MINA HAD BEEN in a few grand homes in her life—her father's new mansion came to mind—but never one as grand as the Duke of Arundel's.

Her gaze lifted toward the ceiling stretched to near infinity above their heads as she and Lucy stood in the foyer awaiting her father. She spied tiny angels peering over fluffy clouds painted onto its surface.

"Too bad ceilings can't be stars all the time," Lucy said.

Mina nodded. Lucy had the most charming way of turning words.

The girl reached out for her hand. "We must make a plan to see each other again. Soon?"

She gave Lucy's hand a testing squeeze, and when Lucy's eyes lit up in a smile, Mina knew it had been the correct action to take. She'd never had a friend like Lucy. Nannies, teachers, servants, and stars had been her friends. And Father. He was a friend, too.

But never a friend like this. A girl. A silly, frilly, delightful girl who used words the way artists used brushes.

The sound of footsteps echoed down one of several hallways that fed into the foyer. Mina turned toward the sound, expecting to see Father round the final corner, but it wasn't he who came into view. It was a boy. No, not a boy precisely—he looked to be a few years older than her—but boyish. Not yet a man.

His face... It would be deemed beautiful on a woman. But on a boy not yet a man? She wasn't sure. Angelic, perhaps, with his blond hair shot through with streaks of platinum and his pale amber eyes. Except he wasn't at all like the chubby babies strewn across the ceiling above. He looked like the heir to the sun.

He caught sight of them, and his feet slowed. His eyes met hers for the briefest flicker of a second before continuing over to Lucy. "Lulu," he called out in the most aristocratic voice Mina had ever heard, "what have I told you about treating the downstairs help like they are one of—"

"Us?" Mina finished for him. Her heart threatened to jump out of her chest, and her skin went hot, then clammy. She'd never said anything so bold in her life.

His eyes cut toward her, this time for a longer second. They held a measure of assessment, curiosity.

"Hugh!" Lucy cried out, "Miss Radclyffe may not be dressed in the first stare of fashion, but she is the daughter of the Viscount St. Alban. You must apologize this instant."

Ever impulsive, Lucy wrapped her arms around Mina. Instead of feeling stifled as she usually did with embraces, she felt buoyed by the gesture. She lifted her hands in reciprocity and gave Lucy's back a few reassuring pats.

"Mina," Lucy said, no move to relinquish her grasp, "I'm so sorry for my dunderheaded cousin."

"My apologies, Miss Radclyffe," Hugh said, not bothering to meet Mina's eyes again. He slid on a pair of kid gloves and offered a slight bow before slipping out the front door.

Lucy released Mina and took a step back. "Hugh, or *Lord Avendon*, as he insists on being called lately, is second in line to the dukedom, behind his father, and I'm afraid it's gone to his head." Lucy's eyes turned sympathetic. "People like him must be terrible for you."

Mina averted her gaze. She had no interest in pursuing this line of conversation with Lucy, a girl she hardly knew and who couldn't possibly understand how terrible people could be.

Once again, footsteps echoed down a hallway. This time it was her father. He joined them and asked, "Are you ready, *meisje?*"

"Yes," Mina replied, the Dutch endearment warming her. She would ever be his little girl. As she was about to rest her hand on his forearm, she noticed that he looked a little askew. "Father, your cravat has gone crooked."

He reached up and tugged the garment straight. "Is that better?"

She nodded and directed her attention back to Lucy. "Thank you for showing me a wonderful evening."

"Perhaps I can introduce you to my modiste, soon?" Lucy asked, uncertainty in her eyes.

"I should like that," Mina said, seeking to reassure her new friend, even as she understood that more fashionable clothes wouldn't alter how London society viewed her.

She and Father stepped through the doorway and into chilly night air. She disliked leaving Lucy on this sour note, but it couldn't be helped. There were certain aspects of her mixed heritage that she must face alone. And fixating on the *terrible* wasn't the way she chose to go about it.

13

NEXT DAY

Olivia squinted and contemplated the cup of coffee before her.

On a usual morning, she took it sweet and creamy. Today, black and bitter tempted the part of her that needed a cleansing, the pleasures of life stripped away. As a lesson in denial.

She risked one tiny sip, then another, and attempted to, if not *like*, then, at least, *accept* the strident brew as her penance. Her face scrunched up, and her resolve slipped away. She reached for the cream and sugar. Just a little. To soften the edge.

What was the use in denial anyway? Look where it had gotten her last night: inside her studio, evidence of her denial strewn about the walls for *him* to see. That was one form her denial had taken.

Of course, it could be said that denial had saved her from herself last night, if not from another restless night. The dark circles beneath her eyes attested to the fact.

And then there was a separate, but related, fact that had plagued her into the night: apart from what they'd done, and *not* done in her studio, what had the dratted man been doing there in the first place?

Lucy bounded into the room on a wave of bright

energy. "Good morning, Mum." She landed a fat kiss on Olivia's cheek and plopped into her usual seat. "Last night was a raging success. Definitely the best soirée you've held in ages."

"Oh?" Olivia replied. She couldn't agree with her daughter. She remembered it as an exercise in humiliation.

A bit more than humiliation, a tiny voice reminded her. As if she needed reminding.

"Mum?"

A particular, tentative note in Lucy's voice sounded Olivia's motherly alarm. "What is the matter?"

"Last night," Lucy began and stopped.

Tension coiled inside Olivia. Was it possible that Lucy had seen her with Lord St. Alban? "Yes?"

"Cousin Hugh mistook Miss Radclyffe for a servant."

Relief surged through Olivia, even as her stomach sank. "Oh, no."

"I've never felt more ashamed in my life."

"Lulu, it's not your shame, dearest." Olivia reached for her daughter's hand and gave it a squeeze.

"I feel ashamed for Hugh and people like him," Lucy said, her reticence shifting into passion with each word she spoke. "I'm ashamed that I belong to those people."

"You can't control the attitudes and prejudices of others, only your own. I'm certain Miss Radclyffe understands this. Besides," Olivia continued, "anyone who has ever met you knows that you belong wholly and only to yourself."

The beginnings of a smile hung about Lucy's lips, but Olivia could see that her daughter's heart wasn't in it. Then Lucy glanced at a point to the left of her plate, and the smile that had begun, dropped. It was another letter from Percy. Lucy slid it out of sight and began buttering her toast with a bit too much force, the knife a determined, choppy scrape across its brown surface.

The duke strolled into the room, a whistle on his lips, and took his customary place across from Olivia.

"Good morning, Your Grace," Olivia said. "Isn't today Monday? Shouldn't you be breaking your fast with Lord Exeter?"

"Michael needed to move our breakfast to tomorrow." The duke's smile reached all the way to his eyes. "Alas, you will have to put up with me this morning."

Olivia couldn't help but return his smile. "You're always welcome at our table."

Six days a week, the duke took his breakfast with Olivia and Lucy in their apartment in the east wing. The seventh day was reserved for his heir and Percy's elder brother, Michael, the Marquess of Exeter, and his ever-increasing family in the west wing, which they had gradually taken over. At last count, there were five boys, the eldest of whom was Hugh, second in line to the dukedom behind his father. It was a boisterous table in the west wing, which even Lucy at her most precocious couldn't match.

Usually, Olivia enjoyed easing into the day across from the duke and Lucy, but not today. Today, she would feel more at ease breaking her fast in a hole in the ground.

"Still reading nonsense, I see." The duke picked up his serious-minded *Morning Chronicle* and gave his eyebrows a waggle.

Olivia lifted her copy of the *London Diary* a notch higher. "Now and then, everyone needs a little nonsense in their lives, Your Grace."

"Not according to Miss Scace," Lucy piped up, her mouth crammed full of strawberry jam and toast.

Olivia was relieved to find her daughter somewhat restored to her usual ebullient self. The world could be such a foul and ugly place.

"Miss Scace says," Lucy continued, mimicking the no-nonsense Miss Scace through her mouthful of toast, "that every bit of nonsense one puts into one's brain forces out ten bits of good sense." She washed down her toast with a gulp of tea. "Or something like that."

Olivia suppressed the impulse to laugh outright at her impertinent daughter. "I'm certain she is absolutely correct, but, at times, I enjoy taking a little nonsense with my morning brew. Now, eat up, Lulu, you're off in five minutes."

"Oh, Mumsy, make it ten," Lucy whined, holding up a book, "I *must* complete this chapter before school, or I shall expire from anticipation. Drummond will understand. He always does."

"And what does the venerable Miss Scace have to say about *that* bit of nonsense you're reading?" the duke asked, his eyes shining with good humor.

"This?" She held up Walpole's *The Castle of Otranto*. Olivia had been equally fascinated with that novel at Lucy's age. "She says it's the worst sort, I'm afraid. A gothic romance." Lucy shivered dramatically and stuffed the rest of the toast into her mouth before opening her book and becoming instantly engrossed.

The duke shook his head in silent indulgence and returned his attention to his morning paper. Olivia squelched a pang of guilt before it surfaced. Contrary to Lord St. Alban's belief, she wasn't acting behind the duke's back to secure her townhouse. She was exercising her right to pursue her future independently. She didn't expect a viscount to understand that which he took for granted every day of his privileged, male life.

Speaking of Lord St. Alban…

Her pulse quickened. It was entirely possible that he could stride into this room at any moment. As the duke's protégé, of course. Not as her…

One kiss didn't make him *that*.

No matter that he might have been if Mrs. Landry hadn't done God's work and interrupted them.

Denial came in many forms.

Olivia stifled the humiliated groan that wanted release. How was she ever to face him again? How badly did she want her own townhouse? How badly did she want her independence?

She could endure the shame of facing him again. What wouldn't she endure for a life dependent on no one for her well-being and happiness?

Why didn't her goal ring as true today as it had yesterday?

"Mum?" A quizzical Lucy stood at Olivia's side. "I said I'm leaving now."

"Oh, yes, dearest. Love you," she replied to Lucy's retreating back. This left her alone with the duke. She peeled away the buttery layers of her croissant until it was nothing more than a flaky mess on her plate. "Will Lord St. Alban be joining us this morning?" The question hadn't aired quite as nonchalantly as she'd hoped.

The duke peered at her over the top of his paper. "He sent a note around this morning that he had other matters to attend."

"Ah," she replied.

"In fact," the duke continued, his gaze fixed upon his newspaper, "I'd be shocked if he returned at all. At least, for my mentorship. Other reasons might bring him back."

Her heart gave a solid kick. "I can't imagine."

"No?" the duke returned, but remained otherwise silent, leaving her to stew.

It had gone too far, and now the duke sensed something between her and Lord St. Alban. She must find a way to put an end to whatever *it* was, but how? She was being swept along by a force entirely out of her control and beyond her experience: her desire.

She needed to be alone. She pushed away from the table and stood. "I shall be in my studio if you need me."

Her feet carried her through the maze of corridors leading to her studio. But the closer she drew to her destination, the heavier, the more leaden, her feet became. She wouldn't be alone in her studio, not really, for *he* had taken it over. In more ways than one after last night. Even in the privacy of her apartments, her face flamed.

What she needed was a restorative rest. Small wonder she was anxious. She hadn't had a proper night's sleep all week. Well, she would remedy that deficit immediately. Instead of pointing right toward her studio, her feet went left and didn't stop until she reached her bed.

She hadn't avoided her studio—and the evidence of her denial—at all.

* * *

THE DREAM HADN'T COME to her in years.

It was the night of Olivia and Mariana's debut ball. Olivia had never seen her parents' ballroom illuminated so magnificently: light casting halos about the hundreds of guests, the servants, too; champagne bubbles effervescing their way up crystal flutes in a glittery little dance; and the chandeliers were too brilliant for words. They sparkled. They glimmered. They twinkled. They received the light and threw it out in a million little ways.

At the head of the grand staircase, she gazed across the crowded ballroom, excitable nerves clanging about her body. This great multitude of people was here for *her*. She brushed her fingertips across the diamond brooch pinned just below her shoulder. Hundreds of sapphires of varying sizes and shapes set in platinum formed a perfect closed rosebud, one petal peeking open, on the edge of coming into full bloom. Mother and Father had given Mariana a nearly identical brooch, hers in rubies and gold.

Mother's steadying hand squeezed her shoulder. "Are you ready, dearest?"

She nodded. She was too full of light and life to speak, to do anything other than glow and smile.

The orchestra struck up yet another waltz. She and Mariana had requested no music other than waltzes be played tonight, and their parents had indulged the slightly scandalous request. The night was perfect.

Almost.

But for the one person she'd prayed would be here...

"Olivia!" shouted Mariana, rushing up the staircase, cheeks flushed. "He's here!"

A rush of anticipation clamored through Olivia's veins, heating her up, body and mind. *He* was the boy, the young man, they'd spotted on Rotten Row, not once, but three separate times this week. Little conversations here and there revealed him to be the Duke of Arundel's youngest son, up from Cambridge.

The mere sight of him had made her heart miss every other beat. What would it be like to be near him? Were his dark brown eyes as deep and soulful up close as they were from afar? She wanted to be close to him and far, far away from him all at once.

Her gaze roved across the tops of heads until she, too, spotted him, laughing and joking with a group of his friends gathered round in a jocular circle. She'd never seen him without a smile in his eyes or a laugh ready on his lips. It was possible that she had enough light inside her to illuminate this entire room, all of London.

She stepped forward in his direction and a staying hand clamped onto her shoulder. A vaguely familiar voice whispered in her ear. "You need not be in such a rush."

But when she turned toward the voice, she saw no one there. Without another second's hesitation, she took Mariana's arm in her own, and the two of them flitted across the ballroom floor.

* * *

IT WAS HERE, at this point in the dream, that an older Olivia began watching her younger self from across the room. Young Olivia looked straight through her. She always did, never seeing her older self.

Of course, her younger self never saw or heard anything that deviated from her own wishes and desires. Such a willful girl. A girl who had never known any troubles, therefore couldn't anticipate any.

As Young Olivia and Mariana floated toward Percy's group, she tried calling out again, "Dance with a few others first."

It was no use. Olivia watched Young Olivia dare to introduce herself to Lord Percival Bretagne under the censorious gaze of the *ton*. A willful, spirited, even foolhardy, girl. The *ton*'s critical eye soon turned adoring as they watched Young Olivia and Percy fall instantly and madly in love. A genuine love match, a testament to true love within their ranks...the kind of love that had eluded so many. Within the hour, they would be the Sweethearts of the Season.

A wave of melancholy stole through her. She would like to wake up now. This dream always ended the same.

In the next instant, her body shifted in sleep, and a riot of conflicting sensation—hot, cold, parched, wet— swept over her. It was the thrill of anticipation, and it drew in toward one specific point in her body: the apex of her thighs. Her legs kicked the sheets off her body, too hot, too sensate. This was new to the dream.

Then she felt it. A presence, sensuous and demanding, hovering behind her. She didn't need to see him. She *knew* him. She should feel shame, but she didn't.

Brazen, unabashed pleasure at the perversity of experiencing *him* in front of the entire *ton* spread through her. Not that they saw her. They only had eyes for Young Olivia, their darling.

A gorgeous, capable hand snaked around her waist and pulled her backward, leaving her no choice but to melt into his hard, unforgiving length. His breath traced a warm trail across the back of her neck, his mouth teasing but never touching, releasing goose bumps down the length of her spine. She was one exhalation away from madness, desiring only that his lips touch her skin.

How could he be so close, yet so far out of reach? Frustration, demand, need, all kicked inside her, clamoring for release. Would he never give her what she needed?

At last, his lips found the nape of her neck, and his hands tightened at her waist before roving up to her breasts, cupping them, his fingertips taking her nipples between them, squeezing them through the fabric of her dress. Her head arched back in mindless abandon.

Through a haze, filtered by lust and hunger, she watched her younger self accept Percy's arm as he led her to the dance floor.

Then, *his* mouth found her ear, and she was lost, utterly lost. That boy across the room had never made her feel like this. But, then, he and Young Olivia had never known the other capable of this level of sensuality.

The expanse between them and herself and *him* stretched beyond the span of a ballroom to a distance of a hundred miles. Suddenly, Percy and Young Olivia were dressed for their wedding day. She wanted to cry out, to warn her younger self that the extraordinary, unique feeling would soon begin dissolving, moment by moment, day by day.

Then *he* pulled at the fabric of her skirts, pulled her

attention toward him, toward matters more urgent, and began lifting the fabric, fold over fold, until her ankles...her calves...her thighs ...her *mons pubis* were exposed. He operated not by sight, but by an expertise driven by instinct and demand, his gorgeous, capable fingers trailing across her hips, branding her with their touch, locating a bud, taut, wet, wanton, orgastic—

A loud moan erupted from her throat, and her eyes flew open...

To find herself alone in her bedroom, bed sheets twisted around her ankles, morning dress tangled above her waist, hand clenched between her thighs.

She flung her arms above her head and released a moan borne of dissatisfaction and denial. She'd made a mess of her sheets.

A perfect, little mess.

Of a sudden, clarity lit upon her.

Her feelings for Lord St. Alban had naught to do with love or matrimony. They didn't interfere with her goals or intentions. This was desire—pure, simple, raw...*implacable*.

She swung her legs off the bed and hopped to her feet in a wave of relief and determination. She must take a risk. It might be her only chance to rid her system of him.

Denial wasn't working. The time had come for her to try the opposite approach.

Before this day was done, she would make another perfect, little mess.

14

Jake sank his battered and bruised body into the steaming salt bath and exhaled a moan equal parts exhaustion and deep satisfaction. How was it possible that he'd gone this long in London before discovering Gentleman Jackson's boxing saloon?

There was something undeniable and purifying about stepping foot in the ring, looking another man in the eye, and tacitly agreeing to do one's worst to each other. It bonded men together in brotherhood at an elemental level.

And it was precisely the release he needed after last night. He'd sent his excuses to the duke this morning and succumbed to the mindless brutality of the ring. Anything to clear his head of *her*, and it had worked. For a time. Until he'd set foot outside the ring again.

He inhaled a deep draught of warm, humid air. There she'd stood in her studio, chest rising and falling in short bursts of air, eyes wide and inquiring. He'd only a few seconds before her questions went from general to specific. A second after that, she'd require serious answers. Answers he hadn't been prepared to give.

With a single second to decide his course, he'd taken a step, then another, a way to silence her solidifying with each inch forward. A simple kiss would do the trick.

He groaned and sank deeper into the water, even as a charge, one specific to her, spread from his gut to his loins. His cock grew thick, and he reached down to give it a testing stroke. There had been nothing simple about that kiss. His eyes drifted shut, the sight of her, the *feel* of her, and he tightened his grip, his body seeking another kind of release.

The low murmur of voices in the corridor caught his attention. He froze and listened, his fingers loosening their grip. Frustration ripped through him. Would he never be allowed release?

The voices resonated no louder than a soft drone, yet he discerned an insistence in the tenor of it, Payne's deep, mournful intonation at odds with one distinctly female. A dogged quality imbued the interaction, replacing frustration with curiosity. The door to his private sitting room turned on its hinges and opened without a knock. What was happening?

He braced his hands on either side of the sunken bathtub and stepped out of its sultry embrace to investigate the situation. His fingers found a towel and wrapped the soft cloth around his hips, droplets of water streaming down his exposed chest and his partially aroused cock.

A surprised, "Oh!" echoed in the other room, and a lengthy silence followed, which in reality could have lasted no longer than a few seconds.

Yet that single syllable was enough to set his bare skin alive. He knew that voice. Even by a single syllable. His ears strained for more, for certainty.

"These are the viscount's rooms?" Her voice, while definitely hers, sounded different, like there was a catch in it.

"My lady, this is most irregular. If you would please—"

"I *please* to wait here for his lordship."

Without delay, he padded across the wet bathroom over tatami mats and came to a stop at the sliding rice paper door separating his bedroom from his private sitting room. He placed ambivalent hands on the door handles and hesitated a brief moment. A moment of self-preservation, perhaps. After all, she was *here*, in his private rooms. No good could come of it.

His jaw clenched in decision. He was master of these rooms.

The door slid open on silent tracks. Framed by the rectangular doorway stood Payne facing down Lady Olivia, her determination apparent in the set of her shoulders and the rigidity of her usually lissome body. She exuded no whiff of the pugnacious, only the quiet assurance that she would have her way.

"Payne," Jake said, eliciting startled glances from the adversaries. "That will be all."

"My lord, I tried—" Payne began in a rush.

Jake caught Lady Olivia's eye, doubt chipping away at the assuredness he'd heard in her voice seconds ago. "And shut the door behind you."

"Yes, my lord."

Jake raised his brow and questioned Lady Olivia with his gaze. Her jaw clamped shut, and her lips drew into a straight line, as if every muscle in her face was bent on keeping words locked away. As if the flow of them would cost her dearly. After last night, he wasn't certain what he'd expected of her, but it wasn't this, to find her barging into his private rooms.

Of course, he'd entered her private rooms uninvited. Perhaps he should have expected a counterpunch of this sort.

"May I inquire why you're here?" he asked at last, convinced they would be engaged in this staring contest all day if he didn't broach the topic.

He reached down to secure the knot at his waist,

and her gaze followed the motion. A second later, she appeared to catch herself, wide, blue eyes startling up to meet his again.

"I, uh—" she began. He watched her struggle to keep her gaze steady on his, resisting the pull to steal glimpses of his bare torso. "I have something I want to say to you."

Her words emerged choppy, the phrasing disjointed. As if her mind was wandering off in a thousand directions. She wasn't acting like herself, her cool composure appearing to fail her. He rather liked this Lady Olivia.

"Olivia," he began, seizing this unsteady moment to take a risk and make a gain, "have I leave to call you Olivia?"

Her eyebrows knitted together in question, even as she nodded her assent to the familiarity.

"In my experience of you," he continued, a rush of satisfaction fueling his response, "those words could lead us anywhere."

* * *

OLIVIA SWIVELED AROUND and pretended to take a look at the room about her.

Somehow the moment had gotten away from her, and the logic and bravado that had propelled her forward had already begun to fail her. How could she possibly say what she'd come here to say with him standing in her line of sight wearing almost nothing?

Too distracting were the corded muscles of his arms and stomach, rippling beneath surprisingly tanned skin. Too distracting was the fine dusting of golden hair scattered across his chest that narrowed to a thin line below his navel as it trailed ever lower to its inevitable destination beneath his towel.

A woman couldn't think with that much flesh on display.

And it wasn't about the quantity, either. This was flesh of the finest quality, even if it was littered with a scattering of newly emergent bruises. What did this man do with his time?

Back firmly to him, she focused on what had first caught her attention when she'd entered this room: the room itself. She'd never beheld one like it.

Despite the rather large amount of wood, a brightness pervaded the atmosphere. A simple, caramel-colored grid of maple outlined the ceiling and walls, which were, in turn, filled in with blank rice paper. Centered in the room stood a sunken mahogany table and four legless chairs.

The room came together in way that suggested open air. One could breathe in this room, so sparse and distinct were its furnishings. With each breath a measure of strain dissipated.

It was all so utterly, simply, starkly beautiful. And all so utterly, simply, starkly *foreign*.

Up until this instant, she hadn't considered how very different Lord St. Alban was from society, from *her*. He so closely resembled the ideal, privileged viscount that one could forget. But who was he really?

A different man altogether, she suspected. One who intrigued her too much. This room, and him in it, wasn't helping her Lord St. Alban problem.

"Did you have this room imported whole cloth from Japan?"

"Nearly."

Her eyes swung up to inspect the expertly latticed woodwork on the ceiling. "I've never seen its match."

"Not even in the mysterious Jiro's studio?"

The mysterious Jiro. The words struck her at a wrong angle. Or rather it was the way he'd inflected the words. Something her ears picked up that she couldn't quite lay her finger on. And turning around to see the expression on his face wouldn't help at all. She would go absolutely tone deaf at the sight of him.

"Is there something you wish to know about Jiro?" she asked. "Does Miss Radclyffe require an art master?"

One second, then another, passed, a resounding silence filling the air. She'd begun to question whether he would reply at all when he said, "No, Miss Radclyffe doesn't require an art master. *That* is a *tansu*."

Olivia saw that she'd begun to feather her fingertips across the intricate ironwork of a chest. "Lovely."

"It's a mobile storage chest used by the Japanese."

She half turned toward him and almost took no notice of his naked chest. Or the bruises strewn haphazardly across its surface. Almost. "It's bold, yet refined, too."

"Boldness can be found in even the most refined objects," he said. "Unexpectedly so, at times."

Again, she pivoted away from him, unable to hold his gaze when he spoke in so suggestive a manner. Yet wasn't he playing into her plan? Hadn't she come here to be bold?

Her courage, nay foolhardiness, failed her with each successive moment, her plan becoming impossible, an embarrassment, truth be told. *Too bold.*

She cleared her throat and focused on the *tansu*. She needed to be gone from this room, now, but her feet felt mired in quicksand.

"There are *tansu* for every use." His voice sounded farther away now. Had he retreated to the sliding door? She wasn't sure if she was relieved or disappointed. "Clothing and food storage, money, linens, even apothecaries use them. Every ship trading along the Pacific carries one onboard for safekeeping valuables and as a sort of status symbol for trading purposes. *Funadansu*, they're called, the most ornate of the *tansu*."

Her eye caught his over her shoulder, and her body

followed. It almost didn't matter that this man, whom she'd kissed with a passion resembling a mystical experience, stood no more than fifteen feet away nearly stark naked.

Almost.

"Did you carry a *funa-dansu* on your ship?" she asked, although she shouldn't. She had an insatiable curiosity about this man.

"I did."

"Did it stay with the ship?"

"It's in the other room."

"The other room?" His meaning caught up to her. "Your bedroom?"

He nodded once, a curt affirmation.

"Is your bedroom the same as this room?"

"Very similar, yes."

She could have left it at that. But she didn't want to. A closeness to him that she couldn't account for stole through her. This room wasn't only a world apart, it was the world within him, and she would know more of it. The feeling transcended simple curiosity. She felt on the edge of something new. She felt on the edge of knowing the very essence of the man.

"May I see it?"

A hard beat of her heart thudded in her chest. He didn't have to say yes. After all, her request fell well outside the bounds of propriety. But what did society have to do with her and Lord St. Alban?

"Certainly, my lady," he said, his tone formal, or as formal as a man clothed entirely in a bath towel could manage. He managed it quite well, actually. "But you will have to excuse me while I clothe myself in something with a little more...fabric."

* * *

JAKE TURNED on his heel and strode through the open doorway, making a straight line for his dressing room. He'd just conducted an entire conversation about Japanese utility chests clad in nothing but a strip of cotton. He'd never blushed a day in his life, but if the heat suffusing his body from head to toe was any indicator, he was now.

What was he thinking? Allowing that woman access to his bedroom?

He tore off the towel, grabbed the first pair of trousers at hand, and yanked them up his legs. Next, he had his arms through a white lawn shirt and over his head. He'd skip the cravat, no time for intricate knot tying as he must return to his *guest*.

But the real question was this: what was Lady Olivia Montfort—*Olivia*—doing in his private rooms? He mustn't let her duck the question again.

The moment he slid open his dressing room door the question fled to the Outer Hebrides. Connective words refused to link the images together: Bedroom. Bed. Floor. Hands. Knees.

Olivia. The very thing of beauty who would surely lead to his undoing.

At the sight of her upturned bum, an instinct—instinct surely passed down from generations of medieval warlord ancestors—to drape her skirts across her back, and take her then and there, surged through him on a wave of unslaked thirst. What in the world was the woman trying to accomplish? His undoing?

He cleared his throat and in doing so hoped to clear his mind. It didn't work. He must say something. "Have you dropped your reticule?"

An honest laugh floated on the air, tinkly and joyous, and at complete odds with the dark seed of lust sprouting inside him. When she sat back on her heels and twisted around to reply, delight lit up her entire being, and another layer of his desire unfolded.

"I didn't bring a reticule with me."

His mind conjured up that word again. The one that described what he most liked about her when she allowed it.

Unbound.

A gentleman didn't allow himself to think in such a base manner about a lady. The gentleman and the medieval warlord battled for dominance.

She would be unbound, and he would be undone.

"I was investigating how your bed is constructed. I've never seen its like," she said, oblivious to the struggle waging within him. "I don't have much experience with beds other than my own." Another melodic laugh sounded.

Her bright mood infected him, and he felt a smile of his own unbind, even if his stubborn medieval hunger hadn't abated a whit. "It's called a platform bed. You see them in the Scandinavian countries."

"From above, it appears to be floating." Her smile turned sheepish and charming. "I had to see if a spell was cast upon it."

She rose to her feet, and he took a seat on the other side of the bed. Oh, how he liked the way she looked in this moment: hat askew; cheeks flushed; unwary, uncool, uncollected smile curving her Cupid's bow lips. Utterly kissable lips, he'd learned from recent experience. Lips he would like to taste again. The bed wasn't the only entity in the room that had a spell cast upon it.

"While I like the simplicity of the Japanese bedroom, it consists of little more than a futon spread on the floor," he explained. For some reason, surely self-destructive, he wanted her to understand him. "The wizened sailor in me prefers sleeping above ground."

"I would hardly describe you as *wizened*, Lord St. Alban."

"Jake," he cut in. He wanted to hear his name, his real name, on her lips.

"Jake," she repeated softly. Her smile took on a knowing quality. "There isn't a woman in London who would describe you that way."

If they'd been surrounded by the glitter and pomp of a ballroom, and she'd spoken those words to him, with that particular smile lifting the corners of her lips, he would have sworn she was flirting with him. But, given their history, he wasn't sure what to make of her words. Only this: they made his insides feel as light and variable as a fall leaf released to the four winds on a blustery day.

He tried to ignore the feeling. "This bed is a solution to that problem."

A wicked laugh escaped Lady Olivia... *Olivia.* "And which problem is that? That too many women find you irresistible? I know women, my lord, and I'm of the opinion that your bed might only exacerbate the problem."

"It addresses," he replied, his voice a husky register out of his control, "my particular desire to sleep at an elevated level, my lady."

What he really wanted to say was, *And you, Olivia? Can I count you among those women who find me irresistible? Might my bed exacerbate that problem for you?*

She focused on a point beyond his shoulder and gasped. "Oh, it's lovely. So intricate, yet subtle."

She'd spotted the *funa-dansu*, and he was enchanted, thoroughly and irrevocably, by her.

Without a consideration for the relation of their bodies to one another, she moved between his place on the bed and the *funa-dansu* to run her fingertips across its intricate geometrical pattern of ironwork overlaid onto smooth keyaki wood. Seeking a wider view of the piece, she backed up by slow increments until her skirts brushed against his knees.

She assumed she was pressed against the bed. He knew it. Just as he knew he must extricate himself from this situation. He'd let matters progress too far. Settled on a direct course of action, he stood, attempting to slide out of her way before she realized her mistake. It was what a gentleman would do.

The point became moot when her spine stiffened and her body went ramrod straight, accomplishing nothing more, or less, than to press herself full-length against the front of his body. It was entirely possible that she felt the outline of his stubborn erection through her muslin skirts.

He held himself stock still and awaited her direction. But there was no question in his mind of how this would end. The medieval warlord had won the battle.

He only waited for her to realize it, too.

15

T iny, electric waves of shock rippled through Olivia, sudden lust licking quick at their wake.

The instant she'd set foot in these rooms, finding Lord St. Alban wrapped in nothing but a length of cotton, she'd known how this day would end. After all, wasn't *this* what she'd come for?

Except she hadn't expected it to feel so immediate, so real, yet so fantastical. As if she'd been granted permission to conflate reality with this morning's dream.

She closed her eyes and sank into his long, hard body with all the resistance of a wildflower swaying to the uncertain rhythm of a summer breeze. Her fingers reached up over her shoulder, seeking out the back of his head, drawing his lips to the crook of her neck, to the exact spot his phantom lips had touched this morning in her dream. An exhalation of his warm breath skittered across her skin, and her nipples tightened into hard buds of anticipation.

Would his lips never touch her?

A soft groan vibrated in her ear, and, at last, his lips met her neck as his hands reached around her waist, his scent intoxicating her with its hint of the exotic and unknown. She was irrevocably lost to the spell of this room. *And this man.*

It wasn't enough to feel him; she would see him. Her lips longed to make contact with his. She found his hands and loosened his grip enough for her to turn in his arms. Facing him, she braved the moment, inhaled, and met his eyes.

She didn't need confirmation of his desire. *That* was pressed against her. She needed to know that she wasn't the only one lost to this insanity between them.

He reached up and tucked an errant lock of hair behind her ear, the gesture intimate and tender. The sort of gesture that could undo her. He was giving her time.

Time to change her mind.

Well, that wouldn't do.

She lifted to the very tips of her toes, and still her lips didn't reach his. A smile, knowing and sensuous, curled about his mouth. "This is madness."

The words whispered across her lips, the promise within them raising goose flesh and emboldening her to say, "Not nearly mad enough."

That knowing, sensuous smile firmed with intent as his head canted to the side and golden lashes lowered to brush against high, angled cheekbones. He pressed forward and touched his tongue to the upturned "O" of her lips, soft, slippery, delicious.

How she wanted to take him in. How she wanted him to let her.

At last, his lips touched hers, a fleeting, tender brush. So tender that she wondered for a wild moment if the passion she'd felt was all her own wishful thinking. Then, in the way a levee will break from too much pressure built up behind it, his kiss deepened, and his fingers tightened about her waist, drawing her body into the long length of his, crushing her into him. A heady, breathless feeling swelled within her. She felt...

Claimed.

Instinct, sudden and animalistic, took over as her greedy fingers snaked inside his shirt and brushed across the expanse of his flat stomach. On a wave of audacity, she found the laces of his trousers and made short work of them. Hot, rigid flesh met her hand, and desire streaked through her as she slid her fingers along the velvet column of his shaft.

A wild, unfettered groan erupted from him, breaking their kiss. His lashes flickered open, and his serious gaze pierced her. "Again," he demanded.

She tightened her fingers around him and again stroked him, up and down his length. Wordlessly, he gathered up the folds of her skirts, handful by linen handful, cool air caressing exposed calves… thighs…*quim*…

"Have you any idea how exquisite is your sweet, wet slit?"

She gasped at the vulgarity of his words. At the ache they provoked along her vulgar, wet slit. He pressed forward, the hot, insistent length of him grazing her, his lips brushing against her ear. "What do you want?"

A heartbeat later, she spoke the one word that could propel them into a realm she understood only at its most rudimentary level. "*This*."

He fell to his knees before her as if in worship, and she transformed into a being created purely for lust. His tongue touched her thigh, and a shudder ripped through her. "I'm not sure my legs can—"

He stroked his tongue across her skin, and she gasped, aching and hollow, wanting and needing *more*. He met her gaze across the trembling expanse of her body. "Support you?"

He reached around and cupped her bottom, bracing her against the onslaught she craved, all the sensation in her body concentrated into the point where his tongue touched her skin. It was everything and not nearly enough as his mouth inched higher, closer, pushing her to the limit of her tolerance. Her body screamed for what he offered and withheld. His tongue on her, branding her with its fiery mark, was all that mattered. It was all that would ever matter.

Madness.

His tongue flicked across her quim, and the world as she knew it folded onto itself a million times over until it ceased to exist. All substance beneath her feet, at her back, above her head, became light and air and black and void all at once until it was only she and he at the center of the universe.

The nascent ache inside her sex became a full-on assault of greedy nerve endings as his tongue languorously stroked her before turning into butterfly flickers focused entirely on the one place she existed in the universe, stripped down to the essence of herself. "Jake," her voice cried out on a note, low and primal. She didn't recognize the sound as her own.

Her fingers wove through, then clutched at his hair, and her body tensed, suspended on the edge of a sensation that provoked, teased, taunted her … just out of reach … her sex swelling from tight blossom toward the verge of effulgence.

All she needed was *one*… "Oh," she moaned.

Two… "Please," she begged.

Three… "More," she demanded.

A fourth flick of his talented tongue, and her back arched as her body shattered and she cried out. The universe reversed itself and unfolded, expanding to an infinity that stretched beyond her wildest imagining on a wave of pleasure that crested over and over, transforming her into nothing more than a heap of tingly nerve endings.

His gaze caught hers from his place below and held as he rose to a stand, corded muscles flexing and releasing effortlessly. He angled his head forward, and her eyes drifted shut in pleasure when his mouth found the sensitive cup of her ear. "Lie back. I would see you better."

Desire flared hotter as she stepped back and did as she was told. Skirts bunched above her waist, again her gaze found his. She felt no shame at this exposure, his eyes, nearly black with desire, taking in her bare legs, her bare sex. Hunger for more of him was all she felt.

Even after the universe had opened its secrets to her, she wanted more. And it was everything.

"You steal my breath away," he said, his voice a ragged whisper.

A surge of womanly confidence buoying her, she came to her knees before him and loosened her bodice, shrugging it off until it lay draped loosely over her hips. His pupils dilated at the sight of her, spiking her desire higher.

She leaned forward, bringing her breasts into contact with the front of his shirt while her hands trailed lower until they arrived at the open fastenings of his trousers. His manhood strained in anticipation of her touch. "This," she whispered as her fingertips glided across his pulsating member, "is what I really want."

Her sex quivered with the want, the utter *need*, to take him inside her. Impatiently, she pressed her body into full contact with his. It mattered not that they were partially clothed, reduced as she was to this need to join their bodies.

With one hand she pulled him forward before pushing him back onto the bed, his body laid out for her like a feast. A feeling of power, heady and bright, overtook and guided her. She swung her legs around to straddle him, positioning herself above him, her fingers reaching down and encircling his long, hard shaft. A sharp hiss sounded through his teeth, ratcheting her desire higher, her gaze locked onto his, the tip of his swollen shaft poised, ready, at the opening of her sex. She'd never felt so empty in her life.

It was slowly and deliberately that she lowered herself onto him, inch by divine inch, until she held as much as she could take, but not all he had to offer. A moan ripped through her, and her eyes fluttered shut from the absolute hedonistic bliss of it. She might have stayed like this forever, luxuriating in the delicious pain of her body stretched to its limit, but he had other ideas.

His hands gripped her waist and began sliding her up and down his rigid length, releasing another wave of pleasure through her. Oh, the pleasure... It was endless.

She felt limitless.

A rhythm to their motion established itself as their bodies moved in unified desire. The now familiar tension in her sex began winding tight, but this time she sensed the same tension coiling his body with every stroke and thrust. She glanced down to find his piercing eyes closed, his beautiful features taking on a quality of abandon, unexpected and strangely intimate. It did something to her insides completely at odds with the uncomplicated liaison she'd sought today.

She let the thought fly away as she closed her eyes and *felt. Him.* Inside *her.*

"I'm not sure how much longer..." He trailed, cupping her breasts and squeezing her puckered nipples between his fingertips. Her back arched, pushing her breasts forward. Raw desire spiraling higher, his hands returned to her waist, and the easy slide became a demanding thrust.

A bead of sweat trickled between her breasts. The muscles of his stomach contracted into hard, defined segments when he lifted his head to catch the salty bead with his tongue on an upward thrust of his hips, his manhood encased to the hilt in her sex.

Again, she cried out. This time with more ferocity, their mutual need escalating. Her legs took over the hard, relentless rhythm. His hand cupped her bottom and stabilized the motion as greed for *more, again* overtook her.

"That's it," he said, his words a muttered staccato. "Oh, yes."

Again, the glorious tension found and teased and licked at her until…until it had toyed with her enough and allowed her release, her sex a fluttery pulse around his hot, rigid shaft.

His fingers reached beneath her chin and tugged, a silent demand. His eyes locked onto hers, and she couldn't look away. Even as he thrust inside her, the slick length of him sliding in and out—the most exquisite pain…the most exquisite pleasure—his gaze held her in its thrall.

His hands clutched her hips, and he flipped them around, reversing their positions, his body now atop hers. His eyes drifted shut as the thrust of his hips, the slide of his cock built, faster, harder toward—

His body tensed, his shout echoed through the room, and release caught him in its unrelenting teeth. At the very last moment, he pulled out of her and spent his seed onto the bed before collapsing beside her, the ragged in and out of uneven breath the only sound in the room.

Through the haze of enervation and satiety came the thought that she'd been a fool in coming here. She hadn't extinguished the flame between them.

She'd only stoked it higher.

* * *

"Ahem," Jake heard as if from a great distance.

His eyes creaked open to the sight of a woman's unclad back. *Olivia's* unclad back.

"If you will please secure my fastenings, I shall be on my way."

He rolled onto his side and pushed himself up into a seated position, his hazy languor giving way to a feeling resembling alarm. He had no idea what to expect from her, but a presented back and a business-like tone wasn't it.

Silently, he reached out and fastened her dress, resisting the impulse to feather his fingertips down her vulnerable spine, resisting the compulsion to influence her to lose that business-like tone. Recent dealings had shown him how.

Task complete, his rational mind asserted itself. "Why was it you came to my rooms?"

She emitted a short laugh. "For this."

"For *this*?"

"Yes, for this."

His mouth clamped shut in exasperated silence. The woman would explain herself sooner or later.

"I was hoping to speak to you today about arranging *this*." She stood and moved to the other side of the room where a small rock garden lay unaffected by their little drama. "To have this tension out from between us. To purge our systems of one another. Simple and uncomplicated."

"And has it worked?" There was no help for the testy note in his voice. "Is the tension gone? Are our systems *purged*?" The words came out more demanding than he had a right to be, given the circumstances of their...*tête-à-tête*.

At last, she faced him. She looked vulnerable, spent, and at complete odds with herself. "Isn't that the way of a fleeting affair?"

"Olivia," he began, "this is no way to cope—"

"And you're the expert on coping?" She glared at his bruised chest. "Is this how you're coping with being a viscount? By allowing yourself to be beaten black and blue?"

He spread his arms wide. "These have naught to do being a viscount. As far as that goes, I find myself settling into the role." He surprised himself with that last bit. It was true.

"Then why?" she whispered.

"You don't know?"

"Perhaps."

That single word confirmed it for him. He'd allowed himself to be pummeled black and blue for the same reason she'd splattered his face across her studio walls.

It was his release…

From her.

And they both knew it.

"Is it working?"

"No." He paused. "Did this?"

"We shall see."

He didn't believe her. She didn't believe her, either. Further, she was scared it hadn't worked. He saw the fear in her eyes.

"Olivia, it doesn't have to be like this."

"You may want to resume calling me Lady Olivia. Decorum matters in our little world."

"*Lady* Olivia, have you ever experienced a fleeting affair?" Silence stretched out between them as he slid off the bed and tied the lacings of his trousers. "What we just shared was simple and uncomplicated?" Disbelief sounded in his voice, and he wanted her to hear it. "And our systems are purged of one another?"

"You are, of course, not obligated to me in any way," she stated, undeterred. "You are free to pursue a proper wife, and I am free to remain a scandalous divorcée." She began sliding her fingers into a gray kid glove, one by one, methodically, determinedly. "In fact, we could keep doing this until—"

Alarmed, he sat forward. "That won't work."

Her gaze, cool, unaffected, met his. He could see her striving to place distance between them. "You're a man of the world. Surely, as a sailor, you had a paramour in every port."

"For us, Olivia," he cut in before she could speak another word. "That won't work for us."

Her gaze refused to meet his as she began tugging a glove onto her other hand. In the space her silence created, he was afforded the distance to think and allow reason to assert itself. He *must* find a wife. To continue with Olivia in this manner wasn't only unthinkable, it was ungentlemanly. He would arrange an outing with Miss Fox and wouldn't beg off this time.

At the edge of his vision, he saw that Olivia... *Lady* Olivia had gone still. She stood in a posture both aloof and expectant, poised on the verge of flight. "I shall be on my way to fetch Lucy from school now."

Without another word, she strode out of his bedroom, out of his mansion, and out of his life for all he knew, leaving him more alone than perhaps he'd ever been in his life.

A series of questions ran rapid-fire through his mind. What had he done? With Lady Olivia... *Olivia?* Had he just ruined his chance of finding the thief? Of finding a wife? Of securing Mina's future?

He shot off the bed, his feet beating a resolute tattoo toward his dressing room. Another bout in Gentleman Jackson's ring was in his very near future.

Within a thing of beauty could, indeed, lie the seeds of one's undoing. In fact, that was where they would most likely lie.

* * *

OLIVIA SAT PERCHED on the carriage seat, her eyes squeezed shut, her thoughts running faster than she could catch them.

That won't work for us.

For a moment, she hadn't been able to breathe. *Us.* Two separate entities, combined, one.

She'd gone lightheaded. From lack of breath, surely, not from that word, the warm, seductive invitation of it. That word didn't have to change anything. This tryst was a purely physical occurrence. She was the same person. She still had the same goals. What had been lurking between her and Lord St. Alban—*Jake*—was out in the open now. They could be free.

But, oh, this feeling knotting her insides didn't feel like freedom. It wanted more. It wanted to become bound to a budding addiction. She could easily envision a future of enslaved dependence on that man, on what his body could provide hers. The thought caused the tender flesh of her sex to swell and ready itself for him again.

She bit back a groan borne of frustration and want. This must end here. She must envision a different future, the one she'd spent years cultivating, one of self-reliance. Never again would she open herself to the uncertainty and unpredictability of dependence on another for her happiness. The inevitable pain of disappointment and abandonment ran too deep. It wasn't worth the pleasure.

Her racing pulse spoke a different truth. She would ignore it.

Eyes clenched tight, she fought for clarity. Her mind evoked the image of her white marble column. As she attempted to relax into it, she couldn't. Something was amiss with her column. Usually, it stood tall and proud, unassailable. Today, it skewed ever so subtly to one side. Not enough to topple over, but...*off*. Try as she might, she couldn't make it stand straight.

The carriage jolted to stop, and Olivia's eyes flew open. She'd arrived at Lucy's school. Before she could compose herself, Lucy bounced into the carriage, her usual ebullient self.

"Hello, Mum." Her daughter leaned across the carriage floor for her customary kiss on the cheek. "Whoa, you smell like...like...like what?"

"Cloves?"

"Oh, yes, that's it. How is that?"

"I've been out and about."

Lucy accepted this and began recounting her day. Just as Olivia relaxed into the excitable rhythms of her daughter's girlish voice, Lucy said, "Mum?"

"Yes?"

"You know who else smells like that?"

Olivia braced herself, her heartbeat doubling its rate, and shook her head.

"Miss Scace."

Her breath released.

"You must bathe immediately when we arrive home. *Immediately.*"

Olivia looked through the carriage window at passing London streets. It had begun to drizzle. "I intend to, Lulu. I'll wash off every last trace."

Even as she spoke the words, she knew they were a lie, that a trace of him would always remain.

Had she truly rid her system of Lord St. Alban...*Jake?*

Or had she set herself up for a lifetime of knowing exactly what she would be missing?

16

NEXT DAY

"I must confess," Miss Fox spoke in the particular haughty tone that characterized her voice. Mayhap the sound would grate less on Jake's ears over time. "I was rather surprised to have received your note yesterday."

"Oh?" He wouldn't confess that he was rather surprised to have sent it.

They encountered yet another mud puddle in the path, this one too wide for a lady to cross without assistance. He leaped the shallow distance and held out his hand for her. She placed her fingers in his and met him on the other side with a dainty, little hop. She strolled ahead while he assisted her chaperone, Miss Markley, who accepted his hand with a giggle and a blush.

Once again, they progressed forward, Jake and Miss Fox arm in arm, Miss Markley falling discreetly behind. "The trails aren't as well groomed here in the Green Park as they are in the more fashionable environs of Hyde Park."

"My apologies, if I was mistaken in suggesting this park for our outing." The lady wasn't afraid to speak her mind. He should find it refreshing, but he couldn't quite. Every word she spoke, and the way she spoke it, contained a sharp edge.

"No need to apologize, my lord. I understand perfectly why you would suggest this park."

He cut her a sideways glance. Her features were composed and placid, but he could see that she did understand perfectly. He'd chosen this unfashionable park at this unfashionable hour—ten in the morning, no less —for the simple reason that he didn't want the curious eyes of society watching him court Miss Fox. If what he was doing could be called courting.

Of course, it was courting. He was an eligible bachelor, she a single young lady, and they were strolling a path together, her chaperone trailing them at a discreet distance. This was courting.

Although he hadn't sufficiently considered all the steps it would take to secure a society marriage, he could see that he'd officially entered the path toward finding a stepmother for Mina.

All the goals he'd set for himself were beginning to fall into place. He'd even made an appointment with a Bow Street runner later today to find Jiro. A Japanese artist living in Limehouse couldn't be too difficult to find. He should've handled the situation this way from the beginning. It was the most civilized and proper approach, he could see that now.

Rather, he'd engaged with a divorcée who society deemed scandalous for her insistence on conducting her life according to her own principles. And yet, yesterday, he'd done more than engage with her in his bedroom.

And there had been nothing civilized about it.

"My lord, are you quite alright?"

His jaw unclenched long enough to say, "Of course, why shouldn't I be?"

"Well, you were glaring at that poor squirrel." She pointed out the animal, its tail twitching in the mid-distance. "Perhaps you thought you could incinerate it with the intensity of your gaze?"

"My apologies if I caused alarm. I can assure you that I harbor no such animus toward that squirrel."

A tight smile pinched at the corners of Miss Fox's mouth. He'd never seen her smile any other way. Had she ever smiled unreservedly in her life? Had she ever looked at someone and poured her entire being into a smile only for him?

A face possessed of just such a smile appeared in his mind's eye.

"You were missed at the Duchess of Dalrymple's dinner party," Miss Fox said. "She let it be known that she was most annoyed at having an odd number at table."

"I'd committed to another engagement that posed a conflict." It wouldn't do to say which commitment came first.

"Two nights ago..." Miss Fox's eyes narrowed. "That was the night of Lady Olivia Montfort's monthly soirée, no?"

"It was," he drawled, certain he was admitting guilt. Miss Fox possessed a specific shrewd quality that he wasn't sure he liked. A possibility occurred to him. "Are you a lover of art? Perhaps you've attended one of Lady Olivia's soirées?"

Miss Fox shook her head. "I've never been invited. Lady Olivia and I don't figure prominently in one another's social spheres."

Another descriptor for Miss Fox's smile came to mind. *Hard.*

"In fact," continued Miss Fox. "I'm not sure she's fully aware of my existence, which is likely for the best."

"And why is that?"

She laughed, the sound tinny and false, as if it had been forced out of her. "Lady Olivia has cultivated quite the scandalous reputation, and it wouldn't do for an unmarried miss, such as myself, to be seen in her company."

"Quite," Jake bit out. Even as their feet progressed forward, he made himself go very, very still, fighting the urge to tell Miss Fox, politely and calmly, that three Miss Foxes wouldn't amount to one Lady Olivia. But it wouldn't do. *Quite* was the only word he trusted himself to say, politely and calmly, on the matter.

He unclenched hands that had curled into tight fists. It wasn't Miss Fox's view in particular that had him wound up, but society's view in general. Society deserved a good drubbing.

Perhaps Miss Fox sensed the storm brewing at her side for she asked, "Isn't this a perfect spring day, my lord?"

"It is a lovely day," he replied, even as a note of disappointment shot through him at this conversational turn, the weather. Possibly, it presaged his future with a proper wife. Proper marriage, proper wife, proper stepmother, proper dull.

"You wouldn't believe the number of poems rhapsodizing about emergent spring that the publishing house gets this time of year."

"The publishing house?" At last, something interesting.

Miss Fox tiptoed around another shallow puddle. "My father won a share in a small press a few years ago."

"*Won* a share?"

"In a card game."

"Your father is a baron, correct?"

She nodded. "A baron, yes, and a publisher." A light blush pinked her cheeks. "My father has his fingers in any number of pies on any given day."

"It was my understanding that gentlemen don't enter into trade."

"As a general rule, they don't. But my father isn't

one to be hemmed in by society's rules, and they indulge him, because he's, well, he's a reliably entertaining dinner guest."

Jake sensed a quiet conflict between father and daughter. In the interest of keeping clear of those murky waters, he asked, "Do you take an interest in the press?"

Her eyes, an opaque gray, darted up to meet his. She really had the most direct way of taking in a person. "Our secret?"

He nodded.

"I love it. At first, it was a bit of a lark, but one day I began sorting through a pile of submissions and didn't look up for three hours. The written word interests me, not only for its ability to communicate ideas, but for its intersection of beauty and power. Take poetry, for instance, the fewer the words—well chosen, of course—the more powerfully it communicates its message. Fascinating, no?"

This was the longest string of words he'd ever heard Miss Fox produce. Encouraging. "Might I read any publications the press produces?"

"Oh, I, um, I doubt it," she stammered, her eloquence gone. "We don't publish for the serious-minded, such as yourself. Ours is lighter fare."

Her gaze, once clear and direct, now skittered away to study the path ahead of them. He wasn't sure what brought about the sudden change. "You are a most unexpected young lady."

"Young?" Her brow lifted toward the blue sky above. "Society would hardly characterize me as *young*. I turned five and twenty on my last name day."

"Which makes you an aged crone?"

She gave a little shrug. "Perhaps not, but it does place me solidly on the shelf, and a decided spinster in the *ton*'s eyes."

"Do you care how you're seen by them?"

"Not in the least."

His eyebrows creased together, and, of course, Miss Fox caught the movement.

"Does that shock you, my lord? If I cared, I would be a most unhappy person. Besides, everyone can't be who they appear on the surface, or the world would be a very dull place."

"I feel certain you are exactly who you purport to be."

"Do you?" Another laugh escaped her. She knew how to make a laugh sound like a chore. "And who am I?"

"A society Miss with a speckless reputation and a keen, observant eye."

"On the prowl for a husband?"

His brow lifted in surprise. "My apologies—"

"I tease you, my lord," she interrupted. "Well, not entirely. To be on the prowl for a husband is the lot of an unmarried lady. There seems to be no way of getting around it."

He resisted the paternal impulse to pat her hand in comfort. "May I ask your given name?" It was the sort of question a gentleman courting a lady might ask.

"Anne," she replied simply, the sound of it curt to his ears.

"It suits you."

"It does, doesn't it? Short and plain." She waved her free hand before her, as if she was a vendor displaying her wares. "That's me."

Brittle. That would be another word he would use to describe her. But he would keep that one to himself.

He really took her measure for the first time. It was true, she was short in stature. And petite, waifish even, not a curve on her. Indistinct brown hair and gray eyes. She had the lovely kind of skin, translucent and clear, that young ladies likely envied, yet she wasn't the sort who would draw his eye in the normal course of events.

But did that matter? Perhaps those very qualities made her the perfect match for him. Miss Fox would never invite gossip or excite scandal, unlike—

He stopped the sentence in its tracks. It wouldn't do to think of *her* in the moment he was coming around to Miss Fox.

"Short, yes," he began, "but to the point. I was thinking more along the lines of classic and English." He could stop there, but he wouldn't. A bit of kindness might blunt her sharp edge. "I think another word could be used to describe you."

"And what word would that be, my lord?"

"Pretty."

A deep blush spread from her modest décolletage, and he intuited this was no contrivance to display maidenly modesty. Miss Fox didn't want to blush, but couldn't help herself. It was possible she'd never been called pretty. How very young she appeared, how very vulnerable. Likely no one ever noticed her vulnerability, hidden as it was beneath her prickly exterior.

The birds trilling in the trees and the mellow sway of the breeze through the canopy above, they strolled in silence, and unease dissipated beneath the gentle persuasion of a lovely spring day.

They rounded a bend in the path, and she emitted a squeaky, high-pitched, "Yip!"

"Miss Fox, are you injured?"

Her hand disengaged from his arm as she struggled to his right with an adversary he couldn't make out. "My skirts have been caught by a tenacious gooseberry bush," she said as she continued to wrestle with her verdant adversary. "The Green Park is quite a wilderness."

Jake stepped forward, intent on helping Miss Fox, when a familiar figure snagged the corner of his vision.

In the distance, the figure stood bent over a sketchpad, charcoal a whir across paper. Two weeks ago, he wouldn't have given that figure a second glance. Today, it stopped him in his tracks.

Olivia. His gaze drank her in like desert sand consumed the first drops of a monsoon rain.

"She is the sort who draws the eye, isn't she?" a voice with an edge of tempered steel cut into thoughts he had no business having.

Of course. Miss Fox had noticed. "My apologies, if I—"

"No need to apologize, my lord," she said, hands patting and smoothing her rescued gown, pretty blushes a thing of the past. "I'm made of sterner stuff than that."

He didn't think she could have said anything that could have made him feel more like a cad. But Olivia stood in his line of vision, and he was powerless to look away. She hadn't yet noticed them, immersed as she was in the world she was creating on that piece of paper. He found himself in the strange position of envying a piece of paper. This was the man she reduced him to.

Of a sudden, her hand stilled, mid-stroke, and she froze, her gaze trained straight ahead of her. Suspense held his breath tight in his chest. One by one, she slid her materials into a black leather case before unexpectedly pivoting to face him and Miss Fox. Her gaze darted back and forth between them, once, twice, and she swallowed, drawing his eye toward the undulant column of her ivory throat. He'd licked a bead of sweat up its length only yesterday.

His mouth went dry. Only another lick would satisfy this particular thirst.

As he and Miss Fox drew close, he saw that Olivia understood what he was doing in the Green Park with Miss Fox. Hands at her sides, bland smile pasted onto her lips, she awaited their approach, her entire countenance placid and unmoving.

"Lady Olivia, how remarkable to find you here," he said once they'd drawn within comfortable speaking distance.

"Indeed," she returned. Her bland, little smile, the mask she employed for society, hadn't budged a jot. She didn't want to give anything of herself away in front of Miss Fox. Or him.

How unlike the Olivia he'd known only yesterday. For all the world she looked as if she'd succeeded in purging her system of him. A pit opened up inside him, and a roil of nausea flipped his stomach over.

As they stood in an uneasy triangle, awkward silence charged the air. Neither lady appeared willing to speak to the other, and judging by the fact that their gazes rested on indistinct points in the distance, neither appeared willing to look at the other, either. "Are you acquainted with one another?" he asked, choosing a direct approach.

Olivia's lips quirked to the side, and her gaze, at last, found his. The pit in his stomach no longer felt bottomless, not with her eyes meeting his, her mask for society unable to reach there, not with him. "We've exchanged a pleasantry or two," she said, "but never been *properly* introduced."

Another silence, awkward and confused, expanded between them. Miss Fox shifted uncomfortably at his side, and Olivia's eyes rolled to the sky. "Lord St. Alban," she began, her voice longsuffering as if she was addressing a particularly imbecilic pupil, "I believe this is where you introduce Miss Fox to me."

The exasperated huff in Olivia's tone was impossible to miss, but he also sensed her pleasure in giving him another society lesson. "Of course, my apologies." He was forever apologizing today. "Lady Olivia, may I introduce Miss Fox to you?"

Olivia inclined her head, and Miss Fox dipped into a shallow curtsy before her social better. "My lady."

Again, Olivia nodded, her smile cool, bland, and implacable. Then her eyes shifted to meet his, and her head canted to the side. Jake felt Miss Fox's gaze darting between the two of them. It was reckless and contrary to his stated goal of securing a proper wife, but he couldn't summon the energy to care.

As long as he held Olivia's gaze, she couldn't leave. That was his sole concern.

He would hold her gaze for eternity, if need be.

17

She should break from his gaze. But through some strange, tenebrous force unique to them, it held her rooted in place. Didn't he understand that Miss Fox's shrewd, vulpine eyes missed nothing?

Well, he would soon enough, if they began a courtship.

Began? Clearly, they'd begun. And she was here to bear witness to it. Delightful.

She must leave this instant. She couldn't watch Jake court Miss Fox. It was too much. She stepped backward, making her intention clear. "Miss Fox, it was nice to make your acquaintance, but I have some matters to attend and must bid you fare—"

Jake held out his arm, halting the flow of her words. "Lady Olivia, would you care to stroll with us?"

Her heart beat out a hard thud, and her skin tingled with anticipation. Anticipation of what? With her next heartbeat came the answer. *His touch.*

She took one halting step forward, then another, drawn in against all will and reason. She placed her hand to hover above his forearm, wild electricity racing between that half inch of air, invisibly connecting them. She inhaled the irked sigh that wanted release and placed her hand down.

Beneath the layers of fabric that lay between them, she knew the naked feel of the arm beneath her palm, its smoothness, its fine dusting of hair, the flex and release of muscle that ran in hardened rivulets up and down its length. She knew what those muscles were capable of. A flush of heat pinpricked her skin, and she shrugged inside her pelisse beneath confining layers of muslin and light wool.

Miss Fox cleared her throat. "Lady Olivia, do you stroll the wilds of the Green Park often?"

"Never."

"Yet, here you are. I can only imagine what brought you out today." Miss Fox glanced around, presumably searching for Olivia's companion. "Alone."

Olivia had the distinct feeling that she was being hunted by Miss Fox. "I was cutting through the park to calculate a distance when a rambunctious pair of wrens distracted me."

Jake's face angled left, and his gaze caught hers. "What sort of distance?"

Awareness shot through her, and she was powerless to do anything but tell him the truth. "The distance from St. James's Square to Queen Street."

A trio of silent footsteps fell behind them, and she sensed in the quiet that he understood why she'd been calculating that particular distance, the distance from the duke's address to the house she was considering purchasing.

Good. It was good for him to understand that all the loose threads of their association would be tied up soon.

Not that it mattered. He was well on his way to a proper wife, and she wished him the best of luck with her. He would need it.

"St. James's Square, I understand," Miss Fox cut in like a razor blade. "After all, that is the Duke of Arundel's address, but what, pray tell, could be on Queen Street?"

"It was just a notion," Olivia said. She was most definitely being hunted by Miss Fox.

"Speaking of the Duke of Arundel," Miss Fox began. How Olivia was coming to hate the chit's tone, as if each word contained a sneer especially for her. "I received an invitation to a ball to be held two days hence at St. James's Square. Such an impromptu affair in the middle of the Season is creating quite the stir about Town. But, of course, everyone will drop everything for the Duke of Arundel's ball."

"I daresay," Olivia said in the hope that agreement would quash this conversation. Miss Fox would extract no currency for gossip from her.

She risked a quick glance up at Jake, but his features gave nothing away. Likely, he'd never been held prisoner between two ladies politely discussing balls and parks while waging a silent war of wills with each other just below the surface. He had so much to learn about society.

"Curious," Miss Fox pressed on. "One can only wonder why the impromptu ball."

"One will find out two days hence, I suppose."

An unhurried succession of footsteps passed, and Olivia realized that she'd shut the chit up. She almost felt badly for her. Almost. It was deuced difficult to feel badly for Miss Fox.

It was time for her to bid them farewell and best of luck on their future union. Well, maybe not that last part.

As she opened her mouth to speak, Miss Fox beat her to it. "If you will forgive me, I must see to Miss Markley. It seems the tenacious gooseberry has claimed another victim."

With that, Miss Fox excused herself and left Olivia alone with Jake.

Jake. Enlivening sensation scattered across her skin at the mere thought of his name. He would ever be Jake to her. And now she was alone with him.

"My solicitors have informed me," he began, "that you've looked at another house since I last—" He stopped himself. "That is, since we last—" Again, he stopped himself.

But it was too late. What they'd been doing the last time they saw each other solidified into a near tangible presence between them. She swallowed and addressed the first part of his sentence. "That is correct."

"Was it to your liking?" he asked, his voice calm, measured, the fluster of moments ago gone.

For all the world, they appeared to be having a calm and measured conversation. How deceptive appearances could be. "It was serviceable enough," she said, "but it lacked a specific something."

His gaze lit upon her for the span of a single second before returning to the path ahead. "Magic."

How she wished her heart didn't race at that word, at the velvet in his voice when he spoke it. She needed to find a different subject to occupy them, one that had naught to do with magic. "It appears that your wife hunt is progressing nicely."

"It does appear so."

Another silence, charged and stubborn, snapped in the air about them. She should make her excuses and go, but she couldn't. Nor could she stop herself from saying, "Undoubtedly, Miss Fox is the sort who will make someone a proper, spotless wife."

"*Undoubtedly*," he echoed back at her.

She might have detected a hollow note in that single word. But it might be what she wanted to hear. Was it, though? "Well, I wish you the best of luck."

Beneath her hand, the muscles of his forearm, muscles hardened by years of sweat and toil, flexed and released, and an unruly frisson of excitement purled up her spine. She liked his forearms very much.

"Luck won't be involved," he said. A distance sounded in his voice. A distance that was good for both of them. "Marriage is a contract."

His words were the splash of cold water her body needed. Perhaps she liked his forearms too much. "What a romantic courtship you and Miss Fox will have," she replied. "How the ladies will envy her."

"Any lady I marry will understand that romance has naught to do with my needs in a wife. I need a stepmother for Mina and, by extension, a partner for me."

"A partner? What a strange way of putting it. Like a business equal?"

A curt nod of his head was his answer.

"That would make you different from any man and wife I ever heard of. But you may have the right of it. Marriage isn't a romantic enterprise, and yet women keep getting tricked into thinking it so."

"Tricked?"

"Most definitely tricked. If young women truly understood marriage, they would run as fast as their feet could carry them the instant a man got down on one knee. Marriage changes nothing in a man's life. But for a woman? It changes everything."

"And not for the better?"

"Not in my experience of it."

"And what was your experience of it?"

Strangely, a moment that should have scared her witless and sent her fleeing turned sideways and went soft and intimate. A thrill of joy ribboned through her at the curiosity and concern in his voice, at the very gravity of it. It was a seriousness that spoke to the secret craving she had to give up her secrets. His seriousness told her it was safe to do so.

Possibility budding within her, she glanced over her shoulder to see if there was any chance Miss Fox would return. All she saw was an empty path behind them. Miss Fox and her chaperone had quietly taken themselves away. Mayhap that wasn't the most auspicious start to Jake's courtship with the lady, but it wasn't Olivia's concern, now or ever.

It was safe. That was her only thought. It was safe to tell him. He wasn't a suitor to her, not really a friend either, but he was safe. She could tell this man anything.

Even the truth about her marriage.

She inhaled, pulling air deep inside her lungs, and allowed it to expand and buoy her into speaking words she'd never spoken aloud to anyone, not even Mariana. On the release, she said, "Shall I tell you how marriage is for a woman?" Her words sailed forth on a cool, blithe breeze, providing the distance she needed to speak them.

"I wish you would," he said, his words anything but cool and blithe.

"Well, Lord St. Alban," she began, bright, chirpy, and false, the sort of façade she needed to hide behind if she was to tell him. "The newly wed couple steps out of St. Paul's on a bright and sunny day, a future of domestic bliss stretching before the optimistic bride. At last, she has everything she ever desired: a handsome husband, her own household, her own curricle, everything society told her she ever wanted. She's never felt so happy."

"You speak of the husband as if he's an object of the same value as the curricle."

"That is, indeed, how the average society wife views her husband."

"And is that who we're speaking of? The average society wife?"

"Who else would we be speaking of?"

Her question was met with silence, stubborn and unconvinced.

"A week later," she continued, "she wakes to find herself in bed, alone, her husband off to sport his newest horse on Rotten Row. She might feel a bit hurt that he didn't include her, but she has plenty to fulfill her. Remember, she is the mistress of her own household, even if it is technically part of a duke's household and doesn't much involve her. And she has social calls to make, even if she has begun to find them endless exercises in tedium. And, lest we forget, she has the shiny, new curricle. She won't allow herself to consider that she might be the *B* word." She lowered her voice to a conspiratorial whisper. "*Bored.*"

"And why can't she be honest with herself?"

"Because she might search for the root of her boredom, and that wouldn't do at all. She's entirely too young and the marriage entirely too new for such notions, so she tucks them away. It's only when her husband begins excusing himself after dinner to spend the odd evening out with his friends that the notion pokes up its nasty head again. The odd evening soon becomes every evening, and she must admit that she's not only bored, but lonely, too."

"And this wife can't tell her husband how she feels?"

"By the time she's able to put her feelings into words, it's too late, the gap between her and her husband, too wide. You see, by now the rumors have started."

"Rumors?"

"Of his gaming, his horses, his…" Again, her voice lowered to a whisper. "*Mistress.*"

Muscles twitched beneath her palm, but Jake's features remained otherwise impassive. She wouldn't have even known of his reaction was she not touching him.

"That is when she allows it to hit her: hers is nothing more or less than a society marriage. Her husband is no different from the men of his set, and she is no different from the women of hers. Their *ex-traordinary* love has been perfectly ordinary all along."

"Betrayed by an ideal."

"Indeed, my lord," she chirped on the bright note that rang more false to her ears with each word she spoke. Yet she couldn't seem to plug the spring. It would flow until its reserves ran dry. "She's never felt so betrayed. By an ideal. By her husband. By society. She realizes that she's been tricked into this life, that society trapped her with a lie, but such is the life of every other wife. She swallows the bitterness and gets on with her life.

"Then, one day, not half a year into their marriage, her husband tells her that he's bought a commission in the army to fight the French scourge in Europe. He races off to the Continent to involve himself in war and glory, and she never sees or hears from him again. Six months later, she's informed of his death."

"This hypothetical husband," Jake interrupted, "never met his daughter?"

"Never. The wife is six months along when she receives the news." She hesitated, certain her tale had gotten away from her. Yet she needed to see it through to the end. "You must understand that her grief for her husband is genuine. She hasn't forgotten how handsome and charming he was. But after the initial wave of grief subsides, an unexpected and shameful feeling takes its place. Can you guess what it is?"

Lips pressed in a straight, silent line, Jake continued guiding them along the path dotted with puddles wide and deep enough to be a nuisance.

"*Freedom.* For the first time in her life, she feels *free.* The future stretching before her is no longer dull and lonely. It is bright and golden with the opportunity to set forth on a life entirely of her own choosing. Yet the shame stays with her for this future isn't possible without Per—" She corrected herself mid-word. "Her husband's death. So, she locks it away. All society sees is a grieving widow with a young daughter. If the widow is a bit eccentric with her growing involvement in the arts, society tolerates it. She is, after all, one of them."

"A merry widow, it seems," Jake inserted drily.

"Ten years later," Olivia continued, "the unthinkable happens: the husband rises from the dead, and all the wife can feel is the walls closing in on her. An alive husband means the end of her freedom. It means a return to her dull and lonely future. It means a return to being a *wife*. She vows then and there that she will never be wife to any man again. She petitions the House of Lords to set her marriage aside and prevails thanks to the combined power of her noble families and the acquiescence of a Lazarus husband who must have reasons of his own for acceding to her request. To be sure, her reputation doesn't emerge unscathed, but she cares not. What's the point of a spotless reputation when freedom is within reach? What cost is too high?" She took a deep breath. "And that is the story of a marriage from a wife's point of view."

She tried to force a carefree laugh, but it lacked all substance and emerged hollow. She'd never felt more exposed in her life. Beside her, Jake planted his feet and brought their progress to a halt. His hand at her elbow, he pulled her around to face him, an unspoken demand pulsing between them. She wasn't sure how she could meet his eye. Somehow, when they'd been walking side by side, her story had felt removed from her because she hadn't been looking at him. But now she must, even as her courage from moments ago abandoned her.

Calloused fingertips touched beneath her chin and tugged, angling her face up, slowly, by increments, even as her eyes remained lowered, her lashes a soft brush against her cheeks. "Olivia," he murmured, his voice a low, resonant rumble that penetrated through skin and bone to touch the very core of her.

Her gaze lifted, and the breath caught in her chest at what she saw in his eyes. *Ferocity…protectiveness…* The same look he'd directed at the *ton* when he all but dared them to speak a word crosswise about his daughter.

Except now it was protective of *her*.

"Not every marriage has to be that way."

She inhaled a tiny sip of air and composed herself long enough to say, "How would you know? You've never been married or even engaged, I daresay."

"I was engaged once."

"Oh?" she breathed out, her heart a hammer in her chest.

"To Mina's mother."

Olivia's mouth opened and closed. She'd gone speechless.

"Does that shock you?"

She shook her head for no words seemed to be coming to save her from the truth: she'd believed the gossip. She'd believed Mina the product of a lord's tawdry liaison with a servant. She hadn't even questioned it.

But for Jake to have been engaged to Mina's mother, there was a different story, one less sordid, one more honorable, one in keeping with the man she'd come to know. She should feel ashamed, but she couldn't. A curious and ineffable joy sprang up from the pit of her belly and shimmered through her veins. High-born or low-born, Jake had loved Mina's mother.

Why did it matter to her? It confirmed what she'd felt about this man from the first moment she'd laid eyes on him. He wasn't the sort of man who let a woman fall.

It mattered. Too much.

"No wife of mine will ever be subject to such a marriage."

"Of course," she began, protesting his words because she must, "you don't believe so now, but—"

"Never."

She believed him. And, oh, how she shouldn't. It occurred to her that she might be lost, that she just might be in lo—

"Here you are!" a sharp voice sliced through the air some distance away.

He blinked, then she blinked, and they each took a step back, snapping out of the trance that had overtaken them. When had their bodies drawn so close?

In unison, they turned to face a rapidly approaching Miss Fox. "I had a devil of a time finding you. You do realize that you've strayed off the main path, don't you?"

That sounded appropriate. But she would keep the sentiment to herself as it didn't apply to Miss Fox's meaning. Olivia tucked her shoulder blades together and drew herself up straight, even as awareness of *him* at her side pulsed through her with every beat of her heart.

A winded Miss Fox drew to a stop a few feet away. "The rabid gooseberry performed quite a number on the posterior area of Miss Markley's dress, and she had to return directly home in my carriage."

Jake cleared his throat. "Seems the most prudent course."

"And as we weren't finished with our stroll," Miss Fox continued, "I decided to come back. You two are such delightful and fascinating company."

Olivia's head canted to the side. What a curious person Miss Fox was.

"As to my lack of a chaperone," Miss Fox went on like it was of the slightest concern to her audience, "since we have you here, Lady Olivia, you can play the part."

Olivia nearly started out of her boots. Chaperone to

Jake's courtship of another woman? Not in an eternity of years.

"Lady Olivia," Jake cut in, "won't be accompanying us in that capacity."

It was all Olivia could do to suppress the sigh of relief that wanted release. Really, though, the cheek of Miss Fox. "Lord St. Alban is correct. I have a round of calls that I must attend, if you will excuse me."

She stepped away, and Miss Fox said, "But, Lady Olivia, it is too early in the day to pay calls."

Olivia drew up short, flummoxed. It was time to put an end to this farce. Umbrage that had wanted to rise the instant she'd spotted Miss Fox strolling arm in arm with Jake was given its head. "Miss Fox, has it ever occurred to you to mind your own affairs?"

The smug smile froze on the chit's face, and Olivia felt a mean bit of satisfaction at having hit her mark. She inclined her head, chirped a bright, "Good day," whirled around, and marched away, her heels a muted crunch on gravel. Several yards down the path, a realization, hard and true and utterly annoying, struck her: she was heading in the wrong direction.

On a deep sigh—would nothing go right today?— she stopped and pivoted. There they stood, observing her like a particularly curious animal at the zoo, Miss Fox's eyes wide and amused, Jake's eyebrows drawn together in concern. They looked like a couple. And why shouldn't they? They *were* a couple. The thought slid a tiny dagger into her soul. It was wrong that it did, but feelings couldn't be controlled like actions. Right.

Well, she could do something about herself. She set her feet into motion and focused on a point in the distance well beyond their shoulders. Just as she was about to move past the duo, her eyes darted left and locked onto Jake's. How still he could be. How serious. How appealing. But the contact was cut when she sailed past and left him behind.

No wife of mine will ever be subject to such a marriage.

Oh, that she didn't believe him. Such a belief made her feel both warm and wretched. Such a belief allowed the possibility of a different narrative for how marriage could be for a wife.

For Jake's wife. For Jake's proper, stainless wife.

It was too late for her to have that sort of marriage. She wasn't the sort of wife he needed, and she could never be the sort of stepmother his daughter needed.

She strode forward, her pace set at a purposeful clip, and remembered her destination. Queen Street offered a different sort of life, the free life she'd fought so hard to obtain. It would be enough to satisfy her.

It had to be.

18

NEXT DAY

"It appears, Lord St. Alban," Mrs. Bloomquist began, "the tide has turned in your favor, and an exception is to be made in the case of your daughter's admittance to our school."

Determined not to gloat, Jake nodded a simple affirmative. He towered over the formidable woman, separated by an enormous oak desk that commanded most of her otherwise small, plain office. He'd respectfully declined her offer of a seat.

Mrs. Bloomquist came to her feet and swept around the imposing desk. "This morning, Lady Nicholas Asquith successfully championed your daughter's cause at the board of directors' meeting."

"Lady Nicholas? Not Lady Olivia?"

"Oh, there isn't much those two disagree on," the schoolmistress said.

Relief flooded him. Their methods didn't matter one whit. He almost reached out to shake Mrs. Bloomquist's hand before he thought better of it. Viscounts didn't shake hands. "When can Mina begin class?"

"Miss Radclyffe may start tomorrow, if it suits her schedule."

He detected a kernel of censure in the woman's

voice. "Mrs. Bloomquist, I can assure you that once you've met Mina, you will understand how right your institution is for her." He couldn't help adding, "She will be a credit to it as well."

Mrs. Bloomquist bobbed a single dubious nod as if she'd heard hundreds of doting parents crow about their exceptional children and had yet to meet one who lived up to the acclaim. "I look forward to meeting your daughter." She strode to the door and pulled it open, her dismissal of him clear. "Good day, my lord."

He opened his mouth to reply when a familiar figure hurried past the doorway. He darted around Mrs. Bloomquist, who emitted a flustered gasp at his sudden movement, and peered around the doorjamb, just catching the swish of a woman's skirts before the front door closed behind her.

Olivia.

"Good day, Mrs. Bloomquist," he called over his shoulder. He'd intended to bestow a viscountly kiss on the woman's hand for good measure, but he had no time for that now.

In three steps, he, too, was out the front door and treading a forever slick London sidewalk. His eyes swept up and down the street for the Duke of Arundel's crest. No sign of it. How had her driver managed to skirt traffic and clear out so quickly? Unless...

Jake crossed the street, dodging oncoming traffic, and rounded the same corner from last week. He caught sight of her distinctly nondescript overcoat and bit back a smile of triumph. A few footsteps later it occurred to him that he was following Olivia.

Again. And he shouldn't be. The Bow Street runner was handling the search for Jiro. But was he really following her to find Jiro? Or was it to see her, to be near her?

He tested the sound of her name on his tongue. *Ohliv-ee-uh.* He loved the way it began on a broad *O* and ended on an exhale. A vulnerability lay within that soft *uh*. Her name suited her.

Until yesterday, he hadn't understood how vulnerable *and* strong she was. She'd entrusted her deepest, darkest secret to him, rousing an intimacy different from what they'd experienced in his bed. The knowledge made his insides sing.

A smile curled about his lips. Her confession only proved that her system wasn't rid of him. What was the word she'd used? *Purged.*

Their systems weren't purged of each other. Far from it. Just this morning, that point had been made abundantly clear to him when the chambermaid had arrived to change his bed sheets. He'd turned her away. Why? Because Olivia's scent of lavender and sandalwood lingered in his room, and he'd been unable to part with the last trace of her. Yet her scent grew fainter with each passing hour.

He snapped to, his lips assuming their habitual firm line, and exhaled a forceful breath. What was this wretched rot? These were the musings of a lovesick pup.

Only yesterday, he'd been courting a different lady. Miss Fox...*Anne.*

His insides stopped singing.

Ahead, Olivia happened upon a pair of vivacious twins and a scruffy little dog, the three engaged in a boisterous game of tug using a knotted scrap of rope. The twins couldn't be more than four years old apiece. He kept an eye on the lively trio while Olivia presumably sought out a parent to secure permission to sketch the little group at play. Soon, she returned with a short, three-legged stool and began drawing to her heart's content.

Which details would attract her artist's eye? The single lock of hair that curled to the left across one twin's face while curling to the right across the other's?

The way their identical smiles created identical dimples in their cheeks? The dog dancing to catch the bit of rope just beyond its reach? Had she noticed the quick darting glances between the boys signaling their next move, known only to them? A twin herself, she likely felt a kinship with the pair that few others understood.

Before long, the boys and their dog ended up in a cuddle that turned into naps for all. Olivia collected her materials and resumed her progress down the sidewalk. His feet kicked into motion behind her, and he found his gaze straying to rest on the sway of her derriere.

An unproductive thought popped into his mind: two days ago, she'd been partially clothed. It nagged at him, his haste.

She'd been thoroughly pleasured, that wasn't in doubt, but he could've gone slower. He could've controlled the situation better. He could've had her naked, stripped of her clothes, layer by layer until nothing but air and his lips kissed her sensitive skin. He could've viewed every inch of her, touched every inch of her, gratified every inch of her...

Once wasn't enough to *purge* their systems of one another, even if she refused to admit it.

She didn't need to say it. He'd seen the knowledge in her eyes yesterday.

With each passing day, she revealed a new facet of herself to him. Like a diamond, she hid her cuts in plain sight behind her sparkle.

Within minutes of first meeting her, he'd noted her depths, but he'd thought an experienced sailor, like himself, would have the ability to skim along her surface. Yet he felt his vessel taking on water, pulling him into her depths, drop by drop. If he kept to his current course, it was only a matter of time before he was entirely submerged.

Yet, the more he learned about her, the more he

wanted to sink a little deeper, to discover more, convincing himself all the while that he wasn't going too far, that he would be able to find his way back to the surface before he drowned in her.

Yesterday's confession hadn't helped that problem. It had only fed his growing fascination. She was more than a carnal obsession.

She was *principled, brave*. At the same time that he wanted Mina's path in life to be easy and clear, another part of him wanted Mina to be exactly like this woman. She would need to be, no matter how smoothly he paved the way for her.

He exhaled a humorless puff of a laugh. He admired the blasted woman. He was sinking deep, indeed.

Almost too late, he saw that she'd stopped in front of a humble gray door. He ducked around a delivery cart and slipped into the shadow of an abandoned doorway. She knocked and awaited entry, and he marveled at his first impression of her as nothing more than a *ton* frivolity. The rational side of him wished he could still see her that way. Instead, she'd become a mystery who dared him to solve her, and he couldn't get enough, reason be damned. She'd become a physical ache in his body. Not since Mina's mother had he felt this way about a woman.

Reality engulfed him like a cold blast of Arctic air. She, too, had been a physical ache in his body. And look how well that had ended. Disaster. Tragedy. Mina, yes, but heartache and public humiliation, too.

Olivia shifted on her feet and looked on the verge of moving on when the door swung inward and a man of Japanese descent stepped forward into the light. Attired as he was in the garb of an English dandy, it took a moment for recognition to spark and certainty to shoot through Jake. Surely, this was the man called Jiro.

Jake's heart pounded in his chest as a side note to a memory long buried came to him. Fifteen years ago.

Nagasaki. The powerful Kimura family's compound. He'd shared space with this man who was Jiro, sitting unobtrusively in the corner of a state room, recording with his watercolors the events of the trading day.

This man had been a trusted member of the Kimura household, and he'd stolen the paintings and betrayed them, risking his life. For what reason? Not money. The man still possessed the stolen paintings. Then why? And why here in London?

Olivia stepped inside, and the door snapped closed behind her. Jake bit back a curse. He'd been too lax of late. Too focused on Olivia. What she and he shared was secondary to this. *This*—to find the thief and uncover his secrets—had been his reason for bargaining with her, not to understand her better. Not to know her every thought, her every feeling.

He'd been skirting the edge of disaster in his dealings with Olivia... *Lady* Olivia. Not only for his intentions regarding the art thief, but for his intentions regarding marriage, his intentions regarding his heart. Given his past failure at love, it was best if his head ruled his heart, rather than the other way around.

Today, Lady Olivia had fulfilled both ends of her side of the bargain. He must let her go.

He slipped into the shadow of an abandoned doorway and propped himself against mildewed stone, its damp seeping through his woolen overcoat, his eyes fast upon the empty door stoop, settling in for a wait.

Not ten minutes later, she reemerged, pulling powder blue gloves onto her hands, her business concluded. He pushed off the grimy wall. Now it was time to settle matters with Jiro.

He was crossing the street when the door again swung inward. Out stepped none other than Jiro, pulling on a pair of buff kid gloves. With no more than two seconds between him and discovery, Jake ducked behind the stalled delivery cart rank with rotten vegetables and caught sight of the man rounding a corner at the end of the block. Jake rushed forward and immediately stopped, thinking better of his actions.

A public confrontation would do him no good. He pointed his feet homeward.

Tomorrow, he would settle this matter, one way or another, and leave it in the past, where it belonged.

* * *

EVENING

Jake opened a plain, white envelope, and two slips of paper slid out into his palm. One a note, the other a newspaper clipping, each unanticipated. He took in the note first:

Queen Street. 10 o'clock.

He glanced at his pocket watch. Nine o'clock. He had an hour.

He turned his attention toward today's *London Diary* clipping scented faintly of lavender and sandalwood.

A house for his Queen
Perhaps more than a quick fling?
How soon 'til banns sing?

IT WAS ABSOLUTELY about him and Olivia. He should mind, but he couldn't quite muster the outrage. It might ruin his chances with Miss Fox, as her quick mind would remember Olivia's mention of Queen Street, but he couldn't deny, to himself at least, that part of him wanted his chances with Miss Fox to be ruined.

To what end? a voice of reason cut in. He would only have to find another Miss Fox.

The thought chilled him clear through to his bones. Better to stay the path he was on.

The French doors cracked open and into the garden slipped Mina. He crumpled the note and the *London Diary* clipping in his fist.

"Any stars shoot across the sky tonight?" she asked as she lay on a reclining chair and directed her keen gaze toward the crystalline sky.

"Not one," he replied, dimming the lamp so they could better see the constellations. He relaxed his hand and let the tight ball drop to the ground, its only sound a single papery bounce.

She held a small, brass telescope to her eye. "The sky here is so different from the one hanging above Singapore."

He detected a note of homesickness in her voice. "You were born under a sky similar to this one in Dejima."

Telescope tight to her face, she said, "I would like to return there some day."

Jake flinched in surprise. She'd never expressed this desire to him before. "Would you?"

"It's the land of my ancestors. It may sound silly, but I would like to see how I feel there." A dry laugh roughed her voice, even as her gaze held steady through the telescope. "Likely, I won't fit there either, but I would like to go all the same."

Her matter-of-fact tone broke something inside him. "Shall we board the next ship East? It's not too late."

She lowered the telescope to her lap and pierced him with a long, measured look. "I am like a puzzle piece that will never fall into place."

"Mina—"

She held up a staying hand. "I have no true fit in either world, Father. East or West."

"You needn't worry about your place." His hands clenched into fists. "I shall see to it."

"A piece cannot be forced into place. It either fits, or it doesn't." She returned her attention to the ordered night sky. "London is as good as anywhere."

He wasn't certain which was worse: her utter acceptance of these facts, or her utter lack of despair. A gut punch from Gentleman Jackson himself wouldn't have leveled him so completely as did her subdued words, so tolerant of a fate that he refused to accept for her.

"Perhaps," he began, deciding it was past time to broach the subject, "a stepmother from the *ton* would help."

Mina hesitated. "Father, even a stepmother with all the right connections wouldn't help in the ways that matter."

"She would see to it that the best of society welcomes you."

"On the surface, yes, but truly I care not about those people. Besides, a stepmother for me would also be a wife to you. Please don't make a pragmatic choice based on me. From everything I've read on the subject, I think it's best to let the heart have a say in the matter. I shall find my way."

Mina settled back into her stargazing, and Jake controlled the urge to jump up and gather her in his arms. Instead, he reached inside his breast pocket, pulled out a letter, and silently handed it to her.

"What is this?" she asked, setting her telescope on a side table.

"It's a letter from The Progressive School for Young Ladies and the Education of Their Minds."

"Pithy, isn't it?" She leaned over and turned up the dimmed lamp. Her humor was a welcome relief.

She opened the letter and scanned its contents. He

couldn't help but notice that in certain lighting, at certain angles, she was looking more and more like her mother. A full minute ticked by before he asked, "Will you go?"

"Yes."

"Miss Bretagne will be thrilled."

"You are correct, but *thrilled* might not be a full enough word to describe Lucy's enthusiasm. I'm not sure there *are* full enough words in the entire world of languages."

Her lips curved into a secret smile. A girlish smile that daughters didn't share with fathers, only with other girls. His heart lifted on a fragile note of hope.

She collected the letter and her telescope and stood. "Good night, Father. You outlasted me tonight." She bent her willowy form over him and pressed a kiss to his cheek. "An early morning? I should like to begin classes tomorrow."

Left alone, he continued thinking how like her mother Mina had become.

His first memory was his strongest memory of *her*. He closed his eyes beneath the indigo London sky, so like the sky above the Bay of Nagasaki, and allowed it to lead him to that place for the first time in years.

* * *

THE MARKET on the trading island of Dejima was pure bedlam on a slow day.

But the Saturday morning market after a trading ship had docked and unloaded its cargo was a mayhem beyond mere insanity: chickens squawking; goats bleating; horses stamping; fish stinking; traders barking orders; sellers crying wares; customers hustling, bustling, jostling, haggling, dismissing, imploring, leaving, returning, buying, all before moving on to the next stall for another round.

These noises, these crowds, these smells conspired to produce an atmosphere of pure pandemonium that could render the uninitiated claustrophobic within seconds. Add to this intoxicating mixture, pungent spices and miscellaneous goods delivered by the sometimes generous, sometimes miserly, always capricious salty sea, and one had the exact scent of young beginnings.

The twenty-one-year-old Jakob Radclyffe striding through narrow market aisles had long settled into these uneven rhythms of Dejima. Nothing about this world surprised him anymore.

That wasn't to say the life of a roving sea trader had lost an ounce of its charm. On the contrary. There was nothing life didn't have on offer for him. It was just that he was confident, as only a youth could be, that he'd seen it all.

That was, until the day he slipped through a narrow gap in the crowd, turned his head as if by instinct, and saw *her* across the glassy expanse of a still, shallow pond.

She'd been a vision, poised gracefully over the railing of a footbridge arched above languid, undulating koi, while the crowd around her pushed past, each person eager to complete this or that errand. She had a way of remaining completely motionless that was unique to her.

It wasn't this, however, that drew his notice. It was that she stood nearly a head above everyone around her. He was a tall man by anyone's standards, but even from this fair distance, he could see that the top of her head would reach above his chin. Unusual in these environs. There wouldn't be another girl like her for a thousand miles around.

He decided on the spot that he must have her. Brash, young men based such momentous decisions on less.

When he focused on the pleasant side of memory,

he recalled that she'd seemed genuinely amused by his pursuit, granting him a coy smile now and again. She wasn't only beautiful and unusual, but reserved and gentle, too.

Put plainly, she hadn't discouraged his pursuit. And his twenty-one-year-old self hadn't the wisdom to separate *not discourage* from *encourage*.

A year later, she was dead, and he'd known himself to be a man different from the one he'd thought himself to be. A man selfish, unbearably naïve, and capable of cruelty to his beloved in the face of public humiliation.

A long submerged wave of shame washed over him, pricking his skin with tiny beads of sweat. He'd pushed for too much, too fast. If he hadn't been such a blind young man, she might have had a different future. She might have lived.

Likely not. It wasn't the way of the *civilized* world to forgive such a *foolish girl*.

At the end, he'd done one thing right: he'd taken Mina.

Protect her, Jakob...she'll have only you...only you can do it...for Minako, my little Mina.

He had a promise to keep: to protect Mina. Now that he'd secured her school, he would secure her reputation. Tomorrow, he would deal with Jiro, which left only one loose end to tie up tonight: Olivia.

And that must be the end of it, of *them*. He would be able to focus on finding a proper stepmother for Mina, a proper wife for him. Words true in his mind, but ones that were feeling more and more false in his heart. Perhaps if he repeated them to himself, over and over, they would seem less empty.

Perhaps his belief in them would return.

19

Olivia tapped the mother-of-pearl face of her newly fashionable wristwatch. Five minutes until ten o'clock. She'd been awaiting his arrival in the quasi darkness of a dimmed lamp since nine-thirty.

She'd been close, so very close to putting *him* behind her. She'd fulfilled her end of the bargain—Miss Radclyffe would begin school tomorrow—and, as far as her search for a townhouse went, she'd resolved not to involve him further. She only needed the services of his solicitors. Once the house was purchased, they could go their separate ways as if nothing had ever occurred between them.

Then, this morning, she'd opened the *London Diary* and saw *it*, the haiku.

They were known by someone. But who?

Some hack with a pen and an inflated sense of his own power and importance. The individual mattered not, in reality, only the scope of his voice. There was but one way to silence that voice: to truly end matters with Jake. Scandal wouldn't much change her life, but for him it would decrease his chances of finding a perfectly perfect, suitable, spotless wife.

Of course, the *London Diary*'s speculation would become confirmed fact if she bought this house. And

Miss Fox was clever enough to figure it out. Their one saving grace was that Miss Fox didn't seem the type to read such a frivolous publication, which, of course, was none of Olivia's concern.

She lifted her face to the ceiling and took a slow spin, winding round alongside the magnificent staircase that coiled all the way up, up, up to the circular skylight now black with night. She located the small, unobtrusive door she'd missed on her first visit.

Earlier today, Jake's solicitors had passed along an instruction from the house's owners that she enter the gray door at the top of the staircase. No further detail was provided her. All very mysterious.

The girl from her youth, the girl who loved gothic novels and currently resided within Lucy, reared her head. Olivia loved a good mystery. Secret doors at the top of staircases were the stuff of her girlish fantasies.

A frisson of anticipation raced up her spine, which, of course, had nothing to do with the fact that her wristwatch now read two minutes to the hour. Two minutes until Jake's arrival. When had she begun thinking of him as *Jake*?

She was being disingenuous. She liked this diminutive of his given name, Jakob. It was a name at ease with itself, making him feel more accessible to her. Not that she desired more access.

That, too, was disingenuous.

Except, this feeling wasn't specifically about access. The diminutive explained something about him, about the man who wasn't supposed to be The Right Honourable Jakob Radclyffe, Fifth Viscount St. Alban. That man had been Mr. Jakob Radclyffe to many, Captain Radclyffe to some, and Jake to few.

In London, he was Lord St. Alban to all, and Jake only to her. A warm feeling at odds with the chill of the empty house stole through her. It was a feeling she liked too much. A feeling she could nest inside and settle too comfortably within.

She drew in a breath of night-cooled air and glanced again at her wristwatch. Ten o'clock on the nose. One more tick of the gold minute hand, and he would be late.

She picked up the dim lamp and crossed the room to the staircase. Her fingertips feathered across silky smooth walnut. No detail of this house had been ignored. It was light and airy, even in the dark of night. It would have to be *this* house. The one with a memory of him etched into it. She kept getting herself wrapped up ever tighter with him.

Oh, this house would be her undoing. Doubtless, there would be another haiku published within a week of its purchase. One less opaque. One more specific and pointed. One which would possibly name names. Society dined on this sort of gossip for breakfast, lunch, and dinner, at once satisfied and ravenous for more. But there was no help for it. The heart knew what it wanted, and hers wanted this house. She refused to think about what else her heart might want.

She tilted her wristwatch toward the dim light of the lamp. One minute past ten o'clock. Jake was late.

The clear and distinct echo of footsteps sounded down the hallway, drawing nearer and louder at a brisk but unhurried clip, *his* clip.

She tried to relax by clenching, then unclenching her fists. At last, he came into focus in the doorway, which neatly framed his lean form. It was as obvious to her as it was to every other woman in London that he was simply impossibly handsome. Even in the near dark. Maybe, especially in the near dark as the shadows played with the angles of his face.

Yet there was something more in addition to the impossibly handsome: the impossibly sensuous. When had he become *impossibly sensuous*?

A vexed frown pinched her lips.

"Am I late?" he asked in a tone that didn't sound as concerned as his words might have suggested.

"Yes," she replied, sounding distressingly like Lucy on a petulant day.

"My apologies," he said on a shallow bow, even as his mouth, that talented, efficient mouth of his, maintained its familiar firm line.

"No need for apologies, my lord. In fact, your tardiness is promising evidence that you are settling into the viscountcy quite well." She liked the way his eyes narrowed at her stern tone, a tone she couldn't help borrowing from Mrs. Bloomquist. "It is the first rule of the nobility. Everyone can wait."

"Then my apologies for not having made you wait longer."

A begrudging smile found its way to her lips. "Now for the second rule of the nobility." She allowed a beat to pass. A flash of pleasure coursed through her at the very idea that she could hold this glorious man in suspense. It wasn't every woman who could boast that particular thrill. "Never apologize."

He stepped forward, halving the distance between them, and took another bow. "Again, my apologies."

His gaze pinned her in place, and, like that, the power of the moment shifted to him. Oh, how an unmanageable part of her wanted him to use it. This felt dangerously like flirting. Was she flirting?

She was. In the presence of the tease playing about his eyes and mouth, she couldn't seem to help herself. She tried clearing her throat, hoping to clear her head in the process.

He should be more careful with that smile. It could give a woman ideas.

"I take it we're in accordance about what's to be done?" she both stated and asked, desperate to change the subject.

His eyebrows lifted, and now it was his turn to let a beat pass before replying. His turn to hold her in suspense. Mayhap he would ignore her query and make one of his own. One less pragmatic. One more in line with the subtext rippling between them. His reaction to her confession yesterday had the unanticipated effect of only strengthening her desire for him.

No wife of mine will ever be subject to such a marriage.

A shiver, warm and liquid, purled up her spine.

"About this house?" He broke eye contact. "I think you should take it."

A chill spiked through her. As if the cells in her body recognized his switch from warm to cool before her brain could process it. As if she understood him on a cellular level. The only logical conclusion to that thought was that he'd become part of her.

Unsettled by logic surely flawed, she gave herself a mental shake. "No, Ja—*my lord.*" She simply must stop giving herself leave to think of him as Jake. "About the *London Diary.*"

"Ah." He craned his neck and glanced up at the blackened skylight. "Shall we take this conversation upstairs?"

She tore her gaze away from him as a measure of self-protection. His words didn't mean what her body prayed they did. All she could say in return was, "Pardon?" And what a weak return it was.

"An intriguing bit of information about this house has come my way."

It just occurred to her to ask, "Is it related to the gray door at the top of the staircase?" At his nod, she continued, "I know about it." An exaggeration, of course, but short of an outright lie.

"Then you must be as curious as I to see it."

He stepped toward the staircase, and, for a charged second, she thought he was stepping toward her, an idea that made her not unpleasantly uncomfortable.

Then he swerved left, his arm a light, fleeting brush against hers. His step might have hesitated, she couldn't be sure, but then shook off the notion when he slipped past her.

His athletic form took on the steep and winding staircase two steps at a time as if it were an easy London sidewalk. A tiny stab of envy pricked her. If her mode of dress had allowed it, she would have raced him to the top, perhaps even beating him.

Likely not.

Instead, she followed at a sedate, ladylike pace. A pace that might be construed as demure to the observer who lacked insight into her most intimate thoughts. They had gone reliably astray at the sight of his gorgeous form in motion. Impossibly handsome was too tame.

Impossibly gorgeous male. How was that for a more specific descriptor?

Her feet three steps from the top, the impossibly gorgeous male disappeared through the discreet open doorway, connecting to a short hallway that dead-ended into a solid black door. "Do you have the key ring with you?" he called out.

Silently, she extended the keys as she approached. They jangled excitedly in an anticipation mirroring her own. The close proximity to him in the darkness of an enclosed space did specific things to specific parts of her body. Parts of her body that weren't satisfied by phantom memories of his touch.

She was about to take a step backward to put a bit of comfortable distance between them when he turned the key in the lock and pushed the door open. He disappeared through the doorway, and a gust of damp London air hit her. Curiosity propelling her forward, she followed. Her feet crossed the threshold, and the breath caught in her chest.

A rooftop garden, lit only by the moon and stars

above, transported her into another world, one not bound by the rules of this one. One lush with green grass and springtime tulips and lit only by moonlight and twinkling stars. This rooftop was magic, pure and simple.

She whipped around to find Jake—how could his name be any other in this moment?—and detected foreknowledge in his eyes. He'd known, but he hadn't wanted to rob her of the pleasure of discovery.

What a lovely act of generosity.

"This is it," she heard herself say, feeling all distance between them, both physical and emotional, vanish.

The intimacy of this space also worked another sort of magic on her. Her face broke wide into an unreserved smile, uncaring of where such a smile could lead her...could lead *them*.

"This is my home. This is the magic I've been searching for," she whispered, never once breaking eye contact.

* * *

JAKE WAS the first to break it.

He couldn't hold her gaze and say what he must. "Then there is no reason for us to discuss how to handle the *London Diary* haiku."

"Pardon?" she asked, puzzlement in her voice.

"We have each fulfilled our respective ends of the bargain."

Cautiously, he watched for her reaction. Even in the half-lit darkness, he saw her posture go rigid. Fading fast was the openness of one minute ago, her face closing off to him with the beat of each consecutive second. Her tongue began worrying her one wayward tooth, and he tore his eyes away. A pang of loss pierced him for what he must release from his grasp.

"The *London Diary* situation will sort itself out, if we leave any concept of *us* on this rooftop."

He wouldn't blame her if she slapped his face. In fact, he craved the contact, any contact, from her. But she didn't. Her body held as still as the night surrounding them.

His very soul deflated like a sail that was at one moment sailing the boundless blue sea, the next, slack and limp, deprived of the breeze that gave it life seconds ago.

They'd gotten what they wanted out of each other. No, that wasn't precisely true. They'd gotten what they *needed* out of each other.

Yet he wanted her beyond the physical, which wasn't at all what they needed. What they'd needed was simple and straightforward, a bargain struck and a bargain fulfilled.

He turned away and snapped a tiny branch off a potted dogwood. He'd deceived her. He'd used her. He'd fallen for her. An impossible situation, given the preceding two points.

"That is all?" she asked.

Through the fog of a nascent bitterness, he managed to reply, "I would say so." He didn't understand how his voice maintained its cool indifference when inside he felt neither cool nor indifferent.

"You do say so." Her tone dissipated the fog. "You will, of course, understand when I don't acknowledge you at the girls' school or at the duke's mansion. We don't want to promote *any concept of us*, do we?"

"I've informed the duke that I shall be discontinuing our meetings."

He caught a flash of stormy azure eyes just before she pulled her shoulders back, adding a good two inches to her height, and strode toward the door. She grabbed the handle, twisted, and pulled. The door remained shut and unmoving.

She twisted and pulled again. Again, no movement, not even the slightest hint of a hinge turning. It refused to budge.

She gave it a testing jiggle, to no avail.

She began to appear comical in her struggle before going completely still. She was weighing her options. Namely, whether or not to request his assistance. When she began jiggling the handle with more purposeful ferocity, he realized she would rather walk across hot coals than ask him for help.

He stepped forward. "May I be of use?"

Again, her body stilled, her shoulders hunched in thwarted effort. Eyes wide with disbelief met his. "It's, um, locked."

"Locked?" He drew level with her, facing the obstinate door alongside her. "It must be stuck."

She stepped left and away from him. "The wind must have blown it shut."

"Won't the key open it?" He watched her, waiting for her to produce the item.

"I believe the key is in the lock." She stared at the deadbolt. "On the other side."

Alarmed, he took the door handle in hand. He tried every angle with varying levels of force and gentleness in his efforts to alternately compel and coax the blasted door open. He shrugged off his overcoat and absently handed it to Olivia at one point in his struggle.

At long last, his hands dropped to his sides, and he gave up the battle. The door was well and truly locked.

He chanced a sideways glimpse of her, expecting to find her stewing in anger. Instead, he found a perverse little smile idling about her lips. That smile, at once playful and mocking, charmed him. "I thought you were angry."

"It's a trifle difficult to be angry with a man who is trying to save the day." Her smile twisted in mischief, and she handed his coat back to him. "And one who looks ridiculous while doing so."

He lifted his hands and shrugged. It wasn't the first time this woman had called him ridiculous. He didn't mind it in the least. He enjoyed pulling smiles from her.

Additionally, he wasn't all that bothered by a situation that held a very real potential for calamity. If they were discovered and forced into a scenario where he would be compelled to do the right thing, well, he wasn't certain he would mind all that much.

As if she could read his mind, the smile dropped from her lips, and she took a step backward. In a flurry of skirts, she swiveled around and began following the graveled path that wound tightly through the garden between potted trees, blossoming tulips, and classical statuary.

"I'd thought to be discreet," she called over her shoulder, a languid fingertip brushing across a Venus' cheek. "But apparently the gods have other plans for us."

"Such as?"

"Whoever finds us will have quite a valuable story to sell to the gossip rags." She hugged her arms tight across her body. "Perhaps she will be a housemaid who would like a new frock. Perhaps she's never owned a single new thing in her life. Perhaps one must forgive such a girl for selling our tawdry little tale." She stopped and pivoted to face him, her hands lifted in surrender. "Well, here we are, my lord, a housemaid's chance at a shiny new dress."

"I'll consider raises for my staff in the near future."

A wry chuckle scraped across her throat, and a few drams of tension drained from his body. A feeling of ease, a natural ease that existed between them when they allowed it, settled over him.

She took a step back, holding eye contact, before spinning around to continue along the path, her again ahead of him, silently taking in the beauty of the garden on this rare, clear night. They happened upon a pair of reclining chairs, and she settled herself onto one, again hugging her arms across her body.

"Are you chilled?"

"A bit."

He extended his overcoat toward her. Her eyes, wide and watchful, considered him for one, two, three heartbeats before she reached out and draped the woolen mass across her supine body.

"Consider it yours for the night," he said, settling into the chair beside hers. "Who knows how long we shall be up here." A deep contentment settled over him as they gazed side by side into the infinite sky spread above them like a blanket. "At least it isn't raining."

"There is that."

"Mina knows every star and constellation up there by heart."

"Oh?"

He liked the enchanted quality in her voice as they shared this wondrous night sky together. "She was quite taken by the ceiling at your soirée."

"You must install the stars on her bedroom ceiling. Mayhap for her name day."

"I wouldn't know which one to give her: the one of her birth, or the one of her childhood, as she was born in Japan, but raised in Singapore."

"The one she misses most, I think."

"Her mother loved the stars." Before Olivia could reply with the requisite platitude that Mina must take after her mother, he continued, "She spoke to me once of her childhood sky. How she wanted to see it again."

"How so?"

"She claimed the sky was different in the Orient, but in Japan it was mostly the same sky."

Olivia sat upright and cocked her head. "I don't understand. Different *how*?"

His brain sounded the alarm. He'd become too comfortable with her and slipped up.

A decision stood before him: continue the lie or speak the truth. A truth known only by him, Mina, and one other man in London. A truth that he suddenly, and instinctively, knew he could entrust this woman to keep secret.

There would be no turning back from here. Before his head could convince him otherwise, he met her questioning blue gaze and followed his heart. "Mina's mother was Dutch."

Olivia's brows creased as if she was trying to add one and one together and kept coming up with three. "How can that be?"

"Mina isn't my daughter by blood."

20

"I sn't your daughter by blood?" Olivia asked, her voice little more than a stunned whisper. "How is that possible?"

"I'd just reached my twenty-first year when I saw Clemence on the trading island of Dejima. Her father was Dr. Oelrichs, the island's resident doctor. I fell for her instantly in the way only a young man can fall in love with a woman."

"Yes, well," Olivia said, "young women aren't immune to the feeling, either."

A wry smile of acknowledgement crossed Jake's lips. "I found a dozen reasons a day to pass her house. Sometimes I could make her smile, even laugh, but she was an utterly serious girl. I did little more than muddle through the entire courtship process."

Olivia's brow lifted in surprise. The polished Right Honourable Jakob Radclyffe, Fifth Viscount St. Alban, wasn't the sort of man she associated with smiles and jokes and *muddling through*. He was a man who most would characterize as utterly serious himself, a man who shouldered the weight of his responsibilities, dutifully and honorably.

It was a quality she found most attractive. So many men in the *ton* took nothing seriously and frittered their lives away. *Like Percy.* At least, the Percy she'd known and married in London. She hadn't the faintest idea of the sort of man he was now.

"I asked for her hand in marriage before the month was out," Jake continued. "I wouldn't return for another six months, as only two ships a year were allowed on the island, and I wanted to ensure that she would still be mine when I did." The shake of his head was near imperceptible, but Olivia caught it. "Dr. Oelrichs nearly laughed me out of his house before shoving a tumbler of whiskey into my hand and asking me what I thought I knew about his daughter. 'Maybe it will turn her head straight again.' Those were his words, and that was it. Clemence came home to find herself an engaged woman." He paused as if weighing his next words. "Later, I realized Dr. Oelrichs must have caught wind of Clemence's activities."

"What activities?"

"Clemence was in love, but not with me."

"Then with whom?" Olivia asked impatient to know. She'd never been able to stop herself from racing to the end of a story.

"I sailed the next day," he said, making it clear that he would tell his story in his own time, "confident and arrogant in my belief that Clemence may as well become accustomed to my long haul trips sooner rather than later. I made such a hash of it." His mouth twisted in bitterness. "I'd been raised by a mother and aunts who bore the long absences of husbands as a natural part of life. I couldn't imagine Clemence would be any different. Brash, young men can have surprisingly small imaginations."

"I am well acquainted with the worldview of brash, young men," Olivia inserted.

"When I returned, we took a moonlit stroll to the bridge where I'd first seen her. Very romantic until she told me that she'd fallen in love with another man while I was away and was now increasing."

"Increasing? With another man's child? How—"

"Devastating?"

Olivia nodded. She detected a shadow of that devastation in his voice fifteen years later.

"Mostly it was my pride that was devastated. And like any young man whose pride has taken a slicing, I lashed out. I demanded the man's name, determined to exact satisfaction. Clemence laughed humorlessly and told me there would be no satisfaction for either of us." He paused a beat. "A better man would have softened in that moment."

Regret soaked into the air and weighed it down. The past could do that to a person. Yet Olivia detected another emotion, too. In his refusal to meet her eyes, she sensed shame. A shame he'd carried these last fifteen years.

"I pressed her for the name," he continued, "until she told me that her lover was the younger son of a noble Japanese family, Kimura of Nagasaki. He was too powerful to touch. Then she asked for my help getting off the island before she started showing signs of the pregnancy. She knew I'd have no problem smuggling her onto my family's ship." He inhaled deeply. "I told her she could go to the devil and live with the consequences."

Olivia gasped. "Oh, no."

"My fiancée was with child, and not just any child, but a Japanese child." His gaze, bitter, raw, shamed, met Olivia's. "It was unbearable to me that the instant the child was born, the world, *my* world, would know that I couldn't be the father, that I was a cuckold. I won't relate back to you the entirety of my words, but they were cruel. My overriding thought was that the world mustn't know I was betrayed by her. I fled the night our cargo was offloaded and didn't look back."

"Then how did Mina become yours?"

"By the grace of whichever god you worship." He swung his legs off the reclining chair and stood, tension coming off him in waves. "Six months later, one of my uncles fell ill with a malarial outbreak in Singapore. The company needed me to captain the ship the rest of the way to Dejima to offload the cargo. It was my first opportunity to captain a long-haul ship, and I couldn't refuse. My first night back on the island, a note slipped under my door. Clemence wanted to see me. I would have ignored it but for a line that caught my eye, *There isn't much time.*"

He strode to the edge of the roof, placed a hand on a low parapet, and peered down at the street below. He was half a world away and completely alone in his memories.

"I rushed to Dr. Oelrichs' house, and still I was nearly too late. Clemence had contracted a childbirth fever." He faced Olivia, his back propped against the low wall, catching her gaze with his tormented one. "I don't remember ever having been afraid of anything in my life until that day, not the way Clemence brought the fear of God home to me. Fading before my eyes was a Clemence quite unlike the one I'd known. Or, I should say, the Clemence I thought I'd known. I hadn't taken the time to truly know her, or to truly love her. Not the real her."

Olivia wanted nothing more than to go to him. To lay some part of her body on his. To comfort him. Her feet, however, possessed more sense than her heart and refused to move.

"She begged me to take the child as my own. Neither her father nor the Kimura family would agree to take the babe."

"Who wouldn't make that promise to a dying woman?" Olivia interjected, unable to help herself. "Even if it was a lie?"

"Maybe they had. I don't know. But Clemence understood the truth of the matter."

Olivia's hand found its way to her mouth as the horror of the dangerous and bleak future that had stretched before a motherless and fatherless Mina unfolded in her mind.

"Clemence died in the small hours of morning. I found a wet nurse willing to travel to Singapore, and we left Dejima within two days' time. I let everyone believe Mina was my by-blow from a relationship with a Japanese servant, and, in the blink of an eye, I was the father of a beautiful, squawking baby girl."

Olivia saw that the fact bewildered him to this day, but that it also enlivened him. Pride sounded in his voice, powerful and fierce.

"And that was the end of it until recently."

Olivia's head cocked to the side. "Until recently?"

Jake startled as if her query had drawn him out of a trance. "It is none of your concern."

Curiosity bade her probe the point, but good sense had her hold her tongue. His tone brooked no rebuttal. Instead, she pivoted and asked, "Does Mina know?"

"She always knew the basics, but I told her the full story two years ago."

Olivia thought her heart might burst with unnamed emotion. There was something he needed to hear, and she would say it. "You should feel proud, not only of Mina, but of yourself."

His eyes shifted, as did his feet. Her words didn't sit right with him. His was the bearing of the guilty. "Pride isn't the first word that comes to mind."

"You took Mina when no one else would," Olivia persisted. "She is yours as surely as if she was your flesh and blood. You did what no one else would do."

She paused to slow down the conversational pace, to consider carefully her next words. To consider whether or not they should be her next words. "I am quite in awe of you."

His mouth twisted. "The threat of public humiliation is a powerful motivator. Never underestimate its ability to reveal the true measure of a man."

"You were a *young* man. None of us can account for our twenty-one-year-old selves. We move beyond who we were then, if we're lucky."

Again, she paused. Again, she considered. Again, she spoke. "You aren't the sort of man who lets a woman fall."

"Aren't I? Haven't I?"

"I'm not speaking of the man you were then. I'm speaking of the man you became. You did right by Clemence. Your true measure was revealed. Adopting a child is an uncommon step in our society. It was brave of you."

"Hardly brave," he said. "Some years ago, one of my uncles took in a boy named Nylander. He and I were near an age, and we came up together. I knew from early on there was nothing to the nonsense that blood will out, but to the world, Nylander carries the stigma of illegitimacy." His arctic-blue eyes went hard and cold, impenetrable ice. "No such stigma will ever attach itself to Mina's name."

Fierce. Protective. Olivia now understood the reason behind that ferocity and protectiveness. An emotion that she refused to name, or even acknowledge, slithered through her body and wrapped its tentacles around her heart.

"This is the real reason you need a wife of impeccable reputation. A society marriage would be the deflective shield Mina needs to protect her. Yet I'm curious," she continued, a thought just occurring to her. "Why is it you never married? Surely it would have been easier to raise Mina with a wife all these years."

An ugly chortle escaped Jake, one directed at himself, not at her. "No woman would saddle herself to the likes of me, not if she knew the truth. I'll take a society marriage and have the stepmother Mina needs."

"Every woman in London would leap at the chance of being saddled with the likes of you," she shot at him.

"*Every* woman in London?" he shot back.

On a different night, his question would fluster her and send her running for safety, but not tonight. She'd intuited something vital to this man, and she wouldn't let it go. "You seek to punish yourself. That is the reason you won't allow yourself to marry for love. It's the reason you allow yourself to be beaten to a pulp."

"I wouldn't say it's the only reason." His translucent blue gaze pierced straight through her. "Or even the primary reason."

Her body went hot, but she wouldn't be unsettled or distracted. "You're afraid."

"Aren't we all?" he threw back at her.

"Of yourself," she returned. He flinched as if she'd physically struck him. "You don't trust yourself when it comes to love. You think love will turn you into a monster. But look at Mina. You will never let her down."

"It's different when it's your child, but Clemence... I discarded her like a worthless piece of lint."

"She betrayed you. One doesn't easily forgive that sort of betrayal, or forget it. You must find someone worthy of your heart."

His inward gaze suddenly reflected out and struck her with a penetrating acuity. "Such idealistic words from a woman who has sworn off love and marriage."

Her heart thundered in her chest. "My circumstances aren't the same."

"Are they so different?"

The intimacy of yesterday and tonight's confessions hung between them. The truth of her marriage. The truth about Mina. He should understand those confessions revealed the past, but changed naught in the present. He needed the sort of wife that she could never be for him.

She'd found her house, and Mina had found her school. They were done. Utterly done. Nothing bound them together. Except for one thing: they remained stranded on this roof together.

As if he'd arrived at the same conclusion, he said, "We may be here all night."

"Oh, dear," Olivia began, her voice cracking at the feeble attempt at a rejoining lightness, "the duke and Lucy think me at a supper party. My first act as owner of this house will be to have that lock repaired."

"My man Payne knows I'm here, so rescue will arrive at some point. We shan't starve." He took his seat beside hers. "We could start shouting. That might yield quicker results."

"I would rather starve than pay that particular price." Even as the words left her mouth, she was uncertain they were as true now as they'd been a few days ago. Very little from a few days ago seemed as true now.

His eyes searched hers. "Would you?"

Her insides tumbled over themselves, and her body gave an involuntary shiver.

"Are you cold?"

She nodded. Exhausted by the revelations and near revelations of this night, she lay back and snuggled deep inside his voluminous wool overcoat. "Silly on an April night."

Before she had a chance to review the import of her words, he'd already begun a course of action.

Namely, he slid off his chair and knelt beside her. "As you already have my overcoat for warmth, all I can offer you is the rest of me."

21

Olivia rolled onto her side and lifted the edge of Jake's overcoat.

His gaze serious and, oh, so attractive, he asked, "Are you certain?"

"Quite." These last few days, she only felt this certain when her body was near his and instinct was given free rein. Except it wasn't simple instinct that drove her.

Something deeper.

Something *right*.

Something so wrong.

He slipped in beneath the coat, their bodies close, but not touching. The cool and crisp night air turned warm and soft in the space that lay between them, the world shrunk down to him and her.

"This doesn't have to lead anywhere," he said, his words a low rumble that shook every cell in her body.

She nodded, closed her eyes, and allowed her other senses to take over. Indeed, the warmth of his body did satisfy a certain skin-deep need. But it also sparked another want deep within her. Experience had taught her that this budding feeling of desire wouldn't be placated by the constrained nearness of his clothed body. Such an obstacle only increased its appetite.

Two days ago, she'd allowed her desire to conflate reality and fantasy into an extension of her dream state. As if the self-deception absolved her of culpability in the matter. Tonight, separated from his body by a stretch of air at once insignificant and unbearably tremendous, she didn't want absolution. Tonight, she would claim and own her actions.

On this particular night, beneath these particular stars, in this particular moment, this particular man would be hers. He would never be husband to her, but he would be her lover one last time.

Her eyes blinked open, unsurprised to find his serious gaze steadily, patiently, observing her. What an aphrodisiac his seriousness was. She'd never been the focal point of such reflective attention. It emboldened her. It made her want to act in a way outside herself. It made her want to seduce him beyond the limits of his self-control. She reached out to touch his face, her index finger trailing along the fine ridge of his cheekbone.

"Olivia—"

The tip of her finger continued its trail to his firm lips before pausing. "And if I want this to lead somewhere?"

Across the few inches separating their bodies, could he feel her pulsing with desire for him? It had begun with a simple, excited acceleration of her heart that with each successive beat spread a thrum through her body. She would vibrate off this reclining chair if she didn't steady herself with the full length of his body hard against hers. The light touch of her index finger wasn't nearly enough. Too few nerve endings made contact with his skin. She wanted more. But not yet.

Her finger continued its way across his chin, its golden stubble picking up flickers of moonlight, and down his neck before hooking his cravat and untying its knot in a few economical motions. Then her finger resumed its course, sliding along the seam of his shirt until it fell open to his waistcoat. She pushed it wide for a better view of his chest when she noticed the shadow of a bruise located directly over his heart.

On an impulse, she bent her head and pressed her lips to bruised skin. Her eyes lifted and found him quietly regarding her. The kiss might not solve anything, but sometimes an instant of grace was all one needed to get through to the next moment.

Ever lower, her finger trailed until it reached the top of his trousers. His hand darted out and covered hers, stilling it. "Not like this. Not again."

She arched an eyebrow in silent query.

"Are you still cold?"

She shook her head. "I'm burning up."

"Good."

He swept away the overcoat and sat across from her. Drawn in by his action, she followed his lead, now facing him, each anticipating the other's next move. He leaned in and reached around to flick open the three pearl buttons that held her bodice together. Her eyes fluttered shut and she inhaled as his open shirt brushed the silk of her bodice, completing her sensory overload with his scent and his heat.

Task complete, his hands fell away. Her eyes flew open. She was both needled and aroused by his action, by the idea of him withholding himself from her. The light of challenge within his eyes spiked her desire higher. The next move in their game was hers.

She unfolded her legs and came to her feet beside him, his mouth a breath's distance from the hollow of her neck, this self-assured man in the supplicant position. Her position as woman on top felt good. Better than good.

A feeling stole across her body, inch by inch. The feeling of power. She went lightheaded with it. To have a man like this, the most desirable man in London, at her feet...

A single shrug of a shoulder, and her bodice fell to her waist. A bolt of triumph shot through her when his gaze could no longer hold hers. As if he would starve if he didn't feast his eyes upon her flesh this very instant.

When his eyes traveled their unhurried way back to hers, they were near black, pupils dilated to the outer edge of the iris. Oh, how wicked and gratifying.

He shrugged out of both his waistcoat and his shirt in a single economical motion, leaving his own chest a bare feast of corded muscle. A man's hardened body was new to her. Percy had been lean and thin in the way of a youth recently become a man. But Jake was lean and *muscular*. His body was just so indecently carnal.

Again, it was her turn. With a subtle undulation of her hips, her dress slid to the ground, leaving her clad in only silvery blue garters and white stockings with slippers to match. She'd never acted so brazenly, so without fear. Neither had she been so aroused. Her *mons pubis* must be dripping its arousal for his un-blinking eye.

His move.

His hand snaked down to unlace his pants as he made to stand. On a sudden whim, she laid a staying hand on his chest and lowered to her knees before him. She wasn't sure what had come over her, but she had an overwhelming desire to touch him with her tongue as he'd done to her.

Her fingers slid down the tensed muscles of his chest and lower belly to tease apart the opening of his pants, freeing his turgid member from the confining fabric. Straight and long and impossibly thick, his shaft was perfection. Reverent fingertips brushed across its velvety surface.

As she held his gaze, her tongue touched his thick

base and slowly stroked the length of him all the way up its pulsing column to its very tip. A shudder ripped through him, and his head arced back. "Olivia," he growled.

She repeated the motion, squeezing her thighs together as her own lust threatened to overwhelm her intention. Then she drew him into her mouth, inch by inch, her hand holding him at the base to guide him in. Tongue swirling around the tip, her mouth and hand moved in unison up and down his smooth length in a steady rhythm.

"Olivia," he all but growled, "I might lose my mind."

Sucking him in deeper, she increased the rhythm, carried along by a lust stoked hotter by the pleasure she gave. She moaned in a mixture of frustration and desire.

"Olivia," she heard again as his hand cupped the side of her face. "I've reached the edge."

She pulled away from him, inch by excruciating inch, giving him one last lick before sitting back on her heels. "Your move."

He reached across the empty space between them and lifted her to a stand. Unexpected move. She'd thought he would ravish her on the ground, perhaps, even hoped it.

He slipped thumb and forefinger into his mouth before reaching out to take one of her nipples between them. Her breath caught in her chest. She might never breathe again. She grabbed his shoulder lest her legs give way. Pleasure cascaded through her in tiny waves that grew larger, bolder with each ensuing ripple, insistent, demanding *more*. He feathered his other hand down her stomach to the mound above her quim.

More was so close, so very, very close…

A groan borne of lust and deep, unfiltered frustration tore through her.

His head snapped up. "Do that again."

Again, she groaned, and his fingers slid along the wet folds of her sex. Her hand clutched tighter at his shoulder. *More* was almost...almost...*there.*

"Again," he demanded.

Again, she complied. One finger slipped inside her as his thumb began strumming her outer sex. Her nails dug in, and another moan escaped her.

Another finger slipped inside, filling her, taking her higher than this rooftop, higher than the sky above. Oh, how the stars twinkled for her tonight.

"Jake," she called out, unsure of how much more of this exquisite pleasure she could take before she shattered into a million sparks of light. She wanted him inside her, his skilled fingers suddenly a poor substitute for the real him. "I want you. *All* of you."

The words had barely left her lips before the two of them were on the ground, him poised above her, his eyes locked onto hers. In a sure swift motion, he sank into her, and nothing else mattered.

"Yes," her voice ground out.

* * *

THAT CARNAL, breathless, mad *yes* was all he needed to hear.

Never had a woman pushed him to the brink of losing all control before he was ready, not like Olivia. Only she had the power to reduce him to this primal state. As if his survival depended on fucking her into oblivion.

His hips gave a hard thrust, and her eyes drifted shut in involuntary abandon. Her swollen lips parted, a moan escaped, and he was lost.

He stilled his hips, and she opened her eyes, a protest in her depths. He pulled nearly all the way out and thrust hard again, and now *she* was lost.

Even as he drove her to the brink, he must be

careful that she reached it first. Her hands held fast to the bunched muscles of his arse, spurring him to increase his rhythm, her hips bucking up to meet him at each downward thrust, her passion driving him into a near frenzied state. Just when he began to question his ability to keep up with this madly impassioned woman beneath him, she broke in release, shouting her climax to the stars above.

Her quim pulsing around him, he could no longer restrain himself and gave in to the animal need clamoring for its own release. He gathered her sweet, supple body into him, one hand at the nape of her neck, the other at her hips, driving into her, relentless thrusts one after the other, her moans and gasps tickling his ear, urging him to the precipice, toward his edge.

"Olivia," he called out as release claimed him in one, two, three thrusts, promising for a wild moment never to let him go, to hold him suspended in the dark, delicious limbo of bliss, need, and satiety for all eternity, for as long as his body was joined with hers.

No more than a spent slab of flesh, he collapsed on top of her before rolling slightly to the side to relieve her of some of his weight.

Their bodies exhausted, the race of their hearts slowing, reality began to creep in at the edges of awareness. He'd spent his seed inside her. Careless.

The thought, however, lacked urgency. What was the worst possible outcome? That she would turn up with child? That he would have to marry her?

He could think of worse repercussions. *Like not marrying her?* came a thought. *Like walking away from her tonight?* came another.

No. It couldn't be possible.

Tonight, he'd been set free from a past that had burdened him alone for too long. It was only when she'd spoken the words aloud that he'd been able to see it. He was years removed from the foolish young man he'd once been. She'd offered him grace—and a glimpse into the man he would be...*for her*.

He would never let this confounding, fascinating woman down. His heart knew it down to its core.

"Olivia," he began, unsure where his words would lead him...*them*.

"Will you hand me your overcoat?" she cut in. "I find myself chilled of a sudden."

He reached for the discarded garment, and a sharp knock sounded at the door. "Lord St. Alban?" came a voice muffled by dense oak. "My lord?"

A muted scraping of metal-on-metal sounded as the key began turning in the lock. Without hesitation, Jake's voice boomed, "Payne, do not open that door if you value your position in my household. You will immediately step back and await further instruction."

All went perfectly still.

A nude Olivia tugged at his attention. She sat with her slender legs crossed to the side of her upright body, golden tresses tumbling in loose waves about her shoulders, casting her in the light of a sated Aphrodite.

A new burst of lust coursed through him. He could take her again this very moment. But lust wasn't the only emotion guiding his response, and she needed to know. "Olivia—"

"It seems we've been found," she interrupted, her voice husky and unlike itself. She reached for her dress. "We shan't starve after all."

His eyes caught hers. "I might be starving already."

* * *

OLIVIA SLID her gaze away from his, avoiding the meaning of his words. With all the passion of an automaton, she concentrated on dressing herself, her movements mechanical and rote, and an ineffable sadness stole over her for what she was about to lose.

The fact of the matter was that she'd gotten too close to the too attractive viscount. And kept getting too close to him, which wouldn't do. He needed the sort of wife who could protect and guide Mina through society's slings and arrows, who wouldn't allow a single one to find its mark.

Besides, had she forgotten that she didn't want to be a wife again? She'd hated being a wife.

No wife of mine will ever be subject to such a marriage.

She wouldn't think about that.

The last few strands of her fine hair tucked into place, her feet began carrying her toward the door, toward freedom. Except she didn't feel free at all.

The image of her once-comforting, steady, white marble column rose up in her mind. But its original meaning had evolved into something dark and unappealing. It now resembled nothing so much as a prison tower.

She wouldn't think about that, either.

"Your man can be trusted?" her voice questioned.

"Yes." Jake drew level with her on the short walk to the door. "But for insurance purposes, I shall see to it that he has a shiny new frock on the morrow."

He'd made a joke, and it was funny, but all her lips could do was curve upward into what felt like the memory of a smile.

"We shall not be able to avoid each other, I'm afraid," she said. "It seems our daughters have become the fastest of friends, but don't worry. I shall do my best not to promote any *concept of us*." She didn't understand why she'd said that last bit. Wasn't it what she wanted?

"Olivia—"

"Nothing has changed, Lord St. Alban."

Her knuckles gave a single rap on the stubborn door. The next instant, Jake's man pushed it open and stood aside, his eyes discreetly lowered. Her quiet, slippered feet carried her across the hall and down the coiled staircase, leaving behind a visibly bewildered Jake.

He needed a wife, and she didn't need a husband. They were completely wrong for each other. She almost believed it, except when they were together, they felt so right.

No wife of mine will ever be subject to such a marriage.

She must do herself a favor and forget he'd ever uttered those dratted words. Only then would she be able to free herself from the unnamed emotion that had wrapped around her heart and refused to let go.

22

NEXT DAY

Veins jumpy with anticipation, Jake cleared the short trio of steps leading up to the humble doorstop and tapped the rusted door knocker twice. He took a wide-legged stance and waited. The day had arrived for him to silence the man on the other side of that door.

He leaned his long body back and peered up at the building's façade, plain, gray, paint flaking, decrepit. He wasn't certain if it was gray from age or coal soot, but one thing was certain: the building hadn't been white in a great many years. Nothing could stay white for long in Limehouse.

An aged servant cracked open the door, and a wary eye examined him up and down as if he was street riff-raff. "Are you here for an art lesson?"

"No," came his clipped reply. "Tell your master that Lord St. Alban is calling."

"Mr. Jiro is not receiving," the servant replied, succinct and implacable.

When she began to close the door in his face, his hand shot out and held firm against surprisingly sturdy oak, preventing her from shutting it. She wouldn't block him out. He'd come to resolve this matter. "Tell

Mr. Jiro that we have a mutual acquaintance. The Kimura family of Nagasaki."

The servant nodded once. No light of recognition registered on her lined face as she closed the door against Jake's slack hand.

It was just as well that he was standing out here in the gunmetal gray mist. After a few days of respite, the typical dreary London weather had reasserted its supremacy. Perfect weather for his current state of mind.

He'd awakened this morning to a brain the consistency of a wet woolen sock, sodden and listless. After last night, well, he'd had a difficult time motivating himself to rise. Then Mina had strolled into his bedroom. "Father, I've had the carriage sent round to deliver me to school."

A reason to leave bed suddenly struck him. He swept the blankets off his body and swung his legs off the bed. "I'll be ready in two minutes."

"I'm quite content to take the carriage alone."

"I insist on seeing you settled."

Mina's eyebrows met, befuddled, before releasing in acceptance. "I shall await you in the sitting room."

If not hope—he knew that was lost—then something else bright and happy bloomed in his chest. He would see Olivia. That was all he needed, a glimpse of her. The scantest morsel would be enough to sustain him. He'd been sure of it.

However, as they'd passed in the corridor, she'd been true to her word and cut him dead. Her eyes held not even the slightest glimmer of recognition or acknowledgement, and a hollow of despair opened inside him.

He'd been wrong: he couldn't live on morsels of Olivia. It would be better to do without her altogether. Which, of course, he must.

He shifted on his feet, restless and frustrated. He

needed a bout in Gentleman Jackson's ring. At least, the ring offered a man a straightforward fight.

The door swung open on silent hinges, and the taciturn servant beckoned him inside. As he stepped across the threshold, he saw that he was entering a proper Japanese household, spare, clean, and open. Even as he wanted to exhale in the specific sort of relief one felt in familiar surroundings, he wouldn't. He must remain alert. This house sheltered his enemy.

The servant bade him stop and pointed toward a low wooden rack. He intuited her meaning and removed his boots before following her to a windowless, low-ceilinged room lit by a dim lamp centered on a low rectangular table. Plain seat pads set atop the tatami floor were the room's only other furniture.

He stepped into the room alone, and the rice paper door shushed shut behind him on wooden tracks. Before he could gather his bearings, the door slid open to admit a man clad in plain white tunic and trousers, today dressed in clothing more Eastern than Western. *Jiro.*

He was taller than Jake remembered, but he'd only seen the man seated unobtrusively in a corner, once. Jiro lowered himself onto a mat, fluid and sure. Although his mode of dress and bearing conveyed the impression of an older man, Jake could see that the man was younger than he by a few years.

He was handsome, as well, but not in the narrow Western ideal. No doubt the strongly defined features of his face—cheekbones, jaw, chin, lips—would catch the attention of even the most small-minded society lady, his appeal extending beyond that of a novelty here for the pleasure of the nobility.

Nobility. Another word that applied to this man. Strange and not at all what Jake had expected of an art master, or a thief. None of the individual pieces were coming together in a neat configuration.

The servant returned with tea service, and the floral scent of jasmine permeated the air. She poured tea into two cups and hastened out of the room on quick cat feet. The man wrapped long, elegant fingers around the cup and lifted it to his lips. *Unhurried* was yet another word for this man.

Jake's patience ran out. "Who are you?"

"You know who I am." A tight smile formed about the man's mouth. "Jiro." He took another insufferably long sip of his tea.

Jake curbed his annoyance and remained silent. The man would have to ask him to state his business sooner or later.

Jiro blew across the surface of his tea, the liquid a muted ripple, and took another sip. "At last, you've found your way to me."

Jake shifted on his feet and tried to find his balance, both physically and mentally. His opponent had all the control. "You know me so well? I don't recall two words ever having been exchanged between us before today."

At last, Jiro's eyes lifted to meet his. Those eyes were as impenetrable as the deepest, blackest night. Yet, in some strange way, they were familiar to Jake. Again, the feeling that there was a piece, a piece that eluded him, missing from this puzzle tickled the back of his brain.

"A father's love for his daughter is that predictable," Jiro replied, a flicker of emotion, unfathomable and quick, fleeting across his features. "I was counting on it."

Twin flushes of anger and fear pumped through Jake. "Explain yourself lest I misinterpret your intent."

More than ever, it struck him that he had no understanding of this man's wants, only his own, which was to reach across the table, grab Jiro by the throat, and silence him forever. As quickly as it came, the impulse passed, leaving him seething with frustration, hollow and acid. More than one piece was missing from this puzzle.

Jiro uncrossed his legs and rose. "Follow me."

* * *

JAKE STOOD before the otherworldly glow of gold overleaf and vibrant color, basking in the beauty and warmth of the paintings that had stirred so much trouble. He'd never viewed them in full light, only in the semi-darkness of a windowless room and only once. He gravitated toward the bottom left corner of the final painting.

There *she* was. *Clemence*, soft and luminous, exquisite. Her loveliness had become almost an abstract idea these last fifteen years.

"Stunning, yes?" Jiro asked.

Jake's gaze darted toward a more neutral spot. "Stunning, indeed," he replied, on his guard. He couldn't be sure of Jiro's meaning. In all honesty, he hadn't expected to be led straight to the paintings. He'd expected more of a struggle.

Jiro drew abreast with him, and they faced the paintings together. "Only noble families own such beauty, yes?"

Jake nodded. It was a fact of their time. For all time, he suspected.

"They were produced by the Kanō school during the volatile Momoyama period. It amazes that a time of such chaos yielded a work of such serenity."

"They weren't produced fifteen years ago?"

"No."

He pointed toward the figure of Clemence. "Then how did *she* come to be in the painting?"

Jiro stiffened. "A later artist placed her there."

"And who would that have been?"

Jiro cleared his throat. "The Kimura family of Nagasaki acquired the paintings when their family were little better than warlords."

"Until you stole them," Jake said, hoping to catch Jiro flatfooted.

"Until I claimed them. You and your daughter were living in Singapore at the time, yes?"

Jake's body tensed. Again, the man mentioned Mina. Was he interested in blackmail? "What is your concern in the whereabouts of my daughter?"

Jiro peered out the window. "The Kimura were great lovers of art through the ages. The older generations had seized power and influence for the younger ones to wield and waste as they chose. Choice is the privilege of the rich, yes?"

Jiro glanced at Jake, perhaps expecting a reply. Well, too bad. He had no interest in a history lesson.

"The youngest son of the current head of family wasn't inclined to wield power or influence like his father or older brothers. Kai cared only for Beauty." Jiro's lips curved into a faraway smile. "You English have an expression for him: his head was in the clouds. Being the youngest son of many, his father indulged this quality, accepting it as proof of how far the Kimura had come since their warlord days." Almost as an aside, he added, "An art master from the Kanō school was employed."

"You?"

Jiro inclined his head. "The boy loved art in all its forms. His focus was like that of a butterfly, lighting upon one beautiful flower after another, be it music, painting, or poem. Beauty was life for him. Then one day, he saw the Dutch physician's daughter at the koi pond in Dejima."

The familiar pang of dread stirred within Jake. "I know about them," was all he could trust himself to say.

"Kai needed his art master's help to—how do you

say?—*court* a girl from the West without his family's knowledge."

A thought occurred to Jake. "You didn't fall in love with her, too, did you?"

Emotion, pure and raw, fleeted across Jiro's eyes, and the hair on the back of Jake's neck stood on end. Certain pieces of the puzzle were beginning to snap together, but not in the configuration he'd expected. The picture that was emerging made no sense.

"She was Beauty personified to Kai," said Jiro. "I believe he loved the girl with all his heart. What could a loyal art master do in the face of such love?"

Jake held his tongue. He could think of a number of things.

Jiro placed his hands flat on the room's central table as if to shore himself up for what he must say next. "Then she was with child. Kai knew what he would do. He would marry her, and they would be a happy family. An indulged youngest son had no reason to believe this idea was anything other than possible. Of course, his father quickly disabused him of such romantic delusion. Clemence and the child were to be cast aside like so much Western rubbish and forgotten. Kai nodded his agreement to his father and began formulating another plan."

"To take Clemence and the paintings and to flee," Jake intuited.

"Kai had this idea that he could sell them and live off the profits until he and Clemence found a way to establish themselves."

"Did she know of this plan?"

Jiro shook his head, and his fingers clenched into fists. "Kai made the decision to bide his time and wait until after the child was born. He'd not wanted to risk her health or that of the unborn child by sailing on the open sea. Besides, his father's spies would know if he attempted any communication with her. After all, they would have the rest of their lives to be together. But then—" An unreconciled note of grief choked up Jiro's voice.

"She died," Jake finished for him.

Jiro nodded and cleared his throat. "Before Kai could surface from his grief, you left Dejima with the child."

Jiro's eyes found his, and Jake saw recrimination in their depths. Compelled to explain, he said, "Clemence requested I take her daughter. No one else would."

"I thought this must be the case. Otherwise, why would you of all people—"

"Yes, why would *I*? Her cuckold?" Jake threw at the man like a rebuke.

"Unless she'd requested it," Jiro finished as if he hadn't heard Jake. "She had nowhere else to turn." A low flame lit within the man's gaze. "Did she have to beg you to take her child?"

Jake felt like he'd been gut-punched. "Yes."

"She did nothing wrong," Jiro stated. "Her only crime was to love in the wrong place at the wrong time. There was nothing wrong with her love."

Jake wouldn't argue with this man about the world's opinion on that love. It was an entirely different conversation. From his perspective—and the only one he cared to consider—Mina came of that union. There was, indeed, some right to it.

Again, Jiro cleared his throat. "Kai resolved to carry through with his plan anyway. The child was his, and all that was left of Clemence. He would claim her from you."

Apprehension churned Jake's gut. "I never received word from him."

"Six months after Minako's birth. That is her name, yes?"

Jake nodded, feeling more unbalanced by the second. His brain refused to speculate where this tale might lead. Certain possibilities were too extraordinary.

"Kai found a ship captain willing to take his gold and turn a blind eye all the way to Singapore. I agreed to accompany him as I had more connections in the art market. But bad luck followed us across the water, and by the time we docked in Singapore, we had contracted breakbone fever."

Jiro reached for a sketchbook and flipped it open to a blank page. Charcoal in hand, he began scratching across paper. "We found our way to a cheap boarding house in a neighborhood of vice to wait out the fever. Both master and servant were sick among strangers. One couldn't discern who was who." He glanced up from the paper. "Who is servant in that circumstance? Who is master? Sickness renders all men equals in that way."

Jiro lay down his pencil and eyed the sketch before holding it up for Jake's inspection. "You thought to find this man when you came here today?"

Jake studied the drawing. Without consciously realizing it, that was, indeed, the man he'd expected to see today. Certain extraordinary possibilities began to appear, unexpected puzzle pieces clicking into place. *Impossible.*

He looked up to find Jiro studying him with narrowed eyes.

"When the fever passed," Jiro continued, "one rose and the other did not."

Jake's gaze darted from the sketch to Jiro's face.

"And master became servant."

Possibility became reality. The picture was clear.

"*Kai.*"

23

"It has been nearly fifteen years since I've been called the name of my birth. I must confess, it feels good to be known."

The impossible collapsed down on Jake as irrefutable fact.

"I am now called Kanō Jironobu. Jiro, if you will."

Jake now recognized what he'd refused to see earlier: Mina in this man…

Kanō Jironobu…

Kai.

Pain borne of fear and desperation spiked through him. Mina was *his* daughter, not this man's. No matter what biology might argue to the contrary.

"After a few months, I recovered and came to your household by the back door, selling cheap watercolors. I saw that Minako had a good home with you, a better one than I could provide her as a fugitive. I was cured of my romantic notions."

Kai flipped to a fresh blank sheet and began sketching again. "I also knew that I could not stay in Singapore. My Japanese features stood out too distinctly, and it was only a matter of time before my father's spies found me, living as I was with several other boarders. People had taken notice and were asking questions. I'd heard that there was a community of us from Asia in London, so I boarded the first ship bound for England. Of course, my features stood out here, too, but the English tend to lump all *Orientals* into one group, which would keep my secret safe. I knew you would arrive here with Minako someday. I set up a studio and waited."

"Have you seen her?" Jake ground out. "In London?"

"Yes."

"Where?" Jake asked, his equilibrium beginning to return, as if he'd been knocked down in the ring and was regaining his footing. In such moments, a determination came over him to see the fight to the end and to win it. This moment was no different.

"In Hyde Park."

"Did she see you?"

"Yes," Kai hesitated, "and there was something in her eyes when she saw me."

Jake assessed his opponent. For all his refined appearance, Kai could throw a punch. "And what was that?"

"Hunger."

There it was: the truth. A truth Jake had known on an elemental level for some time. A truth he hadn't the means to satisfy.

"I want time with her."

"Impossible," came Jake's gut response.

"She must know her heritage."

"She's the daughter of a viscount. What other heritage does she need?"

Kai knew nothing about Jake if he thought he wouldn't fight. A deeper and more important truth lay at the heart of this matter. Mina was *his* daughter. She was as much of him as any biological daughter ever could be. This man wouldn't come between them. He wouldn't destroy them.

"*I* am Mina's father," Jake all but growled.

"By blood," Kai countered, scrappy and persistent.

"Blood doesn't matter."

"In London?" Kai scoffed. "It matters."

"London knows what it needs to know."

"But does Mina?"

Sudden anger burst to the surface, an anger Jake could barely restrain. "You think you know what's best for her? You think you're her father? You understand nothing about being her father."

Kai shifted forward, his eyes ablaze and intense. "But I want to. She needs a place where she can be Japanese, too, a place where she fits with ease," he finished, delivering his knock-out punch with a swift assuredness that floored Jake.

As suddenly as the anger had flared, it faded. Jake's next words fell from his lips like a burden that had become too heavy to bear. "Like a puzzle piece just the right shape."

A glimmer of hope lit within Kai's gaze. "Let her meet me. Is she aware of her true parentage?"

Jake nodded. "Society cannot discover the truth of her birth."

Finally, he'd said the words he'd come here to say, and they felt empty and odd now that he'd spoken them aloud. Kai was no threat to Mina. He never had been.

"It won't," Kai said.

"You have dealings with society," Jake began.

"Society such as Lady Olivia Montfort?"

Every muscle in Jake's body tensed. "Yes, such as Lady Olivia Montfort."

Kai inclined his head. "Her knowledge of the situation is at your discretion."

Like that, it was done. "I shall speak to Mina," Jake said. "She makes the decision, not you or I."

Kai nodded and gestured toward the door. "May I show you out?"

Jake followed Kai through a tight maze of hallways,

simultaneously worn down and strangely relieved. Already, he could predict Mina's decision, and it would be the right one. A part of her unreachable by him craved what Kai offered. He wouldn't stand in the way of his daughter's fulfillment and happiness. She wasn't his possession to keep for himself.

Yet it was another part of the conversation, one not as tidily concluded, that nagged at him. He'd detected a specific knowledge within Kai's eyes when the man had spoken of Olivia. It was clear that he'd intuited the true nature of their relationship.

A few days ago, such insight might have concerned Jake, but not now. Now he wanted it out in the open. He wanted to shout it from the rooftops. Another opportunity he'd missed last night.

Of course, he had only himself to blame. The moment he'd allowed Olivia to step through that rooftop door and out of his life without fighting for her, he'd made a mistake.

Ahead, Kai reached the front door and hesitated, his hand resting slack on the handle. His back to Jake, he asked, "I can trust you to tell her?"

"I've given my word."

Kai hesitated for a quick beat before nodding. He turned the deadbolt and pulled the door open. Jake had already taken a step forward when he noticed. There, just beyond Kai's shoulder stood Olivia, hand raised as if she'd been about to tap the knocker.

An easy smile on her lips, she said, "Oh, good, you're in. Yesterday, I forgot—"

"Lady Olivia," Kai interrupted as he stood aside, "I believe you are acquainted with Lord St. Alban?"

The smile froze on her face, and her eyes went wide. Her mouth snapped shut.

Clear as the ting of a bell, Mina's words came to Jake. *I think it's best to let the heart have a say in the matter.*

Now that Mina was safe, at last, he could hear them. He wouldn't be marrying Miss Fox.

"If you will excuse me, I have a matter to attend to," Kai said, and vacated the tidy foyer.

But Jake hardly noticed. Only Olivia mattered. She blinked and seemed to remember herself.

He wished she wouldn't.

"Lord St. Alban, how unexpected."

* * *

UNEASY, unbearable silence stretched between them, and all Olivia wanted to do was shift on her feet. Any sort of movement to disperse the nervous energy rioting through her body.

But she wouldn't. He would know his effect on her, that she'd gone anxious and twitchy over him, which must be avoided at any cost. She should slip past, and forget she ever saw him. But her curiosity wouldn't allow it. "Are you here about Mina?"

Intense, inscrutable emotion flared within his eyes, but was gone in a flash. "Yes."

"I thought she wasn't interested in an art master."

"Mina has many interests."

"Undoubtedly," Olivia said, at once certain he wasn't going to tell her how or why he'd come to be in Jiro's studio. But since she had him here, there was something she might as well ask him. "Have you seen the latest haiku today?"

His head cocked to the side. "There's another?"

"Oh, yes, and it's a delight," she said, hard notes of sarcasm inflecting every word. "I suspect it will be the talk of the duke's ball tonight."

"The duke's ball," Jake repeated softly as his gaze narrowed upon her. "You will be there."

The foyer walls drew close, and Olivia found it difficult to drag in her next breath. "Of course. I live there. At least, for the present."

"For the present?"

"I sent notice to your solicitors this morning that I shall take the house on Queen Street." She attempted to swallow the lump in her throat. "I believe that severs the connection between us."

He took a step forward, and all that remained between them was a tiny patch of air that would become insignificant in an instant, if they chose. No longer inscrutable, fire snapped in his eyes. "It will take more than that to sever the connection between us," he spoke in the velvet rumble that made her insides go molten.

"Jake," she whispered, her pounding heart suddenly in her throat, making her voice go weak and breathless, "nothing has—"

"Changed?" he cut in. "You do keep saying that."

She glanced away, unwilling, unable, to hold his gaze any longer. Yet when his fingertips reached beneath her chin and gently tipped her head back, her eyes had no choice but to meet his. "You and I have more to say to each other. Much more."

"I seriously doubt that, my lord," she said without a dram of conviction in her voice. Still, she must try. "I do believe we are finished."

"We are far from finished, Olivia. In fact, we've only scraped the surface of our beginning." His gaze held hers for one, two fraught heartbeats, and again her breath suspended in her chest. "Don't forget to save a dance for me tonight."

With that, he let go of her chin and stepped past her. It wasn't until he'd rounded the corner at the end of the block that her breath could release. A shiver, warm and delicious, purled down her spine at the promise in his voice, at the promise in his eyes.

Her feelings were wrong, utterly, utterly wrong. But there was no help for them. That man affected her at a level, deep and true and elemental, over which she had no control.

She would have to do a better job of steeling herself against him in the future.

Her brows creased together. Why had he said that last bit? Wasn't he on the hunt for a proper wife? Then why would he dance with her at a ball in front of the entire *ton*?

Added to that, she'd found him *here* of all the places in London.

None of these factors added up to an explanation that made sense.

A soft harrumph ushered her back into the present. She turned to find Jiro, waiting for her to enter. A few seconds later, she stepped inside his studio and realized that she'd always seen it in the afternoon, never seen in full morning light. It was a glorious distraction from the strange interlude of minutes ago.

Well, almost. The idea that Jake was so recently here called out to her. As if an essence of him lingered in the air and, with every breath, she inhaled him instead of oxygen.

What romantic rot.

She may be many things to many people, but romantic wasn't one of them. No longer was she a romantic, green girl. Marriage, widowhood, and a set-aside marriage had put an end to the girl she once was.

Jiro stepped forward, an object in hand. "Is this the item you seek?"

She looked down to find her set of charcoals. "Ah, yes, thank you. Although I'm not sure why I bothered, other than to get away from the frenzy of ball preparations. My pencil hasn't produced anything worthwhile these past few days."

"One cannot predict such things," he stated, his fingers busily organizing his own tray of charcoals. "Your pencil will find its way again."

"Jiro," she began without thinking, "about Lord St. Alban—" She paused, hoping he would complete her sentence. He didn't. "May I ask—?"

"No, Lady Olivia, you may not," he replied softly, firmly.

Those last three words were so simple. *You may not.*

Monosyllabic, light words. Neither heavy nor complex. *You may not.*

Yet they landed in the room with a solid thud.

She averted her gaze, stung. A confirmation lay within those simple words that wasn't at all simple, confirmation that something didn't add up. Jake was withholding information from her.

Her pulse jumped as a swirl of emotion threatened to catch her up in its whirlwind. Hurt, yes, but other emotions as substantial. *Pique...curiosity...* A righteous sort of hurt, pique, and curiosity. Feelings to which she had no right.

Tiny, invisible splinters, they burrowed deep beneath her skin.

"Is that all you need?" Jiro asked.

Olivia nodded, already on her way out. A spark of vitality flared inside her. "I believe my pencil has found its way."

We've only scraped the surface of our beginning.

What on earth could the dratted man mean by speaking such words to her?

24

An olive to pluck
A viscount fair dares to dream
Far more than a good—?

Olivia was right: the latest *London Diary* haiku was a delight.

Except Jake wasn't being ironic. To be sure, it was crude, uncivil, and even made a crass stab at rhyme. No matter. It served his purpose that he and she be known.

He stepped foot inside the Duke of Arundel's opulent ballroom, and immediately found himself the recipient of no fewer than five knowing, appreciative nods from his own sex and five knowing, flirtatious smirks from the opposite sex.

Oh, yes, they were known. That feeling from the night he'd met her infused him with its galvanizing spark—*interested, engaged, and alive.*

But the feeling had been inconvenient, so he'd shut it away—or, more accurately, *tried* to shut it away. Suppression hadn't exactly worked.

Tonight, the feeling would be given free rein.

Tonight, he was a man with a purpose, and no one would stand in his way—not even himself.

"St. Alban!" His name emerged crystalline and bright through the dull, monotone roar of the ball.

He braced himself and turned toward the dowager duchess. Avoidance would be futile. He bowed at her approach, and she placed her palm on his forearm. "Take a turn with me." As their feet found a pace conducive to conversation, she said, "Do not cut out early tonight. There will be an announcement later, and I'm requesting the presence of all my family."

"Whatever you require, Your Grace."

She squeezed his arm. "Speaking of marriage, how goes your courtship of Miss Fox?"

"We found that we don't suit," he replied in a carefully neutral tone.

"Oh? I'm so rarely wrong about that sort of thing. Take Nathaniel and me, for instance."

"Nathaniel?"

"The Duke of Arundel, of course."

Jake's brow lifted, and a smile worthy of the Sphinx softened the duchess's features. He intuited in an instant the subject of tonight's announcement. "May I be the first to congratulate you?"

"I accept your congratulation, my dear, but you are not the first to congratulate me. I have congratulated myself aplenty." Her smile transformed into one triumphant and not a little self-satisfied. "The Duke of Arundel is quite a catch. And I know of, at least, one other lady who'd set her cap at him. But *I* landed him."

No one could accuse the duchess of false humility.

She began twirling a string of pearls with her free hand, a signal that she was about to state her business. "Now, let us discuss your marriage prospects. Even if Miss Fox won't do, you've made a splash this Season. If you play your hand capably, you could be married by Michaelmas, or, at the very least, engaged."

"I shall take that under advisement."

"What sort of bride would you like?" The duchess pointed in the direction of a girl dressed in pale pink muslin. "One who blushes for the first year of your marriage?"

A note of alarm clanged inside Jake's head. "I'm not certain Mina would be well-served by a mother so near her own age."

"You're seeking an older woman?" A tiny frown of concentration pulled at the duchess's mouth. "Not many men in your position show that sort of fortitude when presented the array of possibilities that lie at your hand."

A snort escaped him. It wasn't fortitude guiding his choice of wife, but the duchess needn't know that. What he felt for Lady Olivia Montfort had naught to do with strength of character. It was its very opposite, in fact.

Weakness...powerlessness... Something deeper, too.

Something they must discuss tonight, privately, away from the prying, knowing eyes of the *ton*.

The duchess jutted her chin toward a lady seated next to the punch bowl, blissfully unaware of their scrutiny. "How about a lady who has been on the shelf for a few years?" Her fingers stopped mid-twirl. "I know what you're thinking, St. Alban, and you couldn't be further from the truth. Certain ladies are like fine wines, and the shelf only enhances their flavor. Take my dear friend, Miss Dunfrey, never married, poor dear, but the details that woman knows..." The duchess's countenance took on a dreamy aspect. She gave her head a shake and resumed twirling her pearls. "Suffice it to say, she let me in on a few secrets the duke will appreciate on our wedding night."

Jake fought to keep his gaze expressionless and trained ahead of him, all gentlemanly concern for the safety of their progress. He wouldn't betray a thought on that particular matter, not even to himself.

"Or how about a respectable widow?" the duchess persisted. "One with children of her own, but safely within childbearing years, of course. The viscountcy must be secured, St. Alban. Now don't get the wrong end of the stick. I don't begrudge you the fact that the viscountcy fell out of my branch of the family tree. I made my peace with that turn of events a year ago. But if you die heirless, the title will revert to the Crown. Not a felicitous state of affairs, not in the least."

He nodded, pretending to seriously consider the matter. In truth, he didn't give a fig about the security of the viscountcy. However, a widow did coincide precisely with his intentions. Well, a former widow. An outright *un*respectable, former widow.

"Ah, here we are," said the duchess, her tone grown soft and very unlike itself. Jake glanced up to find they were approaching the duke. "Your Grace, St. Alban and I are discussing his prospects for an advantageous marriage, and we are agreed that a respectable widow is exactly what he needs."

Jake couldn't help noticing that wives and husbands were nothing more or less to the duchess than commodities on the marriage market. A wife was *what* he needed, not *who* he needed.

Not so very long ago, he'd been in agreement with her. No longer. A wife must be more than a thing. She was a *she*, a person. A person with no value on the open market as she would be invaluable...*priceless*.

Only one woman lived up to that standard.

The duke's piercing blue gaze lit upon Jake and turned hard and assessing. "A widow, you say? I think I can see exactly the sort of widow Lord St. Alban wants."

Jake held his peace. The word *want* could mean

lacking. It might have even sounded that way to the duchess, but he caught the duke's true meaning. The man was speaking of desire. Specifically, Jake's desire for Olivia.

The duchess clapped her hands together and held them clasped before her. "Now that's settled, whispers are floating about that the champagne may be running dry, and I must see to its resolution. There is no happiness at a ball where there is no champagne."

With that, the duchess flounced away and disappeared into the crowd, leaving Jake and the duke alone.

"Lady Olivia," the duke began in a voice that wouldn't carry beyond them, "may not be my daughter by blood, but she is my daughter in here." He jabbed his thumb into his chest just above his heart.

"I understand." More than the duke could possibly know.

"And her interests will ever be mine."

Jake understood what the duke needed to hear. "I hope to make them mine, as well, Your Grace."

The duke nodded once in approval, and muscles that Jake hadn't realized were tensed relaxed in relief. He watched the duke follow his future duchess at his own ducal pace and vanish into the crowd.

A waiter appeared at his side with libation, but he shook his head. Champagne was all well and good, but he found himself in need of a more substantial drink. A drink conducive to plotting out one's plan for the evening. In short, he needed whiskey.

He located a stocked sidebar and poured himself a finger of the silky, amber liquid, downing it in a single, grateful gulp. He and Olivia were known by the duke. *And* he'd secured the duke's approval. Two hurdles cleared, but ultimately meaningless if he didn't secure Olivia's as well. Speaking of Olivia...

His gaze cut across dancing couples sweeping

gracefully atop glistening parquet floors, certain he would find her amongst their number. He didn't.

He began singling out small groups of ladies scattered about the periphery of the dance floor, engaging in lively conversations, again certain he would find her amongst their number. Again, he didn't.

His brow knit in confusion, and his search expanded toward the outer edges of the room, over the old, the infirm, the spinster, and the wallflower, certain he would *not* find her amongst their number.

He did.

There stood Olivia, her back pressed against a wall, her eyes following the dancers. He wasn't certain if it was the atmosphere of the ball—enthusiastic violins singing the rhythms of a mazurka; golden light filtering through chandeliers vibrating alongside the hum of music and crowd; fashionable bodies radiating the excitement and tipsy joy that only a ball could induce—but she was part of it and above it all at once.

Clad in a distinctly *un*virginal ivory gown of near-transparent silk shot through with threads of gold, light and music swirled, casting her as the goddess of the ball, its Aphrodite. And like a goddess, she stood apart, alone. Yet *alone* didn't quite capture it.

Olivia looked lonely.

Comprehension of her place along her little spot of wall hit Jake all at once. Amongst the old, the infirm, the spinster, and the wallflower, she was the divorcée, equally odious to polite society. Protectiveness and outrage warred inside him until his blood coursed hot and fast through his veins.

Olivia should be dancing.

Englishmen were a lot of spineless cowards if they couldn't traverse the treacherous distance of a ballroom floor to ask the crowning jewel of this ball to dance. No woman in this room—nay, in all of London —was her equal. She was a diamond cast before swine.

This couldn't stand. His feet moved forward. Though she may resist, he would coax her onto the dance floor to take her rightful place, and they would stand before this lot, united.

Before this night was through, he and Olivia would be known, properly.

25

O livia's lips ached.

Blithe social smiles held for hours on end tended to have that effect on the muscles of one's face. Yet soldier on she would, for this was the duke's ball, a wild success, judging by the number of luminaries populating the room. Was that the Duke of Wellington leading Mrs. Arbuthnot onto the dance floor? Those two couldn't help but invite scandal.

She tapped bored fingers against her thigh, but remained glued to her spot of wall. For the last decade, she'd played default hostess at the duke's gatherings, but not tonight. On this occasion, nothing was required of her. The moment the duchess had arrived, her part had become entirely superfluous. The woman had issued a series of commands to the staff and seized control of the room.

Really, there was nothing for Olivia to do but stand aside and observe, which wasn't the worst thing. Really.

After all, it was impossible to be indifferent to the thrum of exhilaration whirring around the ballroom. The guests understood why they were here: to witness the engagement of the Duke of Arundel to the Dowager Duchess of Dalrymple. It mattered not that the marriage would be the second for both bride and groom. The union of two grand families generated excitement and reinforced the rightness of their enclosed world.

She was happy for the duke, truly she was.

Across the cavernous room filled with sparkling diamonds and eyes to match, she watched for *him*. A few minutes ago, she'd left Lucy with a newly arrived Miss Radclyffe, so she knew *he* was here. The man who said words like, *We've only scraped the surface of our beginning.*

She exhaled a clearing breath. He'd been absolutely and utterly wrong: he and she were finished. *Finished?* That wasn't correct. They never were. They would have had to have begun to be finished.

Except hadn't they begun something?

Was he so absolutely and utterly wrong?

Placid, social smile affixed to her lips, she snatched a glass of champagne off a passing waiter's tray and gazed across the crowd before closing her eyes and allowing the music to seep into her at the cellular level. It really was lovely. *One-two-three...one-two-three...* The human body was meant to move in time to such a rhythm.

Of a sudden, her feet longed to swirl around the ballroom. She settled for tapping out the rhythm with her fingers against the glass. Was this how spinsters and confirmed widows did it? Tapping out rhythms with fingertips and feet hidden by skirts as they sat virtuously by the wayside. Was *this* her future?

Her eyes flew open. She might need another glass of champagne to brave the thought further.

Yet the thought refused to wait. When she'd petitioned the House of Lords to set aside her marriage, this was the fate she'd carved out for herself, forever to be on the periphery of events, but never in the stream of them. She'd known that freedom would have its price. Tonight, she was beginning to understand how society would exact payment in the years to come.

Yes, another glass of champagne would be necessary.

A voice, sharp and vulpine, cut into her thoughts. "Lady Olivia, may I congratulate you on the Duke of Arundel's impending nuptials?"

Olivia's eyes startled left and found Miss Fox at her side. She nodded and kept her silence, unable to trust herself to discuss nuptials with Jake's future bride.

"I now understand your need for discretion a few days ago," the chit continued. "Might this marriage shift your position in the duke's household?"

Olivia felt her mouth start to gape open and snapped it shut, clenching her teeth together. The cheek of Miss Fox.

"Unless, of course," Miss Fox added slyly, "you have other plans."

She was referring to the haikus, Olivia knew it. "Miss Fox, you mustn't rely on gossip for your facts. How surprising that you read the *London Diary*."

Miss Fox's gaze shifted toward the dance floor. "Something like that."

Emboldened, Olivia said, "Of course, soon your own wedding banns will be read." She was being imprudent, but she couldn't seem to help herself. Miss Fox never failed to provoke her.

A tight, knowing smile hinted about Miss Fox's mouth. "You needn't fear that particular outcome, Lady Olivia. I shan't be marrying Lord St. Alban."

"That is rather a surprise," she said, somehow managing to suppress the lightning strike of joy that bolted through every cell in her body.

Yet it changed nothing. Mina needed a *proper* stepmother.

Miss Fox's brow lifted. "Is it? I would think it rather obvious that we don't suit. The man is a thoroughbred stallion to my one-eyed cart pony."

Startled by Miss Fox's words, spoken with such

clarity and confidence in their truth, Olivia looked at the other woman, really looked at her. The chit was of a height with Olivia, but slighter, airier in some way, as if a strong wind could blow her off a cliff. While some might deem her features unremarkable, the more discerning would see finely wrought bones beneath translucent, milk-pale skin that a Michelangelo marble would envy.

"Miss Fox, you speak too ill of yourself. One would be a fool to miss your delicate beauty."

A blush the soft pink of a spring rosebud stained Miss Fox's cheeks. The chit had the prettiest blush Olivia had ever seen. Still, she stared ahead, clearly unused to flattery of this sort.

"Flashy beauty isn't the only sort," Olivia continued.

"No?" Miss Fox asked, notes of her familiar acerbic tone returned. She gestured toward the dance floor. "It does seem to arrest people in their tracks, though, doesn't it?"

Olivia glanced across mahogany buffed to a mirror shine and caught sight of a familiar figure. *Mariana.* A relieved smile found its way to her lips. This night wouldn't be so bad, after all. Then she remembered the woman at her side. "Mariana does manage to attract a few eyes," she conceded.

In parallel, Olivia and Miss Fox watched the string quartet strike up a waltz and Nick appear at Mariana's side. Mariana didn't light up at the sight of her beloved in the way of some women with a wide, glorious smile. Instead, a radiant blush softened her cheek, and the heat of her gaze increased tenfold.

"She does love him rather a lot, doesn't she?" Miss Fox asked, her tone rhetorical. It was obvious to anyone with eyes.

Nick took Mariana's hand, and from across the room Olivia felt the electricity of that touch. Miss Fox must, too. Mariana knew the secrets of that magnificent man, and he knew the secrets of her. He led her into the stream of the waltz, and they were swept away in its current.

A crystalline memory of their first Season came to Olivia. While Olivia had pursued Percy, a boy full of light and near her own age, Mariana had abstained from giving herself over to London's entertainments. It wasn't until a year later that Olivia understood why: Mariana had been waiting for the return of the elusive Lord Nicholas Asquith from the Continent, a man the polar opposite of Percy. *Experienced. Worldly. Opaque.* Where Percy was a boy, Nick was a *man*.

"Look at the way he gazes upon her," Miss Fox said. "They do make one feel like an intruder for watching. But…" Her voice fell away.

"Just try *not* watching," Olivia finished for her, forging an unexpected kinship between them. She might like this Miss Fox, fellow intruder.

"Right. They're just so…so…" Miss Fox's mouth twisted to the side in search of the right word.

"*Perfect*," Olivia said.

"Perfect," Miss Fox agreed. "They have what everyone wants."

Yearning, fierce and pure, shot through Olivia, threatening to unravel her thread by thread until nothing remained but the raw, quivering core of this longing. Miss Fox's words were the simple and absolute truth. She wanted what Nick and Mariana had. Wanted it so bad, she could taste it.

It tasted of…

Jake.

If she was being honest with herself, she longed for a different sort of freedom from the one she'd fought so long and hard to obtain. She longed for the freedom to gaze upon Jake the way Mariana gazed upon Nick. To claim him in front of the *ton* for a single dance as hers.

As hers?

She blinked, once, twice, and snapped to. He wasn't the man for her. And she wasn't the woman for him. They'd made those facts very clear to each other.

Another tray littered with bubbly champagne appeared to her right, tempting her with its happy dance. She found her own glass empty—when had that happened?—and traded it for a full. She took one... two...*whoo!*...bracing gulps. The bubbles effervesced all the way up to the tippy top of her head, and she felt lighter, floatier, even if she didn't feel precisely *better*.

"They waltz as if no one else in the world matters," Miss Fox said.

"Mm-hmm," Olivia assented around the lump in her throat.

There was a proper way of dancing the waltz that involved distancing oneself from one's partner, back held straight and rigid, arms stiff and unyielding, eyes averted and aloof. It was entirely possible to remain separate from one's dance partner, both in body and spirit, during a waltz, if one put enough effort into it. If one *cared* to put enough effort into it.

Clearly, Nick and Mariana didn't, their bodies flat up against each other, the entire length of her body pressed full length against his. Mariana, feline and sensual, stretched up to whisper into his ear. A quicksilver smile flickered across Nick's lips, and his eyes glowed with promise.

"It looks like the prelude to a coupling," Miss Fox whispered.

Olivia ripped her gaze away and stared down into her champagne glass. It wasn't only yearning that was turning her stomach into knots. It was jealousy, pure and primitive. She wanted what her sister had.

She wanted the carnality and the passion...the love and the ease...

She wanted it all.

And it wasn't possible.

Not for her.

What Nick and Mariana shared was unique to them. Olivia would wager her new townhouse that no other couple in this room experienced that sort of love, singular and true. During their courtship, she'd thought she had it with Percy. Their marriage had shattered that particular illusion. But she now understood she could have it with the right man. And in her very soul she knew who the right man was.

But she couldn't have him. She was the wrong woman.

The music ended on an upbeat flourish, and the couples cleared the floor to make way for a new set. Nick and Mariana melted into the crowd.

"That was quite an elucidating experience," said Miss Fox, a bewildered smile belying her sardonic tone. "Is it only me or has this room warmed by a few dozen degrees?"

A wry chuckle escaped Olivia. "I'm afraid my silk fan may not be up to the task of cooling me sufficiently after that display."

Miss Fox's familiar vulpine smile spread across her face, even as an unfamiliar warmth reached her eyes. "Lady Olivia, I rather like you."

With that, Miss Fox departed on a shush of silk skirts, taking the moment of levity with her. Olivia closed her eyes and exhaled a sigh on the hope that her breath could force out the horrible feeling gnawing at her stomach.

"You should be dancing."

Her eyes startled open on a surprised gasp. "Jake?"

Could it be? She blinked. It could.

He bowed. "In the flesh."

Flesh. The word caught between the chinks of her armor, and her heart hammered in her chest. It was possible that her heart would break free of her ribs and reveal itself to him. "It's really too bad that yours is—"

She stopped herself from finishing that sentence. *So thoroughly covered.*

Had she been about to speak those words aloud?

The smile that curled about his lips and reached all the way up to his eyes told her that she didn't need to. He'd done it for her in his head.

A flurry of anticipation shivered up her spine. She liked that he had. And the way he was looking at her...

She liked that, too.

It was entirely possible she liked everything about this man.

On a reckless wave of abandon and desire, she stepped forward, a slight wobble in her step. From two glasses of champagne? Lord, she was light as a titmouse when it came to wine. He likely noticed, but she cared not. She lowered into a deep curtsy that might have listed left. She steadied herself before rising and extended her hand. "Lord St. Alban, would you do me the honor of the next dance?"

The arctic blue of his eyes warmed, and the distance between them melted. He reached out and wrapped his gorgeous, capable fingers around her hand. "It would be my utmost pleasure."

He led her onto the dance floor just as a quadrille struck up. Tittery, gossipy shock rattled the air around them, its silky sibilance ascending into a soft buzz, continuing to rise in volume until it crescendoed into a roar, excited and delighted. The music ceased on a jarring and discordant note, eliciting disgruntled rumblings from everyone eager for a little scandalous drama. What could be more delightful at a ball?

Two familiar-looking young bucks brandished what appeared to be a bundle of bank notes at the musicians. Next, a violin bow swept across strings, and the quadrille transformed into another waltz. The *ton* wanted a show, and she and Jake were to provide it.

She moved with him on a wave of champagne bubbles. She'd never felt so light, so free, as when she placed her hand onto his shoulder, felt the sinewy flex of hardened muscle, and their feet glided into motion to the buoyant one-two-three rhythm of the waltz.

His warmth enveloped her in a cocoon at once safe and precarious, and she was absolutely lost. It was dangerous to be here with him, to expose her vulnerability to the *ton*, but she couldn't help herself. Her entire being pulsed with the particular joy that sprang up from one's heart when its desire was fulfilled. She was powerless beneath its sway.

She should set her gaze over his shoulder. She should keep her posture rigid and her arms stiff. She should keep him at a proper distance. But, oh, how she didn't want to be—

Safe.

The word jolted her out of this sugar-spun fantasy borne of want and ache and unbridled joy. What was she doing? This waltz, this night, would end, reality would reestablish itself, and what would she have done?

She had no business dancing the waltz the way Nick and Mariana had. A mortified blush crept up her décolletage, and she aligned her spine into an upright rod and set her arms at a stiff angle.

How close to the edge she'd come. How close she still wanted to come.

Oh. That sounded wrong.

And true. Oh, so true.

And wrong. Utterly wrong.

Champagne.

Tomorrow, she would blame it all on champagne, bubbly and bright, seductive and beguiling temptress.

Next to them, a couple danced too close and brushed Olivia's skirts. A usual occurrence at a ball. It was somewhat odd, however, that this was the first such occasion during this dance. She glanced around, and her heart jumped into her throat. They were one of only four couples dancing. Of the two hundred or so guests, at least half formed a loose circle around the dance floor, watching...

Her and Jake.

How had she forgotten them?

Abandoning her arm's length distance, her erect posture, and her stiff arms, she gathered into him, pressed full-length into his body, and strained toward his ear. "Do you see how they watch us?" she asked, keenly aware of the *ton* intently, delightedly observing Lady Olivia Montfort make a spectacle of herself with the Right Honorable Viscount St. Alban.

"Of course." His warm breath tickled the fine hairs of her neck. "The haiku."

How had she forgotten the haiku? She spoke her next words before they stuck in her throat. "They assume we are lovers."

"We *are* lovers."

"*Were*," was her automatic reply. But she wasn't certain there was enough conviction in that word to give it the weight of truth.

As if scalded, she pushed away from him, their only points of contact where their hands rested on necessary stretches of clothed skin. She resolved to ignore the side of her that longed to luxuriate in the long length of him flexing and moving beneath his form-fitting superfine. He was long in more ways than one.

Oh. Where had that sprung from? She could blame it on the champagne, but it was no use.

Soon, not soon enough, she recognized the final bars of the waltz. It was finally, blessedly, coming to an end. She made to step backward, to separate from him, but he pulled her in, reducing her physical rectitude to bits. Again, his body pressed against hers, his mouth brushing her ear. "Meet me in the center of the duke's labyrinth thirty minutes hence."

She opened her mouth to reply that she had other plans for the evening. Plans that involved at least two more glasses of champagne and no trace of him.

"Say *yes*, Olivia," he said, his voice low, raspy, a masculine rumble in his chest that sent shivers racing across her skin, down the length of her spine, threatening to reduce her to jelly right here in front of the *ton*.

She couldn't think of what to say, her mind wiped clean by him. So she nodded her acquiescence once, a light brush of her soft cheek against the rough stubble of his, imperceptible to the avid crowd hemming them in.

The music ended on a stirring flourish, and the two young bucks alone shouted a raucous cheer that the rest of the assembled indulged with rolled eyes and inflexible smirks.

Jake walked her to the edge of the dance floor, bowed, and strode in the direction of the billiard room. Refusing to give the *ton* what they wanted by watching him walk away like a love-struck girl, Olivia turned to seek out another servant bearing the nectar of the gods. Ever more and more champagne would be needed if she was to survive this night intact.

But he'd been correct: they did have a few matters to unravel between them.

And the tight center of an elaborate labyrinth seemed the perfect setting.

26

Jake rounded yet another leafy corner and found himself facing a hedgerow identical to the one he'd just left behind. He was late, not having accounted for the fact that he hadn't the faintest idea how to find the labyrinth's center. Olivia would know it like the back of her hand.

A memory from last night stole in: her hand feathering across his bruised chest before pressing her lips to it. That kiss had penetrated all the way through to his heart, and he still felt it there, filling him to bursting. No longer was there room for the hurt, shame, and regret that had plagued him for years. Before him lay a future different from the one he'd envisioned since setting foot in London.

And he was free to pursue that future. If he could ever find her.

Fifteen minutes ago, he'd watched her duck out of the ballroom, champagne flute in hand, wobble in her step. Since it wouldn't do for them to leave together, he'd stood in affable silence for a full five minutes while a lively matron extolled the virtues of her daughter, who stood quietly to the side, eyes cast down to the tips of her white satin slippers. The girl couldn't have been more than a few years older than Mina. The idea of selling Mina off to a man old enough to be her father churned his gut.

He'd offered the pair a succinct bow and excused himself, taking a different exit from Olivia, in case curious eyes tracked their movements. One couldn't be too sure with these people.

He snorted and shook his head to clear it. Here he was: a formerly capable man reduced to prey for the *ton*. He made a sharp right, and stopped dead, the breath frozen in his chest. Suddenly, he stood inside the labyrinth's center, his future laid out before him.

Awash in moonlight, luminous and sublime, lay a supine Olivia stretched atop a marble bench, gazing up at the night sky, champagne flute lolling gracefully at the end of an outstretched arm. A vision of aristocratic elegance, her ball gown cascaded toward dewy grass that stretched across the space between him and her. The statue of a long-forgotten saint stood vigil, poised to grant a special indulgence only for her, this Aphrodite.

He stepped forward, snapping both a twig and Olivia out of her reverie. She shot up and swung her legs around, eyes flashing, lips drawn in a straight line just turned down at the corners. She resembled less amorous Aphrodite than vengeful Hera.

This wasn't at all the mood he wanted, or expected, for the question he would ask.

"In the excitement of the ball, I forgot to ask you a question that has been bothering me since this morning." The glare beneath her furrowed brow intensified. "Why were you really at Jiro's studio?"

Her question struck him like a swift left hook to the jaw. An inauspicious beginning to say the least, but one he must address if he was to salvage a night that had begun to slide away from him. "Jiro knew of Mina from Japan."

Olivia's head canted to the side. "*Knew* of Mina from Japan? I thought she was a few days old when she left."

"She was."

"Then what would it matter to Jiro that Mina is in London? Were you acquainted with him in Japan?"

Jake stilled, body braced for a blow from a larger opponent. "I'd never spoken to the man until today."

Her eyes narrowed. "Either you're talking nonsense or the champagne is dulling my mental faculties. And, for the record, while I think it could be the latter, I'm leaning toward the former."

"I didn't know he was here until I saw the sketches."

She leaned forward until she perched on the very edge of her seat. "What sketches?" she asked, her voice a low and hard mirror of the cold stone beneath her. Dread stole into the air and hung about her in heavy waves.

He must speak the words aloud. "The ones I knocked from your hands."

"What is it to you that either the paintings or Jiro are in London?"

"Have you ever noticed the group of young women in the final painting of the set?"

"Bottom left corner."

"One girl stands slightly apart, reading."

"A book."

"Pardon?"

"A Western-style book."

Olivia's eyes widened. She knew.

Her eyes narrowed. She knew.

"If she looked anything like she does in the painting, Clemence was really quite lovely."

"Quite." It was possible the moment could go soft and pliable, and he might be able to slip inside it.

"Then what?" Olivia asked.

"Pardon?"

"After you saw my sketches. Then what?"

"How do you mean?" Sometimes in the ring, it was necessary to shuffle around, to avoid an opponent's blows, to regain one's bearings and devise a way forward.

"What incredible serendipity that you and I travel in the same circles." Sarcasm laced her every syllable. "What fantastical serendipity that our needs happened to align so neatly."

The moment closed with a snap, firm and definite. He shifted on his feet, absorbing the impact of her words.

She began ticking items off a list, finger by finger. "The duke's mentorship. The house hunt. Seeing Mina placed at school. Those were all secondary to what?"

"I needed to get closer to you."

"You *needed* to get closer to me? Well, you certainly succeeded on that front." Her sharp laugh sliced through the air. "What is so important about Jiro and the paintings?"

"They were stolen from the most powerful family in Nagasaki, the Kimura."

Her eyebrows knit together. "And Jiro—"

"Stole them."

Sudden understanding dawned across her face. "He could know the truth about Mina."

Jake nodded. Again, he felt that the moment could grow soft, that opportunity, fragile and skittish, was presenting itself.

"Why didn't you simply ask me for his direction?"

He inched forward, his footsteps muted by springy grass underfoot, encouraged by the direction of their conversation. "I couldn't risk anyone connecting him to Mina. I didn't yet know the sort of man he is."

A loaded heartbeat passed. "Or the kind of woman I am?" she asked, steady and controlled.

Too steady. Too controlled.

Jake stopped cold. Separated by a few feet, the

chasm that opened between them spanned the bound-less sky.

"Did you think I would betray her?" A note of hurt ribboned through the question.

"I couldn't risk her."

"I wouldn't have risked her."

He knew that. But he couldn't say it. Not now. It would only sound like so many manipulative words.

"Jiro wouldn't have risked her. He's not that sort of man."

"Olivia," he began, anxiety curling through him. The sort of anxiety when it sank in that he'd lost a fight, but must stay in the ring and take his pummeling like a man. "His name isn't Jiro. He is Kai, Mina's—" He hesitated, the next word twisting his throat into a hard knot. The truth would become more definite, *final*, spoken aloud.

Olivia's pupils flared, pushing her irises into thin, blue rings. "Father," she spoke for him.

Another layer of betrayal slipped between them and pushed the chasm wider. She glanced at the half-empty glass in her hand as if wondering how it got there. She lifted it to her lips and downed the champagne in two great swallows. With a simple flick of her wrist, she tossed the empty glass into dense shrubbery. She cleared her throat. "You used me."

"Yes," he replied.

"Thoroughly."

"Yes."

She heaved a great sigh and shot to her feet. "And now Jiro isn't even Jiro anymore. He is Kai." A mirthless laugh escaped her. "Mina's father."

She closed the remaining distance between them. Fortunately, she wasn't required to travel far or in a straight line. She tipped her head back to hold his gaze and poked a finger into his chest. Despite the fact that she was undeniably three sheets to the wind, her eyes

held his with clarity and control. He would take whatever punishment she chose to dole out, anything she
threw at him until she was finished.

"But there is one question that remains unresolved."

"Ask."

"How did you find Jiro...*Kai?*"

There would be no use in hesitating. So he didn't.
He ripped the bandage off in one swipe, swift and sure.
"I followed you."

* * *

HER BODY WENT numb at the confirmation, even as her
heart doubled its erratic beat. "Followed me?" Betrayal
and exposure blossomed, robbing her of breath.

He'd used her. He'd lied to her. He'd *followed* her.

Her afternoons spent roaming the East End were
part of an intimate life that no one had the right to vio-
late. How dare he?

"You bastard!" She reared back her right hand and
swung it around to slap his lying face.

Except her hand never made contact. He caught her
wrist and held it fast, suspended in the night air. His
gaze pinned her in place, and her body flushed hot, her
focus concentrated on the point where his gorgeous,
capable hand wrapped around her wrist.

A succession of thoughts flowed in a rapid cascade.
She could ignore his scent...his warmth...his powerful
body...his piercing eyes...his gorgeous, capable hands.
They needn't affect her as they had in the past. But...

How closely her body was positioned to his... How
their breath mingled together in a ragged cadence of
uncertainty and...

Was this anticipation making her heart race? Anticipation of...

What?

At once, she was certain of a single, irrefutable fact:

more than she wanted to slap his perfidious face, she wanted this man one last time.

Every time was supposed to be the last time. Yet it never was.

Tonight was different. Tonight, he didn't have to be more than a body, his only function to be a source of pleasure for her. They didn't have to solve anything between them to do this temporary act. They both wanted it. She saw the truth of that reflected back at her in his eyes, irises flared black with desire, surely a mirror of her own.

Oh, he wanted her. And she would have him.

She reached up and touched fingertips to the dimple in his chin, traced the outline of his stubbled jaw until she found the back of his neck, her fingers threading through his sun-kissed hair. Gently, insistently, she tugged, pulling his face down, even as she rose to the tips of her toes, her mouth reaching, straining, toward his. In a final push of the sweetest anxiety, her mouth took his...

* * *

...IN A KISS THAT RAVISHED, urged, insisted, left nothing in reserve, left Jake no doubt how this night would end.

Her tongue pushed inside his mouth. Her body carnally rubbed up the full length of his, her intent clear. He released her wrist, and her hand snaked between their bodies until it reached the laces of his trousers, already strained to their limit by the bulge of his swollen cock. The cool tips of her fingers feathered down the hot length of his shaft, once, twice, a taunt, a tease.

A growl, rough and demanding, sounded from the back of his throat. He needed... "More, Olivia."

"When I say."

Her palms pressed flat against his shoulders, and

she pushed his yielding body onto white marble, his hard cock exposed to the night air and the avarice of her gaze. She took her skirts in hand and slowly lifted, exposing ankles, calves, thighs...*mons pubis*. He heard an animal moan and realized it came from him.

The knowledge of Eve lit within her eyes. "I know what *more* you want." Her tongue grazed her crooked tooth. "And what I want." She braced her hands on his shoulders and straddled him, her naked, wet quim poised inches above his cock, another taunt, another tease. Her lips met his ear. "Beg," she whispered.

"Olivia, if I could take back—"

"Not for forgiveness."

Relief, dirty and wrong, pulsed through him. He didn't want her forgiveness. He wanted her hot, slick cunny wrapped around his cock. He throbbed, he ached, for her to... "Fuck me."

She pulled away and met his eyes. "Did no one ever teach you how to grovel?"

His gaze fixing hers in place, he allowed a heartbeat to pass, then another. "Please."

A triumphant smile curved one corner of her kiss-crushed lips, and her hand wrapped around his length one deliberate finger at a time until she held him firmly. It was all he could do to keep his hips still, to not press up and into her, to keep his hands fast at his sides and let her control the situation. This night was hers to use him as pleased her.

Unhurriedly, she lowered her body, her bare flesh brushing his throbbing head before lowering to take him in, inch by slick, agonizing inch, until he was fully immersed in her. She went still, her breath ragged, her cheeks flushed, and her eyes drifted shut, intoxicated by her own private nirvana. She'd never looked so unbound, so unknowable.

Eyes closed to any world outside her own, she rose up, then down, a slow, intentional rhythm with every rise and fall of her hips, his shaft a tool for her pleasure. His hands clenched the back edge of the bench as she took him.

Her eyes fluttered half-open. Desire darkened their luminous blue into opaque navy. She reached inside his shirt and gripped his shoulders, her nails digging in deep. Blood surely mixed with the sweat trickling down his spine.

Lust, hot and swift, ignited, and he reached the limit of passive endurance. His fingers found her hips and squeezed. Her legs wrapped around his waist, allowing him further entry until he pushed against the core of her.

"Harder," she moaned, wild abandon freeing her, him, of the past, the future, freeing them to this moment, this pleasure, pure and raw, blazing and demanding. He thrust his hips and drove inside her in a swift, slick stroke, relentless. Her moan encouraged, begged, pleaded with him, for more, for all he had.

Her head arced back, and her body tensed, suspended, still, except for the relentless thrust of his cock. Her breath came and went in staccato bursts as her body broke and pulsated her release atop him, her quim fluttering in rhythmic pulses around his manhood, all but begging him to follow her lead.

But he wouldn't. Not yet. He wasn't done.

In a quick, sure movement, he tightened his grip on her hips and lifted her up and off him. Confusion crinkled her brows together. "But you didn't—"

He pressed a silencing finger to her lips. "Turn around," he demanded, more imperious than he had the right to be.

Dark, fierce lust flared her pupils, her irises a thin blue ring, and she obeyed, bending over and bracing herself against smooth stone, her luscious, heart-shaped derriere naked and waiting for him to take her again.

He took his cock in hand, slick and sweet with *her*, and guided himself into her, and she released the longest, most sultry moan ever to cross a pair of lips. He stroked in, then out, her moans sliding into gasps. Her hands gripped the edge of the stone bench, her back arched, and her sex bloomed more with each thrust of his hips, ready for more, harder, faster.

He and she were nothing more than animals, devoid of reason or concern. This was fucking. They took from each other what was needed. He wanted her to take from him until he had nothing left.

Her gasps became short, hard bursts, as if she'd wound herself into a knot. He drove inside her, again and again. Only he could release her, unbind her. Gasps transformed into aching groans, and he felt her unfold beneath him as her wet, hot pussy seized her, quaking its release around him. This time he had no choice but to follow her to the precipice and over its edge.

He came hard, spending his seed deep inside her, each thrust an intentional branding, a claiming, animal, primitive. She was his. He would have her any way he could get her.

A bead of sweat trickled down the side of his face, and his animal nature began to recede, reason and reality, heartbeat by beat, reasserting itself. He glanced down and found himself still joined with her. He never wanted to separate from her. Yet he must.

He stepped back and slipped out of her. With one hand, he reached for the laces of his trousers, and with the other, he tugged her crushed gown over her pale bottom. The fine muscles of her back contracted, one by one, and she straightened. Her dress fell to the ground in a soft shush. It was almost possible to convince himself that what had just happened hadn't. But why would he want to?

She turned around and braced herself against the bench before sliding to the grass in a graceful cloud of gold and ivory silk, her back supported by white marble. He'd never seen her so gorgeously and thoroughly spent.

"I wish you'd allowed me to land that slap." Her voice carried to him across crisp night air swirling with the vibrations of a distant raucous mazurka, the antithesis to the quiet and unsettled mood pervading the space around them.

"No, you don't."

"Don't I?"

He lowered his own spent body and settled back onto his elbows. Her gaze seemed determined to fix on the patch of night sky beyond his right shoulder. Now, in the quiet of this rare moment, he must ask a question. "Olivia?"

She must look at him.

"Olivia," he repeated.

Her gaze, wide and wild, flashed to meet his.

"Marry me."

Ephemeral emotion flickered across her face.

"Not replying isn't an option. You cannot run from this."

A laugh, sudden and mirthless, emerged from her parted lips. "No? But I am so good at it."

"Olivia—"

"No. The answer must be *no*."

27

A light rush of joy coupled with deep, dark despair swept across and sank into Olivia.

Jake had asked her to marry him. She'd said no.

His brow wrinkled in disbelief. "No?"

His inability to take *no* for an answer was almost comical. Almost.

His brow released, and his entire bearing took on a pugilistic set that didn't appear remotely defeated. "What if there's a babe?" he threw out like a rebuke.

A possibility she'd considered. But there were ways of concealing pregnancies, country estates and such. Besides, the *ton* would expect nothing less, or more, of her. Her resolve strengthened. "You mustn't marry me."

"Stop using that word. *Must*," he growled, thwarted, frustrated. "It's wearing thin."

"Jake, stop and take a listen." The strain of violin strings and the monotonous hum of the party drifted over the dense labyrinth. "Can you hear them? Discussing me? Dissecting me? Even in the duke's own house."

"That hardly matters to—"

"It matters to you. Don't you remember?" She inhaled deeply, sharp, midnight air frosting her lungs, steeling her for the conversation that must be had. "It matters for Mina's chances with that lot." She pressed on, insistent. "You see their refined, glossy smiles. What you don't see are the sharp, vicious teeth hiding behind those civilized smiles. But I do. I've felt the fine points of those teeth sink into me. Mina is innocent. She deserves better than that."

"I'm her father. I know what's best for her."

"It's not me."

He opened his mouth to speak and closed it. He shot to his feet and began pacing the length of the enclosed space, calling to mind a caged tiger who hadn't yet made peace with the narrow confines of his cage. Welcome to your life in the *ton*, Right Honourable Jakob Radclyffe, Fifth Viscount St. Alban.

The reality of their situation had begun to sink in for him. Good. Great. Brilliant. Like a tenacious barrister pressing her point home, she continued, "Mina needs a stepmother of impeccable reputation. She needs a protective shield. We've accepted this in our hearts."

He stopped mid-stride and swiveled toward her. Silent accusation pinned her in place. She'd read him all wrong. He hadn't accepted her version of their reality. Not in the least.

"Our hearts? Do not speak to me of our hearts, Olivia."

He stalked toward her, an unpleasant glint in his eye. A frisson of worry tingled down her spine, not for the safety of her person, but for something more important: the safety of her intentions.

"Mina isn't your reason for refusing me...*us*."

Olivia sprang up, her heart threatening to pound through her chest. She stepped behind the stone bench, placing it between her and him. As if it could protect her from the havoc he was wreaking inside her. "If you must know," she began from what she thought was a safe enough distance, "I'm not certain we are well suited to one another. That the, um—"

"Passion?" he supplied.

"Yes, that the passion we share could be enough to sustain us over time."

"The heat between us burns hot and bright enough to sustain us through not one lifetime, but a dozen." His words emerged clipped, Dutch in intonation. He was definitely upset.

He rounded the bench. Now nothing was between them. Nothing in the physical world, anyway. But it wasn't a physical barrier that stood between them. It was the one invisible to the naked eye that was most impenetrable. Solid enough to prevent one heart from accepting another.

"Try again," he said, words that penetrated clear through to her core. "Your refusal isn't about the fickleness of passion. It's about your marriage."

Her entire being stilled as if caught in an invisible snare, held in thrall by intense ice-blue eyes that dared her to look away, to refute the veracity of his words. He wanted the truth? He would have it. "What if it is? Surely, you can see the parallel."

"What parallel?"

"Between you and Percy."

Incredulity spread across his face. "Not a single similarity exists between Percy and me."

"No?" Cold steel wrapped around her heart and braced her for the words she must speak. "Percy withheld facts from me. *You* withheld facts from me. How are you any different?"

She knew how in so many ways, but she couldn't let that knowledge see light. It might grow roots and undermine her purpose.

"I had—"

"Your reasons?" she interrupted. "Of course. And I understand them, truly I do, but lovers, husbands, *men* always have their reasons. It's the prerogative of your sex. It places you above the women in your life and makes them less than equal. I shall never place myself in that position again."

"I've told you that I seek a partner."

No wife of mine will ever be subject to such a marriage.

She gave her head a clearing shake. She mustn't lose focus. "I believe that you believe your words, but they can't be true. The fact is you are a man, and I can never know you truly."

"You know exactly who *I* am. Not as a representative of my sex, but *me*, Olivia. This conversation isn't about generalities, but about *us*."

"I thought that about Percy. Then we married. The truth is—"

"The truth is," he interrupted, "you don't trust your judgment when it comes to love."

Her gut twisted and sank to her feet. She'd uttered similar words to him two nights ago on that magical rooftop. Now he was throwing them back at her. She deserved them. "I've been wrong before."

"But we aren't speaking of *before*. This is *now*."

"Can't you see? The stakes are too high to be wrong. What of the stepmother Mina needs?"

"Don't throw Mina at me. That is pure evasion."

Chastened, Olivia allowed the steel around her heart to release. He was right. Using Mina was an avoidance. "We are quite a pair of damaged goods, aren't we? We both have sound reasons for swearing off love. Why can't you leave it?"

"Is it so easy for you?" he asked.

"*Easy* isn't the right word. Nothing in life is easy. Consider the price if we fail."

"Olivia, is there a price too high?"

The gently spoken question hung in the air for a

moment. It was the sort of moment that could go either way. To answer *no* was an undeniable temptation. But to answer *yes* was the more rational option. "I've done a fine job of avoiding that price these last eleven years until—"

"Until?"

"Until you came along," she admitted. The admission needn't change the outcome of this conversation. "But it's too late for us. You see how capricious the universe can be?"

"You'll never start truly living until you trust yourself and let your fear die."

The compassion of those words threatened to deplete the last shreds of resistance left inside her. Her feet carried her past him and around the stone bench until they found the patch of grass bearing her imprint. She folded herself down into the spot and leaned against the bench.

There were a few angles from which to view the word *living*. It could describe the basic functioning of the body: blood pumping through veins; muscles contracting; brain processing. Or it could describe the very heights of human existence. To *truly live* meant to take life beyond its basics, to seize hold of it without a plan for the next step.

One had to risk all to *truly live*. One had no room for fear in such a life.

The air swirled around her as he settled onto the ground beside her. Her next breath caught the soft heat of his body and took it deep inside. It was a perfect breath. She closed her eyes and held it inside for as long as her lungs would allow. She would hold it inside forever if she could. Salty tears pinpricked the backs of her eyelids. Oh, that they, too, would stay inside forever.

"What if I loved you?" he spoke into the space between them.

The breath arrested inside her lungs, and hope swelled. Within that *what if* nested her chance to truly live. The next moment, her breath released, and the flight of fancy tucked itself away. "Love isn't enough. It's chaotic and fleeting."

"Look at the stars, Olivia."

Her eyes fluttered open, and she took in the fathomless indigo sky.

"That isn't chaos. It's order. The past, present, and future suspended above our heads. *Our* past, present, and future are written there. If you squint hard enough, you can see it: a future so bright that the shadows of the past can never dim it."

She averted her gaze. The stars now offered no comfort or respite. He'd managed to insinuate himself into the wide universe.

"But one must brave it."

His words were perfect. Words that were years too late for her. She no longer put her faith in perfection. "Brave in love?" Even she could hear the hollow bluster that carried her words. "Madness, given all you and I have experienced." She exhaled, and the fight left her. All that remained was a single stripped-down, implacable truth. "I can't have you."

His brow furrowed. "*You* can't have *me*?" He leaned in, and her eyes fluttered shut. His lips brushing the sensitive cup of her ear, he whispered, "Olivia, *you're* the prize. Has no one ever told you?"

A lone ripple of exultation fanned through her, holding her suspended in a warm, protective cocoon. She could stay here forever, waiting for him to say more words like the ones he'd just spoken. Words that would make her world, *their* world, right, possible. But the wider world lay beyond her closed eyes, pressing in, reminding her how impossible *their* world was.

A soft rustling sounded beside her, and she kept her eyes shut tight against reality. Still, her ears would hear his feet padding softly across the grass, receding away from her. Her eyes blinked open in time to catch a glimpse of him rounding the corner and out of sight.

She released a breath and the last of him.

No one would ever mistake her for someone brave.

28

"One-two-three, one-two-three," Lucy counted out over Mina's shoulder.

As Lucy led her through the simple steps of the waltz—surely a silly sight as she stood a head taller than Lucy—Mina marveled over how she'd gotten herself into this position.

"Ouch!" Lucy cried out.

"I'm so sorry." Mina had stepped on Lucy's toes no fewer than seven times this waltz alone. "We can stop, if you like."

"I definitely do *not* like. Now, I never thought I would say this to you of all people, but you must concentrate." An impish grin curled about Lucy's mouth. "Besides, ten broken toes wouldn't be too high a price to pay for waltzing to a string quartet. Even if the musicians are a room removed, their music is heavenly."

Mina tried to concentrate on the dance steps, really, she did, but it held little interest for her. For Lucy, this dance, every dance, even the minimal act of breathing, was an adventure, and she was ever on the lookout for the next one.

At school, some impertinent question was always erupting out of Lucy's mouth, not from malice or to cause trouble, but out of a need to *know*. No subject was taboo. This was where Mina felt a deep connection to Lucy. She, too, was a curious person.

It was from this place that she viewed their friendship, even if others couldn't see it. Their curiosity manifested itself in different ways, but once stimulated, they stopped at nothing to satisfy it. Which was how Mina found herself in this small, forgotten room one wall removed from a ball, stepping through the waltz with Lucy. Even if Lucy's ebullience wasn't inspirational, it was most definitely motivational.

"Oh, my dear," Lucy said, all stuffed up matron. "This music is divine. Simply the music of the gods. Why, I haven't heard this song since my debutante ball." A few beats of the waltz skipped by for dramatic effect. "One hundred and fifty years ago!"

A laugh, shocked and delighted, startled out of Mina. She liked that about spending time with Lucy. She made it easy to believe that the world was a bright, fun place.

"Now, try setting your arms like so." Lucy demonstrated a loose, elegant turn of arm, one Mina could never come close to mirroring in an eternity of moons.

"You mustn't be so...*stiff*. What will all your lovers think?"

"I shan't have any lovers," Mina replied matter-of-factly. "I shall dedicate myself to—"

"Science," Lucy said, her tone dry as a dinosaur bone. "But Mina? Why isn't there room for both?"

Before Mina could reply, Lucy's gaze fixed on a point in the distance, and the next moment she flew out of Mina's arms on a high-pitched squeal. "Huey!" her voice sang out as she shot across the room toward her cousin, Lord Hugh Bretagne, Earl of Avendon, heir to a future duke...and heir to the sun, Mina remembered thinking the night they'd met in the Duke of Arundel's foyer.

"I knew I would find you in this very room," Lord

Avendon said, a mixture of supercilious reserve and genuine amusement infusing the words.

Into an unlit corner, Mina shrank, hoping to avoid his attention. Of course, he'd seen her dancing with Lucy, but perhaps he hadn't really noticed her. Members of the *ton* tended not to look directly at her. Except when she wasn't looking at them. Then they feasted their greedy eyes on her to their heart's content.

"Lulu, Grandpapa has sent for you to meet him in the ballroom."

"Me?" Lucy squealed. "At the ball?" She fled the room without a single backward glance as if the slightest hesitation would render her invitation null and void.

Mina's attention remained fixed on Lord Avendon. Instead of following in Lucy's turbulent wake, he strode deeper inside the room and stopped in front of a bookcase, clearly perusing titles. She stood still as a statue as if he was a wild animal, and the smallest movement would scare him away. Or invite his notice.

She wasn't certain which would be worse.

His gaze scanned gold embossed titles, down the line, one after the other. Which books interested someone like Lord Avendon? What did the heir to the sun read?

Now no more than ten feet from her, his eyes continued roving left, toward her, and stopped, a particular title catching his attention. He reached up and began to slide it out. She opened her mouth to ask which book and snapped it shut. She was trying to remain unnoticed, after all. Still, what book could it be?

She tried to make herself smaller in her little corner, her heart pounding, anticipation racing through her veins. Perhaps he wouldn't notice her.

His head angled left, and his translucent amber eyes unerringly landed upon her, not a speck of surprise in their depths. He bowed, and she lowered into a polite curtsy.

"You may want to come, too, Miss Radclyffe," Lord Avendon said, pushing the book back into place. "I believe your father is looking for you."

"Thank you, my lord."

He stepped aside, clearly waiting for her to pass. As she drew level with him, her eyes darted sideways to see which book it could have been, but she couldn't tell. They all looked the same. She continued forward and felt a seed of frustration crack open. Curiosity must always be satisfied, no matter the cost. Her feet planted in lush, Aubusson carpet, and she swiveled around, the question on her lips, ready to be asked.

She gasped. He was closer than she thought. Taller, too. Taller than her. A rarity. Her gaze lifted to meet his, and she cleared her throat. "May I ask which title you were perusing?"

A confounded look crossed his features, and he appeared his age. A few years older than her. No more than that. He mostly didn't look like a future duke. He reached over, slid the book out, and cleared his throat. "*Emile, or On Education* by Jean-Jacques Rousseau, it appears." He turned the book over in his hands a few times, as if to test its weight, and met her gaze, his head cocked to the side.

A smile sprang up from the soles of her feet. "*Emile* is the foundational text of my and Lucy's school, The Progressive School for Young Ladies and the Education of Their Minds. Of course," she added, "as applied to females instead of males."

His eyes clouded over, and her smile dropped, suddenly conscious of itself. He pushed the book back into place, and his usual air of...*dukeliness*...returned. "Honestly, Miss Radclyffe," he replied in a voice that reeked of disinterest, "I took it out at random. I don't give a fig about it."

In the face of such a provocative remark, Mina's curiosity chased away her self-consciousness. "But why?" she asked. A possibility occurred to her. "Can you read? I've heard that some members of the English nobility find it too tiresome ever to learn."

A surprised laugh startled out of Lord Avendon. "Of course, I can read."

"Then why wouldn't you care about that book? You held it, felt the weight of it in your hands. Not to mention the fact that it's one of the most influential books of its time. Doesn't anything interest you?"

Lord Avendon drew himself up to his fullest, noblest height. "I'm interested in everything appropriate to a gentleman of my age and rank."

"Appropriate?" Mina asked, nonplussed. "But that isn't how curiosity works. It has nothing to do with appropriateness. One is either interested in the world, or one isn't. It's a true measure of one's intelligence."

Lord Avendon's eyebrows drew together into an expression that could only be characterized as utter shocked bewilderment. "Miss Radclyffe, are you calling me a simpleton?"

The tips of Mina's ears burned in sudden mortification, and her heart became a hammer in her chest. She'd been too bold, gone too far. Why was she speaking this way to this young man of all people? She hadn't the faintest idea, but now that she'd started, she couldn't seem to stop. "I wouldn't say I've directly called you a simpleton, but in my word choices, I might have implied it. In my experience, someone who is interested in little is of little interest."

Lord Avendon's mouth gaped open for an instant before he recovered himself. "Miss Radclyffe, I've never met anyone quite like you."

"That's because you only associate with your kind."

"My kind?"

She nodded. "You might try casting your social net a bit wider, so to speak."

Lord Avendon opened his mouth to reply when the exterior French doors opened and in walked Lady Olivia Montfort, Lucy's mother. She was a vision in ivory and gold, the epitome of the English lady. The sort of lady Mina never would be.

Never *could* be.

Lady Olivia's eyes darted between Mina and Lord Avendon. "Have I interrupted something?"

"Not at all," Lord Avendon said smoothly. He appeared to have recovered himself. "Miss Radclyffe was just educating me on some of the finer points of society and questioning my intelligence."

Again, embarrassment flared inside Mina, and something else, too. The weight of her place in society, or lack thereof, pressed down on her, and she wondered for the first time if she could bear it. It wasn't only her exterior that marked her as different to the *ton*, it was her interior, too. Lord Avendon sensed it, she could tell by the way he watched her, speculative gleam in his eye. Indeed, he was a young man very much of his class. Someone who actively strove to be uncurious and idle, someone who not only didn't understand her, but who was someone she couldn't understand.

"*Meisje.*"

All three sets of eyes swung toward the voice, and the room startled into complete stillness. Relief swept through Mina at the sight of her father, but something kept her from going to him. In a way that felt new and strange, she sensed this odd tension between her and Lord Avendon was theirs alone to sort out.

"We're needed in the ballroom," Father said. Concern radiated about him, and a look might have passed between him and Lady Olivia. Something lay within the look that might have piqued Mina's curiosity another time. Right now, the exterior French doors called to her. Beyond them lay a quiet garden and an open night sky.

"I need a breath of fresh air first," Mina said, her feet already moving toward freedom. "If you'll excuse me."

* * *

WITH THAT, Mina slipped out the door and faded into the gray night. Olivia returned her attention to the two men still occupying the room with her, neither of whom she'd expected to encounter when she'd entered it not five minutes ago. Unable to look the one man in the eye, she started with the other. "Hugh, have you anything you would like to say?"

"I believe the duke would like you join everyone in the ballroom, too."

Olivia suppressed a groan. "Please inform the duke that I'll see him later." She didn't have it in her to face that ballroom of nobility again tonight. The duke would understand. He always did. "Before you go, Hugh, what occurred between you and Miss Radclyffe?"

Before Hugh could answer, Jake cut in, a glower darkening his expression. "What do you mean *what occurred* between him and Mina?"

Had Hugh noticed that Jake's hands had clenched into fists at his sides? Likely not as Hugh released a disinterested sigh. "Nothing *occurred*," he drawled. "I came to find Lulu for the duke, and Miss Radclyffe called me a simpleton. That's the basic long and short of it."

Jake's hands released, and a gruff laugh escaped him. "I believe I'll see to my daughter now."

Without thinking, Olivia held up a staying finger, stopping Jake in his tracks. "Let me."

His eyes met hers and held a moment. It was a moment that could last until the end of time. It was a moment that couldn't end soon enough.

He nodded his assent, and Olivia pivoted, her skirts a silky swish about her slippers as she stepped into the duke's garden for the second time tonight, filled with both relief and despair for having left Jake behind—for the second time tonight. But she wouldn't think about that now. She needed to tend Mina. It didn't take her long to find the girl perched atop a gleaming marble bench in the informal section of the garden, a small, brass telescope held to her eye.

"A brilliant night for stargazing," Olivia said.

Mina startled and instantly lowered her telescope as if chastened.

"Do you mind if I rest a moment beside you?"

Mina shifted over and made room. Olivia gestured toward the telescope now resting on her lap. "What a lovely little telescope."

The girl flushed. "Thank you."

Olivia's brow lifted in silent question, eliciting a shy smile from Mina. "I constructed it."

"Indeed?" Olivia asked and held out her hand. "May I?"

A companionable silence fell around them as Olivia gazed through the eyepiece, the wondrous universe a little bit closer.

"This telescope isn't powerful enough to see all that far into the cosmos," Mina said, her voice equal parts pleasure and pride. "But the brighter constellations and odd shooting stars aren't out of its reach."

"From up there, we must all seem the same," Olivia said, her voice faraway, even to her own ears.

"It's only down here that the differences matter."

Olivia lowered the telescope and glanced at Mina. "Would you like to be the same as everyone else?"

The girl's fingers worried the silk of her skirts, a

gesture that spoke of unease. "It might be a nice experiment."

"Perhaps," Olivia began and stopped, hoping the right words would come to her. "Perhaps you might try viewing the matter from above, away from your place down here. Might it be possible that being different in one obvious way affords you the freedom to be truly yourself? Sometimes when a person looks like everyone else, society forms certain expectations about who that person should be, rather than who that person really is. You, Miss Radclyffe, are young, beautiful, wildly intelligent, and talented with a magnificent future stretched before you. You can be exactly who you are, don't let anyone tell you any differently. I know that's the future your father wants for you."

Beside her, Mina held still, clearly considering Olivia's words, before she nodded once, and the breath Olivia hadn't realized she'd been holding, released.

"Expectations and surfaces matter not to me," Mina said. "It's workings beneath the surfaces that interest me most. But I've observed the English to be wholly different. They would be content to build a society composed *entirely* of surfaces. They don't seem to care about the substance behind them."

Olivia handed Mina's telescope back to her. "Don't be too quick to paint us all with the same brush. Some of us may surprise you."

A smile found its way to Mina's lips, and relief flowed through Olivia. "For all that you and Lucy are very different, she's also very like you," Mina said as she came to her feet. "Lady Olivia, thank you for joining me out here. I've enjoyed our conversation very much, but I must join Father in the ballroom. I hope we have the pleasure again soon."

As she watched Mina rush toward the ballroom, Olivia rose and followed slowly in Mina's wake. She liked the girl and saw how easily she could form a maternal attachment to her. Mina would turn out all right, Jake would ensure that. And he would find exactly the correct stepmother to help him, too.

A little voice reminded her that he'd asked *her* to marry him. He'd asked *her* to be that stepmother. And she'd said *no*. A strange numbness that insulated her from the devastation of his proposal and her refusal filled her from the far depths of her soul to the surface of her skin, her entire being insensate to the very air around her.

Across the green expanse of tufted lawn, rendered slate gray by the indifferent moon above, stood the duke's mansion, blaring its chorus of music, light, and general gaiety. The stars dimmed their collective glow, overtaken by so much ducal glory.

She touched fingertips to the tense patch of skin between her eyebrows and applied pressure. The beginnings of a headache stirred as her feet delivered her to the outer terrace beyond the edge of light.

Inside the ballroom, the quartet stopped mid-stroke, and the crowd quieted to a monotone hush at the sound of a metal object purposefully striking glass. *Ding-ding-ding*. There was to be a toast.

From her vantage point, she could all but see a frisson of excitement ripple across the ballroom floor. The duke and the dowager stood at the top of the grand staircase. Below them, arranged on the steps like a descending waterfall of privilege, gorgeous and aristocratic, stood the entirety of their two families. She located Lucy. Mina, too. She knew every face shining out at the gathered multitude, all reaffirming examples to the *ton* of the rightness of a world where they made its rules. If she were to put this scene to canvas, her color palette would barely extend beyond stark whites and yellow golds, so bright was their combined glory.

She didn't give much credence to the *right to rule*, but many of those gracing the staircase did. Take the duke's heir, for example, Lord Michael Bretagne, the Marquess of Exeter. As Percy's elder brother and the duke's only other surviving child, she'd had plenty of time to observe him, and he most definitely believed in divine right. To Exeter's left stood his heir, Lord Avendon. Lucy called him by the diminutive Huey, but she suspected only Lucy could secure that particular right with a self-serious young man like Hugh. What had she interrupted between him and Mina? Had she really called him a simpleton?

Her eye swept across the staircase. Both families claimed descent from the reign of William the Conqueror and all made jolly on this joyous occasion, but their place in the world was a serious business, and none of them would stop at anything to keep it secure. In a way, she could relate to the feeling. It was that particular feeling, the need for security, that had bound her life together this last decade and kept it from falling apart. It was the same need that had predetermined the outcome of this night.

She couldn't give up the security of the life she'd built around herself for the uncertainty of a life with Jake. The trade-off was too fraught with instability. A moment's grief now was nothing to a lifetime's worth of mourning should their experiment fail.

The stately rumble of the duke's voice cut through the still night. "I would like to thank everyone for gathering here tonight to celebrate this most special of occasions." The duke's hand extended toward the dowager, who brusquely swiped at tears that dared stray from her eyes. "Please raise your glasses in a toast to the Dowager Duchess of Dalrymple, soon to be Her Grace Lucretia Bretagne, Duchess of Arundel."

A little "squee!" of excitement sounded from the staircase, eliciting delighted snickers all around. Olivia's gaze found a flushed Lucy, and a grateful smile for the moment of levity crinkled the corners of her eyes, even as every single one of tonight's unshed tears rushed forward.

"Hear, hear!" chorused the crowd while the quartet struck up a lively country reel.

The duke, majestic and assured, led his future duchess down the staircase and into the center of the ballroom. They instantly fell in step with the music that would have been popular in their youth. The assembled nobility lost all awareness of its aristocratic airs and joined together in clapping a beat to the rhythm of the strings, harkening back to roots that no city aristocrat ever left completely behind. The land was in the blood of every English nobleman. They were nothing without it.

As her eyes picked over the two families soon to be one, Olivia finally allowed herself to settle on the one head she'd been most carefully avoiding. Apart from Lucy, he shone the brightest of all, his serious gaze sweeping across the crowd as if he was looking for someone.

A shard of pain stabbed through Olivia. He was looking for her.

He might love her.

Her breath caught in her chest.

He'd lied to her. He'd followed her. He'd betrayed her trust.

She'd vowed years ago never again to put herself in the position where a man could betray her. And, yet, she had.

He'd asked her to marry him.

What if there's a babe?

A babe was the least of her worries. She would never marry without love.

What if I loved you?

She would never marry *for* love.

Olivia, you're *the prize.*

She shook her head and forced her breath to release. She must go it alone. As she'd done for so many years. Surely another decade wasn't a problem.

Happiness may be held at arm's length, but so, too, would heartbreak. She would be safe from the inevitable betrayal of marriage inside the marble prison tower that she'd so carefully and thoroughly constructed for herself.

29

ONE MONTH LATER

Espied in Mayfair
A discreet retreat for two?
Chits weep: lucky who?

"Pish, these *London Diary* haikus are becoming truly atrocious," Lucy exclaimed. In disgust, she dropped the paper onto the breakfast table, where it landed with a light, papery slap. "Whoever could they keep referring to? I thought it was Mina's father, but what was the 'A house for his Queen' one all about?"

A house for Lady Olivia Montfort on Queen Street, Olivia didn't tell her too astute daughter.

Her stomach filled with acid, and she pushed her croissant away. This was how it felt to be mocked. Of course, the writers at the *London Diary* had no idea that they were mocking her. They thought they were taunting her.

Well, it wouldn't be long before they realized how very wrong they were. Today marked the anniversary of her and Lucy's first week in their new Mayfair townhouse. The matter had been settled at the discreet office of Mister Tobias Dilbey, Esquire, Jake's solicitor.

Money had efficiently changed banks and signatures solemnly scratched across deeds.

On impulse, Olivia had reached across the table to shake hands with Mister Dilbey. He'd stammered a bit before he'd haltingly reached out and tapped her palm with the tips of his fingers.

Life had a relentless way of moving forward. With or without one's permission.

A movement at the corner of her eye drew her out of philosophical musings doomed to reach no good end. Lucy had cracked open *The Bride of Lammermoor.* "How was your day, Lulu?"

Lucy stopped mid-chew, and her eyebrows drew together in consternation. If Olivia was reading her daughter's expression correctly, she was looking at her as if she'd grown horns. "The day has barely begun, Mum," she said around the food in her mouth. "I'd say that the tangles brushed out of my hair without too much fuss, and it was a pleasant surprise to find that this dress still fits. It seems that my body has decided to grow *outwardly* of late." Her head tilted quizzically to the side. "Shall I ring for another pot of coffee? You might need another cup. Or three."

Olivia grew warm beneath the acuity of her daughter's gaze.

"Seriously, Mum, you might need a holiday."

"A holiday?" Olivia asked in all sincerity. She'd convinced herself that she'd hidden her glum state of mind quite well. After all, she was busier than ever.

"How are your art lessons progressing?" Lucy asked in an obvious attempt to change the subject.

"Splendidly," Olivia replied brightly, too brightly, earning a penetrating double-take from her daughter.

It was a lie. She hadn't seen Jiro...*Kai* since he'd all but told her to stay out of his affairs. It was too soon. Besides, she was busy with her new life. Kai might be part of an old life better shed and left behind.

"And, of course, I've been so busy with the move."

"Hmm," Lucy began, her voice a hum ripe with disbelief. "Mum, it's like you're everywhere and nowhere at once." She tapped the small, rectangular missive to the left of her plate, and her eyebrows drew together. "I suppose you know about the letters Lord Percival has been sending me."

"I'd noticed."

"Tell me something."

"Anything."

"Why did you marry him?"

The question took Olivia by surprise, but she wouldn't give Lucy any answer other than the truth. She deserved that much. "Simply, I took one look at him and knew I must, that I would perish of unrequited love if I didn't. There was no other man in the world like him. I was very young."

"He broke your heart," Lucy stated, the words flat.

"He did."

"Don't you regret him?"

"Never."

"Why not?"

"He gave me you."

A small frown pinched Lucy's mouth and released. "That's something you must say, isn't it?"

"Can I speak freely?"

"It's the only way to speak," Lucy said with her characteristic certainty.

Olivia smiled for the first time in days. "Now, that is something the Lord Percival I knew would have said. In some ways, you're very like him."

Lucy shook her head, protest in her eyes. "I don't want to be like him."

"He had some bad qualities, your father, but he had some good ones, too," Olivia continued. "He was open. He spoke his mind. He loved to laugh." She reached across the table and squeezed Lucy's hand. "You're allowed to embrace the good. You won't be betraying me, Lulu. It's your choice to open that letter or not, to forgive or not, but sometimes it hurts the person withholding forgiveness worse. It can turn into the sort of hate that eats away at a person."

"Have you forgiven him?"

"Yes," Olivia said, surprised that she meant it with every fiber of her being.

Lucy turned the missive over in her hands a few times before slipping it inside her book. A bittersweet joy sprang up inside Olivia, even as a thread of misgiving ribboned through it. Percy had better prove worthy of her.

A movement outside the front bow window caught Lucy's attention. "Drummond has arrived."

"I'll be here when you come home."

A month ago, Olivia had stopped picking up Lucy from school. She simply hadn't been able to brave it, not since Jake was there in mornings and afternoons. Further, it had been hard to miss the steady increase in the number of mothers, all impeccably groomed and polished, personally seeing their daughters off to school and crowding the corridors. Motherly concern for the safe passage of their daughters was at an all-time high at The Progressive School for Young Ladies and the Education of Their Minds.

Surely, it had naught to do with the recently admitted Radclyffe family.

Ha. One mother had run smack into a doorjamb whilst craning her neck for a glimpse of him. The mothers simply couldn't keep their eyes off him.

"Oh, Mum," Lucy called out from the doorway, snapping Olivia back into the present, "may I invite Miss Radclyffe for a visit this evening?"

Olivia's heart stomped out a hard thud in her chest, even as she willed the rest of her body to remain very, very still. "Do you have a project together?"

"Oh, nothing to do with school." Lucy pulled a disgusted face. "I've told her about our rooftop garden, and she would like to observe the sky from up there tonight."

Sweat slicked Olivia's palm. Another response she couldn't control. She could, however, continue to hold herself very, very still. "Of course."

"Excellent." Lucy threw her a quick smile and dashed off toward her day, calling out over her shoulder, "And please ask Cook to bake up a batch of her scrumptious shortbread."

The front door slammed shut, and Olivia sagged into her chair. That name, *Radclyffe*, was like a long, razor-sharp sword that stabbed through to the hilt every time she heard it. Over time, mayhap its blade would dull and shorten to a more manageable state. A short dagger could be handled. And then, perhaps, someday she would feel nothing at all when she heard the name Radclyffe.

Her stomach twisted. That day hadn't come. If their lives continued to be intertwined through their daughters' friendship, it would inevitably happen, correct?

Of course, it would. It must.

She clenched her fists at her sides and allowed the nails to dig in deep. One sort of pain could replace another and draw her more fully into the present. Lucy hadn't been wrong. Lately, she *was* everywhere and nowhere at once.

Since the day after the duke's ball, she'd filled every moment of every day with one task just completed, another task to complete. She couldn't remember a time in her life when she'd been more occupied, both physically and mentally. After all, she had a new house and a new life. A life she'd striven tooth and nail to achieve. A life that offered freedom, independence, security, predictability. Everything she'd wanted, she'd gained. She'd secured the predictable life cycle of an English rose.

And if in the quiet of the night, when the house fell silent and only the whisper of her breath broke through the stillness, her mind protested that this life felt empty and lonely, that she'd never felt so empty and lonely, she rolled onto her side and began compiling mental lists for the next day's tasks.

"My lady," she heard as if from a very far distance. She glanced up to find her butler, Wilkins, standing in the doorway not ten feet away. "His Grace, the Duke of Arundel, has arrived."

Olivia's spirits experienced an immediate lift, and she pushed away from the table. With a somewhat renewed spring in her step, she rushed to the foyer and found the duke taking in the room.

"This house suits you, my dear." His eye followed the coiled staircase up to the skylight, bright and cheery, even on a gray and dank day like today. "I can see why you chose it."

She landed a quick welcome kiss on his cheek. "I'm glad you like it."

He took her hands in his and stepped back, assessing her. "You're looking...*well*."

She looked peaky, at best, and they both knew it. The duke noticed everything.

"Has Lulu left for school?"

"You've just missed her, I'm afraid."

"Good," he pronounced, eliciting a start of surprise from Olivia. "Now, show me this magnificent rooftop garden everyone is talking about."

"It would be my pleasure," she replied smoothly, even as dread blossomed in her gut. He'd all but pronounced that he wished to speak with her privately, and she couldn't help feeling she wouldn't like what he had to say.

With the duke at her heels, she placed a balancing hand on the banister and a few short minutes later, they reached the rooftop. Despite the London morning oppressive with soggy clouds, she experienced the same rush of love for this oasis that she'd felt from the very start. Unlike her dark and wintry state of mind, this rooftop, with its colorful riots of peppermint tulips and marigold forsythia, illustrated life's ability to move forward into spring, bright and effulgent.

She couldn't bear the glory of it and looked toward a sky indistinct and fuzzy with cottony mist.

Indistinct...fuzzy...

The words nestled inside her with disconcerting familiarity. Nothing lately was sharp or acute. Like the clouds hanging above her head, so close she could reach up and touch them, she'd gone indistinct at the edges, like a walking blur. Would she ever be sharp again?

"When my solicitors first informed me of your intention to purchase a townhouse in Mayfair—"

"Your solicitors?" she asked, his words jarring her out of her cloud.

"Of course, my dear. Did you think they would keep your correspondence from me? They understand who butters their bread." He held out his arm to her, and they began strolling along the crushed granite path. "My first thought was that it would be a fitting endcap to these last several months of courage."

"I'm not certain *courageous* is the word I would use to describe myself."

"I agree, my dear. You've turned out to be quite the little coward, haven't you?"

Her body drew up in a rigid line, and she opened her mouth to speak, but only a rough, unformed croak emerged. When she began to pull her hand from the duke's arm, he subtly tightened his hold. It appeared he'd only gotten started. "I thought you'd finally allowed yourself the opportunity to move forward with your life, to fully unburden yourself of the ghosts of your past."

"I have," she said, her voice still a raw scrub against her throat, but, at least, she could now form words, even if only monosyllabic ones.

"Percy was a boy," the duke began, "a boy I loved with all my heart, but a spoilt one, I can admit. He was the spitting image of his mother, and I couldn't help doting on him. A willful child can be charming, no? A willful man, on the other hand, can be decidedly less so."

"I know exactly the sort of man Percy was…*is*," she retorted, a snap in the words. She had no desire to speak of Percy.

"Yes, I'm afraid you do." He hesitated. "I didn't want the two of you to marry. Did he tell you?"

"I had no idea." Betrayal and hurt rushed through Olivia, feelings that had become too familiar of late. Tears welled up behind her eyes, and she dare not blink lest they break and stream down her cheeks.

The duke squeezed her hand. "Oh, my dear, it isn't like that. The rush of your young love was so sudden and complete that I advised Percy to extend the engagement, to give you time to know one another. I rather think my advice had the opposite effect as you were married by the end of the Season." He shook his head, bemused. "Percy wanted what he wanted, and he found a way to have it. He wanted you, and he had you."

"Until he didn't." She hated the bitter note that sounded.

"I won't defend him, but I shall say this. Percy was like every other young man of wealth, popularity, and rank in London. But you, my dear, weren't like every other young lady. I saw from the beginning that you would want more from your marriage than he would. Percy wanted a marriage that would allow him to skim across its surface. You wanted something deeper. But once you married, I was powerless to do anything about it. Then Percy ran off to the Continent and got himself blown to bits." He pinned her into place with his piercing gaze. He wanted her to know that she was seen. "Do you know what I saw through the dark haze of my grief for him?"

She shook her head, unable to speak.

"I saw a ray of light for you. You were free of my willful, spoilt son, and my guilt lifted."

"Guilt?"

"I could have stopped your marriage. I could have saved you from the misery of it."

"We would have found a way. Percy wasn't the only willful, spoilt child in our relationship."

"Over the years, I watched you grow and blossom into an accomplished woman, a woman who I was and remain proud to call daughter. Then Percy rose from the dead, and I've never been more grateful to God in my life."

"Of course."

"But when you told me the news, I heard the tremor of your voice, saw the tremble in your hands. Before me stood a woman fearful, but determined, to set her own course. At once, I knew I would move heaven and earth to see you free to pursue the life you wanted, not the one imposed on you by an unhappy marriage."

"Even if it meant helping me divorce your son."

"Percy was...*is* my son, but you, my dear, are my daughter."

Wind sharp with the last remnants of winter gusted across the rooftop, and Olivia closed her eyes, allowing the duke's words to surround her in warmth and love. As a newlywed, she'd come into his house, and he'd accepted her like a long-lost daughter.

The feeling, however, was short-lived when he cleared his throat and said, "Now, getting back to that one pesky word, *courage*."

Her eyes flew open, and she steeled herself.

"It takes a good bit of courage to pursue a free and happy life. I thought you understood that."

A hot, shamed blush flared across her skin, pinpricks of perspiration pushing to its surface.

"May I be bold?"

"Please," she replied, bracing herself against the shifting sand of this conversation.

"St. Alban is no Percy. Percy was a boy, not yet formed into a man. In fact, I haven't the faintest clue what sort of Percy will someday find his way back to London. But St. Alban is very much a man who can be depended upon. The sort of man who will make an excellent viscount and an even better husband. According to Lucretia, quite a few chits have set their caps at him."

"I'm sure they have. Perhaps one will even convince Jake to fall in love with her."

"*Love?*" the duke scoffed. "How many unions of our class have naught to do with love? *Jake* knows his responsibility and won't shirk it. He will marry for reasons other than love, if he must."

"I'm not certain how much you've gathered about my relations with *Lord St. Alban*." Olivia considered the possibility that he'd gathered quite a bit. "But a future between us is impossible. His daughter needs a stepmother of impeccable reputation and social standing."

"And you think you can't be that stepmother?"

"I know it."

"Well, I agree with you on that front, but I think you're viewing the matter from the wrong angle," the duke said. "I met the young lady in question yesterday at Lucretia's manse. She's a remarkable girl, but an unconventional girl, wouldn't you agree?"

"Most definitely."

Her mind traveled back to the night of the duke's ball. Of the way she'd found Mina in the study with Hugh, after she'd called him a simpleton. How Olivia wished she could've seen the impact of that word on his face.

"So what sort of stepmother does Miss Radclyffe need?" the duke continued. "One who would render her into an unoriginal copy of a thousand other young ladies?"

Olivia remained silent, even as butterflies began fluttering in her stomach. What was he getting at?

"Would she be happy with the life a conventional stepmother would impose upon her?"

"I...I," Olivia stammered, "I can't imagine."

"What Miss Radclyffe needs is a stepmother who will nurture and reinforce the remarkable young lady she is. One unafraid of the unconventional and extraordinary. Viewed from this angle, the stepmother Miss Radclyffe needs is—"

Olivia interrupted the duke without a single, staying thought. "Me."

30

"I am the right stepmother for Mina," Olivia said for good measure, the idea gaining traction with each word she spoke. The strong maternal feeling she'd experienced for the girl was no fluke. She was exactly the correct stepmother for Mina. The concept sank in with the uncomplicated weight of truth.

The duke smiled. "I do believe you are."

Long unused muscles stretched across Olivia's face. She was smiling, possibly like a bedlamite, but smiling nonetheless. And now that the words had begun flowing, she couldn't hold them in. There were truths that would see light. "Which means I'm the right wife for Jake. My feelings for him weren't wrong. A woman could give herself fully to a man like him without fear. In fact, she would be a fool not to."

Another truth would be spoken.

"I've been a fool."

"He will have a viscountess before the year is done, mark my words," the duke predicted. "Now ask yourself: have you truly seized the opportunity to move forward?"

Her smile grew hard and determined. "No one else will have him."

"No one else?" the duke asked, a canny twinkle in his eyes. She'd played right into his hands.

"No one else," she all but growled. She'd never felt so ferocious.

"Now, what will you *do* about it?" he asked, the question the nudge she needed.

The heavy numbness that had been plaguing her since the night of the duke's ball lightened and lifted away. An airy and buoyant being was she, untethered by the physical world. It was entirely possible she might up and float off this rooftop.

This was her chance to *truly live*, and this chance at happiness far outweighed the risk. She must *seize* it this very instant. What was the alternative? That she would live a life of uncertainty and unhappiness?

That was the life she was living now.

Her prison tower, dependent on no one and nothing for support, listed to the side and, at last, toppled over, crumbling to dust.

The only life worth living was one dependent on another. A person worthy of trust and love.

Jake.

Her view went from limited and confining to unlimited and utterly wide open all the way up to the stars.

Oh, the stars…

He'd been right about them, too.

Her heart accelerated, and she flung off the last vestiges of the haze that had hung about her this last month. She was alive, *truly alive*, her edges distinct. She shuffled backward, and the duke released her hand. "How can I ever thank you?"

A discerning smile crinkled the corners of his eyes. "If your father is still out of the country, allow me to walk you down the aisle?"

She nodded once before striking out across the garden and down the stairs, her feet a swift tattoo of lightly descending steps. One foot moved faster than the last, her pace and resolve increasing with each successive stair. She reached for the front door lock and jerked it open with an impatient twist. She shot through the doorway with nary a backward glance.

And with nary a consideration for overcoat, bonnet, parasol, sensible boots, or reticule. Clad in nothing more substantial than a muslin morning dress and paper-thin slippers, her feet hit the sidewalk at a near run. The fact that the duke's carriage stood waiting and could be at her disposal never crossed her mind.

She hurried to the end of the row of townhouses, weaving through the few pedestrians braving the London damp, eyes on the lookout for a hackney where her quiet street intersected with Curzon. Her hand shot toward the sky and began waving, fingers waggling, uncaring that she might be attracting unwelcome attention.

What did she care what strangers thought? Or acquaintances for that matter? She only cared for the opinion of one man.

Just when she thought all the hackneys in London were conspiring against her, one rolled into view. She blew a short, sharp whistle, and her hand increased its frantic bid to entice him her way. The driver crossed a lane and pulled his lone horse to a stop in front of her.

"Where canna I take ye?" he called down from his lofty perch as he flipped up the collar of his overcoat against the unseasonable wind.

"Cleveland Row, if you please."

"And if ye don't mind me askin', how will me fare be paid today?"

She glanced down to find her hands empty of reticule or any form of currency for payment. "Oh," was her reply before she dodged right and set her feet in motion at a hurried, and decidedly unrespectable, clip.

If she'd been paying attention, she might have overheard the driver mutter a discontented diatribe against, "That lot o' 'oity-toities 'oo 'speck to get sumpin' for nuttin' off tha backs o' tha workin' folk."

Olivia, however, had no intention of dithering about when she could be making her way toward Jake. A second without him was a second wasted. Her slippers had curdled into a sloshy mess, and the lightweight muslin of her dress may have turned transparent due to rain now falling in drops heavier than a drizzly mist. No matter. If she kept her focus, she could be on his stoop in twenty minutes.

She cut a quick right through Shepherd's Market, her clip developing into a steady jog. By the time she reached Green Park, she was sorely tempted to shed slippers that had begun to blister her heels. She banished the idea. She couldn't arrive on his doorstep unshod. That would be too much.

She was rounding an overgrown corner when, just ahead on the path, she spotted Miss Fox strolling toward her, arm-in-arm with a man...

A tall, powerfully built man.

Without thinking, Olivia ducked behind the nearest bush, her heart racing and threatening to break. She closed her eyes and waited and tried not to think of who that tall, powerfully built man could be, or the deep pit of despair that had opened inside her at the sight of him.

A throat cleared politely, and her eyes flew open. Before her stood Miss Fox with...

Not Jake.

Her lungs released. She could breathe again. Her heart could remain intact.

"Lady Olivia?" Miss Fox asked, genuine concern in her eyes. "Are you quite the thing?"

"Oh, yes, quite," Olivia said, her words a breathless rush. "I'm inspecting this gooseberry." She gestured toward the shrub that should have done its job and protected her from view, feeling very much like a gooseberry herself.

"Actually, this gooseberry and I know each other rather well. But who am I to tell you?"

Miss Fox pointed toward Olivia's skirts, drawing her gaze. The devil take it. The dratted gooseberry had ensnared her in its diabolical grip.

As she quietly attempted to wrest the delicate muslin from the tenacious shrub, Miss Fox's companion asked, "Aren't you going to introduce me to your fine friend?"

He pronounced *fine* like *foin* and placed himself decidedly out of her and Miss Fox's social class, a fact Olivia would have found curious any other time.

Miss Fox hesitated before relenting, "Lady Olivia, may I introduce—"

"There!" Olivia exclaimed after one last twist of gossamer muslin. The tear was no wider than four, maybe six, inches. No matter. She was free. "Miss Fox, I'm turned around. Could you point me in the direction of —" She stopped cold, good sense preventing her from finishing that sentence.

Miss Fox finished it for her. "Queen Street?"

Good sense would prevent her from reaching Jake if she didn't finish her sentence for herself. "Cleveland Row."

Miss Fox's brow lifted, even as she silently pointed the way.

With nary a care for proper etiquette, Olivia's feet kicked into a rapid walk that increased into her former steady jog, her chest heaving, droplets of sweat trickling down the sides of her face, the obstinate gooseberry and the curious eyes of Miss Fox forgotten. She had more important matters on her mind. Like not stepping through the fresh rip in her dress.

After what felt like forty days and forty nights,

Jake's Cleveland Row mansion came into view, and within moments her feet were taking the front steps two at a time. Propriety be damned. She had a future to begin.

At the top, she paused, just a breath to collect herself and attempt to tame her stampeding heart. She combed back strands of wet hair off her clammy and surely flushed face and smoothed them down as much as she could. Fat droplets of rain had accumulated over her entire person like so many glittering diamonds.

What a ridiculously glamorous metaphor for the mess she must appear.

No matter. She drew herself up to her fullest height and reached out before her nerve failed her. Once, twice, she rapped the knocker, and waited.

She tapped out the seconds that followed, forefinger striking thigh, and reached thirty before the door cracked open. Jake's man, Payne, stuck his head out the opening. "May I be of assistance—" He stopped midsentence, recognition lighting within his eyes. "It's *you*."

To his credit, the man didn't shut the door in her face.

"Please announce my arrival to Lord St. Alban," she intoned in her haughtiest voice, conjuring up generations of aristocratic forebears who in no way had ever resembled her current state of dishabille.

"Is his lordship expecting you?"

"No," she had no choice but to reply.

The valet probably had to accommodate all manner of deranged women banging down his employer's front door. Even ones wearing nothing but a destroyed pair of slippers and a ruined muslin dress the color and consistency of a well-used dishrag.

"His lordship is not in. Good day," the butler offered respectfully, but inflexibly.

To Olivia's horror, the door began to shut. She'd come too far to allow that to happen. Her foot kicked out, and she tried not to wince when it became wedged between the solid door and the unforgiving jamb.

She pinned the valet beneath her stubborn gaze, reminding him ever-so-subtly that she outranked him, even with a wet string of hair stuck in her right eye. "Is he *not in*? Or is he *out*?"

There was a difference, and they both knew it. If Jake was *out*, then he wasn't here. If he was *not in*, then he could be here and had instructed his butler not to admit her.

The first option was a minor set-back, the second a soul-destroying defeat.

"My lady, if you will please…" The servant directed a pointed stare at her obstructive foot.

She removed it, and the door shut with a firm snap.

Jake was *not in*?

Gutted, she stood staring at the closed door for an indeterminate amount of time, all the energy and life that had brought her here, draining out of her. At last, she pointed her feet homeward. And stepped through the rip in her dress. Of course.

She bent and finished what her foot had started, tearing off the bottom eight inches of muslin. She must look fit for Bedlam.

Without Jake, perhaps she was.

31

J ake rocked forward onto the balls of his feet before settling back on his heels, his feet as restless and tetchy as the rest of him. Sweat-slicked palms clutched the package he'd brought for Olivia. He refused to think of the package as a present.

Payne had nearly gone apoplectic when he left the manse carrying the package with the intention of delivering it himself. Viscounts didn't deliver packages. They had them sent by post or delivered by footmen.

His intention had been to hand the package over to Olivia's butler, pivot, and leave. It had been a good plan. Except he hadn't followed the plan. Instead, he'd stepped inside the foyer and said, "Will you inform Lady Olivia that Lord St. Alban is here to see her?"

Those had been his exact unplanned words. Now he stood tarrying in her foyer while the household staff searched the house for her. It appeared they'd misplaced their mistress.

He was, in fact, under no obligation to stand here and wait for her. He should place the package on the receiving table and leave, saving them both the embarrassment of his presence. It was what she wanted. She'd made that much clear.

He didn't need to see her unknot the twine and pull

the parchment paper apart. He didn't need to see her face light up from what lay inside.

Rationally accepting what he didn't need to see, he set the package down. "Right."

Behind him, he heard a muted click and the soft creak of a hinge. His head whipped around, and his body followed a beat behind. The front door stood wide, the silhouette of Olivia framed within its opening. She resembled an angel, light and lithe, illusory.

Except, when details began coming into focus, his first impression was replaced with a different reality of her. Hair set at an odd angle...dress fabric strangely heavy and frumpled...

She was...*disheveled*.

Jake took an alarmed step forward. Olivia wasn't merely disheveled. She was nothing less than a complete mess. Hair stringing down her face, half up-half down. Feet bare on cold marble tiles, rainwater pooling beneath her. Dress ripped to shreds and translucent with wet and clinging to her body in ways that cleared all decent thought from the mind of any sousing male who happened upon her, who happened to be him at present.

She closed the door and rested her forehead against oak. Her body language spoke of defeat. Another wave of concern crested inside him.

He cleared his throat, and her body went stiff, but she remained with her back to him. "Olivia, are you *well?*" It was all he could do not to launch across the foyer and gather her in his arms.

She twirled around at the sound of his voice and froze in place. Startled azure eyes met his, and an involuntary, "Oh!" passed through her parted lips. Her entire person was so pale from head to toe that she nearly blended with the stark white walls behind her.

They stood like this, eyes locked, hearts racing, for the blink of an eye—for the longest moment in history.

"Have you been in an accident?" His hands clenched into fists, ready to do battle with the world. "Or attacked?"

Her eyebrows drew together in bewilderment. "Of course not. But Jake," she continued, "I have given some thought to the stars."

He took a concerned step forward. "Would you like to take a seat? To rest yourself a moment?"

"Why? I'm perfectly well. I mean, look at me, I'm a perfect mess, but well." She splayed her arms wide and looked slightly maniacal to his eye.

"Mayhap you've taken a fever?"

She shook her head, sending droplets of rain flying. "Not in the least. Getting back to the stars, you said they were orderly."

"And you said they were chaotic," he countered. "Shall I find you a towel, at least?"

"I don't need a towel, Jake. I need to tell you something."

She inhaled deeply, and he made sure his gaze didn't stray toward her chest, for he was fairly certain he'd detected the dusky outline of a nipple through sopping wet muslin.

"Could the truth be located somewhere in the middle?" she asked, the question breathless and rushed. "Within the stars lies a capacity for order *and* chaos. They quietly watch us from above until, one day, they decide to shoot across the sky in a searing blaze of light until they have nothing left."

"Perhaps," he drew out slowly.

"Perhaps," she drew out equally slowly, "people are like stars in that way. Perhaps within us lie those same ingredients for order and chaos. Except, what if that searing blaze of light isn't chaos? What if there's an ordered catalyst that triggers a star to take to flight across the sky?"

"I'm fairly certain Mina could give you scientific answers to your questions."

"I'm not talking about science. Can't you see?"

"I'm not sure I can," he admitted.

Her head canted to the side, and her brow crinkled. "What are you doing in my home?"

Was that wonder in her voice? Likely a figment of his imagination, conjured up by his own desires.

"I thought you weren't in," she continued.

"I'm not," he said. "I'm out. I'm here." What precisely were they talking about? He gestured toward the receiving table at his side. "I've brought a package." *Not* a present. "For you…your house."

"Oh?" She stepped toward the package, toward him by default. "What is it?"

As she neared him, his body anticipated a passing contact. He could move aside, out of her way, allow her a straighter line to her goal. But a self-defeating part of him wanted her to have to curve around him so he could breathe her in. Her shoulder passed scarcely an inch wide of him, and he inhaled.

There it was: her scent of lavender and sandalwood, yes, but also *Olivia*, womanly, enigmatic, a scent he could almost taste on his tongue. Except he also detected the distinct reek of London street. Again, the alarm sounded in his head, and it was all he could do to keep his hands at his sides and not reach for her. "Olivia, what has happened to you?"

"I was, um, out for a stroll and was caught in the rain," she mumbled and avoided his gaze.

She was lying. It had been raining for a solid week, no end in sight. Ladies didn't *stroll* in such weather, even ladies as unconventional as Olivia. He'd never seen the cool and collected Lady Olivia Montfort as *un*collected as she appeared right now.

"Are you unwell?" he asked again.

Singularly focused on the package, she waved away

his concern with a flick of her delicate wrist. She picked up the package and turned it over in her hands a few times. Light, reverent fingertips feathered across its plain surface as if she was savoring and prolonging the moment. His heart lifted on a doomed note of hope.

Her tongue began worrying the tip of her one crooked tooth, and lust, base and unworthy, shot through him. He was ever fluctuating between lust and love with this woman. Both must cease. He couldn't have the one without the other. Not with Olivia. It didn't work that way with her.

Her eyes caught his and brightened. "It feels almost insubstantial, it's so light."

"A mere trinket. It might fit somewhere in the house," he said on a nervous rush, his words the green jumble of a young man. Her fever of restless energy had infected him, too.

"Oh?" Her fingers set about working the twine loose.

He needed to be gone from this place before she opened the package. "I shall be on my way. Good day."

He offered a shallow bow in her direction and stepped toward the door, determined to leave this place, and Olivia, in the past. She didn't want him in her present.

"Jake," he heard behind him, "stay."

He stopped, for her words, for the fervent hitch on which they hung suspended between them. But that didn't mean he had to watch her like some lovesick wretch. His gaze fixed on the iron detailing of a rather ordinary wall sconce.

Behind him sounded a gasp, followed by another faint, "Oh!"

His body tensed. This was the moment. Like Lot's damned wife, he couldn't resist a single, last glance. If it turned him into a pillar of salt, so be it. He must see her face.

It was exactly as he'd envisioned: rapt and ravenous in its exploration of the small painting. Her head popped up and luminous eyes met his. "It's exquisite."

Those words and the joyous expression blossoming across her face drew him back into the room, back into her sphere. His resolve to leave her, broken. His mouth began moving, words spilling out of their own accord. "It isn't the original. That wasn't for sale." According to the Dutch government, this Vanmour didn't have a price, and he hadn't enough time to find out if that was true.

A canny, speculative gleam entered her eye. "You didn't just happen across a reproduction of *Whirling Dervishes in Mevlevihane in Pera*."

"Kai knew of an artist who could reproduce it. I thought perhaps you might hang it—"

* * *

OLIVIA HELD up one silencing hand, even as the other clutched the painting tight to her chest, to her heart. It was the least insubstantial gift she'd ever received. She pointed to a specific patch of wall, the same patch she'd mentioned weeks ago. "Right there."

Of a sudden, she felt overwhelmed by the gesture and a little shy of this man. This painting represented everything she admired about him.

No. Nothing as cold and distant as admiration. This painting was a pure expression of love, daring and true, lacking expectation. She as good as held his heart in her hands. After having his heart crushed underfoot at the duke's ball, he'd taken a risk by bringing this painting to her. Now, it was her turn to take a risk.

She set the painting on the receiving table and stepped toward him, her slow and careful pace belying the urgency of her emotions. As she made her advance, he watched her from beneath a speculative brow. He thought she'd gone mad.

Perhaps she had. Mad for him.

She stopped, her body a foot removed from his, reached out, and took his gorgeous, capable hands into her cold and wet ones. His hands were warm and dry and safe. A shiver purled down her spine, one vertebra at a time. "About those stars," she began.

"Olivia, perhaps you fell and hit your head. Oft times, one doesn't remember such an occurrence. One of my crew once cracked his skull—"

She touched a fingertip to his lips, at once quieting him. "Shh, hear me out. You didn't ask me to marry you because I might carry your babe. Or because you need a stepmother for Mina. You didn't ask me to marry you because you *might* love me." She deliberately inhaled and deliberately exhaled, once, twice. "What if the catalyst for our stars is love? It takes us out of our orderly, mundane existences and makes it possible for us to truly live." At once shy and bold, she continued, "Without you, I am an orderly star lacking the ability to come to life. You are the flame who sets me alight."

Oh, the way his serious eyes took her in. How could she ever have thought she couldn't trust herself in love when a man like Jake wanted her?

She dropped to her knees before him, his hands clasped within hers. His intensity only strengthened her resolve to pursue this path. To have him as hers. "I thought love needed to be perfect to be real, but I see now that is a fragile sort of love. It can't last." She shifted back and settled her bum onto her feet, her knees no longer able to support her, trembling as they were. "I don't want perfection. I want you."

His lips quirked to the side. "Flattering."

"True love is hardy and messy. I want to spend the rest of my life making a perfect, little mess with you.

Would you consider making an exception to every rule that states what a wife should be and take me as yours?"

He sank to his knees so they faced each other on an equal plane, his serious gaze giving nothing away. A tremor of misgiving streaked through her, and a possibility stole in. What if he no longer wanted her? What if she'd read this situation wrongly?

"What of your freedom, Olivia? Your freedom to be an unwed lady of means. Your freedom to pursue the life you choose. You defied society to achieve it." He hesitated, weighing his next words. "I can't have you resenting me for taking something so precious from you."

The fear grew claws and sank into her. She could lose him. She must find the right words. "You told me that no wife of yours would ever be subject to an unequal marriage." She took his face in her hands. "I *believe* you. I *trust* you. I *love* you. Freedom doesn't have to be a lonely endeavor. When shared with the right person, with *you*, how much more liberating. Let us be free together."

He reached up, calloused fingers gently stroked the side of her face, and the fear released from her body. Her eyes drifted shut, and she surrendered to the moment. The granular rumble of his voice sounded at her ear. "Yes, Olivia. You have undone me." His lips touched her neck, and she thought she might melt through the floor.

When his mouth, at last, found hers, she fell headlong into his kiss, and her heart expanded until she felt it must burst with joy. Her arms wrapped about his waist, bringing his body into hers, surely soaking his clothes through to his skin. She hadn't realized how cold she was until now, his warmth seeping into her body at the cellular level. The chemistry between them was undeniable. It always had been. The love they now openly shared heightened it.

An impatience to discover what new heights of passion they could reach seized her, and her greedy hands found the knot of his cravat and tugged. He tore his mouth from hers, a flare of desire darkening his eyes to near black. "The servants," he intoned on a low murmur.

Reality hit her, and her fingers froze. She'd been about to make love to Jake in the foyer of her new house in the broad daylight. What new heights, indeed.

He stood, lifting her with him. "How about we make an exception to another rule?" he whispered, his words a hot, velvet temptation that snaked across her body, raising goose bumps, tightening nipples, caressing her clear through to her very center.

"And what rule would that be?" she asked, the question a breathless expulsion of words.

"I seem to remember one about not anticipating the wedding night…"

A sly smile curved her lips. "I cannot think of an exception I would rather make."

EPILOGUE

ONE MONTH LATER

"I certainly never did *that* on one of the Montfort family trips to Skye," Olivia exclaimed as she fell back onto lush goose down and silk. She squeezed her eyes shut and inhaled a delicious breath.

"Well, you're a Radclyffe, now," Jake said on a dry chuckle. How she loved the sound of joy on his lips.

She rolled onto her side, fit her body into his stretched alongside her, and allowed the gentle sway of the boat to lull her.

"You know the place Mina and Lucy are exploring?" he asked, the low rumble of his voice making her want to do *that* again.

But even her virile husband needed a rest, so she answered him. "I know the Faerie Glen of Uig well. The valley was forged when a massive glacier crashed through here thousands of years ago, leaving behind an odd assortment of jagged pinnacles and miniature mountains. The locals believe faeries live there, so they stay away, but I think it's magical."

She snuggled deeper into pillows, blankets, and Jake.

"The duchess certainly raised an eyebrow when we informed her that the girls were coming with us on our honeymoon, and this after denying her the big society wedding she wanted for us."

"I've already set in motion a plan for making it up to her. Kai has agreed to paint a wedding scene from her and the duke's upcoming nuptials. As far as bringing the girls along, I couldn't bear the idea that they would miss the magic of Skye." Olivia's heart began to accelerate with anticipation. Now was the time to tell him. "Besides, there was no point in leaving them behind."

Jake shifted away before rolling onto his side and facing her, his eyes bright with curiosity. "I could think of a few points." Perhaps to illustrate one of said points, he feathered a fingertip across the curve of her hip.

She shook her head. "Nope. No point in leaving them when we're already bringing along one of our children, possibly two."

She watched, delighted, as his brows knit together in perplexity before releasing, his eyes wide with understanding. His fingers continued their progress from her hip to the subtle curve of her belly. "One...possibly *two*?"

His awe and excitement transferred into her, and her face broke into the smile she couldn't contain any longer. "Oh, very possibly."

He took her hips in his hands and rolled her atop him, intense blue eyes locked onto her. "I love you, Lady St. Alban."

"And I love you, Jake." He was Jake to her, now and forever.

This was what it was to truly live.

It turned out the life cycle of an English rose suited Olivia not at all.

ALSO BY SOFIE DARLING

All's Fair in Love and Racing
Odds on the Rake
The Duchess Gamble

Shadows and Silk
Three Lessons in Seduction
Tempted by the Viscount
Her Midnight Sin
To Win a Wicked Lord
At the Pleasure of the Marquess
One Night His Lady
Nell and the Runaway Duke

ABOUT THE AUTHOR

Bestselling and award-winning author Sofie Darling's passion for historical romance began in middle school the moment she cracked open *Wuthering Heights* by Emily Bronte. An instant and enduring love affair was born.

Sofie spent much of her twenties raising two boys and reading every romance she could get her hands on. Once she realized she simply must write the books she loved, she finished her English degree and set pencil to paper. (Ticonderoga #2 is her quill of choice.)

When she's not writing heroes who make her swoon, Sofie enjoys a nice weekend hike, a visit to a crumbling medieval castle whenever she gets the chance, and a slightly codependent relationship with her beagle, Bosco. Visit her website.